Under Her Wings

By: Anne Marie Citro

Table of Contents

Chapter 1

Please Take Me

Gabriella stared out at the stormy water of Loch Snizort, five minutes away from the town of Portree on the Isle of Skye, Scotland. She sat on the edge of a cluster of boulders that were half-submerged in the loch. The spray of the water mingled with the tears streaming down her face. She was soaked, shivering, and not even aware the daylight was escaping from the night.

"Goddammit! God, if I believed in you—which I don't—I would ask you why! *Why!*" She sobbed. "Why leave me? Please take me. I have nothing." Her stomach muscles ached from the constant, racking sobs she couldn't control.

She had contemplated suicide, but the fear that God did exist had stopped her. If by any chance an afterlife did exist, by killing herself, she would be denied the privilege of entering Heaven, of holding her beloved boys in her arms again. She would be stuck in

1

the hell that was her never-ending existence.

It had been years—three to be exact—since her world had been turned from light to dark. Everyone had said she needed to deal with her grief, and she had tried. Regardless, it hadn't worked.

Besides, who the fuck were they to say what stage of grief she was dealing with? What if the next stage never came, and she never recovered? Then what? Did people actually believe it was a conscious choice not to move on? Was it depression? Abso-fucking-lutely! Did seeing a shrink help? No. Did talking about it help? No. Did medication help? No, because no one seemed to understand Gabriella's pain.

She had lost her world through no fault of her own. It was marred not just by loss, but also because of the rumours surrounding her family's deaths…

***

Edward awoke to the sound of haunting sobs. A chill went up his spine, thinking if ever there were such things as ghosts, that would definitely be the sound they made. The sound triggered déjà vu in the recesses of his mind, and he searched his memory for something he couldn't put his finger on.

The curiosity of the lost memory and the wailing sound drove him up and outside to either help whatever was making that noise or put the thing out of its misery. His mind was so busy trying to place the sounds that were haunting him that he inadvertently forgot to give Liam, his guard and best friend, a heads-up that he was leaving.

Night had descended hours ago, and even with a shirt and heavy sweater on, the chill still seeped into his bones. Combine that with the relentless sound, he was uneasy.

He cautiously walked through the gardens connected to the side door of his suite, which were stunning in the summer yet now looked lifeless and sad. He was on alert because of who he was. People were forever trying to catch him in compromising situations and always tried to take a piece of him, befriend him, and not because of friendship, but for gain. However, late April wasn't a popular time to visit; the temperature could be downright nasty, and the sun rarely shone in the summer, let alone spring.

The inn they had chosen for its solitude was named McIntyre Country House, a beautiful, old estate that looked lonely with its regal, black roof and white exterior walls. Phone reception and Wi-Fi were on again, off again, tending to be more off.

The inn only had one other guest, and the innkeeper had tried to cancel that reservation to accommodate Edward's privacy, but he had been unable to reach the guest in time. Instead, the owner had asked Edward if it was okay to put them on the other side of the building with the assurance they wouldn't disturb the men. Edward had hesitantly conceded.

Just as the moon moved out from behind the clouds, the light allowed him to see.

"Good God," he gasped.

There was a wee woman crying—no, howling—on the boulders

3

by the loch. She must have been hurt, maybe had gotten her leg caught between the rocks, and was now crying out for help.

Edward ran at top speed then stopped just a few feet from the boulders so as not to alarm the woman curled up and cradling herself.

"Are you okay?" he asked. "Miss, are you all right?"

No answer, but her sobbing turned softer.

"I don't want to frighten you, but I am going to join you on the boulders. Miss, can you hear me?"

Still no answer.

He approached her with caution, thinking she might have been attacked, that a man or an animal had hurt her. However, something about the sound of her agony led him to believe it wasn't a physical pain, but something much deeper.

When Edward got closer, all sounds stopped from the woman. That frightened him more than the thought of ghosts.

Did he dare touch her? What if this was another setup to make him look bad in the eyes of the world?

Edward pushed all negative thoughts aside. He had to help her.

He touched the woman's cheek. Holy Mother of Mary, she was either frozen, or she had died before his eyes.

"Miss...? Please, are you okay?"

Bloody hell, I have to get her warm, he thought.

Edward bent down and checked for a pulse, breathing with a sense of relief when he realized she had one. Next, he checked her body for wounds, running his hand around her skull and down her neck then checking his hands continuously for blood. Nothing. Next, he ran his hands down each arm, her torso, and finally down each of her legs. She appeared not to be bleeding or, by quick assessment, didn't have any broken bones. His military training had its rewards, one being he was efficient in field combat first-aid.

He gently lifted the woman into his arms, which wasn't an easy task since she was soaked to the bone. He had a dilemma. His arms were full, and if he made any sound or someone spotted him carrying a hurt woman, the press would explode and crucify him in the tabloids.

Shaking off those thoughts, he progressed carefully across the boulders; carried her quickly through the gardens; and, in mere moments, was back at the inn.

He gently laid her down on the ground and searched for his key.

Damn it to hell! He had forgotten to grab it.

He felt it before he heard the words, a gun pressed against the back of his skull. *Fuck, could this night get any worse?*

"Take your hand off the door and back away from the woman."

Edward released a thankful breath.

"Liam, man, it's me, Edward," he whispered.

"Jesus fucking Christ," Liam cursed. "I could have blown your fucking head off. What in God's green earth are you doing out here? And where the bloody hell did that woman come from?"

"There is something wrong, very wrong, with her," Edward

answered. "I think she's hurt."

Liam secured his weapon in his chest holster, gave Edward the key to both suites, and then gently lifted the woman into his arms. He had to wonder if Edward had dragged her body up from Loch Snizort. Had she almost drowned, or had she been trying to commit suicide?

Whatever had happened to this woman, Liam couldn't even fathom. She was soaked and frozen. They needed to get her inside, and Edward out of sight.

Liam walked through Edward's suite and told him to unlock the connecting door into his own. Once there, Liam laid the woman on the chesterfield. Even in an emergency, he had enough sense to do his job and protect Edward first. He also had to consider any gossip that could surround Edward, especially if anyone knew there was an unconscious woman in their lodgings.

After re-establishing she had a pulse, first-aid 101 stated she needed to be warmed up as quickly as possible. Therefore, Liam instructed Edward to go into his closet and grab his workout clothes, consisting of sweat pants, a T-shirt, and a hooded sweatshirt. Liam also wanted towels.

Liam looked down at the girl and assessed her age to be mid- to late-twenties. She looked like a drowned rat with her long, dark hair hanging in wet clumps around her delicate, tiny face. Her bone structure was fine and reminded him of a bird. Her skin was a grey colour, wrinkled, wet, and goose bumps covered every inch. Her lips

6

were purple, and she had dark circles under her eyes that made her look even younger. Liam noticed all this as he started to remove her clothing.

He tried to give her as much dignity as he could, which wasn't an easy task when the jeans were so wet they clung to her like a second skin. Regardless, he finally managed to peel the pants off along with a turquoise lace thong. The woman's lady bits were hairless, much like the slags from porn movies.

Liam, feeling a little guilt and shame for noticing, and quickly averted his eyes, moving on to pull her coat and sweater off. As he did, he couldn't help noticing she had on a matching turquoise bra that he removed to reveal her shapely breasts. What really knocked the breath out of his lungs were the stretch marks and scars that lay all over her lower belly. This young woman was someone's mum, and it was his responsibility now to make sure she was reunited with her loved ones.

Why was she alone, wet, and nearly frozen to death? Where was her family?

Edward approached with the items Liam had requested, but before he reached the girl, Liam stopped him.

"Throw the clothes and wait until I cover her."

"Really, Liam? Sod the fuck off. She isn't the first female I have seen naked."

"But she is someone's mum, and if it were Raven, she would have been devastated by one strange man seeing her naked, let alone

7

two."

At the mention of Raven, Edward stopped dead in his tracks, tossed the clothing, and turned his back. Liam very rarely mentioned Raven, so this meant something to him.

Liam worked quickly and efficiently to warm and dress the mysterious woman. Now all tucked in the chesterfield with his clothing swimming on her tiny frame and blankets wrapped around her, she appeared to be resting peacefully.

Liam turned to Edward. "Where did the lass come from? Who is she? And why did you not call me to give assistance?"

Edward painstakingly retold the tale of the last forty-five minutes, wondering why things always happened to him.

Liam wouldn't call the authorities or Scotland Yard yet, not until they were certain the young woman wanted or needed police help. He wanted Edward far away from whatever was going on. Nevertheless, they would have to wait to get answers when she awoke.

Chapter 2

Trust No One

Gabriella moved, feeling the pains in her muscles before she could even open her eyes, which was taking all of her concentration.

She was desperately trying to gain her bearings when her memories flooded back. Maybe God had finally answered her prayers, and she was back in time. She assumed, if you travelled back in time, it should hurt—it shouldn't come for free.

Finally, her brain connected with the muscles in her eyelids, and she slowly opened them, moaning from what would normally be an unconscious act, but now took all her effort and strength.

The moan alerted Edward, who had been working on his laptop not far from the young woman. He placed his laptop down and moved to kneel beside the chesterfield.

"Miss, are you all right?" he asked then saw her flinch. "I won't hurt you. Be assured, you are safe."

Gabriella's eyes flew open, unfamiliar with the voice or accent. She pushed herself up so quickly she nearly blacked out from the movement. Her breathing was laboured, and her heart rate was off the charts.

His voice lowered, assuring her again she was all right and that he wouldn't hurt her.

As Gabriella got control of herself, she asked in a scratchy voice, "Who are you? What do you want? Why are you in my room?"

"I am not in your room; you are in my friend Liam's room. I pulled you off the boulders by the loch two nights ago. I am still unsure if you are hurt, and I have no idea who you are. My name is Edward, by the way."

"Am I hurt?" She paused. Why would she be hurt? "Where am I? And why are you with me?"

Gabriella's mind was working overtime, trying to figure out what on earth was going on. She searched her memory, but the last thing she remembered was going to the Callanish Stones on the Isle of Lewis. The stones were said to have mystical powers.

"Oh, my God, it didn't work." A pain stabbed her heart, and she grabbed her throat.

She had whispered so faintly Edward almost didn't catch it.

"What didn't work?" he asked.

Tears of failure trailed down her hollowed cheeks, and pain emanated from her eyes. It was so powerful it took Edward's breath away.

So caught up in pain the woman was experiencing, he failed to hear Liam enter the room.

"Ah, I see the lass has awakened."

Gabriella, also lost in her thoughts, had failed to hear Liam, but upon seeing him, she screamed.

Liam moved back, and Edward moved forwards, grabbing Gabriella's shoulders then leaning into her personal space as he repeated gently, "We won't harm you. But you have to let me know you are okay and what your name is."

Gabriella looked closely at the man. He was young, good-looking, and around six-feet. He had slightly curly, thick, light brown hair with a trace of red; a clean shaven face with a smatter of freckles covering the bridge of his nose; and big, beautiful, hazel eyes. She pegged him at about twenty-four years old. And he was patiently waiting for her answers.

"My name is Gabriella Dante, and physically, I am fine." She didn't state that her mind was so fucked up there was no fixing it.

Liam again pushed into view as Edward took a relieved breath and moved back. She lifted her eyes to Liam and had to strain her neck to look into his face. He had to be at least six-foot-one. He had a military cut to his dark hair; light, crystal blue eyes; beautifully shaped eye brows; and lines in his face that indicated he had dimples when he smiled. She estimated him to be in his early thirties. He was well-toned, muscular, and his black T-shirt stretched across his well-defined chest. He wore black cargo pants and black motorcycle boots.

The man had an air of authority about him that instantly made Gabriella think of the many police officers she had known over the years. The thought chilled her, and she pushed herself as far back as she could from him.

Liam noted the instant change in Gabriella's face; the panic was so real it felt tangible.

"Gabriella, I won't harm you."

Edward quietly asked Liam to give him a few minutes with her, seeing that Liam was upsetting her.

"Gabriella, you don't know me, but let me assure you that we wish you no harm."

"Is Liam a police officer?" she asked.

Edward's mind raced, trying to figure out, if Liam was an officer, how that would matter to this woman. What was she hiding?

Edward had learned the hard way to trust his instincts, which were telling him something was off. Her fear was so real it seemed like it was bleeding from her pores. She was terrified of the police.

"No, he isn't an officer; he's military. Out of anyone I know on earth, I respect and trust him most in the world. Although, if you tell him that, I will deny it." He chuckled at his inside joke.

As serious as the situation was, anytime he got one up on Liam, it was worth a little smile.

Gabriella visibly relaxed, something he would ponder at another time.

For some reason, she trusted this young English man with a kind face and a twinkle in his eyes.

"May I ask you a few questions? Nothing too personal."

She didn't answer yes, but she also didn't say no. Therefore, he took that as a silent yes. However, just as he was going to ask his first question, there was a knock on the door, and Liam walked back in.

"I'm sorry, but I can't stand in the next room and wait." Liam looked directly at Gabriella. "I mean you no disrespect, but we need answers, and we need them now." His gut said she could handle a firm lead, and he had to grasp control of this situation. Edward was his first and only priority.

She didn't look up at him, but she nodded in agreement.

Liam watched Gabriella as Edward started to ask her questions. She showed absolutely no recognition of whom Edward was. How could that be when everyone on the planet knew Edward and his family?

He was the third son of the beloved Princess Emma, and the son everyone believed had been fathered by a famous actor the princess had danced with at a charity event held in the US twenty-six years ago.

Her accent sounded American, although she was definitely of Latin descent. Her hair was in desperate need of a wash, hanging in long ringlets that fell almost to her waist; and her eyes were large, brown pools of pain. It almost broke his heart to look into her eyes. She was a wee thing, just slightly over five feet. She wore a single band of yellow gold on her left hand, but the band was probably not as thick as it looked on her tiny hand.

She was married and had a child or children, and it was now his job to look out for her until he could safely hand her off to her family. He needed to find out who she was, and he wasn't getting the answers he wanted fast enough, probably because of her exhaustion and lack of sustenance in the last forty-eight hours. Liam knew he could fix one problem.

He called the front desk and ordered three traditional Scottish breakfasts, a pot of coffee, a pot of tea, and juices to be brought immediately to his suite. Next, he concentrated on the answers she was giving Edward.

Gabriella revealed she was from Toronto, Canada and was traveling alone. This took fifteen minutes to get out; she was leery of sharing personal information, trusting no one.

Breakfast arrived, and when Gabriella saw the amount of food, she was pleased. She shuffled up to a seated position and began to eat.

After shoveling half the plate in, she raised her head and paused with her mouth full to ask what the dark thing was on her plate. Edward explained it was black pudding made with sausage, oatmeal, and pork blood. She gagged, and her stomach heaved. It took all of her concentration not to throw up. She hadn't eaten for two days, so it was probably better she didn't overeat, anyway.

Now that she was done, Liam felt it was time she continued to answer some of their questions. He looked at her, realizing he needed to be firm yet gentle with her. She had the appearance of a broken bird—fragile, lonely, and sad.

He had never really believed you could see into someone's soul through their eyes, but Gabriella's told a different story. She had suffered and still was. Maybe Edward pulling her from the Loch had been a thwarted attempt at suicide. Consequently, he needed to proceed with caution but persistence. Gentle but firm. Coaxing was the only way to deal with this delicate, little bird.

"Gabriella, how can we help you?"

He waited for her reply, watching her eyes turn downwards. He didn't think she was going to answer him, but then she very quietly responded with, "There isn't a thing you, Edward, or anyone can do for me."

Before he could respond, she lifted her eyes to him, and he saw they were filled with tears. His heart clenched.

It became too much for Edward, who was also witnessing her pain. His breakfast sat like a rock in his stomach. He had seen many terrible things in his life and had lived through his own pain and losses, but what he witnessed in Gabriella's eyes was devastating. The woman was suffering beyond reason.

He felt a streak of protectiveness over Gabriella. She reminded him of his own mother—all alone, even though she had been surrounded by people.

Liam stopped the questions immediately, not wanting to lose the ground they had already gained with her. Instead, he suggested they continue after she napped, showered, and changed. Maybe, if she felt more like herself and not so uncertain about her surroundings, they could gain her trust and get her to share what had broken her.

In the meantime, Liam could use his Scotland Yard contacts to get a background check done on Gabriella Dante.

***

To the outside world, Edward's mum was the princess who had possessed everything. She had been stunningly beautiful, kind, compassionate, and she had lived a fairy tale life. However, her heart had been broken when she had found out her husband had been repeatedly unfaithful. She had kept up the appearance of a happy marriage for her children's sakes, while suffering greatly in private.

She had been a lost soul through much of her adult life. It had always bothered Edward that, at the time of her suffering, she'd had no one. He had just been a little boy and couldn't help her. In the back of his mind, he remembered hearing her cry when she had thought no was listening.

It occurred to Edward that maybe it was that memory that had alerted Edward to Gabriella's crying on the boulders. He remembered the helplessness he had felt after watching his mother read the headlines of the *London Times*, seeing his mum's tears when yet another story of her husband was splashed all over the newspapers.

Much of what he knew about his mother was hearsay, because he had been a mere five-year-old when she had died. Nevertheless, he remembered the woman who would snuggle with him at bed time, called him her little prince, and read him the book *I Will Love You Forever*. She had promised he would have a charmed life and constantly reiterated not to let other people's viciousness determine the course of his life.

What no one in the world knew was that his mother had written them letters every few months and had put them in a safety deposit box in a London bank. When she had passed on, his uncle had brought all the boys into his office and explained that his mum had loved them with all her heart and soul and that she had left them letters to be given to them on their twenty-first birthday. Edward had celebrated his twenty-first birthday five years ago and now carried a piece of his mother everywhere he went.

Most of the world believed Edward was the son of a famous Hollywood actor. Instead, he knew through the letters that he was, indeed, his father's son—a last ditch effort to save her marriage.

Edward liked to blame his "Pops," as he liked to call him, much to his father's annoyance. The future king thought it was a derogative term, which only egged Edward on, because in Edward's mind, someone had to pay for the hurt and betrayal that his beautiful mum had suffered.

Edward had learned the hard way to trust no one. His mum had written many times in his letters that "Courtesy was given. Respect was earned," and so far, he only trusted three people: his two brothers and Liam. Everyone else had eventually betrayed him.

As that thought struck him, he realized maybe this was why he needed to help Gabriella. She, too, had lost everything she believed in. He might have been too young to help his beloved mum, but he could help Gabriella.

His thoughts were forced back to reality when he heard the shower turn off. After she had napped in Liam's room, Edward had taken Gabriella back to her own room where he was now sitting and waiting for her. He was afraid to leave her alone for fear she wouldn't have enough strength to carry out basic grooming tasks.

Edward needed to fix her. One way or another, he had to right the wrongs in her life and show her there was still beauty in the world.

Chapter 3

Nice to Meet You…I Think

Gabriella turned off the shower and began wringing the water out of her long hair. She was still incredibly numb, and her thought process was still not at peak working order. Why had she allowed these men to care for her? More importantly, why were they caring for her? She had nothing else to give. She was empty. She was a shell of her former self. Her last bit of hope had died at the standing stones.

How desperate was it to travel across the ocean on a whim in the hopes of going to some standing stones that were said to have mystical powers to travel back in time? As a child, her Scottish great-grandmother had always told stories of the Druids. It had sounded like a crazy idea, but it had been her last desperate attempt to bring back all she had lost. That was her sad existence—grasping at straws.

Gabriella was the daughter of Manual and Eileen Capello.

Manual, or Manny, had been born and raised in Avilla Spain, and Gabriella was every inch her papi's daughter. She had olive skin; huge, dark brown eyes ringed with black, long, dark eyelashes; and long, dark, curly hair. If you pictured the perfect little Flamenco dancer, it would be Gabriella with her tiny, delicate body and a dancer's grace.

Eileen—Elia—her mother, had been born and raised in Glencoe, Scotland. Gabriella's brother Philippe was the spitting image of their mother: tall, auburn hair, light green eyes, and fair skin. No two blood siblings looked less alike than Gabriella and Philippe.

As teenagers, their parents had immigrated to Canada where Manny and Elia had met, fallen in love, and built a better life for themselves and their children.

They owned and operated a Spanish restaurant in Toronto that went by the name of his beloved home town, Avilla. Their home and restaurant were warm and welcoming environments that friends and clients loved to visit in order to share a great meal and a great sense of community. It was an honour to grow up in such a close-knit family, which was one of the reasons Gabriella couldn't be around them right now.

She dressed in faded jeans she couldn't keep on her hips without a belt and a lilac, lace, square neck top over a dark purple tank. Underneath, as always, she wore a beautiful In Your Dreams push-up bra and lace thong set, this one in a lilac colour. It was out of habit, not for the fact that anyone would ever again see her underwear.

On second thought, maybe it was in tribute to Marco, her beloved husband. He had loved her in sexy lingerie, even encouraged it and made sure she always had every colour of the In Your Dreams collection.

Early in their marriage, they had been watching an entertainment show that featured clips from the In Your Dreams fashion show. Gabriella had thought the women looked beautiful, and Marco had tried to convince her that she was equally as beautiful, if not more.

The next time Marco was in the US, he had stopped at an In Your Dreams store and bought her two sets, one in black and one in white. When he had come home, he had made Gabriella model them. She had come out with the white set first, her eyes cast down with embarrassment. He had made sure she saw how hard he was and what was going to follow the little fashion show. But before that happened, he had asked to see the black set.

She had giggled at his reaction and thought to push it up a notch by wearing a pair of thigh highs she had received at her bachelorette party, pairing them with black stilettos. Giggling, she had put the music on in the bedroom and curved her leg around the wall before coming out.

Marco had spoken in Spanish, saying, "Dios, proteja mi corazón." *God, protect my heart.*

It had turned out to be one of the most erotic nights of their marriage. Marco had made her keep the stilettos on while she rode him on the couch, not able to wait the thirty seconds it would take to make it to the bedroom. That had been the prequel to the erotic underwear collection Marco had started.

The second most erotic day of her life was the day In Your Dreams entered the Canadian retail market. Marco had gone to the launch and stood in line for three hours to purchase five different coloured sets. It had cost him a mortgage payment, but he had said the change in Gabriella's confidence was priceless.

In the Latin culture, some families celebrated namesake days. It was sort of like having two birthdays. Marco had decided the store was the saint of his heart, so they had celebrated Saint In Your Dreams Day every August 26th. On that day, Marco took pleasure in buying every set they sold. Then Gabriella chose one of them, a sexy dress, and matched it with a pair of fuck me heels. She then spent an hour in preparation, making everything perfect, before Marco spent the night lavishing all his attention, love, and pride on her.

In one small way, still wearing the collection was a way Gabriella kept Marco close to her each and every day.

Back to reality, Gabriella took the time to put on some mascara and cover-up to hide the dark circles under her eyes. She finished it off with pink blush and the mauve lipstick she wore every day of her life.

Her mother had always taught her children to get up, shower, and dress, even when they were sick, because she believed, if you looked better, you would feel better. Right now, Gabriella agreed. She would never feel well again, but at least she felt like she was presenting herself better.

Gabriella then took a deep breath and opened the door to a surprised Edward.

"Wow." Edward was blown away, his mouth hanging open. Gabriella was stunning. He could easily fall for her if she weren't already taken.

Gabriella's lips curled up a little. She was nearly old enough to be his mother—well, not really, but she bet she was closer to his mother's age than his.

"Okay, let's meet up with Liam. He has been patiently waiting to make sure you are okay."

***

Liam had been doing a background check on Gabriella via Scotland Yard.

When Liam had joined His Majesty's Royal Army, he had never envisioned himself as a personal bodyguard to one of His Majesty's grandsons.

Special Reconnaissance Regiment—SRR—had recruited Liam as a division of the United Kingdom's Special Forces. Terrorism had changed the world, and if a terrorist group got their hands on a member of the royal family, it would change the world, because the government couldn't negotiate with kidnappers for political gain. Therefore, Liam took his job seriously.

Liam lowered his head, breathed deeply, and blew out. "Oh, no. Fuck me."

Gabriella's life wasn't hard to uncover. In fact, it was highlighted in every newspaper in Canada and the Northern US.

She had lost her husband and two sons when an off duty police officer had set her husband up to take the fall for a car accident that had killed four Russian youths. The group had been chased by the off duty officer in an illegal chase through the streets of Toronto after a corrupt deal between the officer and the kids had gone wrong. The youths had crashed their car into Marco's, and Marco had ended up in the hospital for three weeks with no memory of texting and driving, which was what he had been charged with, along with vehicular manslaughter.

While waiting outside the courthouse, Gabriella's family had been gunned down, a hit by the Russian mob. One of the mob members had been the brother of one of the youths who had been killed in the accident.

Only two days after Gabriella's family had been killed, the police officer's accusation had been proven false. Gabriella's husband hadn't been texting and driving. In fact, he hadn't even had his phone.

"Bastard! What happened to serve and protect?"

That was the media report. The official report was even more heart breaking. Thankfully, Gabriella would never know that version.

Liam closed his computer with a heavy heart. How could he of all people help this girl with her grief when he didn't have the skills to deal with loss? The three of them were a fucked up triangle of Freudian bullshit.

Liam, forever cognizant, heard Edward and Gabriella before they were at the door. Two seconds later, it felt like Liam had been punched in the gut.

Gabriella entered the suite like angel on a cloud. Not only was she graceful, but she was also drop dead gorgeous.

He thanked his lucky stars he was sitting down, because he had a hard-on in one point three seconds flat.

Liam heard Edward's smirk from across the room. Edward knew what Liam was feeling. In fact, any male from the age of twelve to eighty would feel the same way. It wasn't just her looks; it was how she carried herself and how vulnerable she appeared. It made him want to wrap her in cotton and keep her safe from the world. The softness of her voice and those Goddamn soul searching eyes of hers.

"Fuck me," he breathed out. "You look totally different than you did an hour ago. But that doesn't excuse my behavior when I saw you." Liam dropped his eyes in embarrassment. "The King's Army would be ashamed of my conduct." Liam caught himself before he said, "while on duty." He didn't want Gabriella questioning why he was on duty. As far he could determine, she didn't recognize Edward, and he wanted to keep that from her for as long as possible. No matter who you were, it changed how people reacted and treated Edward.

She raised her eyes to question what he had said, slightly amused anyone would apologize for their language when all of her friends and family constantly told her she had the mouth of a sewer rat. Her father had often prayed to the Heavenly Father, and always in front of crowd, to forgive his precious daughter for her foul mouth, as he had said many times, she was raised better than that.

For her, words were like paintings. They represented something more than just one meaning, and "fuck," if said right and in different tones, meant different things. No other word got the attention "fuck" did.

Edward exploded with laughter to the astonishment of the other two. "What load of bollocks is that, Liam?" He held his stomach in the best belly laugh he'd had in months.

Edward couldn't contain his laughter; it was contagious. Soon, even Gabriella was giggling and not really sure why.

"Excuse my friend, Gabriella, but as long as I have known him, he has never spoken like that."

Once he could breathe again, Edward finally said, "You sound like a stuffy, English lord with a pickle up his arse?" Edward started uncontrollably laughing again.

Gabriella realized this was the first time she had laughed or even smiled in over three years. The feeling was so freeing, and for a few minutes, she had peace in her heart. She knew it wouldn't last long, so she embraced it while she could.

She was brought back to reality when Liam suddenly crossed the room and threw the laughing Edward flat on his back.

Liam growled, "Enough."

Were these two men for real?

Gabriella watched as a still spirited Edward took Liam's hand and was yanked up before Liam pounded Edward's back in a friendly gesture. Gabriella could see they were close friends who didn't mind showing it. It was nice to witness. She didn't know why she thought that was strange, but she was under the illusion that British men were cold.

Gabriella wondered whether her sons, Gianluca and Mateo, had they been given the chance to grow into manhood, would have had the closeness Liam and Edward had. With that thought, all the freedom she had just felt dissipated.

Edward instantly noticed the change in Gabriella. It was like a storm moving across the loch.

The two men exchanged a quick glance.

Edward instantly wanted to do something to bring the light back into Gabriella's eyes, and Liam decided it was time to get some food into this wee bird.

Chapter 4

The Little Angel Has Fangs

Edward beat Liam to the punch and pulled out Gabriella's chair in the private dining area that had been reserved for their use in the inn's restaurant.

Gabriella was surprised. No one back home pulled out chairs anymore.

After settling in and ordering a glass of wine, Gabriella asked, "So, I know Liam is in the military, but what do you do, Edward?"

"I am also in the RAF; I just completed my first tour. When I'm not flying, I do some charity work for children living with AIDS. My mum was passionate about the cause, and after she passed away, my brothers and I continued to support it." Edward went on to explain about what the foundation did and how far research and education had come in the fight against AIDS.

Gabriella couldn't get over how proud he was about the foundation and how his face lit up when he discussed the children and how their mortality rate was decreasing with the new medicines that were available because of the money his mother's foundation had raised. Edward truly believed that, in the next decade, the world would see a vaccination to prevent HIV. Her admiration for him grew in leaps and bounds.

Liam then took control of the conversation and asked Gabriella what she did for a living. Gabriella's face changed, the corners of her mouth curving up.

"I am a nutritionist for Reach Within. I work with parents, caregivers, and group homes with children who have severe developmental, behavioural, and physical disabilities. We've found that children with behavioural issues are calmer when provided with healthy, nutritious food instead of processed food."

Liam was impressed and wanted to know more about how she had ended up doing such a job. Edward also had many questions.

She explained that the high school she had attended had offered an afterschool program she had volunteered for.

"Part of the Canadian school system requires all students to do forty hours of community service in order to graduate. I chose to do mine at Reach Within and fell in love with the special needs population. I volunteered in a behaviour room that had a girl with autism. She was very violent, and her mother was on social assistance and couldn't afford good food. The girl was always searching for extra food because there was no real substance in what she was eating, just empty calories." Gabriella took a deep breath and went on to explain that Gabriella's parents owned a restaurant, and at the end of the night, they threw out any food that went uneaten.

"I asked the administrator if I could bring in the leftover food for this girl. The administrator asked the mother, and the mother was thrilled that her daughter would have good food. After about a month, the staff noticed a change in her behaviour. She was calmer and a lot happier."

Liam could feel her excitement as she talked about a career she was proud of, and he continued to listen intently to every word.

Edward, although captivated, drifted for a moment and wondered if this was how his mum had felt about her foundation. Showing such a love for something you believed in, captivating every audience, it was no wonder his mum had raised so much money. Gabriella graced him with something no human had ever given him before: a real glimpse of his mum. What else could he learn from this incredible, beautiful woman?

Gabriella continued, "I went to university, studied nutrition, and after graduation, I approached Reach Within with a proposal to teach underprivileged families how to make simple, nutritious food on a low budget. They hired me on contract to see if it was successful, and a year later, I was hired on full-time."

"I have to say I am impressed. I'm sure there will be a special place for you in Heaven," Edward stated.

"I hate that fucking saying! Being a good person means shit to a heartless God."

Holy crap! Edward recoiled like he had been slapped.

Liam was also surprised that the little angel had fangs, but he knew why her bark was as bad as her bite. He made a mental note to let Edward in on why Gabriella had lashed out.

"I understand what you're saying, but Edward meant no harm. He meant it as a compliment," Liam stated.

That brought Edward's shocked face into Gabriella's line of vision, and she immediately realized she had crushed Edward's feelings with her totally inappropriate response. She was humiliated and embarrassed.

In a quiet voice, Gabriella said, "You didn't deserve that, Edward. Please forgive me." She took a deep breath. "I am normally not that rude. The only way I can explain my reaction is to tell you that I used to be extremely religious until my world blew apart three years ago, and I lost my faith in God and the Church. But that is no excuse when you have been nothing but kind to me. I didn't mean to be impolite. I guess I am still not fit to be with people." With that, Gabriella stood up and thanked them for dinner.

Edward grabbed Gabriella's hand. "I forgive you. We all have times when we speak before thinking. I am sorry your world fell apart, and believe it or not, I understand. I may not have walked a mile in your shoes, but my shoes have seen many rough roads. I promise you I don't take it personally." Edward saw the guilt in her big brown eyes and continued, "I beg you, Gabriella. Don't leave me alone again to listen to Liam's stories of when he was a wee lad in Scotland."

Gabriella hadn't expected that response, and she started to laugh, which broke the tension.

Now that things were back on track, they ordered more wine with their supper. Gabriella made sure to know exactly what she was ordering for dinner. She didn't want a repeat performance of breakfast. Therefore, she ordered a steak and ale, pie, and a salad, making sure the waiter told her every ingredient.

Liam watched with a smile, absorbing all that was Gabriella. He asked if she cooked in her families' restaurant, and Gabriella's response was filled with enthusiasm.

"I love to cook. I love the smell, the taste, the textures, and I like to create something wonderful out of fresh ingredients. From the time I could walk, I helped my papi in the kitchen, absorbing and learning everything I could. He always says I will one day take over the restaurant. So, yes, to answer your question, I do cook at the restaurant."

Edward smiled. "That's brilliant. I think you should cook for Liam and me. I can honestly say I can't remember the last time I had a home-cooked meal."

"What! You're bullshitting me." Gabriella couldn't fathom that. It had to be lie.

"Nope, it's the God's honest truth," Edward stated, wincing when he realized his reference to God again.

Gabriella turned to Liam to see if Edward was giving her the run around. To her surprise, Liam nodded.

"It's true for Edward and myself. It's been about three and a half years."

"Really? Well, in that case, you boys are taking me to the market tomorrow, and I am so cooking you dinner. It's the perfect way for me to repay some of the kindness you both have shown me."

"We don't expect you to cook for us. Edward's only joking."

Edward turned his shocked expression on Liam. "I'm not joking. Rest assured, I would sell my soul and yours—if you had one—for a home-cooked meal. I am salivating just thinking about it."

"That settles it, then. You are getting the Capello family's recipe for Spain's most famous paella."

Already Gabriella's mind was working overtime, thinking of all the ingredients.

Maybe she would sleep tonight and not dream of the family she had loved, lost, and still missed so much it made it hard to breathe. That thought made her realize she hadn't cooked for anyone in at least three years. It felt good to have a purpose again.

She had a close-knit group of friends back home. They would laugh if they knew she was getting excited over cooking for a couple of men she had just met.

As their evening drew to end, Liam approached a subject that could cause Gabriella to lash out or send her running.

"Gabriella, I am going to ask a favour of you, and I want you to think a moment on it before you give me your answer…I want you to move into my bedroom. I'll either sleep on the chesterfield or stay in Edward's suite with the bypass door open."

She tried to answer, but Liam cut her off.

"Before you say no, I'll give you the reasons I want you to take my bedroom." He started to tick off on his fingers. "One, you were exhausted and near frozen to death when Edward found you. Two, you slept for two days straight and still don't have your strength back. Three, tonight was the only the second real meal you've had in almost three days. Four, you need someone to watch over you. Fifth and final, I won't sleep a wink if I'm concerned you may need something and no one is there to help you. I am pleading with you. Please, just let us move you into my suite for a couple of days."

"Uh…I don't know. I don't even really know you two. And truth be told, I'm scared. Please don't be offended or take it personally, but life has taught me that, just when you think everything is going to be okay, you get kicked down."

Liam instantly picked up on her vulnerability and decided to play on it to get his way. "You stayed in my bed for the last two days. You had nightmares and woke up, screaming and crying, and I rocked you in my arms until you calmed down. Edward made you drink broth, and we watched over you until you fell back to sleep."

Edward jumped on the bandwagon. "If we wanted to hurt you, we could have done it while you slept. We wouldn't have healed you

34

just to re-injure you. Please believe me; we wish you no harm."

Gabriella was stunned to hear all that they had done for her. She was also embarrassed by her behaviour and her lack of appreciation.

"I am so sorry for all the shit I put you both through, but how can I expect you guys to do anything else for me? You have already sacrificed so much of your vacation to help me, and I have been nothing but a burden."

Liam grabbed Gabriella's hands and looked her in the eyes. "When you saw a child was in need, you fed that child. Did it feel like the child was a burden?" Liam could tell by the look in her eyes that he had hit the bull's-eye. "Some caregivers are great at giving, but suck at receiving. I bet you have given your whole life and never taken for yourself. Gabriella, you have brightened this holiday from the minute we laid eyes on you. You need a little extra TLC right now, and we have a little to spare. Trust me; if you want to pay us back, we will trade our TLC for some home cooking."

"And if you can bake, I will be your servant for the rest of time," Edward added.

"Enough, enough. Okay, I give up. I will stay in Liam's room, and he can stay on the sofa."

"Sofa? What's a sofa? You Americans say the weirdest things." Edward chuckled.

Gabriella drew her eyebrows together and took on an edgy tone. "How much do you value your life? Because, if you call me an American one more time, you will be acquainted with my cobra. I am Canadian through and through. Just because I come from North America, it doesn't make me an American. They are citizens of the United States of America; I am from Canada and, therefore, Canadian. Not, I repeat, an American." She blew a piece of hair out of her face.

The edges of Liam's mouth raised, and again, he thought the beautiful, little angel had fangs. He found that appealing.

Edward threw his hands up in surrender and bowed. "Again, my good lady, I must apologize for my wayward tongue. Though, I must say, it has never gotten me into as much trouble in one sitting as it has tonight. I meant no disrespect, my lady."

Gabriella chuckled. The man could twist any situation around, and you couldn't help adoring him. Somehow, she trusted these men, and she was growing to like them very much.

Chapter 5

Sangria and Churros

*S*he had gone back to the car to get her sweater, leaving her family standing in front of the court house, when multiple bangs made her jump.

As she turned around, she saw a car with its tires screeching and a man with a balaclava over his head, hanging out of the car with a gun in his hand.

Time stood still.

Then, in slow motion, she saw the bullets rip through her boys. Gianluca's body flew back with the impact of the bullets. Mateo's body hit his father's then fell forwards onto the ground, and Marco crumbled, his hand still around Mateo's shoulders.

The stairs leading up to the courthouse were awash in blood. There was screaming all around. Regardless, something kept her feet glued to the spot. She tried to move, but her feet wouldn't obey until someone bent down to touch her Mateo. Then, whatever force was holding her still suddenly released, and she ran with all her might before that person could touch her son.

"Leave him alone! Don't touch my baby!" She jumped over a man who had drop to the ground.

The good Samaritan bending down to help Mateo jumped back, still freaked out after the shooting.

Gabriella fell to her knees and grabbed the limp body of Mateo as she shook Marco, screaming at him to help her.

"Marco, help me, please! I can't do it by myself. Please, Marco!"

The police from inside the courthouse were now by her side, trying in vain to help her husband and children. One started CPR on Marco while another yelled at her to let him help Mateo. Gianluca was being tended to by a woman in civilian clothes.

It was mayhem all around her, and again, time stood still as she sat, holding her knees to her chest, rocking back and forth, covered in her baby's blood.

"No, God. Please, God, save my babies. Please save my family. No...God, please. God, save my husband. No...God, save my family," she repeated over and over.

When the ambulances arrived, and the paramedics took over, one of the officers then turned and took her in his large, strong arms, as she silently wept. She hardly noticed him, watching as the blood drained from her precious family, as did all her hopes and dreams.

The police officer continued to rock her as she sobbed, and

when she opened her eyes, instead of the police officer holding her, it was Liam.

He was wiping her tears as they fell. He had placed Gabriella in his lap like a child, rocking her, as she leaned against his bare chest while he comforted her.

She was so fucking tiny, so fucking broken. He would give anything to see her fangs at that moment.

Edward was beside himself, as white as sheet and breathing heavily from the fear of being woken up by her earth shattering screams then witnessing her suffering again.

"Get me some tissues," Liam ordered Edward gently.

Edward moved to the loo to grab a box of tissues. On his way back, giving Liam a chin lift with knitted brows, silently inquiring what was going on.

Liam just nodded, indicating he would fill him in later. He felt guilty for not letting Edward know sooner, but they hadn't let her out of their sight since he had found out, and he wasn't ready for her to know what he had uncovered.

As he wiped her tear-stained face with the tissues, Liam couldn't help wondering why fate was so cruel to some people. This little angel didn't deserve what had happened to her and her family. He had to make it better for her. He had to teach her there was life after death.

Fuck, she was beautiful, delicate, and gorgeous.

As that thought hit him, he realized the irony. Well, maybe they could learn that lesson together.

Liam continued to rock her for another hour before she settled and fell asleep in his protective arms. She mewed as he moved her under the blankets and onto his chest, enveloping her with his arms. For the rest of the night, she would be protected from the night terrors as he stood guard, rubbing her back and arms to insure she knew she wasn't alone.

***

Gabriella felt the warmth of the sun shining through the window onto her face. It felt glorious. She kept her eyes closed and just enjoyed the feeling of the sun beating down on her. Then she heard the rhythm of a heart beat and felt the tickle Marco's chest hair. A small smile came to her lips, but that quickly changed when she took a deep inhale to breathe in all that was Marco. She froze. That wasn't Marco's scent. This scent smelled warm and spicy with a hint of citrus.

Gabriella jumped back and bumped her head on the night table, knocking the lamp over and onto Edward's head.

Everyone gave a startled gasp, trying to figure out where they were and what was going on.

"What the hell is going on here?" Gabriella gasped as she recognized her bedroom mates.

"Damn, did you have to throw a lamp at me?" Edward accused, rubbing his head.

All the heavy breathing and yelling came to a halt when Liam's laughter was heard.

Both Gabriella and Edward turned to glare at Liam. Together, they asked, "What's so fucking funny?"

Liam had to take a minute to compose himself. "Look at the three of us. Imagine if the maids were to walk in now. We would never be able to explain this."

Gabriella held the sheet up to her neck. "I don't find this funny. You two told me I could trust you last night, and now I wake up to find you in my bed—well, actually your bed, but you gave it to me with the assurance that you would be on the couch. Why is Edward sitting beside us? What the freak gives?" She was looking down at the sheets, embarrassed to be in such a compromising position with two men. Had she drunk too much last night?

"Gabriella, look at me," Liam demanded, pushing away from the headboard. "No, not at my chest; look in my eyes. You had a nightmare last night, and you were inconsolable. We felt like we couldn't leave you alone."

Gabriella was thankful he had on track pants. It almost took her breath away to look at the perfectly sculptured body Liam was rocking. She also noticed he had a tattoo on the left side of his chest. It looked like a black bird emerging from inside his chest.

When she realized she was staring, she quickly looked away, only to turn her blushing face towards Edward, who was also only in track pants. She noted he had no tattoos, and his chest was as smooth as a baby's bottom.

Edward fell to his knees beside the bed and grabbed Gabriella's hand, the one that held the sheet to her chest, and looked into her eyes. "Tell us what happened to you. Why are you suffering? Why are you alone in a foreign country? Let us help you, please."

A single tear travelled down her face, followed by a stream of them. "I'm so sorry. I had no idea. Truth be told, I haven't slept through the night in over three years." She sobbed, continuing, "Three years ago, my family was killed, and I am afraid I will never recover from it. I relive their deaths every night."

"Oh, bloody hell, Gabriella. I am so sorry," Edward replied.

"There's no need to explain now," Liam jumped in, sensing she wasn't ready to give them details. "When and if you are ready, we will listen. Whatever makes you comfortable. Let's move on and regroup."

Liam talked about plans to shop for Gabriella's dinner, and the mood lightened. Gabriella was thankful she didn't have to relive the story again so soon after her nightmare.

Gabriella went to take a shower, and as soon as the men heard the water turn on, Edward approached Liam.

"I can read you like a book. What happened to Gabriella's family? How were they killed?"

Liam took a deep breath then told Edward all he knew. Edward was devastated for her. He wasn't sure how someone could recover from that kind of loss. Liam reiterated not to let on that they knew about her husband and sons. He thought it was important that she

42

share how they had died as part of the healing process. She had to be ready to share that kind of pain and loss. It wasn't something that could be forced. Then, and only then, could they help her move on.

When everyone was dressed and ready, they again went to the private dining room and had breakfast. Gabriella simply ordered potato scones with blackberry jelly and a coffee. The men ordered the traditional Scottish breakfast again with hot tea.

It was odd for Gabriella to see men drink tea. In the Spanish culture, they drank espresso, and in Canada, no one started their day without a large Tim Horton's coffee. *Oh, well,* she thought, *when in Scotland, do like the Scottish.* She scoffed at that. She would rather have her coffee, thank you very much.

When they were finished, Edward said he needed to go back to the room to get his hat. And when he came back out, Gabriella swallowed a giggle.

Edward was wearing a jacket and a baseball cap with sunglasses. She hardly recognized him.

"You didn't tell me we were going incognito to the market," she teased.

"Ha-ha, Gabriella. Very funny. I like wearing baseball caps. It makes me feel more North American, emphasis placed on the north and not the American."

"Smart man. You're learning."

They drove into the town of Portree and down to the port where an open air market was in full-swing. The town was quaint and beautiful with its colored row houses surrounding the port, and the shops were beautiful.

They wandered in and out of a few shops, and at one, there was a rack filled with little fairies in front of the cash register. When Liam saw a couple with long, dark hair and wings, it reminded him of Gabriella, a beautiful, little angel. Fairies, angels—they all looked alike to him. So, as she was searching through the store, Liam bought three fairies; one with long, dark, curly hair in a white dress that looked like Gabriella to him, and two with straight black hair and pink dresses. He quickly stuffed them in his jacket.

Gabriella was in her glory shopping for fresh food, although they didn't have the selection she was used to. She knew she was still going to have to visit a grocery store for the staples, but she was enjoying bartering for goods, nonetheless.

She gathered many different ingredients, intending to cook for the rest of the week for the men. She gathered fruits for authentic sangria and flours and sugar for desserts. Liam insisted on paying for all the groceries and wouldn't take no for an answer. He was stubborn and bossy as shit.

Gabriella turned to him. "You do know we women have been given the right to vote and work and earn money outside the house, Mr. Caveman. I can pay for my own groceries, thank you very much."

"When you are with me, I pay, plain and simple. No argument," Liam calmly responded.

Gabriella had noticed people were staring at them and whispering. She was sure it was because the two men escorting her were drop-dead gorgeous. They were intently looking after all of her needs, and people were probably trying to figure out who was with whom. Regardless of the reasons, it was really starting to get on her nerves. The gawking bordered on rude. The women were the worst, giggling and shyly flirting.

On the way back to the car, Gabriella was telling them how beautiful she found the town, and they told her about some of the sights around the Isle of Skye, like the fairy pools, Dunvegan Castle, and Kilt Rock.

Liam was proud of his homeland and wanted to share all of its glory with Gabriella. Therefore, they agreed to take her to all the sights in exchange for all the meals she was going to cook.

They carried all their purchases into Liam's suite and unpacked. The first thing on Gabriella's list was to make sangria. The first thing on Liam's list was to go to the front desk to see if they would store some of the goods. Also, Gabriella couldn't find a pan big enough to cook the paella in, so Liam needed to talk to the chef to see if they would loan her one. The inn's management knew who they were hosting, so Liam was sure they would bend over backward to accommodate them.

Two hours later, the suite smelled mouth-watering good as Gabriella cooked like she was teaching one of her classes at school. She had Edward and Liam cutting onions, garlic, chorizo, and meats.

They laughed while they worked, sharing the sangrias Gabriella had made.

Watching Gabriella was like watching those fancy-ass cooking shows. She captivated her audience to a point where they were working as hard as she was, but you felt like you were being honoured to have her guide you.

Now that everything was in the pan and cooking, they had about forty-five minutes before dinner would be ready. Therefore, they took their sangria outside to enjoy the sunset over the Loch.

Liam had to run back inside after ten minutes to get the other pitcher of sangria, and when he came back out, Gabriella asked him if he had touched anything else while he was inside.

"No, of course not. You asked me not to touch the churros, and I painstakingly did not."

Gabriella looked at Edward, and they burst out laughing. Offended, Liam challenged them to prove him wrong. Gabriella stood up, lifted Liam's shirt, and blew all the cinnamon and sugar in his face before she laughed again. He begged for forgiveness in light of the fact that he had never tasted anything so scrumptious in all his life. Liam, who could take down a man with one punch, was terrified, if this wee lass didn't forgive him, he wouldn't get any more of his new favourite piece of fried heaven.

"You have no idea how hard it is to be from the United Kingdom and smell that kind of goodness," Liam excused himself. "We don't do flavour in our grub, so you can't blame a man for his stomach being a weakness, can you? You would never understand, being that you're Spanish."

"Actually, my mother is Scottish. She was born in Glencoe."

"Are you bloody serious? You're going to try to tell us that you—with your olive skin; dark, curly hair; and deep brown eyes— have a hint of Scottish in you?" Edward was aghast.

"I am telling you that Eileen *Miller* Capello was definitely born and raised in Scotland." With that, she went inside to check on the paella.

Liam turned to Edward. "I think I am falling in love."

Edward, just having taken a sip of his sangria, spit the contents of his mouth all over his friend and bodyguard. Choking and coughing, Edward pounded at his chest. "What the fuck did you just say?"

Liam looked pissed off. "Never in this life have I thought I would be this attracted to another woman, but there is something so fucking special about that angel. I can honestly believe I'm falling in love with her."

Well, that was another punch in the stomach to Edward. He felt the same way. Even though Gabriella was older than him, he believed he could very easily lose his heart to her.

Chapter 6

Mama's Niños

The men rubbed their full bellies. Never had either one of them eaten more food nor had anything quite as delicious as Gabriella's paella. The favours exploded on their tongues, the chicken so tender it melted in their mouths. The mixture of meat and seafood together was amazing, and the yellow colour from the saffron just made you happy.

"Gabriella, I have to tell you, I have had orgasms that weren't half as good as the supper you made us."

"Edward!" Liam bellowed.

Edward continued. "What else can I do to insure you will cook more meals like that? And on that note, no matter how full I am, I want another churro please."

Giggling to herself, Gabriella got up to get the last plate of churros. She had thought they would have at least a five-day supply, but she never anticipated two full plates would be consumed in one sitting, and the third was on its way out.

"Don't come crying to me when you bust a gut. That said, I must tell you that I enjoyed making the meal as much as you enjoyed eating it."

"The more I get to know you, Gabriella, the more I appreciate all that you are," Liam chimed in.

Gabriella blushed and looked down at the table, embarrassed by all the attention. "You guys sure know how to butter up the chef, even though you are English and, therefore, easy to impress." She outright laughed at the indignity on their faces as they pouted after her comment.

She giggled and then continued somewhat more somber. "To tell you the truth, I haven't felt this alive in so long, and you two make me feel like I can see the clearing beyond the trees. I also think I owe you some explanations."

Liam feared it might be too early for her to regurgitate her heartbreaking story, or maybe he was just afraid of how hard it would be to listen and watch this beautiful angel fall apart in the daytime. He had been able to comfort her in the dead of night because she wasn't conscious of him holding her and giving her strength.

Gabriella braced herself, took a deep breath, and organized her thoughts. "I had the perfect life, but between two crooked cops...God, I lost everything that was important to me. I had a husband who worshipped me and was my soul mate. From that union, we had the two most loving and beautiful sons in the world." Gabriella's eyes filled with tears. She wasn't sure she had the strength to carry on.

When the men realized her struggle was getting worse, Edward placed his hand on her shoulder, and squeezed it while Liam took her hand and rubbed circles with his thumb.

"Angel, you don't need to do this. We get it," Liam stated.

"Please don't look at me with pity, Liam. It's my life now, and I need you to understand why I am so messed up."

She freaked both of them out when she switched from a whisper to a scream. "Do you know why I'm in Scotland? Let me tell you. No *sane* person would do what I have attempted!"

Liam bent down in front of her and grabbed both her hands in his larger one. With his other hand, he grabbed her jaw and angled it to look at him as he yelled, "Angel! For fuck's sake, stop and look at me!"

Gabriella jumped and stopped yelling.

Liam knew he had frightened her, but he had to reach her now or risk her falling back into her depression.

Looking into her big, brown, beautiful eyes, he said, "If you want to do this, you need to pull yourself together. We promise not to judge anything you say. And, Gabriella, both of us have lost people in our lives. We feel your pain. Do. You. Get. Me?"

After pulling herself together, Gabriella lowered her head. "I am so sorry. Of course, you must think I am freaking nuts. Everyone has lost someone, and they don't act as crazy as I do. But, Liam, they were my whole existence, my whole fucking world. I am nothing without them.

"Why, Liam? Why would God leave me behind? I tried my whole life to be a good person. I believed in good versus evil, right over wrong. I raised my children to believe that, and yet, I am still being punished for some unknown reason. I just want my family back. Please, Liam, please help me. I just want my family back!"

Grabbing her face with both hands, he pulled her closer so they were nose to nose. "Sweetheart, I can't bring your family back, but you can keep them alive by sharing your memories of them. Tell me their names, what they looked like, what made them who they were. Please, angel, tell me." Liam wiped the tears from her face after Edward passed him some tissue.

Gabriella nodded. "My husband's name was Marco. We were high school sweethearts—well, not really high school. I met him my first year of high school, but he graduated the year before and was giving tours of our school because he had a week free before he started university. There was an instant connection. He had seen me in my family's restaurant, but since I was five years younger than him, he decided to befriend me and wait until I was old enough to date. He would come to the restaurant the days he knew I was waitressing."

Gabriella took on a peaceful look as she told the love story about her and Marco. She talked about him asking her papi if he could take her on a date the day after she had turned eighteen. After three months of dating, he had asked for her hand in marriage, and although it was fast, Manny and Elia had known in their hearts it was coming. Marco and Gabriella had become inseparable, and their love had been visible to everyone who had happened to be in their presence.

She described how her brother Philippe had possessed major issues around their engagement and would often argue with his parents that the engagement was way too quick. It had gotten to a point where Philippe had refused to speak to his father. What Philippe had failed to realize was that they were going to get married whether or not they had their parents' consent or blessing, so her parents had known it was better they blessed the union and kept their daughter close.

One year and a month after their first date, Gabriella had a huge Spanish wedding for three hundred fifty guests with a seven course meal and flamenco dancers. Philippe had finally conceded the day of the wedding that maybe he had been wrong, and he had wished his beloved sister all the happiness in the world.

Gabriella had continued to finish her university degree, and when she had started working, she had met a group of girls who would become her closest friends. Although, that was a story she would tell them at another time.

"I never dated another soul. It was like Marco was made for me. He treated me like a princess. I would come down the stairs, and he would ask, 'Is that my hot wife?' He used to tell the boys that they had the prettiest mama in the world."

Every day with Marco had been a gift, and the only other thing she had wanted was his child, but they'd had priorities and dreams, so she had finished university and then had been offered a permanent position with Reach Within after the one-year preliminary contract was up. Then all of her dreams had come true when she had become pregnant. Nine months later, they had a baby boy.

"Gianluca was the spitting image of his papi, and he also had Marco's easy disposition. He was mythological, quiet, and smiled a lot. He was fearlessly protective over his mama. At school, he had a ton of friends and was adored by all of Marco's buddies because he was a real man's boy."

He had loved sports; played hockey in the winter and competed with the swim team in the summer, but his number one love had been soccer. He had been the goalie, and Gabriella explained that she had done everything in her power to convince him to play another position, because she was afraid he would take the teams' losses on his own shoulders, but there had been no swaying him.

"Marco and I made sure one of us was at every game he ever played. I was so proud of him."

"How old was Gianluca and your other son?" Edward asked.

"Gianluca was ten, and Mateo was eight." Gabriella had a bittersweet smile from the memories. "Mateo was a little joker. Everyone loved him, and he knew everyone on our street and anyone who ever dined at Papi's restaurant by name. It didn't matter whether you were eight or eighty, Mateo befriended you. He loved to make people laugh. I miss that so much."

Gabriella began to cry again, and again, Liam steered her away from her grief by asking her to share what Mateo had looked like.

"Mateo was big for a baby. He weighted ten pounds two ounces when he was born."

"No bloody way a tiny, little thing like you could give birth to a baby that size," Edward stated, shocked.

"Well, I did, but because he was so big, he got stuck in my birth canal. I had to have an emergency C-section and nearly died. Mateo was the last child I would ever be able to carry.

"Marco was so thankful that Mateo and I survived, and because of his fear, he was relieved I couldn't have any more children. He always said he couldn't go through that again, though we had always wanted a daughter. Still, we were both thrilled with the two little men God had granted us. I didn't know at the time that God would snatch all that he had blessed me with away and leave me in purgatory."

"Did Mateo play soccer, too?" Liam inquired, again moving her to safer thoughts.

"No, he tried it, but it just wasn't for him. He hadn't yet found exactly what sport he wanted before he was murdered. He loved to cook and bake with me, though, and he was forever stuck to my papi's side at the restaurant. I truly believed he would have one day taken over the restaurant, and I think my papi was grooming him to do just that.

"Mateo loved churros almost as much as you," she said to Edward. "And he even convinced my papi to serve them with Nutella. It was a huge hit at the restaurant.

"Mateo had beautiful, laughing eyes and chubby cheeks you just wanted to squeeze. When he hugged you, it felt like everything was good in the world. We could never discipline him, because he would make us laugh or would talk circles around us until we weren't quite sure why he was in trouble anymore. We used to joke that, if the restaurant didn't work out for a career, he could always be a lawyer."

"Your family sounds like they were beautiful, Gabriella. I can almost visualize them by your description," Liam shared with her.

"I have pictures of my family just before they left me. I carry them everywhere I go. Let me go and get them." She jumped up and ran into the bedroom to her suitcase. She opened her iPad, pulled the case off, where three pictures of Gabriella with her family sat. One was from their last Christmas together, one was at the beach, and the last one was at Mateo's communion.

She got lost in her memories until Liam walked in to the bedroom to see what was taking so long.

"May I see?" Liam spoke softly so as not to frighten her.

She smiled through the tears as she handed them to him. "This one here was the last family photo we took together." She showed him the one taken at Christmas.

"Such a beautiful family, and you look so happy together. I can see a lot of both you and Marco in the boys. Mateo definitely has your eyes, but Gianluca has your nose."

Gabriella's smile widened. "Do you really think so?"

"Yeah, I really do." He nodded. "Let's go and show Edward." He grabbed her hand and dragged her into the main room.

Edward stood up, and Gabriella showed him the photos, smiling as she told them the stories surrounding the photos.

Hours passed as she told them story after story, laughing and crying until she ended up falling asleep on the chesterfield, absolutely exhausted and emotionally drained.

Liam took her into the bedroom and laid her on the bed. She looked so peaceful for once and a little less tortured. He moved a strand of hair from her face then ran his knuckles up and down her cheek. He would do anything to take her pain away. She was such a giving woman and had so much love. He wished her peace in her sleep tonight, although he wasn't leaving it to chance. He would sleep beside her and hold her close to try to keep the nightmares at bay then leave her bed at the crack of dawn so that she didn't know, like he had every night since they had found her.

He would protect her and love her if he could ever heal her broken heart. Never had he expected to feel this, not ever.

Chapter 7

Beautiful Skye

Waking up refreshed was a new feeling for Gabriella. She stretched her body, and for once, it wasn't sore from being cramped up in one position—the fetal position—fighting the memories and the nightmares. She jumped out of bed, went to the loo, showered, and dressed in record time. It was a new day, and for the first time in forever, she wanted to experience what was ahead of her.

"I'm ready to cash in on the deal we made. I fed you two, and now I want to see the sights. Come on, Liam, get off your phone. You promised."

Liam continued in a muted voice, holding a finger up to indicate he would only be another minute. Edward knew Liam had to let Protection Command or, more specifically, the Royalty Protection Branch—SO14—the division responsible for the royal family's security, know their itinerary and whereabouts.

57

Edward decided to keep Gabriella busy for a few more minutes.

"Have you decided what you want to see first?"

"Yes, I want to go to the fairy pools first. Don't ask me why, but I feel like I need to see the mystical part of Skye. Next, and not necessarily in this order, I want to see Dunvegan Castle, Kilt Rock, Neist Point, and I know you mentioned a couple of other places I should see. Gabriella continued with a newly discovered enthusiasm, "My gram grew up not too far from the isle, and she always spoke of the uncut beauty of Skye, so in a way, I am connecting with my Scottish roots."

She beamed at him, talking a mile a minute. "I feel good. This is the first time I slept through the night in over three years, and I feel lighter and not quite so lost, if that makes any sense at all."

He knew what she struggled with during the night. After all, last night was the first night since he had met her that he had slept through the night instead of waking up to her screaming.

"That is aces. You feel great, the sun is again shining—for how long we are not sure—and we are off to see the fairy pools. The legends say that the pools hold the secret energy of the Seelie Fae, and on a full moon, you can see the creatures gathering energy. Last night was a full moon, so maybe we will get lucky and spot the little buggers. It is said they are not always visible to the naked eye, but with smart phones, we might be lucky enough to outwit them." Edward winked at her when he saw the smile she was trying to contain.

Liam caught the folklore Edward was feeding Gabriella, and it gave him an idea. Maybe he could bring the magic to life for Gabriella. Of course, to do that, he would have to let Edward in on his little scheme.

He carefully stuffed his surprise in his pocket then walked back into the main room where Edward was putting on his baseball cap and sunglasses. Liam wasn't quite sure how they were going to explain Edward wearing the sunglasses on a rainy day to Gabriella, but they would cross that bridge when they had to.

They ate the rest of the churros, had some coffee, and then Gabriella and Edward finished getting ready. Then they jumped into Liam's truck and headed to the fairy pools.

Gabriella rushed to the public washrooms before they started the hike to the pools, and Liam used that opportunity to pull the fairy ornament out of his pocket and show it to Edward.

"I have a wee fairy I want to use when taking pictures of Gabriella, so if you are taking pictures with your phone, then I will hold the fairy, and vice versa so it appears in the pictures. I want this to be a fun and mystical experience like you were describing in your folklore story."

"That's brilliant!" Edward laughed. "I am seeing a side to you I had no idea existed. I must say, she definitely brings out the best in both of us." In truth, Edward wanted to protect her and look after her; make sure she saw the good and the wonder that life still had to offer her.

Liam had to agree. "For the first time in five years, I feel like I am capable of making someone happy and that her happiness exceeds mine. I want to fix that tiny wee angel's broken wings so she can fly and soar and be free to live again, not just exist."

Gabriella appeared then, ready and anxious to discover the sights. They took the path towards the base of the Cuillin Mountains, and she was amazed to discover sudden openings in the ground where little brooks, pools, and waterfalls appeared.

After witnessing them, she turned to Edward. "You know, I think I understand why they call them fairy pools. To me, it looks like miniature valleys and waterfalls that you would see in, like...I don't know...let's say Victoria falls in South Africa, but on a much smaller scale."

Edward smiled. "Let me take a picture of the waterfalls. I will crop out the scenery around it, and let's see if your theory stands true." Edward did this then turned the phone to show Gabriella.

"Yes!" she exclaimed excitedly. "That is exactly what I see. Cool. It looks like it could be one of the largest waterfalls on earth when it is cropped like that. Thanks, Edward. Do you guys mind taking a few pictures for me? I didn't even think to bring my phone. I want some memories of this enchanting place, even if I don't get to see a fairy," she said on a pout.

Edward winked at Liam. "Liam, go and stand next to Gabriella. I will take a picture of the two of you with the waterfall in the background. It will give perspective to the dimensions of the pools and the waterfalls."

Liam stood beside Gabriella and placed his arm around her waist where he held the fairy by a string. It dangled a few inches beside them. Edward then traded spots with Liam, discreetly exchanging the fairy. The next shot had Edward with his arm around Gabriella's shoulder, and it appeared the fairy was in the tree to the right of them.

As they walked down and then up the trail, the pools got bigger and the water changed to a turquoise green. The pools were still hidden from view until you came upon the opening in the earth. A young couple were also taking selfies, and Gabriella offered to take a couple pictures of them together if they took a couple of photos of the three of them.

"Edward, please take off your glasses and hat. I feel like I can't see you."

Like every other time Gabriella requested something, Edward did her bidding without question. Meanwhile, Liam placed the fairy right beside Gabriella's shoulder.

The man was taking the pictures when his girlfriend said to Edward, "You remind me of someone...I feel like I know you from somewhere, but I just can't place where."

Edward and Liam both tensed, and Gabriella felt it. The air also seemed to thicken around them. She was taken aback by the change, noting how Liam was no longer the carefree, good-looking male. She actually took a step back and bent her head way back to look him in the eyes. In the meantime, Edward put his glasses and hat back on and started to walk away.

"Liam, what's wrong? Why am I picking up weird vibes from you two?"

"It's nothing. Let's get moving; we have a lot to see and do today, and the weather can change at the flip of a coin. The clouds have already begun to move in." Liam took her arm and turned her around after retrieving his phone from the man and thanking them.

Gabriella might have been oblivious to many things that were going on around her over the last few years, but she knew down to her soul something important had just passed between Edward and Liam. She had started to trust these men, but she was beginning to wonder how well she actually knew them.

While on the way to Kilt Rock and Mealt Falls, Gabriella encountered a road she thought was unbelievably cool, so much so that she made the men pull over and take some pictures.

"Liam, I don't want to offend you, but the miniature waterfalls at the fairy pools and now this tiny, little road...I mean, really, how cute is that?" Feeling a little mischievous, she said, "I hope everything in Scotland isn't quite so small."

Edward burst out laughing, tears running down his face.

Liam took two large strides to bring him in front of Gabriella then bent down so he was face to face with her. With a lethal stare, tried to intimidate her, "Another comment like that and I'll pull you over my knee and give you a spanking for being the naughty *little* lass you are. If you are curious about the size of everything in Scotland, let me know; I can prove to you just how *large* Scotland can be. Do. You. Get. Me?" He had whispered the last part seductively.

Holy freakin' hot pissed off man. Gabriella tried to keep her laughter at bay so as not to piss Liam off any further, but with one glance at Edward, who crossed his eyes at her, knowing it was taking all her willpower not to laugh, she lost all control.

She was having trouble breathing when she realized Liam was laughing as hard as Edward and her. Then it occurred to her, he wasn't laughing with her, but *at* her because she was so out of control. The laughter stopped dead when she realized that. And the guys stopped due to her reaction, apprehension in their eyes.

Liam asked her if she was all right, and she turned to both of her saviors and said,

"Yes, I finally think I am going to be okay."

Without a word, Liam and Edward led her back to the SUV. No one said word for the rest of the drive. It wasn't an uncomfortable silence; it was peaceful. Each one of them was lost in their own thoughts.

***

The guys directed her through a gated area to get to the edge of the cliffs that overlooked Kilt Rock. They explained to her that the rock was aptly named because it looked like the pattern on a kilt, and the vertical edges of the cliff gave the illusion of pleats.

"It truly does look like a kilt," Gabriella whisper in awe.

They took a few pictures, and Edward took a selfie of the three of them with Kilt Rock in the background.

As they stood there, admiring the sights, the wind picked up, and an eerie whistling sound could be heard.

"Do you guys hear that?" she asked, a little spooked.

"Hear what?" Edward asked.

"Come on, guys; no screwing with me. Tell me you hear the creepy whistle. Liam, you hear it, right?"

"No, angel, I don't know what you are talking about. What do you hear?" He really did hear it and knew exactly where the sound was coming from.

"I hear a whistling, almost musical. Could I be hearing bagpipes from somewhere around here, and the sound is carrying on the wind?"

"That's not really possible, angel. One, because we are nowhere near a town, and two, if that were the case, we would all hear it," Liam answered.

"If you guys are bullshitting me, I'm warning you, I will push you both off the cliff and hitchhike back to the inn."

Turning away from the guys, she saw the most beautiful sight. Combined with the whistling, she felt a weird sense of being closer to Heaven up here.

"Oh, wow, look! There's a rainbow over Kilt Rock. It's beautiful, but still a little creepy with that whistling."

"It's raining over there, meaning it will be raining here in few moments. I think we should head back to the SUV and carry on tomorrow with your tour," Liam suggested.

"Not only that, but I'm getting hungry, and you promised us another great meal tonight," Edward said.

Gabriella turned to the men, asking a question she wasn't sure they would grant her. "I need a few moments alone up here. Do you guys mind?"

She saw the conflict on their faces, exchanging looks amongst themselves. In the end, though, as uncomfortable as they were, they knew she needed this, so they walked away and left her.

Feeling closer to Heaven, she needed to say a few things.

Gabriella turned to the wind and the water, looked out at the sky, and had her first conversation with her dead husband.

"Why did you leave me, Marco? Why did you have to go away? I was counting on you to give me my forever. I fucking love you and miss you and the boys so much my heart aches. I'm not sure why God left me alone, and I am still so very angry at Him, but I am getting better...I think. I know you are with me and watch over me constantly. I feel your presence. I think it was you who sent Liam and Edward to me. Please tell me this is true, because I feel guilty for laughing and having fun when you and our babies aren't here to share it with me. Is this how I move on?

"I know. I can hear you telling me that you can't rest until you know I am settled. Still, we were soul mates, yet I find I am attracted to these two men, one more than I should. Help me, Marco. What do I do?

"I had to leave home. Everything reminded me of you and the boys. Everyone treated me like broken glass, afraid to touch me, afraid they would crush what little was left of me, and thinking they might not be able to be to put me back together again.

"Marco, reassure me you are okay with me having a relationship with these men. Does that make me a bad wife? A bad mother? You have the boys and are looking after them. Do they cry for their momma? I cry for them. I know, I know. I am breaking your heart."

Just as she made that statement, it began to rain, and rain hard. It came down in sheets, carried by the strong wind.

She wrapped her arms around herself, fell to her knees, and began to cry, knowing these were Marco's tears from Heaven.

She was so tormented, and he couldn't help her find peace. And until she did, he wouldn't rest in peace.

All of a sudden, she was wrapped up tightly in Liam's embrace. He swept her off her feet and into his arms, carrying the sobbing Gabriella back to the truck.

Edward jumped out and opened the back door, and Liam shuffled himself in with Gabriella positioned on his lap. Edward then jumped into driver's seat and drove them back to the inn.

Liam played with her hair, twisting his fingers in the wet ringlets, calming her sobs and letting her know she wasn't alone.

By the time they were back at the inn, Gabriella had pulled

herself together. Just after Edward turned off the ignition, she spoke in a soft voice.

"Believe it or not, I am getting better, and I have you two to thank for that. I am trying so hard to move on, but sometimes it hits me and takes me down to my knees. I can't ever thank you enough. One day, the shoe will be on the other foot, and I will repay your support and friendship." She sniffed and wiped her face. "You guys are going to pretend that never happened, and you're going to help me make our next meal. Are you with me?"

Both men smiled, and then they carried on like her breakdown had never happened.

Chapter 8

Chapters

Gabriella, I am almost convinced you could take a piece of shoe leather and make it into something delicious," Edward praised.

"Aw, Edward, you could charm the rattle right off a rattlesnake. You're already in my good books, so there's no need to keep buttering me up unless, of course, you want dessert." She winked.

"You know"—Liam sat back and patted his full belly—"you accomplished something many people have tried yet failed."

"And what great feat was that?"

He smiled. "My mum would never believe I ate fish and enjoyed it. And, not only did I eat it, but I willingly helped myself to seconds."

"Why didn't you tell me you don't like fish?" Gabriella felt horrible. "I would have cooked you something else. Although, I would have teased you." She had a mischievous smile on her face.

"Now that I know you aren't partial to fish, I will have to cook it more often so I can bring you over from the dark side."

Chuckling, Liam responded, "Maybe if my mum had added an abundance of flavours to her fish like you just did, I could have eaten it and saved my arse from many whippings for wasting good food. However, if you ever meet her and tell her that, I will deny it."

"Well, it is sacrilege to be from Britain and not eat fish and chips," Edward stated rather pompously.

"Let's not forget, ye wee bastard, I am Scottish, not English."

"Oh, yeah, that's right, a wannabe Brit."

The air changed in the suite as Liam growled, "Ye just never kent when to shut yer yap, do ye? Ye would think ye were brought up with more class than that."

Gabriella heard a hint of Liam's Scottish accent usually, but when he was defending his homeland, the accent came out thicker, and he really rolled his Rs. It sent a tingle south to a place Gabriella had thought long dead.

"Well, I have to say that I find this conversation a little amusing seeing as Edward can't understand why I don't like being called American, and Liam doesn't like to be called British. Care to explain to wee Edward why that is, Liam?"

Liam said, "Aye, I would, but it would just fall on deaf ears, like it has for the last five hundred years. Big brother countries just don't get that we smaller countries don't want to be just like 'em. We like our culture, our heritage, and we are proud of who we are."

"If I'd known you were both going to be sanctimonious and whine, I would have brought some cheese," Edward replied. "But I didn't, so I am raising the white flag. I concede that you are both right, and I am wrong. Now, can we have dessert?"

"Wait, can you say that again so I can record it on my phone, and every time you question one of my decisions, I can play it back for you?" Gabriella questioned.

"Ah, Liam, the quickest way to a woman's heart is to agree with whatever she wants to hear. So, milady, if you want a recording, then by all means." Edward cheekily bowed.

In the blink of an eye, for the second time in less than a week, Edward was again flat on his back with the wind knocked out of him and Liam growling at him to be careful.

Gabriella laughed, loving how they interacted with one another. Theirs was a friendship that had experienced many ups and downs, built a tremendous amount of respect, and the banter was just another layer to the friendship. Gabriella decided to break the tension and serve the yemas—small cakes covered in powdered sugar.

The men enjoyed another sweet treat that was covered in powdered sugar, and Gabriella conceded and allowed them to enjoy it with a cup of hot tea while she indulged in a café latte.

"Guys, do you mind emailing me the pics you took of us today? I want to make a slideshow of all the things I see so I can show my mom and see if she remembers any of these places. Also, the Sistas of the United Nations like to send and receive video diaries of each other to keep up with everyone's lives."

Edward's face screwed up as he replayed in his mind what Gabriella had just said. Finally giving up, he inquired, "Sisters of the nation; what's that? Some weird Canadian cult?"

"Ha-ha, very funny. No, I said the *Sistas* of the United Nations. They are *my girls*. I met most of them at work; the rest are friends I've had since forever. We hung out together and called ourselves sistas because we share everything like blood sisters. The United Nations part comes from not one of us having parents from the same country. We are all hybrids and enjoy and share our diversity and cultures. We embrace the differences. Most women compete and try to knock other women down in order to make themselves look and feel stronger. We are the opposite. We are stronger and more powerful as a group, and we empower one another."

"Wow, you have your own gaggle of women. That's cool. Are any of them single? Because I am in case you didn't know."

"They would be too old for you," she told Edward. "You need someone your own age."

Edward pouted. "How old do you think I am?"

She narrowed her eyes, studying him. "I would say twenty-three."

"Aw, that's rich. Twenty-three...No. In fact, I am twenty-six, and when I first found you, I believed you to be younger than me, about twenty-four."

"Oh, get the fuck out! You did not believe that. Really, Edward." She shook her head at him. "I am thirty-four; soon to be thirty-five. And that, my young friend, is an eight-year difference and too much of one for any of my gaggle, as you call it."

"Well, my mum was thirteen years younger than my pops, and if I remember correctly, you were five years younger than Marco."

As soon as he made the reference, poor Edward cringed, afraid it would send her into another downwards spiral of grief.

Gabriella caught the cringe and let him off the hook. "You don't have to be afraid to say Marco's name or the boys. It might hurt, but I don't want any more people in my life pretending that my family didn't exist. It makes me so much sadder to only have them alone in my mind. They did exist, and I am so proud of who they were. And I want to share in their existence, no matter how short it was or how sad it makes me."

Edward set his hand on hers. "You're right; keep them alive with us." He paused then smiled devilishly. "So, back to my statement, I am very close to the age difference between you and Marco, so I would be an excellent candidate for any of your gaggle. Or, if you keep cooking as you are, a candidate for you when you're ready to move on." He winked.

"Move on...? Fuck." Gabriella felt like someone had punched her in the stomach. She started breathing heavily, almost hyperventilating.

Liam, knowing exactly what she was experiencing, moved to

her and placed both his hands on her shoulders, telling her to breathe deeply. He then gave Edward a look to reassure him that it was okay. She needed this to happen if she was going to continue on the road to recovery.

"Angel, I know it hurts," Liam started, "but a wise woman once explained life to me like this: your life is like a book, and on the cover is your name. Marco, Gianluca, and Mateo are all very important chapters. Even though they are gone, your book still continues on, and you will write new chapters. That's life."

"Like your trip to Scotland," he continued. "For whatever reason, you ended up here, and it is now written in your book. Nothing can erase that. Edward and I are also part of that book. One day, someone special will come along, and that man will be lucky enough to have a relationship with you. It doesn't erase Marco or the boys, or us, for that matter; it's just another chapter."

He knelt down to get closer to her. "Gabriella, you didn't die that fateful day, and it is your responsibility to live the life you were given, continue to write new chapters, and honour all of the people who have touched your life."

Liam looked up at Edward and saw tears swimming in his eyes. He knew Edward understood who had imparted those words of wisdom.

Liam swallowed the lump in his throat and thanked the heavens above for that woman's wisdom so he could pass it on to the wee angel shaking with quite sobs in his arms.

A few minutes later, Gabriella hugged Liam as tightly as she could. When she pulled back, she said, "Moving on."

The men understood.

"Do you talk to your girlfriends often?" Edward asked after regaining his composure.

"Yes, we email and group chat constantly. If truth be told, I know there must be tons of emails from many worried people right now: my sistas, my parents, my brother, my work friends. I have a huge network of people who love and worry about me."

"Edward and I will email you the photos from today, and then you can let everyone in your network know you are alive and well. There is no need to say more if you don't want to, but please give them peace of mind."

"You are so right, but I've tried, and I'm having so many troubles trying to connect to the internet here."

"I am hooked up to satellite Wi-Fi through the British Intelligence Agency," Liam responded, "so we can create a hot spot, and you can piggyback off my Wi-Fi, therefore insuring all the important people in your life know you are okay."

Gabriella totally missed the reference to the British Intelligence Agency when she jumped up to get her iPad, but Edward caught it and held his breath until she made no reference to it.

Liam took the iPad and hooked her up to the hotspot he created. Instantly, two hundred fifty-five unread emails popped up. If Liam had been the sender of one of those emails, he would be out of his fucking mind with worry. She was the type of woman people took care of and worried about, not because of her size, but because she spent her life caring and loving everyone else unconditionally and neglected herself. Therefore, everyone felt honoured to repay the debt and look after her.

Instead of reading each email, because that would take hours and would be emotionally draining, she sent a mass email to everyone.

I am alive and well.

Dear loved ones,

First, let me apologize. I know I have been out of contact for a long time, and I have just now gotten internet. I am so sorry if I worried you. I assure you all that I am fine.

I have made some new friends and am working through a lot of issues. For the first time in a long time, I believe I am beginning to heal. My new friends are helping me work through my grief.

Although I love you all and know you wanted to help, I realized we just have too much history, and I needed to try to learn to stand on my own two feet. If I stayed and let you all carry the load, then I would never be strong and would spend the rest of my life leaning on you.

One of my new friends said I have to write new

chapters in the book that is my life without ignoring the old chapters, but instead, build on them.

I came to Scotland because I was desperate. I thought, if I went to a place that I heard had magical powers to send me back in time, I could save my family from being murdered. As I write this, I know how crazy it sounds, but that was me hitting rock bottom. I was truly at the lowest point of life.

That night, I believe Marco sent these two people to me to bring me back from the brink of madness. Every day since that faithful night, I have grown stronger and learned a lot about myself.

Please don't be hurt by my next words, but I have to be honest with each and every one of you. I am not ready to read your emails or answer them or speak to you on the phone. This journey is about self-discovery. Because you all care so much for me, you would willingly take that burden over for me, but it is something I have to do alone. Rest assured that, although I have to go through this journey alone, there are still two people watching over me and carrying me through the rough spots when it gets to be too hard. I will be strong if you all will. I will come back to you, but I will come back, not as a broken person, but one of strength.

I love you all.

Love always and forever,

Gabriella

She pushed send and looked at her emails, seeing even more now. She scrolled to the top and saw the three new ones were from Liam Connor and one from a Yesherson.

"Edward, is that your email, *Yesherson*, and if so, is it your last name?" she asked as she began downloading the pictures from the emails.

"No, it isn't my last name. Yes. Her. Son, Yesherson. Get it?" Edward responded.

"Yeah, but do you mean her son, as in, your mother?"

"Yes, in honour of my mum."

"Cool. Maybe I can change my email to lovedherboys. That way, every time I write an email, I could honour all my boys."

"We all find ways to honour the ones we have lost. You will find your own ways to do that. If changing your email helps that process, then do it," Edward said.

"How did you get so freakin' smart for a man your age?"

"Everybody has a story, and I have mine. One day, I will tell you all about my life. My life lessons have taught me to hold those I love close to me and walk away from those who just want to suck the life out of you. I have to say, though, that I admire you and all your sistas. I can't imagine having that many close friends. I have hundreds of acquaintances, but I can count my close friends on one hand, and I consider you one of them."

Gabriella smiled. "I am honoured to hold such an important position in your life."

Gabriella was looking down at the photos she was downloading, admiring them, when her mouth drop opened, and then she suddenly burst out in laughter.

"How the fuck did you accomplish that?"

"What are you talking about?" Edward asked.

"Oh, come on. Seriously, how did you get that fairy in the pictures? When did you have time to Photoshop them?"

"I didn't Photoshop anything, and I am not sure what fairy you are talking about."

While Edward spoke, she looked at the photos Liam had sent. The fairy was also in his pictures. *How did they do this?* she wondered.

"I don't know how you did it, but I freakin' love the fairy." She raised her head and looked at Liam, knowing he couldn't bullshit her like Edward.

Liam smiled the most beautiful smile, exposing his gorgeous dimples, and winked at her. She instantly blushed and felt heat surround her. It surprised her since she believed that part of her had died the day Marco had.

She truly was coming back to life.

She smiled back at Liam, but she couldn't wink, so she squinted and blinked both eyes.

Liam burst out laughing at her adorable attempt.

Chapter 9

Motorcycle Mama

I t rained, and it rained hard, for the next few days. The threesome spent most of their time indoors, getting to know each other by sharing stories of their lives. They laughed, Gabriella cried, and they learned there was a lot they could teach one another.

Gabriella continued to teach the men how to cook, and Edward became curious when Gabriella had mentioned wanting to make s'mores.

Confused, he asked, "What is a s'more?"

"A treat that every kid learns to make. You roast a marshmallow over an open fire, and then put it in between two graham crackers, but not before you put a piece of chocolate on top of the hot marshmallow, then smush it into a sandwich. It's the best thing you will ever put in your mouth.

"Mateo loved s'mores. One night in the backyard, we were all eating s'mores, and Mateo was out of control with a sugar high. He was jumping all over the place and acting silly. He jumped into Marco's arms, and Marco had a s'more. Needless to say, it was all smashed into Mateo's hair. Mateo thought it was hilarious."

They all laughed at the story, and this time, she didn't have tears. It was a big step in her recovery.

Gabriella was eating so much she had actually gained weight, in the time they had been together, and it looked great on her. She no longer needed a belt to keep her pants up. Both men liked her new curvy look, and they were often caught appreciating the scenery a little too much.

"Edward and I have decided that, if we continued to live with you, we would both weigh six hundred pounds. Thank Christ for our morning runs; otherwise, we would be badly out of shape."

"What? You guys don't run. I've never seen you run in the mornings."

"We run before you wake up," Edward answered. "We start at five a.m."

"No shit? And for the record, morning starts at seven. Anything before that is simply the middle of the night," Gabriella stated with conviction, and both men laughed.

Edward taught her all about polo and chess. She thought it was neat that Edward could ride a horse and steer with just the muscles in his legs. She was very impressed and admitted she had never seen a polo match, so Edward promised he would bring her to one of his polo matches one day soon, and she could watch firsthand how it was done.

Chess was another thing altogether. Gabriella was an easy mark for Edward. She was way too expressive, giving away every move she intended to make. Liam tried to get her to give it up, declaring poker was probably another game Gabriella should stay away from.

Liam spent a lot of time on the phone and always left the room to have his conversations, and Gabriella thought it was weird Edward never asked who he was talking to. She guessed he knew, although they never discussed it in front of her.

After learning the guys ran every day, she also learned Liam was a certified instructor of self-defence with the British Air Force and begged him to teach her some skills. No begging was required, however, since Liam believed all women should learn to defend themselves. Could these men get any cooler in her eyes? She didn't think so.

One day, they moved the furniture out of the way in the main room in Liam's suite, and Gabriella changed into her yoga pants and a cute little workout tank. Liam began to give her the basics about defending herself against anyone larger than her, which he pointed out, was most of the population. Anyone smaller than her was most likely a child.

That pissed Gabriella off, and she went to kick Liam in the leg, but just as her foot was ready to connect, Liam turned slightly then grabbed the back of her ankle, twisting it slightly and toppling her to the ground. With a screech, she landed hard on her back. First lesson learned: avoiding confrontation was the best defense.

Liam taught her the most effective areas to hit if being attacked: the eyes, nose, neck, knees, and groin area. Even though she was tiny, he taught her how to throw a man twice her weight and a foot taller than her. Needless to say, poor Edward, the guinea pig, was black and blue by the time the other two called it quits.

Gabriella couldn't believe what a great sport he was to humour her, and she rewarded him by giving him the choice of anything he wanted her to cook. She realized she had created a monster when he chose another double-batch of churros.

While Gabriella was in the kitchen, Edward and Liam went outside to sit on the terrace.

Edward whispered to Liam that Gabriella didn't really have to make him churros; having her wrap her arms around him and landing on top of him was payment enough. Poor Edward again found himself on the ground with Liam holding his arm against Edward's throat.

"Don't say shit like that."

Coughing, Edward sputtered, "What the fuck?"

"Damn. Sorry, Edward, but fuck, man. I feel something for her. I can't control my actions when I feel she needs defending. Don't fuckin' say shit like that. Everything about her makes me want to make sure nothing ever hurts her again. She has suffered more than any person should."

"You don't need to tell me this shit, you asshole," Edward snarled. "I have been along for the whole ride. I care about her as much as you do, so don't get all holier than thou with me." He picked himself up and started walking away. "I am going for a walk to blow off some steam. Don't fucking follow me."

"Edward, I apologize, man, but you know I can't let you go alone."

"I am a grown man. I don't need a fucking babysitter. Back the fuck off."

"Don't be stupid. Where you go, I follow, and if that means battling it out in front of Gabriella, so be it. I can't allow anything to happen to you, and not because you're the prince, but because you're my friend."

All the steam building up in Edward released on that last word. "Why did you have to go all girlie on me and say that shit?"

"What did Liam say? What did I miss?" Gabriella came around the corner with hot churros in hand.

"Mm...I will tell you later. Right now, I have plans for my mouth, and it doesn't involve talking. Hand over those little gems."

Gabriella laughed, handing off the hot churros, knowing she wouldn't be conversing with them until the plate was clean.

Just then, she heard a motorcycle pass the inn. She couldn't see it, but she knew it wasn't a Harley. Still, the sound brought her back to another place in time.

Liam never missed a thing—that was what made him so good at

his job. He watched as she was transported somewhere else.

Bringing her back to the here and now, he asked, "Where did you go, angel?"

"Did you hear that motorcycle? I love motorcycles. Marco had a Harley, and I loved getting on the back of it and feeling the wind on my face. There is a freedom you can't get any other way than on the back of a bike."

"Edward and I ride and have motorcycles. In fact, the inn is storing our bikes. Do you want to go for a ride?"

Gabriella jumped to her feet and clapped her hands. "Yippee, I would love to! Can we go now, please, please, please?"

Edward jammed the rest of his churro into his mouth with a huge smile answered her question.

"You're going to get dirty after all that rain mudding up the roads," Liam responded.

"I couldn't care less about getting dirty. The only thing is, I don't have a helmet."

"Let me call the front desk and ask if any of the staff have an extra helmet we can borrow. Then we can drive into Portree and buy one," Liam was quick to respond.

"That would be great. This is so cool! I can't wait. What type of bikes do you guys drive?"

"I have a Ducati Monster 796 Corse Stripe, and Liam has a Ducati Multistrada 1200," Edward responded.

"I have never heard of a Ducati before. All of my friends'

boyfriends or husbands have Harley Davidson's or rice rockets."

Edward was stunned that Gabriella knew about motorcycles yet hadn't heard of a Ducati. "Ducati makes the best motorcycles in the world; how can you not know that?"

Rolling her eyes, she placed her hands on her hips and squared off with Edward. "I mean no disrespect—well, no, that's a lie. I do! Harley Davidson makes the best motorcycles in the world," she scoffed. "And after I learned you played chess, I figured you were highly educated. Now I see my mistake."

Before Edward could chime back in, Liam said, "Ouch, that was a direct hit, but let's not stand here, arguing. Let's go for a ride, and you can be the judge."

Gabriella turned to go inside to get a sweater and her hiking boots, still mumbling about "thick-skulled British men who thought they knew everything about everything, but they didn't know their head from a hole in the ground."

In less than five minutes, the trio were at the front desk to meet the groundskeeper who was lending her a helmet and unlocking the garage where the bikes were stored.

When the caretaker opened the door, two bikes stood at attention, and Gabriella gasped. They were definitely sexy looking bikes.

Edward walked to the red one. The lines of the bike were hot, and the seat was low. It didn't have a bitch pad on the back, so Gabriella knew she wouldn't be riding with Edward. He took his helmet that she noted matched perfectly to the red of the bike.

Liam's bike was bigger and not so streamlined. It was built for comfort with elegant lines, all in black and chrome. She couldn't wait to go for a ride.

She watched Liam put on his full-faced helmet, shoved the visor up, and backed the bike off the kickstand. Once in position, he told her to jump on. She placed her left boot on the peg and threw her right leg over the back of the bike then wrapping her arms around his waist.

Liam got an instant hard-on. Fuck, he hadn't considered what it would do to him to feel her wrapped around his body. He adjusted his position, his dick pushing against the gas tank.

Edward erupted into a fit of laughter at the sight of Liam's discomfort, but Liam didn't say a word. He just flipped him the bird. Gabriella was too enamoured to try to figure out what was going on between the two men.

Liam started the bike, and Gabriella was in her glory. She lifted her visor and bent her head so Liam could hear her. "I want to go fast. I want to forget for a while."

That was a wish he could grant.

He nodded his head, pushed his visor down, pulled out of the garage, and took off like a shot.

Gabriella's heart was pounding in her chest. She was flying! She was free!

Edward pulled up beside them and gave her a thumbs up to

make sure she was okay. She didn't take hers arms off Liam, too nervous on her first ride after not being on a bike for a while. Therefore, she just nodded her head to indicate she was good.

She had missed riding on a motorcycle, and damn, but this bike was sweet, not that she would admit that to Edward. It was a totally different ride than a Harley, and it was incredibly exciting.

Liam brought her back to reality when he rubbed her hand and patted it. She knew he was also checking on her well-being. She just squeezed him more tightly to relay she was better than good. She was fucking great!

She couldn't get over how good it felt to have her arms around Liam's steel abs. She had awoken that one morning with her head resting on him as he held her through her nightmares, but that was by accident. Holding him now was for necessity. It felt nice to have some human contact, and somehow, it felt really right with Liam.

She had convinced herself that she would never again feel anything for another man, because there had only been Marco for her. However, she hadn't realized how very lonely that would be.

Time had seemed to drag on when she was alone, but that hadn't been the case the last couple of weeks she had spent with her two saviours. She wondered for the first time if she could ever love again, and then realized it was an odd thought to have on the back of Liam's bike.

Then again, she was learning the next step in her recovery was that she had to live again. Not just exist and breathe, but to honestly want to live and share herself with others. For the first time, it hit her that she *was* starting to move on. How and why it had happened, she wasn't sure, but Liam and Edward were teaching her there was life after death. She might never be the Gabriella she had been before Marco and the boys were killed, but she could be a new Gabriella. With that thought, her body relaxed, and she started to cry.

When Liam felt her body shake with what he assumed were sobs, he immediately pulled the Ducati over, worrying that maybe it was too much, too fast.

He jumped off the bike, took off his helmet, unhooked Gabriella's helmet, and yanked it off.

"What it is, sweetheart? Why the tears? Were you scared? I'm sorry." He grabbed her head and shoved her face into his neck just as Edward pulled up and jumped off his bike.

"What the bloody hell happened? Gabriella, why are you crying? Did we go too fast?"

Wiping her nose, she lifted her head and looked from one to the other. "No, I just realized for the first time that I am alive, and I"— she sobbed—"am going to be okay." She hiccupped.

Edward grabbed her off the bike and threw his arms around her. "Welcome back, Gabriella," he whispered into her hair.

Liam waited until they'd had their moment then turned Gabriella into his arms and hugged her. He grabbed her jaw in both his hands, kissed her softly on the forehead, and said, "Angel, I am proud of you. That makes me the happiest man in the world."

She thanked them for their kind words and smiled, realizing she meant something to these beautiful men.

She turned to Edward. "Last one to Dunvegan Castle does the dishes tonight." She threw on her helmet and buckled it up as she urged Liam to hurry. "Let's get this puppy moving and show him who's boss."

Both men laughed and jumped again to do her bidding. Another challenge had been raised, and Liam was going to make sure she won this one.

Chapter 10

Don't Poke the Bear

It had now been over a month since the three had met, and if you asked any of them, it was like they had always been friends. The attraction between Liam and Gabriella continued to blossom into sexual tension that was so strong it was nearly tangible.

Gabriella insisted they go out on the motorcycles every day, so they did. She loved to have an excuse to wrap her arms tightly around Liam, and Liam loved to have them there.

She was thankful she had brought hiking boots. It became a habit for the trio to ride the motorcycles then hike to different sights, exploring every inch of the isle. They started to bring lunches and some drinks every day that it didn't rain so they could spend more time in remote parts of the isle.

A pivotal moment happened the day they went to see the Point of Sleat. The walk was an incredible hike through the southernmost point of the isle, but what the guys really wanted her to see, besides the lighthouse at the end of the hike, was the beautiful, white sand beach named Sandy Bay.

Most of Skye had rough terrain, so to go from the rough path to the most beautiful, little white beach was spectacular, and they knew she would love it. It was located at about the halfway point to the lighthouse. Liam was hoping the tide was out so they could have their lunch at the beach.

The trio had been hiking for an hour and half when they veered off the main path to a smaller one. When it ended, the beach appeared in all its glory, and the view captured Gabriela's breath. It was like an oasis in the desert.

"Wow, I have seen some beautiful places, but this little beach has to be one of the most spectacular."

Liam was pleased with her reaction. "And it is even more beautiful because you are in it."

Oh, shit. He realized by her reaction that he had said that out loud. He held stock still, waiting for the full-force of her reaction.

"Gabriella makes this beach memorable, and it would be even more memorable if I got to eat a churro here."

Liam glanced thankfully at Edward, the tension broken, trouble averted, a job well done. Edward was a hero in his books.

He had never really given thought to why he kept extending his contract to watch over and protect Edward, but he knew in his heart why. Edward was a man you wanted to spend time with, a true brother, even if not by blood. He had honour and integrity, loyalty, and was a free spirit. Liam had never personally met Edward's mother, but he knew Princess Emma would have been proud of the man Edward had become.

Jokingly, Gabriella turned away from Liam and said to Edward, "I would rather pay your rent any day than I would your grocery bill. No wonder Liam refuses to let me pay for the groceries. I would have been flat broke in the time we have spent together."

"Never mind the cock and bull and just feed me, woman." Edward laughed, pounding his chest like an ape.

"Keep that cock and bull up, and the only thing you will be eating is bull *shit*."

"Gabriella's fangs are showing again." Edward laughed, running away from the crazed, little, dark-haired woman chasing him and yelling.

"Did your mother not teach you never to bite the hand that feeds you?"

"I wish she'd had the time." Edward smiled, holding Gabriella's arms back so she couldn't punch him.

She instantly went relaxed in his hands, realizing what she had said to him.

"Edward, I apologize. That was uncalled for. I didn't mean—"

"Stop, Gabriella. No harm, no foul. I know what you meant, so cut the shit and feed me."

She turned from him to grab the backpacks that contained their lunch, mumbling about British men having more wit than brains. Then they sat on the beach and shared yet another delicious meal. They also shared a bottle of wine, and much to the shock of the men, Gabriella took a swig from the bottle.

The first day they had decided to pack a lunch and wine, they had forgotten to pack paper cups and ended up swigging from the bottle. Ever since then, they had teased her about it, saying she was more a tomboy than a delicate princess. Therefore, she kept drinking from the bottle.

They loved the fact that she wasn't high maintenance like the women they were often acquainted with. She had class that couldn't be bought. She was low maintenance, high-class, and all real woman—a rare mix these days.

She had just taken a swig of wine when, out of the corner of her eye, she caught movement. She started to cough as she choked on the wine, and Edward patted her back. She pointed at the animal that had caught her eye, and the men saw what had startled her.

"It's a sea otter, and look, she is being followed by two pups."

When she regained her breath, she exclaimed, "Oh, my God, how cute is that? I love animals, and don't ask me why, but I have always been fascinated with otters. Although, I have never seen one in person. That is so cool."

"Why are you fascinated with otters?" Edward asked.

"Dakota, my sista, believes in sprit totems, and she taught me about them. This is going to sound so dumb, but I have always believed, if I were an animal, I would be a sea otter because they love the water as much as the land. They carry a stone to use as a utensil to break shells to provide food for their family, are excellent parents, and are faithful to one mate."

Edward and Liam definitely thought that sounded like the woman they had gotten to know over the last four weeks.

"It isn't dumb at all. In fact, I think Liam would agree that sounds very much like you. What animal do you think I would be?" Edward was curious to know.

Without hesitation, she said, "Hyena. Yes, definitely a hyena. You're always hackling. Your appetite is never ending, yet you don't cook; you wait for the scraps of someone else's hard work. You're crafty and always looking for trouble. Yup, I nailed it. You're a hyena."

Edward threw a piece of bread at her, laughing. "I changed my mind. You aren't a sea otter; you're a badger, one of the meanest animals known to man."

"Point made." She grinned.

"If we sit here a little while longer, we have a good chance of seeing some other wildlife, like seals, dolphins, or whales," Edward told her. "The chances are about fifty-fifty as the tide comes in. This is the time of the year they migrate back to their home waters. You will lose the pretty beach, but you might see some other amazing things."

"Get the fuck out! You're kidding me, right? Liam, is he shittin' me?"

"Point made about you, you foul mouth, little badger." Edward smirked as she smiled back at him.

"No, beautiful, he isn't *shittin'* you. I am starting to get why your father prays to God about that potty mouth of yours. Your mouth is truly as bad as any sailor I have ever met."

"Very funny. But honestly, does it really bother you guys that I swear? Because if you find it offensive, I can stop. I don't speak like this all the time. Of course, I never spoke around my sons like this or around anyone at the restaurant or at work."

"Gabriella, stop," Liam told her. "I didn't mean you had to stop swearing. Honestly, it's just another side to you that I feel honoured you share with us. I don't think less of you. I just look at you, and truly, to me, you look like this little angel. Then you say things that are so contradictory to that picture. I like the fact that there are different layers to the beauty. And I like the fact that you are who you are and don't excuse yourself for it. I respect that."

"Thank you. No one has ever really gotten that; even Marco would try to get me to tone it down. He used to say I would grow out of it and it was just a phase. I like the power of language, good or bad, and it has always amazed me it was acceptable for a man but not a woman. And trust me when I say that, if someone uses bad language to demean or embarrass someone, I find that offensive."

"As you Canadians say, rock on, sista." Edward lifted his closed fist to tap knuckles with Gabriella.

She laughed. "With all that you are, I am amazed some young girl hasn't snapped you up and married you." For the first time since she had met Edward, she saw sadness enter his eyes that was painful to witness. "What did I say?"

"Nothing. Don't get your knickers in a knot. It's nothing you meant to say."

Gabriella grabbed his chin and turned it towards her. "Seriously, you know all my secrets; what are you not sharing with me?"

Damn, that was a loaded question both men wanted to avoid. The list was endless for both of them, and eventually, all their secrets would come out. Nevertheless, it had been nice for the last month just to be Edward Norwich and Liam Connor.

The only way to save the day was to give a little bit of honesty, so Edward started.

"I was engaged to a beautiful woman I adored and loved. I assumed I would spend the rest of my life with her. Not only assumed it, but looked forward to it. But unlike you, her beauty was only on the surface. She betrayed me about six months ago, and it has left me bitter and very untrusting."

"Oh, Edward, I am so sorry, but she is an idiot. She lost the best thing that could ever have happened to her. You're a catch, and any woman would be thrilled to become your wife. In fact, if I weren't older than you and unable to give you children and hadn't already been married, I would jump at the chance to be with you."

Edward felt privileged that she felt that way. He wrapped his arms around her and just held her. She was one of the good ones, the ones who were always taken.

He glanced over at Liam and saw uncertainty in his friend's eyes. Edward knew he was reading too much into her statement.

He would always regret she wasn't the one for him. He could look past the age difference and the fact that she had been married. And he would have adopted children if she wanted more to love...if she would just look at him like she did Liam. Neither of them could see it, but to him, it was visible. They were slowly falling in love, and he wanted to help push them together. They needed one another.

Edward released Gabriella and stood up. "I'm going to make a trip to the bushes. Be right back, chums."

"I feel so bad," Gabriella told Liam once Edward had walked away. "I didn't know about his ex-fiancée. What stupid bitch would cheat on a guy like that? I mean, really? He is gorgeous, funny, caring, loving—what else could that girl have wanted? I feel like he is my brother, and I want to beat the crap out of her for hurting him like that."

It was apparent how deeply Gabriella felt for Edward, but it was also a relief to Liam to hear she thought of Edward as a brother and not a potential lover. Liam's attraction to the beauty beside him, however, was the furthest thing away from being a brother.

He turned to Gabriella. "Let's give Edward a minute, and then we'll leave the past in the past where it belongs." Liam stood up. "Let's take a walk before the tide comes in."

Gabriella conceded. After being married to man for twelve years and living with her own brother and papi, she knew men didn't like talking about things that hurt their hearts.

She followed Liam's lead and untied her hiking boots. Then she wiggled her toes in the sand and turned to Liam who was rolling up his cargo pants.

"Do you own any other type of pants? I mean, I know you have six pairs of these black cargo pants since I have seen you folding your laundry, and you carry a million gadgets in all those pockets, but really!"

Liam laughed. "Yeah, when I'm not working, I wear jeans. And believe it or not, I even own one suit besides my full dress uniform." He realized his mistake the instant the words fell out of his mouth. Fuck!

"You're not working..."

"The simple answer is I didn't go home after leaving my last tour. We came straight to Skye."

"But why does Edward have an array of clothing and you don't?"

By the Grace of God, he was saved from answering her question by a spectacular sight. Just in the distance was a pod of Orcas jumping and crashing in the water.

"Angel, look! There are some killer whales!"

"O...M...G. Those are just like the one we took the boys to see in Orlando. I didn't ever think I would see one swimming free and playing. That is the most beautiful thing I have ever seen in nature. I wish my Gianluca and Mateo were alive to see it."

"You're unable to share it with them in the flesh, but just mentioning their names lends credence to the fact that they are probably with us right now. They are seeing it through your eyes."

Gabriella turned to Liam and looked through his eyes and right into his soul. This was a man she could believe in and care for. Maybe, just maybe, she could even love him more than a friend.

Liam read her expression and made his move. He turned three times to check on Edward's whereabouts, constantly professional and always concerned for his well-being. Then he tilted his head down and brushed his lips across hers. He pulled away slightly then kissed her again, this time feeling the softness. He licked along the seam, hoping to gain entry, placing both hands on each side of her petite face to hold her steady.

Out of shock or curiosity, she opened her lips, and he got the first taste of his angel. His tongue met with her hesitant one, and he patiently stroked it. She tasted amazing.

He breathed in deeply, all of his senses confirming that he indeed had her where he wanted her. He could taste her, feel her in his hands, and smell the fragrance that was solely her.

She allowed him to roam freely in her mouth, her heart pounding. She wanted this, so why was she holding back? He deserved this, and she had made her choice. She was going to give him this one kiss.

She wrapped her arms around him and attacked his mouth. If she was going to only have this one kiss, she was going to make it count.

As Gabriella and Liam were having their moment, Edward came back and sat on the boulders to give the two some privacy. The kiss gave Edward a chance to stare at his two friends.

Damn, but they were a good-looking together. She was his beautiful angel, and he was her knight in shining armor, saving Gabriella from her self-imposed nonexistence.

Unbeknownst to them, Edward knew she was doing the exact same thing for him. She was making him realize that he still had a heart for love, and not the type you gave to your family, but the kind you gave to your lover.

Edward took his smart phone out of his pocket and took a few pictures of the whales for Gabriella, and then he took a picture of the couple kissing. He got creative, getting a picture of them kissing with the whales jumping in the background. Even he was impressed with that shot and thought he would one day blow it up and gift it to his closest friends.

The couple finally broke their kiss. Gabriella blushed and looked over to see Edward sitting on the rocks. She then glanced down in embarrassment.

Liam put a finger under her chin and lifted her face up to his. "Don't ever be embarrassed for sharing something as pure and as good as what we just shared. Understand?"

"I get you, but in front of Edward…That is so insensitive after what he lost not six months ago, and I'm not sure I am ready to take this next step, Liam."

"No one knows more than me that life goes on. It has to. I mean no disrespect, but I wouldn't take that kiss back for all the tea in China. It was that good."

She didn't lie when she whispered, "Me, too."

He smiled then grabbed her hand as they walked back to where Edward was packing up the leftovers from their lunch.

"Ready to see the lighthouse and maybe another glance of those killer whales?"

"Yeah," she barely whispered.

"Gabriella, don't be embarrassed. I didn't really see you sucking face with my best friend, but thanks for coming up for air and allowing him to breathe."

Oof! Down on the ground again, and not from Liam this time.

Pointing her finger, she said, "Don't. Poke. The. Bear!"

Chapter 11

Sharing is Caring

By the Friday morning of their eighth week together, not one of them had discussed how long they would remain together. They all just hoped this little piece of paradise would last forever.

Liam had just come in from paying the inn's owner for another month, uncertain if they were going to remain that long. However, the owner had to contact and cancel his future clients who had already booked. Luckily, the man felt honoured that a prince was staying at his establishment.

Liam also wanted to make sure the owner was still storing the package they'd had delivered earlier in the week. He had reassured Liam they had done as was requested.

Liam had been working with Edward for three days to try to make their next adventure possible for Gabriella. They had arranged for a private tour on the Seaview, a semi-submersible glass bottom boat. She would get a rare glimpse of all the marine life in the conservation area of Lochalsh. Now that they knew she had a love for wildlife, they hoped to give her a unique experience.

After the boat tour, they had also arranged a surprise to move her into the next phase of her recovery process. Sometimes, the logistics were the easiest part of surprise. Her reaction, however, could go one of two ways. One, she would love them; or two, she would feel betrayed.

"Come on, lady; move it, or we are going to be late, and you don't want to miss this adventure," Edward encouraged.

"Coming, coming. Sorry. I got caught up writing an email. I felt like I needed to reach out. Sometimes, I forget what it is like for the people I left behind. I thought, if I could write it now, then maybe when we got back, Liam wouldn't mind hooking me up to his Wi-Fi."

"You never have to ask. I'll gladly do that. The boat we rented has to be back by noon so that will give us enough time to eat lunch and come back here."

"Thank you so much! That means the world to me."

"Now that we have that settled, let's get on the road. The boat leaves soon." Edward pushed the duo forwards as he placed he cap and sunglasses on.

They loaded up in the Range Rover since it was a little cool for the motorcycles this beautiful June morning. Everyone was quietly thinking during the ride, and Gabriella's mind wandered to her friends. She thought about, if the roles were reversed, how she would have felt if Jocelyn, Dakota, or any of her of other girlfriends had disappeared. She would be frantic. Therefore, she had decided she needed to right some wrongs in her life. She needed to respect other people's feeling and stop being so self-absorbed.

She had lost her family, and it hurt like hell, but by pushing those away who loved her most, it wasn't helping her to heal. Instead, it was punishing them for still having their lives intact. Liam was right; she needed to start living again and write some new chapters. She would start today by sending the email.

Suddenly, a beautiful song that Gabriella recognized came on.

"Oh, that is Blue Rodeo singing "Dark Angel." They are a Canadian band I love, and this is my favourite song from them. I saw them in Toronto four years ago. My brother Philippe bought me tickets for my thirtieth birthday, and he and I went."

Both the men promised to listen to her playlists on her iPad to hear more songs by Blue Rodeo. However, Liam wanted to hear this particular song again. The lyrics definitely reminded him of Gabriella and her dark struggles.

"Guys, let me ask you a question, and your answers could determine whether or not we can remain friends, because this is very important to me. If you answer wrong, we are done and can't be friends anymore."

Both men looked at each other with leery curiosity.

"Ask away," Liam answered with a confidence he didn't have at that moment.

"What kind of music do you listen to? And, Edward, I swear, if it is classical, I am so pushing you off the boat the minute we get into deep water."

Laughing, Edward said, "How did you know that I would say classical or opera? Honestly, I really do like many different genres of music, and I can't name just one. I am going to change it up a bit. Instead of asking the type of music you like, how about: what is your favourite song of all time?"

"Fair enough. I guess I would agree I could never just choose one type of music. I would probably say classic rock, and The Rolling Stones are my most favourite, but I also like artists like Barbra Streisand and the Zac Brown Band. It would be equally hard to pick just one song, so I need to think about that."

"I knew you were my kind of girl," Liam said, "but now that I know you like The Rolling Stones, I think I have instantly fallen in love with you. They are the best band of all times and the best band to ever come from the UK. See? We were meant to meet and become friends."

She didn't respond, worried she wasn't able to give Liam—or herself, for that matter—what they both wanted. In her head, she knew Liam and she were growing closer. He would hold her hand, kiss her forehead, and give her earth shattering kisses. He made her laugh, held her when she cried, and listened to her talk for hours about her family. But was she ready for the next step? She desperately wanted to be, yet she felt like she was cheating on Marco or disrespecting her kids' memory every time they shared a moment.

She felt the first tear she had shed in over two weeks travel down her cheek. As she lifted her head to wipe it away, she saw Liam staring at her in the rear view mirror. He lifted a perfectly shaped eyebrow then winked at her. She realized from that gesture that he got her. He understood her internal battle.

If she still believed in God, she would almost believe He had sent her Liam and even Edward after the mistake of taking her family. She was falling for Liam, but she wasn't sure she was capable of having a physical relationship.

The days he hugged her to his body, she could feel his hard dick against her tummy and knew she was drenched down there after hugging and kissing him. She didn't have the answers. In truth, she didn't even have the right questions.

They reached Lochalsh, and Gabriella saw the unusual boat they were about to board. It looked like a tug boat with seats, but you could see the bottom was shaped differently.

"Welcome aboard the Seaview. My name is William, and I will be your captain. We will tour the conservation area for three hours this morning, and you will get an opportunity to see wildlife above and below the surface. I will point out different sights and guide you to some you might not have seen before, so if you will all take a seat and get your cameras ready, we will get on our way."

The boat was well on its way when Gabriella turned to the men.

"This is so cool! I can't believe you guys organized this. Thank you. How am I ever going to repay your kindness?"

Liam grabbed Gabriella's hand, kissed her knuckles, and said, "Every day that you put a smile on the beautiful face, you pay us back." He kissed her forehead. "It makes us happy to see you happy."

Tears filled her eyes, but she was determined they wouldn't fall. As she concentrated on pulling herself together, she heard a weird *ork, ork* sound. Turning, she saw an inlet filled with seals.

"Holy crap! Look at those seals, Liam. Can you believe it—real live seals? Edward, are you looking? Wow, I didn't know all this marine life surrounded Scotland. I am blown away."

While she was watching the seals, the men were taking pictures for her. Gabriella would have beautiful pictures to remember the fabulous memories they were giving her. She was like a little child seeing Santa Claus for the first time. The excitement in her voice and the smile on her face made Edward think this was the reward for all the crappy things that had happen to each of them over their lifetimes.

The captain came over after about an hour and asked them if they would like to see what was going on under the water. The trio got up and followed the captain down to the hull where it looked like a submarine with large windows.

"Are you kidding me? This is unbelievably cool. Oh, my God; look, Edward! Look at the seals swimming. And look over there."

She pointed. "There are a ton of fish. And look at the seals coming up to look at us."

She squeezed Liam's hand so tightly he felt real pain, but she was oblivious to it, too absorbed in what she was seeing. She was like a kid in a candy store, not knowing where to look first. She was beautiful, breathtakingly beautiful.

Just then, Edward pointed out a family of otters as three more jumped in the water from the above outcrop of rocks.

The captain explained they were heading to the underwater kelp forests and then to a shipwreck. As it was a beautiful, sunny day, they saw every aspect of the ship that lay broken at the bottom of sea. It looked creepy, but also intriguing. They also saw more seals, porpoise and fish.

It was a wonderful morning, and Gabriella was still smiling from ear to ear as they sat down in a pub where they all ordered bangers and mash—sausage and mash potatoes—along with pints of Guinness for the men and a cider for her.

Liam excused himself to make a call before they headed back to the inn. Gabriella was a little restless to get back. Now that she had made the decision to contact her friends, she was eager to send off her email.

When they arrived at the inn, Gabriella went into the bedroom to retrieve her iPad; Liam went to living room where his luggage was stored to grab his computer; and Edward went into his suite to organize the surprise they had for her.

Liam placed his computer on the table in the kitchenette and went about setting up the satellite Wi-Fi.

"Angel, if you don't mind giving me a minute to set this up in private, I have some sensitive emails from work I have to answer. It will take me about five minutes."

"No problem. I will be outside, looking at the photos you and Edward sent me." Instead of looking at photos, though, she was busy rereading her email to the girls.

When Liam called her in, she walked over to the computer. And just as she reached the table, she spotted a drink beside the computer. It couldn't be...

"Liam...is that what I think it is?"

"Yes, angel, it is Caesar Friday, and what kind of a Caesar Friday would it be if you didn't have a Caesar? Go on; give it try. It's the first one Edward has ever made, but he followed your instructions to the letter. And please note no celery since that would just take up room."

She couldn't believe he remembered her telling him how she and her girls always had Caesar Fridays.

"Holy shit! You guys rock. I can't believe this. Wait, I only see one glass. Tell me I'm not drinking alone."

Edward was smiling, watching how the whole event played out over her expressive face.

Liam walked over then turned the computer to face Gabriella, and two familiar faces were smiling back at her from the computer.

110

"Hey, Mingo. Happy Caesar Friday, sista!" Jocelyn and Dakota yelled.

Gabriella threw her hand over her mouth and started to shake. She was having trouble processing what she was seeing. Her two closest friends in the world were on Liam's computer screen.

"How did you guys do this?"

Liam walked up and guided her into the chair. "Visit with your girls. We will talk about that later. For now, Edward and I are going to grab a couple of pints and head outside."

As soon as the ladies heard the door shut, Jocelyn said, "Gabby, that man is abso-fucking-lutely hot. I mean, hotter than hell. I mean, burning my retinas hot. I mean, Chris Hemsworth freakin' hot. Who is he, and who is Edward? Is he as hot as that one? How are you, and why have you been off the grid for so long? We have been so worried." Jocelyn kept firing questions at a fast rate, not giving her a chance to reply.

Gabriella just picked up her drink and took a sip.

"Mm..." She closed her eyes as the flavours flowed over her tongue. Jesus Christ, that sip tasted amazing. It tasted like home.

"Gabby, pay attention. We need some answers."

Gabriella laughed at Jocelyn. "Are you going to stop talking long enough for me to answer? And by the way, you both look fabulous. I have missed you guys so much. Please forgive me."

"You never, ever, ever have to ask for our forgiveness," Dakota answered. "We love you and understand, but it does our hearts good to see you are in a way better place than you were when you left."

"Yeah, I was in a really bad place when Edward and Liam found me."

"Gab, why didn't you call me? You know I would have been there in a New York minute. Honey, I would have dropped everything to be with you."

"I know, but I needed to be away from everyone associated with my old life," she told Jocelyn. "I wasn't healing. I just existed."

"When are you coming home?" Jocelyn asked.

"I don't know. I do know that I am not ready yet. Toronto reminds me too much of all I had and lost. Everywhere I look, I see something that reminds me of the boys or Marco. Can you guys understand that? If I'm going to be totally honest with you girls, I can't see myself ever moving back."

"Oh, Gabby, I get it, but it still scares the crap out of me," Dakota whispered, close to tears. "I know this is so selfish, but I miss not being able to see you all the time. I want what we had back."

Gabriella responded the only way she could. "I know how you feel, but I am learning a lot about myself: how I still need to be needed and to set boundaries for myself. Pretending that everything is okay just so other people won't hurt is killing me inside, and it can't work anymore. My friends here are teaching me to discover a new Gabriella, one that is learning to accept the fact that I had a family and now I don't."

Both her closest friends were crying.

"Girls, I am sorry. I never wanted to hurt you guys, but I have to figure out what works best for me in order to keep myself sane." She took a deep breath then asked, "Jocelyn, how are my parents? Do you know if they received the email I sent to everyone?"

"Yeah, they did, and I drop by to see them at least once a week. They know we are chatting with you today. We are going to have dinner at the restaurant tonight so I can tell them all about how you are. They miss you, Gabby. They were so scared when no one could reach you. In fact, they were talking about hiring a private investigator to find you, but your friend Liam called the restaurant and reassured them that you were alive."

"What! Liam called Mom and Papi? How did he know how to reach them?"

"He phoned the restaurant and talked to Manny. Liam told him that he met you and that you were in a crisis, that they were watching over you, and that you were doing better. He told Manny you had talked about your family and the restaurant, so he googled it and got the number. He also gave your dad his name, cell phone number, and rank in the military. Manny was able to check up on him so that he could rest easy that you weren't in danger from some psychopaths."

Gabriella shook her head. "This freakin' man just gets better and better. I swear, girls, I feel like I have known these two guys my whole life." She went on to tell the girls all about her two guys.

113

"And Liam...Well, he hasn't told me yet whom he has lost, but I know he has, and it was someone very close to him. He totally understands my breakdowns, and even when I can't describe how I feel; he just gets it. I haven't asked him yet. I don't think I am ready to take on someone else's sorrow. Wow, that sounds selfish after all the man has done for me."

"No, that is a woman who now understands her boundaries," Dakota jumped in, "knows what she can handle, and what she can't handle. That is growth. Keep getting stronger, and one day, you will be able to come home, even if it is only for a visit."

"You're right. Another lesson I have learned today is that I am getting stronger. And now that I have talked to you two, my next step will be Mom and Papi."

"Go slowly. One step at a time, because whatever you're doing is working. Next, I hope I don't upset you, but Philippe and Nina are expecting another baby. They are due in late September."

That felt like a double-edged sword into the stomach. On one hand, Gabriella loved her brother and his wife and their other two children to death and was thrilled for them, but now that she had lost her precious babies and would never again have another child, it hurt like a son of a bitch.

"Please tell them congratulations for me," she managed to get out.

The friends continued to chat for over two hours. In that time, Liam brought her three more Caesars. It was only when Gabriella had to go the bathroom that they all decided to hang up.

"Before I go, I want you to meet Edward, too. He is adorable and hilarious. You girls will love him.

"Edward!" she called out to him. "Will you come in and meet my friends? And hurry, I have to pee."

Liam laughed and yelled back through the window, "Sorry, angel. Edward went to the restaurant to get more ale. Next time, okay?"

"Sorry, girls, you're missing out on some serious eye candy, but next time for sure. How about same time next week if I can manage it? I'll let you know through emails, okay, my friends?

"I love you girls with all my heart. Please let all the other girls know that we will touch base soon. Jocelyn, give Mom and Papi a big hug tonight and make sure Papi doesn't cry. Tell him I am good and getting better, and I will talk to him as soon as I am a bit stronger." Gabriella had to again wipe tears that started to fall down her cheeks at the mention of her beloved Papi.

"Mingo, stay strong and get stronger. Love you, girlfriend!" Dakota said through her own tears as she blew kisses.

"Gabby, know that we understand where you are. If you need me, I am a phone call or Skype away. Love you, my little Mingo." Jocelyn also was blowing kisses as she wiped the tears away before the screen went to black.

Chapter 12

Unwrapping

Gabriella bounced outside after running to the bathroom, and before Liam could fully stand, she threw herself into his arms. He laughed and hugged her tightly, enjoying the feel of her body against his as he rubbed her back. They had done the right thing by contacting her friends. In a small way, they had given them back to her, and she had taken one more step forwards in her recovery.

When Edward walked up, she kissed Liam's cheek then turned to Edward and threw herself into his arms, even though he was holding two pints.

"You will never know what you did for me." She also kissed his cheek then stood back to have her conversation. "Edward, I wanted you to meet my friends."

"Sorry, *Mingo*, I didn't know you were going to end your conversation then. Otherwise, I wouldn't have left. So, curiosity is

116

killing us. How in God's name did you get a nickname like Mingo?"

She laughed. "I think I told you guys that my girlfriends refer to one another as the 'Sistas of the United Nations,' because each of us has parents from two different countries. For instance, mine are from Spain and Scotland. Jocelyn's mom is from the Czech Republic, and her dad is from Japan. Dakota's mom is Native American, and her dad is from France. So, we each have a name associated with our background. We call Jocelyn 'Geisha' because of her Japanese background, and Dakota is 'Pocahontas' because of her being Native American."

"I get that, but I am still struggling to connect Mingo with Spain or Scotland," Liam said.

"Plain and simple, it is the last part of the word flamingo. My parents had these flamenco dancer dolls on display from Spain at the restaurant when we were children, and my papi used to say to everyone, 'Doesn't that magnificent doll look just like my gorgeous, little girl?' I would die of embarrassment, and Jocelyn would laugh her butt off. Since a lot of people mistakenly say 'flamingo dancer,' Jocelyn named me Mingo. Of course, the term 'flamingo dancer' drives my papi crazy, but I think that is part of the charm of the name for my girls."

"Well, it certainly makes the name prettier since we know the origin, although Mingo, Gabby, and Gab are not what we associate with you. I think Gabriella is perfect for you."

Gabriella laughed. "It's okay." She continued with her original statement, turning to Edward. "Next time, you are meeting my friends. Anyway, would you guys mind if I didn't cook tonight? I really feel like hometown takeout. Could you possibly bring me to some place for a good, old-fashioned hamburger, please?"

"Sounds good to me," Edward responded. "I would love a hamburger and chips with mayo. How about you, Liam?"

"We have all had a lot to drink, so let's call a cab. Hamburgers first. Ice cream second. How's that?"

Gabriella promised to be ready in fifteen minutes while Liam called the front desk to request a cab, and the owner said they didn't need to, because he would be more than happy to drive them. Liam assumed he just wanted the prince to ride in his vehicle so he could brag.

At the restaurant, Edward saved their table while Liam and Gabriella ordered their food and drinks. Gabriella had a hard time getting used to the different way the pubs served people. In most restaurants in Scotland, you went to the bar to order your food and drinks.

While Gabriella was thinking about the difference in service, Liam was thinking how amazing it was that, if people didn't expect someone famous to be somewhere, they would look past him. Due to this, Edward was incognito with his cap and sunglasses.

After dinner, Liam and Gabriella walked hand in hand as they went for ice cream. When they were finished, they called the inn's owner for a ride home. Once back at their suites, Gabriella made coffee for herself and hot tea for the men, and they sat outside on the patio to enjoy the sunset.

Gabriella turned to Liam and asked, "Jocelyn told me you called my papi; is that true?"

"Absolutely, and I won't apologize. If you were my daughter and I had no idea where you were, I would lose my fucking mind. You might disagree and think I was wrong not to tell you, but I couldn't in clear conscience let the man suffer needlessly. And I continue to call him every other day because a man deserves to know that his only daughter is safe."

Tears came to Gabriella's eyes. "I don't know what to say. I guess I am thankful, but you could have told me." She paused and reflected for a moment, weighing what she should feel with what she actually felt. "I should feel betrayed, but I know you had the best of intentions, so again, thank you."

"Come here." Liam pulled her onto his lap.

Edward took this as a cue to leave. "I have some of my own emails to catch up on, so I am going to retire early. Good night."

"Good night, Edward," the couple said in unison.

Gabriella curled up in Liam's lap, enjoying the contact. You never really thought about the small things until you didn't have them anymore, like how she hadn't had any body contact since the funeral. Now she loved the fact that Liam had his arms around her. She felt warm and cozy while he rubbed her lower back, resting his chin on Gabriella's head.

Liam was comforted by that fact that she wasn't angry about his conversations with her father.

He nuzzled his lips against her neck, and she instantly forced him away. Then she felt him tense and became worried she had offended him.

"It's not you," she tried to assure him. "I am just extremely ticklish." She giggled. "I can't handle my neck being touched."

"Look at me, angel." He tilted her chin up. "If I do anything that makes you uncomfortable or you don't want, just tell me to stop, okay?"

"Yeah." She nodded.

He lifted her head up until their lips met. They kissed for a few moments before Liam licked the seam of her lips, and she opened her mouth then pushed her tongue into his, taking control.

The taste of him was intoxicating, and he smelled incredibly good. She would have to remember to ask him what cologne he wore.

She wiggled due to her growing excitement, and that move became the last straw for Liam. With a growl, he put his hand under her knees and swept her into his arms before gliding them right into his suite.

They kissed passionately as he placed her on the bed then followed her down. It was going to be a delicate balance. He needed to build her trust yet also keep her so excited she wouldn't have time for regrets, and he was afraid after not having sex for so long and being driven crazy with lust by her presence that he wouldn't be able to control his libido.

She, too, was having an internal battle. She wanted him so badly, but she felt like she was betraying Marco. Gabriella made a conscious decision to shut her mind down and allow her body to take over. She needed to feel, wanted to feel, so she poured her emotions into responding to Liam.

They kissed like teenagers, not able to get enough of one another, but Liam wanted more, much more. He lifted her blouse up over her breasts, seeing she had a hot pink bra on. He would bet his soul that, when he got her jeans off, there would be a matching thong. Before he got that far, though, he needed to taste more of the gorgeous woman.

He kissed her collarbone, staying away from her neck, not wanting to give her an opportunity to pull back. He then kissed and licked his way down to her cleavage.

"Mm...You have the sexiest lingerie I have ever seen. It's almost a shame to take it off. You look fucking hot in it."

He moved down the bed, still kissing her as he started to undo her jeans and pull them down. He got them to mid-thigh before Gabriella knifed up and covered her stomach.

"No," she whispered, trying to recover her breathing.

"Angel, what's wrong? Talk to me. Don't shut me out. Please, baby, what's going on? Why are you holding your stomach? Are you sick? Angel, look at me. Gabriella, I'm not kidding! Look at me!"

He sounded panicked and confused.

"I can't. It's not pretty. It's disgusting," she whispered.

"What's not pretty, baby? We will stop if you are hurt."

She started to shake, and he was at a loss as to how to help her. Then, all of a sudden, she snorted.

"What the fuck?" Liam said.

In less than ten seconds, she was full-blown laughing. Maybe she had finally lost her marbles. He had no other explanation.

"Oh, Liam, shit. I am sorry. It's either laugh or cry." She breathed deeply while trying to control her laughter.

Liam grabbed her face in his hands and growled, "Help me out here, angel."

"Okay, okay. I'm not laughing at you. I'm laughing at your rambling." Turning somber, she said, "My-my stomach is disgusting. I have stretch marks and scars. When you see them, it will gross you out and turn you off. You always say I am pretty or beautiful, but trust me; below the waist, I am brutally disgusting." Even quieter, she continued, "Marco knew me before I became scarred, so he accepted it and allowed me to make love in the dark so that I was more comfortable. Maybe, if we turn the lights out..." She pulled her face away from his hands so that she could tip her head down, and her eyes were again looking down.

He shook her face gently to get her to lift up and look at him without having to ask. When her eyes shifted up, he gently said, "Baby, I have already seen your scars and stretch marks. The first night we found you, I changed you out of your wet clothes. I have seen all of you, and you're beautiful from the top of your head to the tips of your toes. You're perfect just the way you are."

"You saw me naked and still want me?" She thought he must really be nuts if that were true.

He nodded. "You are truly gorgeous, and the fact that you have stretch marks and scars makes you even sexier, because you got them carrying a child. You nurtured and cared for another human being. That is incredible. Liam continued, "Baby, you have no idea whether or not I am scarred or disfigured under my clothes. Tell me honestly, would it change anything for you if I were disfigured?"

Speechless, Gabriella shook her head.

"That's what I thought. So, no, we are not turning off the lights. We are going to leave them on and celebrate the beauty that is you."

"Are you for real?" she whispered. "That was a panty removing statement if I ever heard one. I have never heard another man speak as eloquently as you just did."

"Nice try, angel; you don't wear panties. You only ever wear lace thongs."

She giggled. "From that whole statement, all you heard was panties?"

"Oh, you want to laugh at me again?" He attacked her neck, kissing and sucking.

She laughed and giggled and begged for mercy, but he didn't stop until he saw the brand he left on her neck. Then he removed her

123

jeans, tossing them aside.

He looked down and held his breath as he tried to memorize every detail of his beautiful girl, promising himself that no matter what, this was only the beginning. He was keeping her.

Chapter 13

Tiger Stripes

Gabriella was blown away by the look on Liam's face. When she saw the lust in his eyes, she started to get tingles in her lady bits, as he liked to call them. She couldn't stay still any longer.

She raised her arms and lifted the bottom of his shirt up so she could lift it over his head.

Liam stopped staring and helped her remove his shirt. He was going to run with it if she was participating.

She went to the belt of his cargo pants, undid the buckle, and unzipped his pants. She started to shake as she realized what she was about to do. Could she do this? Should she stop it? She was bombarded by second thoughts.

"Stop it. Just let it happen. I have wanted to sink my dick into you from the second I laid eyes on you, and now I am going to love you until you can't walk. And, Gabriella, know that I do love you."

He lowered his mouth and kissed her breathless.

She closed her eyes while experiencing his taste. *He loves me. Oh, for Christ's sakes, I don't know how to feel about that. I just can't deal right now.* She squeezed her eyes more tightly. *Don't think. Just don't think.*

She didn't hear anything for a moment or two, so she opened her eyes and instantly stopped thinking when she saw him in all his glory.

He was right; not everything in Scotland was tiny. The man was hung, his hard length standing at attention.

Liam smirked at her expression, his dimples on full display. "Lose the bra and thong," he ordered.

She slowly removed her bra, feeling shier by the minute. Liam didn't notice, though. He was staring at her full breasts with their pinkish-brown nipples that were hard and puckered and just screaming to be sucked. He couldn't wait.

He bent his head and licked first one nipple then the other. Her back arched off the mattress as he sucked a nipple into his mouth and swirled his tongue around it, increasing his suction while rolling the other nipple between his thumb and index fingers.

He could feel her heart pounding and prayed to God that it was from passion and not fear. Every other sign she was sending—her laboured breaths, her puckered nipples and, as he lowered one hand between her legs, her wetness—confirmed to him it was passion. He knew there would be repercussions tomorrow; however, they would deal with them at that time. For now, he wanted her to embrace the feelings he had for her.

He loved running his hand up and down between her hairless lips, spreading her juices. He could wait no longer, though. He had to taste her essence.

He slowly kissed his way down her body, stopping just above her belly button when he felt her tense again. He waited to see if she would stop him.

Instead, he heard her say, "Second most vulnerable spot."

He smiled at her belly button and bypassed it then dragged his tongue all over her lady bits while pulling her legs apart. He then pulled her to the edge of the bed, his hands looking huge on her ass as he pulled her down. He loved how it looked and felt, so he squeezed each cheek. Then he dove right into a little piece of heaven.

She tasted like ambrosia. He kissed, licked, and worshipped her core, using his strength to hold her down as she lifted and shifted her hips in her excitement. She had a tight grip on the sheets, and was thrashing her head from side to side as she drew close to climax.

"Oh, please, Liam. I need you now. I need you right fucking now!"

Liam yanked her ass back to the edge of the bed and positioned himself, placing the head of his cock at her entrance and pushed.

"Yes…yes! Oh, Liam, yes! Don't hold back. Faster, faster," she moaned.

Fuck, she was tight. He felt like his dick was being strangled, and it felt amazing. She felt warm and slick as he guided farther into her. She was too tight to go as fast as she demanded. He could hurt her if he lost all control. As a result, he pushed in and then out slowly, and with each push in, he gained a little more depth. He was almost three quarters of the way in when her hips flew up, and she impaled herself on him to the root.

"Argh…yes…Holy Mother of God, yes!" she whisper-hissed.

Not a scream, but on a whispered hiss. Edward would not hear her climax from the next suite.

Liam could feel her muscles contracting around his dick, and he was absorbing all of it. Thank God above he had a good grip on her legs. Trying to hold her while she was wiggling and pumping the lower half of her body was a task. She was the wildest ride he had ever had.

He held her hips up as she grinded against him throughout her climax, only her shoulders still touching the mattress. There was no way this woman would ever be able to fake an orgasm. She was full-out feeling it, body and soul.

After she climaxed, she collapsed into his grip, her body to the bed, and breathed hard, trying to get as much oxygen as possible after holding her breath to ride out the end of her orgasm.

For Liam, it was incredible to watch and even more incredible to feel, but it had taken all of his willpower to let her climax, and now he needed a release more than he needed his next breath.

He leaned over and lifted her shoulders up so he could wrap her close to his body as he pumped into her. One...two...three pumps, and on the final pump, he pushed as far into her as her body would allow, his spine tingling at his release.

When he came back to reality, he thought that, if he died right then, he would die a happy man.

Realizing he had collapsed on top of her, he started to get up before he crushed her. Just as he was rising, though, she grabbed him around the shoulders and didn't let him move.

"Thank you," she whispered.

Was she fucking kidding him? She was thanking him? Did she have any clue how responsive and passionate she had been?

For a few minutes, she had made him feel like a star, like there was no one else on earth but him. He had never felt happier to be a man than he had while making love to her.

He realized she had to love him, even if she couldn't admit it to herself or say it to him. That kind of passion was a gift created through heart-stopping love. He would give her time to come to that conclusion. He was in no rush, knowing in his heart they were meant to meet and fall in love.

"You never have to thank me. I would give you the world if I were able." He kissed her. "Baby, this is just the beginning. We need each other." No truer words had ever been spoken.

Liam wrapped Gabriella in his arms and gently flipped her so he was on his back and she was lying on top of him, still connected. He wanted to clean her up, but he wasn't ready to leave her body yet. He liked the connection.

It occurred to him that he hadn't worn a condom, and he momentarily panicked before he remembered her saying she couldn't have any more children.

"I didn't wear a condom. I am sorry, baby. I've never done that before, but I got so caught up. Are you okay with that? I will get tested to prove to you I am clean."

"I trust you and know you wouldn't lie to me. I'm clean, too. I have only ever had one lover before you."

He smiled against her head. He thought that it was cute she needed to reassure him. Like anyone who had met her for five minutes would think any differently. Above anything else, he absolutely loved to hear she trusted him. She might as well had told him she loved him, because having her trust was exactly the same thing. This woman just got better and better.

He hugged her, one arm around her torso and one down to grab a cheek of her fine, fine ass.

They fell asleep for a while, and Gabriella was awakened by Liam flipping her gently on her back. He was still inside of her, but now he was hard again and moving.

She didn't have time to think before Liam latched on to her breast and suckled it while he rolled the other nipple with his fingers. After a few minutes of playing with her nipple, he moved his hand to her clit and started to rub it in circles. That was her magic button. He was driving her out of her ever-loving mind.

As she got closer to her orgasm, he started to pluck her clit then pinch it, which sent her soaring into her second climax in over three years. He followed seconds behind her.

This time, he got up and started a bath. When it was ready, he walked into the bedroom and lifted the exhausted, little angel into his arms and carried her to the loo. He got in and lowered both of them into the warm water.

She purred when he had settled them in and draped her across his chest.

He reached for the soap and washed every inch of her body, gently smoothing his hands over her skin and paying particular attention to her nipples.

"You know," she whispered, "when Gianluca saw my stretch marks and scars one time, he asked what had happened to me, and I explained to him that I had gotten them when I was pregnant with him and his brother. He was horrified and asked if they had clawed their way out of my stomach. I would have laughed, if I hadn't seen how upset he was at the thought of hurting me like that. I explained that my tummy got stretched while I carried him and his brother, and the scars were from when the doctor took him and his brother out. I told him it was from both of them because I didn't want Mateo to think it was his fault I had scars from the emergency surgery.

"Gianluca started to cry. He was only five. No matter how many times I tried to reassure him, it didn't work until Marco came in. He had been listening from the other room and told him they were tiger stripes. He told Gianluca that it showed how brave his mommy was and that she would protect her little cubs at any cost, at which point I roared, and he laughed. He loved that explanation, and every time he saw them, he would make me roar." She smiled at the memory.

Liam continued to rub the soaped area around her stretch marks, happy she was talking about her family so soon after having sex with him. Maybe he had panicked over nothing. Maybe she *was* ready to move on.

When he moved lower to clean her lady bits, she flinched.

"Sorry, angel. Are you sore?"

She giggled. "Yeah, I guess I am a little raw after all of that friction."

He was thrilled she was so responsive in the aftermath of their love making.

He gently finished washing her then lay with her in the water until it cooled and their skin wrinkled. When it was time to get out, he stood her up and reached for the towel, drying her off then wrapping it around her. He then gave her privacy as he went to lie in the bed, waiting for her to come back.

She opened the loo and walked out as he shook his head.

"Lose the towel. I want nothing between us."

She was going to argue, but it was late and she was exhausted, so she dropped the towel and crawled into the bed. He reached out and pulled her into his side with her head against his shoulder. Then he rubbed up and down her spine like he had done for the last two months as they fell asleep.

At five a.m., like every morning, Liam shifted what he thought was a sleeping Gabriella off his body, kissed her forehead, and then got out of bed. He got ready then left the room to collect Edward for their morning run.

Edward opened his door after hearing the light rap. "Well, look at you, as proud as any peacock. I can now assume everything went well with Gabriella, although I didn't hear any evidence of that last night."

"You can assume right, but I swear, if you tease her, I will hurt you. I don't think she wanted you to hear us. She has been so concerned about your emotional well-being ever since she heard about Gillian and your breakup. The woman cares for you and your feelings, so don't make her feel self-conscious."

"Stop being a bloody arse. I love that girl and would never intentionally hurt her, so sod the fuck off."

Liam sighed. "I'm just on edge, hoping there won't be repercussions after last night."

"No need to say more. I have been thinking about how she is going to handle this next step in returning to the living. I don't envy you right now."

Liam didn't respond as they made their way outside and started to run.

Meanwhile, the minute Liam left the room, Gabriella was up

and in the washroom. She ran her fingers through her tangled hair and looked into the mirror, knowing she couldn't fix the mess. She had to get to Marco.

She raced into the bedroom and got dressed. Then she raced to the side door and across the lawn to the path that would take her to the main road, beside herself with her need to get to Kilt Rock.

She thought of taking Liam's truck, but she had no idea where she was going, and she wasn't sure she could drive on the opposite side of the road. Therefore, she started walking briskly on the side of the road. It was still dark outside, so she should have been a little nervous, but she was only focused on getting to Kilt Rock.

After about fifteen minutes, a truck started towards her. She moved closer to the side of the road as it slowed down. Her heart pounded in her chest, hoping it wasn't Liam or Edward.

She couldn't believe how stupid she was acting, not waiting for the guys to come back. Even if she didn't want to see Liam yet, she knew Edward would have driven her. Now she had put herself in danger, and if anything were to happen to her, Liam would never forgive himself. *Stupid, stupid, stupid.*

The truck pulled up beside her, and the window rolled down. "Where are ye off to this early in the morn, little lassie?" It was the groundskeeper from the inn who had helped them get the motorcycles out of the garage.

"Kilt Rock. Would you be so kind as to drive me into town so I can grab a cab?"

"I can do ye one better. Get in, lass, an' I will drive ye. My sister lives in the next town closest to the rock, an' I promised her I would check her sheep. They been actin' a wee barmy. I will go now and have breakfast with her," he answered in a thick Scottish brogue.

"That is so kind of you. Thank you, sir." Gabriella jumped up into the truck.

"My name is Shamus. No one has ever called me sir in my entire life, little lass."

"Well, thank you, Shamus. I am Gabriella, and I really do appreciate the ride. I will make it up to you and bake you something for your kindness," Gabriella said with a smile.

"That would be very kind of ye. I don't get many baked goods anymore since me Maggie passed on," Shamus said as he rubbed his belly.

After about ten minutes of silence, he could feel the sadness pouring off the little lassie as he saw her wipe a few tears. "Is there anything I can do for ya, little Gabriella? I was married for close to forty years, so I'm a good listener."

"You're going to be sorry you asked when I tell you," she said as she continued to wipe away her tears.

"No, I won't. As ye get older, ye realize that some of your life experience might someday help someone else. I can't ken what you're going through, but I can tell how I have dealt with me own problems, and it might help ye."

For reasons she would never know, she started to pour her heart and soul out to this little old man. She told him all about her loss and her fear that she had just betrayed her husband.

"Even saying the words 'moving on' makes my heart want to explode. I am being so unfair to Liam. I should let him go so he can find someone who isn't broken, someone he can share his love with."

"Gabriella, all I can say is ye have to realize the heart isn't always a logical place. Ye can't tell it what to feel. I can tell ye I understand loving a spouse who has passed on and wantin' to honour dem. But is it honouring dem by not feelin' and not lovin' when that is someting they taught ye to do? Would ye want that for yer husband? Would ye want him to just exist, never feeling love again? Love him by honouring what he taught ye, lassie."

She didn't respond until they reached Kilt Rock. Then she opened the door, looked at Shamus, squeezed his hand, and kissed him on his weathered, old cheek. "You gave me a lot to think about and to talk to my husband about. Thank you for bringing me here and for your wisdom!" With that, she shut the door and walked up to the cliff.

Chapter 14

Words of Wisdom

L iam got back to the suite at about six-ten and started his regular routine. He put on the water for tea then went to his computer to check his messages. When the kettle was boiled, he made the tea and let it steep while he answered some of the more important emails, sent in his daily log, and checked in with his mother back home.

At about seven-fifteen, he got some clean clothes and quietly snuck into the bedroom. He saw Gabriella all wrapped up in the blankets and figured he would wake her up after his shower. He couldn't wait to get his lips back on his beautiful angel.

After he was cleaned up, he came out of the loo and headed towards his girl. When he got to the bed, he bent down to kiss her when he realized she wasn't there. The bed was cold, which meant she hadn't been there for a while.

A cold chill passed over his body. Something was wrong.

He ran out to the living area, but she wasn't there, either. He opened the door to the patio, looked left then right, and still no sign of her. He ran to Edward's suite and knocked loudly until Edward answered, fresh from the shower.

"Please tell me she is here," Liam said as he pushed by Edward.

"Gabriella? Is something wrong with her?" Edward asked with fear in his voice.

"She's gone, man! She's fucking gone! I pushed too hard, and she couldn't handle it. We have to find her! She is alone, upset, and I don't know where she is," Liam said as he paced Edward's room, running his hands through his hair.

"Did she leave a note?" Edward looked at his watch. "How far could she have gotten? Did she take any of her clothes?"

They were both panicked and not thinking straight, which was unusual for the duo since they had been in many situations where level-heads prevailed. The emotional connection they both shared with her made it impossible to think straight.

They ran back to Liam's suite where Edward checked for her luggage and purse while Liam went to the bedroom to check for a note and to see if anything was missing. Nothing was out of place. Her purse remained on the nightstand, and all of her clothes were in the chest.

They met back in the living area, knowing they had to come up with a plan. Then it occurred to Edward there might be somewhere on the property she could have gone, so they both left the suite and ran down to the loch. Thankfully, she was nowhere near the water.

Edward took the lead since Liam was beside himself. Liam frantically rubbed his head, trying to shut out the fear. All he could think of was that he had pushed her too hard. He should have waited longer. He had probably freaked her out by telling her he loved her. If anything happened to her, he was completely fucking responsible.

After they had searched the banks of the loch, Edward decided they should check the front desk and ask if anyone had seen her. If no one had, then they were going to get on their motorcycles and hit the road in opposite directions, trying to find her.

Together, they went to the front desk and checked with the staff, but no one had seen Gabriella, so they headed out after agreeing to touch base every hour. Liam went towards Portree then to Dunvegan Castle. Edward was heading to the fairy pools then Kilt Rock. If they still couldn't find her, Liam was going to the ferry dock to make sure she hadn't left the isle, although it would be difficult without her pocketbook and passport. If they still hadn't found her, Edward would then head towards Neist Point and their little beach.

Liam had only been this scared once in his life, and that hadn't turned out so well. He was at a loss as to how to calm down. Could he lose this woman who had claimed his heart? No. He knew he would fight tooth and nail to have her and to make a future with her.

Once before, he had prayed for someone's soul, but that had gone unanswered. Now, after five years, did he really believe God would listen to him after ignoring him when he had begged before?

But if there were even the slightest chance God would listen now, he had to try.

He drove into town and started searching every store and cafe. Then he made his first call to Edward.

"Anything?"

"No, I just arrived at the fairy pools. I will call you if I find anything. If not, I will check back in an hour."

Edward was as frantic as Liam as he raced up the path towards the mountain range, checking each individual pool. He was out of breath when the next call from Liam came in.

"Anything?"

"No, I am going back to my motorcycle now and heading towards Kilt Rock," Edward answered as he started jogging down the path. "It will take me forty-five minutes before I get back to my bike and another forty-five minutes to drive to Kilt Rock. I will touch base then."

"Edward, I have never left you unguarded before. I can't stress enough to be careful and please find my girl."

"I'll do my best. And, Liam, I assure you that we will find her." He disconnected.

***

Gabriella stood at the edge of the cliff and looked at Kilt Rock. She felt the wind on her face as she thought long and hard about what Shamus had said.

"Marco, I know you can hear me. I can feel you surrounding

me. I miss you, mi amor, so much." She wrapped her arms around herself as she felt a chill over her body. She knew in her heart Marco was listening.

She took a deep breath and decided she had to confess before she lost her nerve. "I betrayed you last night." She started to sob as the confession left her lips. "I am so, so sorry. I broke the vow we made to each other. Do you remember it? We were lying in bed after just making love for the first time as husband and wife. I turned to you and asked you if you believed in Heaven, and you said you believed in an afterlife." The tears spilled down her cheeks as she stood there, not able to focus because of the abundance of water drowning her sight. She blinked, forcing more tears to fall then choked as she started to speak again. "We agreed that our love was so strong we would wait for each other in Heaven so we could spend an eternity together. We knew one lifetime was never going to be enough.

"Mi amor, I broke that vow last night, and I can't lie to you. I feel something for Liam, but how can we have our eternity if I love you and him? What happens, then? Who gets left behind? Oh, my God, what have I done!" She dropped to her knees then to her butt, wrapping her arms around her legs as she rocked back and forth, quietly sobbing. She had ruined their forever.

***

Three hours later, Gabriella sat in the same position, rocking back and forth, and this was how Edward found her. She was near the edge of the cliff, away yet still visible from where the tourists stood to look at Kilt Rock. Thankfully, there were only a handful of tourists, and they looked ready to move along.

Weights that felt like ten thousand pounds lifted from Edward's shoulders as he grabbed his phone and texted Liam, *Found her at Kilt Rock. Approaching now. Text me when u arrive. Fill u in then on what I learn.*

Edward walked towards Gabriella, feeling apprehension, the same as he had two and half months earlier when he had found her half-alive on the boulders. She was so quiet he wouldn't know she was breathing if not for her rocking.

Softly, he whispered as he sat down beside her and wrapped an arm around her, "Hey, love, I'm glad I found you. We have been so worried."

When he gently kissed the side of her forehead, she didn't respond. She just continued to rock as he held her. She was killing him.

"You need to talk, love. You can't keep it bottled up. You deserve to be happy, and I know Liam definitely deserves to be happy."

"I don't deserve to be happy. In one night, I ruined everything," she responded with a hoarse voice.

"How did you ruin everything? Why do you believe you don't deserve to be happy? I have met so many people in my life, and Gabriella, I have never met anyone as pure of heart as you. You *do* deserve to be happy." He continued when he realized she wasn't going to answer him. "You have no idea what you have done for me. You restored my faith that there are still good people in the world. You represent everything that is good in this world. Until I met you, I believed that everyone only wanted what I could give them, but they never gave anything in return. But not you. You wanted nothing from me except my friendship, no strings attached. And why you would want to know little, old me is beyond comprehension."

She looked at him and gave a bit of a smile. It didn't reach her eyes, but it was a beginning.

"Anyone who has ever met you would want to be your friend. You are selfless, gorgeous, funny, and that accent makes me feel like I am talking to royalty."

He tensed and wondered for half a second if she knew who he was, but as she rested her chin on her knees and continued to get lost in her own self-induced punishment, he realized she didn't have a clue. Otherwise, she would have called him out. She called a spade a spade, prince or no prince, and that was one of the reasons he loved her.

"Why do you think you don't deserve to be happy again when I have never met another human being with more love to share than you?" After a few minutes of silence from her, he added, "And believe me, no one in the world needs to be loved more than Liam."

"You don't understand. My husband and I made a vow to each other the night we were married. We promised we would always be true to one another if one of us died before the other so that we could spend an eternity in Heaven together. I broke that vow last night with Liam, and not just by being unfaithful, but…"

"What? Just say it."

"I fell in love with him. I would never have slept with him if I didn't love him. Look at what I have done! I have nothing to give him. I am broken, and he deserves so much more than I could ever give. And not only did I hurt him, but I betrayed Marco at the same time."

"Either you are blind or just plain barmy. You give more to so-called broken people than most would give in three lifetimes. You just have to allow yourself to move on. That doesn't mean you have to forget Marco or the boys. It means you have to continue to live and give what Marco taught you to give, and that is love."

Gabriella looked up at Edward, stunned that two different men in one day had said the same thing.

"Oh, my God, Shamus said almost the same thing."

Edward was taken aback "Who the hell is Shamus?"

"The groundskeeper at the inn. He lost his wife some time ago and said that I should honour Marco by sharing what he taught me about love. But what about the vow I broke to Marco about eternity? How can I move on after that?"

"Aw, love, when you made that vow, you were newly married, young, and everything was roses and sunshine. You couldn't conceive where your path would lead. If the roles were reversed and

Marco had survived, would you have wanted him to live this tortured existence? You are only thirty-four and have more than half your life to live. Would you want Marco to live fifty years in total misery? Would you want him to be angry and sad and never have another person touch him, to grow old alone, to never be around family and friends because it hurt too much to have reminders of what he lost? Would you want him not to laugh, not to feel, but just exist until he became bitter and old? How would he come to you in the afterlife? Would he be the same person you left? No, he wouldn't. He would be someone you didn't recognize, someone who wasn't capable of loving anymore.

"The love Marco gave you and shared with you was a gift that some people will never get in a lifetime. Trust me, I know. And for you to have it and not share it is a sin, especially to someone like Liam who has also come back to the living since meeting you.

"Gabriella, we have no idea what the future holds for any of us in this lifetime or the next, but you can't control it. You can only live it and decide how you want to live it. Make your husband and sons proud of you. Give them some peace. Let them go to enjoy Heaven and all the good and not worry about you. Let Liam take over caring for you and loving you. He, too, needs the freedom to carry on."

Just as he finished, his phone vibrated in his pocket, and he knew Liam had arrived. He had been so absorbed with his conversation with Gabriella he hadn't even heard the motorcycle approach.

He turned to Gabriella and saw she was sobbing again. He took her in his arms, kissed her forehead, and rocked her back and forth for a few minutes until he sensed Liam. He then lifted her jaw so he was looking into her eyes.

"Give him a chance, Gabriella. Talk to him and be honest. You might be surprised what you learn about him. I love you, my little, fanged she-devil. I want the best for you, and the best is Liam." He kissed her lips then hugged her tight before he got up and walked away.

When he approached Liam, Liam asked, "Is she okay? Am I going to lose her?" Liam shook his head. "I can't compete with a ghost."

Edward grabbed his shoulder and squeezed. "It's time to lay it all on the line. Don't hold back. Tell her." Edward hugged his friend, slapped his back, and then walked to his motorcycle. His job was done, and he was heading back to the inn to try one of Gabriella's famous Caesars. He had earned it. It had better be good, or he was making her drink his favourite scotch, and that, too, was an acquired taste.

Chapter 15

Raven

Liam walked up to Gabriella, sat down behind her, and wrapped his arms around her with his chin resting on top of her head. They didn't speak for the longest time, both gathering their thoughts, afraid they had hurt the other one beyond repair.

"Let me start by saying I am sorry for pushing you too hard, too fast—"

"No, Liam, don't apologize for what happened between us. You didn't push. Don't let me fool you. I knew what I was getting into, and I wanted it as much as you." She curled her hands around his forearms, gently rubbing back and forth as she continued her thoughts. "I don't think I could have survived these last few months without you. I was at the lowest point in my life. I was so lost and alone and scared, but you saved me."

"I pray that is true, but it was you who saved me. You see, years ago, I built a wall around my heart, and you systematically took it down, brick by brick."

She tilted her head to look up at him. "Who hurt you? Who could have had that kind of power to hurt someone as strong and confident as you?"

"My wife."

Gabriella tensed and stopped breathing. "What do you mean *your wife*? You're married?" she exclaimed, horrified.

"No. Sorry. Let me rephrase that...My deceased wife, Raven."

She breathed out. "Oh, Liam! I am so sorry. I had no idea. I only knew you were holding something back. Tell me what happened. Wait, that was rude. You don't owe me any explanations if you don't want to share it, I understand."

"Don't mistake me not telling you for not wanting to share. I was just afraid you couldn't handle anything else."

Gabriella looked straight ahead when she asked him, "So, will you tell me about Raven and what happened to her?"

He waited a few minutes, composing himself. "Raven was the sister of one of my Air Force buddies. I met Camden on the very first day I entered the academy. He was from my hometown of Sterling, but I never knew him because he was from the other side. When we found out that we were both from the same city, we became fast friends. Basic training was tough, but as tired as we were, we didn't want to sleep when we went to bed. We were both used to going to bed well after midnight.

"Our bunks were right beside each other, and we would talk for hours every night. We had a lot in common. We both loved our families and found out we had sisters the same age whom we both adored. We promised to introduce each other to our sisters on one of our leaves.

"I learned that Camden had lost his mum to cancer, and Raven had taken over most of the duties of their beloved mum. She cooked and cleaned for her brother and father out of love. She sounded like an incredible girl, and I couldn't wait to meet her. Camden said she was pretty, but nothing could have prepared me for when I met her." Liam stopped for a few moments and tried to find the words to describe Raven.

Gabriella remained facing forwards to give him a little bit of privacy. "It's okay, Liam. Take your time. Don't think so hard; just remember and feel."

Gabriella was right. The minute he started to remember and feel, the words poured out of him. "The first time I met her, I was blown away by how beautiful she was. She had black hair way past her shoulders. She was tall for a girl, five-foot-nine, and had the most amazing sky blue eyes you have ever seen. They were so light and captivating you felt like you were looking into her soul. And, although she was tall, she was delicate, and her skin was alabaster white. Her lips were big and pouty.

"Her beauty wasn't just skin deep; she was the real deal. She was kind, nurturing, and loving. I fell instantly in love with her and

149

asked her out on a date. She accepted, and we went for dinner and a movie. I was only on leave for thirty days, but I saw her every one of them. I didn't get another leave for almost nine months, and when I did, I went immediately back to Sterling to see Raven. This time, my leave was for two months, and again, I spent every minute I had with her.

"Both our parents were a little shocked by how fast and hard we fell for each other, but they had no idea we wrote each other every day that we were apart. You have to know, back then, I didn't have access to a computer for personal use at the base, so we actually wrote handwritten letters. I learned a lot about her that I might not have otherwise face to face because, when you write a letter, it's like keeping a diary. You can pour your soul out without feeling embarrassed. I didn't know I was capable of writing letters until I wanted to share my every thought with her.

"After four years, I graduated and had three months off before starting my career. Raven and I spent all of our time together, and before I left to go back to England, I bought a ring and asked her to marry me. She accepted, and we chose a date for our wedding for the following year when I would get another three months off.

"She planned the whole thing. I told her she didn't need to check with me for anything. The only thing I wanted was for her to have the wedding of her dreams. She missed not having her mum to help plan the wedding, especially since I was on a mission and couldn't help. My mum and sister helped out as much as was

150

possible, but she still wrote and expressed how much it hurt her that her mother wasn't there to guide her.

"We were married on June 29th, and I couldn't have been happier. I was so blessed, and I just knew I would cherish her for the rest of our lives.

"The wedding was beautiful, and it so reflected her personality. She gave a tribute to her mum, and I was so proud of her. Then we moved to London where I was based out of. Shortly after, I was heading out for another mission and didn't know how long it would last.

"Even though she knew full-well what I did for a living, she was still crushed when I left again. She was terrified I would get hurt, and nothing I did seemed to pacify her. We argued that, after losing her mum, she couldn't lose me, too. I made her promises I knew I might not be able to keep, but I didn't want her to be afraid, or suffer because of me.

"I left after making those promises, and then came home safe and sound after my tour, and we got to spend another three months together. I was about to leave on my next tour when I found out Raven was pregnant. I was overjoyed that we were going to have a child and knew she wanted to be a mother more than anything else. This child would give her something of her own to love every day, especially when I wasn't home. Life couldn't get any more perfect.

"Just before the end of her first trimester, my lieutenant called me into his office and asked me to sit down. He informed me that they were sending me home due to family issues, and I would work out of the London base. I was confused as to why until it hit me that something had happened to the baby, and they were sending me back to be with Raven. I asked if it was the baby, but he said he wasn't privy to that information, just that I needed to get ready to leave immediately. I was back in London in less than seven hours.

"I walked into our flat, and my mum and sister were there with Raven, holding her hand. I could tell things weren't good by the look on their faces and tears in their eyes. Raven stood up, and I could see she was still pregnant, so I couldn't figure out what the fuck was going on.

"My mum and sister told me they were leaving so we could talk. They kissed and hugged me tightly then left. I went to Raven, took her in my arms, kissed her, and asked what was wrong. My heart was pounding out of my goddamned chest. I was so afraid."

"It was then, Gabriella, that she told me she had breast cancer, just like her mum. It felt like someone had punched me in the gut. She started to cry, and I hugged her and told her everything was going to be okay. I would make sure of it. I asked her if she knew what treatments were available and when she would be starting them. I told her I wouldn't leave her side. I would walk through the process with her. She would be okay. Then I prayed I was right."

Gabriella started to cry, and Liam could feel her body shuddering. She pulled out a pile of used Kleenex she had been using all day and blew her nose. "I am so sorry, Liam."

Liam tightened his hold on her. "I don't want to upset you. I just want you to understand me, and to do that, you have to know my story. If you can't hear anymore, I understand. You already know she died; we can leave it at that."

"No, I want to know all of it. It makes sense now why you have been able to help me heal. You've had to walk the same path as me."

Taking a deep breath, he continued, "It was then that she told me she was carrying twins. I couldn't believe it. We were having twins. If that wasn't shocking enough, her next statement floored me. Nothing could have prepared me when she told me she'd had a sonogram, and when she looked at her two little babies, she made some decisions without me.

"She told me that she wouldn't have any treatments until after the twins were born. She said she had stage three breast cancer, and the likelihood of her surviving if she had the treatments was fifty-fifty. If she waited till after the babies were born, her chances for survival went down to twenty percent. She went on to explain that she hadn't come to her decision easily, but the doctors had told her the babies couldn't survive if she had the treatment. The doctors advised her to abort and start the treatments immediately. She went against their advice and decided not have an abortion. She said she couldn't murder our children. She loved them too much, and it was her job to protect them.

"I argued horribly with her. I wanted her to abort. I was terrified of losing the love of my life. Can you believe I wanted to kill my own children to save her life? What kind of father would do that?

"I told her we could have more children, but that wasn't possible if she were dead. She explained that, after the treatment, she would never be able to have children. The treatment would kill all her eggs. I didn't give a fuck! I wanted *her*. I couldn't live with any other decision. But she had made the decision for both of us. Her mind was made up. It was her body, her decision."

Liam paused. It was killing him. "I was so fucking mad at the world, and I was so mad at her. How dare she make that decision on her own without considering my feelings? I told her she was selfish, and we both ended up on the floor, holding each other and crying. I was such a bastard, and I wasted so much time being angry instead loving her every minute I had with her. We stayed on the floor all night, her begging for my forgiveness and me begging her to change her mind. I never did change her mind, and she never did get my forgiveness."

Gabriella's heart broke for Liam. What a terrible thing to happen to him. Life was so unfair.

She was sobbing when she said, "Oh, Liam, I am so sorry you lost your wife and children."

"The twins didn't die. Raven carried them to almost full-term and gave birth to identical girls. I have two six-year-old daughters. One is named Enya and the other Ainsley."

"What? You have two daughters? Alive and well? Why aren't you with them?"

"My mother is helping me raise them because of my job. Right now, they are in their second year of school. I promised Edward that I would take this vacation with him because of his devastation over losing Gillian. He helped support me when I lost Raven, so I am trying to return the favour. We will be heading to my home soon."

"When did you lose her?"

"Fourteen months after the twins were born. She got to hold and feed and love our daughters for the first fourteen months of their lives. During her pregnancy and when the girls were born, she made video recordings so the girls would know how much she loved them and to help guide them through different stages of their lives when a daughter might need her mum.

"I'm embarrassed to admit that I wasn't sure I would ever be able to love the girls. I secretly blamed them for her refusing treatment. I resented that she chose them over me. What kind of person does that to someone they claim to love? I was so selfish, and she died knowing that.

"You know, when they moved in her stomach, she was so excited and wanted to share that with me, to feel the miracle that that was growing inside her. I didn't let her see it, but I would cringe when I touched her stomach. I acted horribly, and I have to live with that forever. So, you see, as much as you want to give me credit for saving you, I am nobody's hero."

"You're a hero to me; don't ever doubt that. But please tell me you grew to love your daughters."

155

"Yes. The second Enya was born, I fell instantly in love with her, and I realized Raven was right. Although I never told her, I felt as much for Ainsley as I did for Enya when she was born seven minutes later. They were so perfect and totally innocent. They were the best gift Raven ever gave me besides her love. She left me her legacy in the form of two perfect, little girls. They are the spitting image of Raven, too.

"I hope, very soon, you will accompany me to my home to meet my little hellions. And trust me; those two little sprites rule the roost."

"I would love nothing more than to meet your daughters. I bet you're a fantastic papi. Raven truly gave you a beautiful gift. Children are the best of both their parents. I hope you celebrate and teach those little girls all about their mama. Let her live in your stories."

"That is why I understand the guilt of moving on. You're the first woman I have been able to feel anything for in five years, and I struggle with the fear of loving you and the chance that I could lose you. I don't know if I am strong enough to live through that again.

"Since Raven died, I chose not to date. Now, don't get me wrong; there were women, but only for a few hours at a time. That way, I never had to feel anything. Then *you* entered my life, and I couldn't stop myself from falling in love." Liam tucked himself even closer to Gabriella's back. He rested his chin on her shoulder and surrounded her.

"You think that I have been healing you," Liam continued, "but in reality, you were helping me heal. You taught me that it is possible to love two people in one lifetime. And I do love you...with every fiber of my being. I learned from Raven to always say what you need to say. You can't wait for a better chance, since you may never get it. I love you, Gabriella Dante, now and forever."

Gabriella thought for a few minutes then turned in Liam's arms, looking into his eyes so he could see her sincerity. "I guess Raven is still teaching lessons of the heart. Now I feel free to say that I love you, Liam. We have both suffered, and now it is time to move on. It won't always be easy, but we were given a second chance, and I, for one, want to grab it and run."

She turned and hugged Liam with every bit of strength in her body. When she was done squeezing the breath out of him, she brought their faces together. This time, it was her who grabbed his face in her two little hands and brought his mouth to hers.

She needed to feel, to touch, to smell, to absorb all that was Liam. It was easy to justify in her mind that this beautiful man deserved a second chance at happiness, which made her realize he must feel exactly the same way. She really must be healing since she was putting another person she cared for ahead of herself. And wasn't that really what love was all about—wanting more for your partner than you wanted for yourself, loving them enough to take the good and the bad?

Liam allowed her to take the lead, but the instant they were back at the inn, he was taking control again. After losing all control when Raven had gotten sick, he had vowed never to lose control of any situation again.

"What brought you here, and why didn't you let me drive you?" he asked when she finally pulled back from their kiss.

Gabriella looked around. "The last time we came here, I came to the edge of the cliff where we are now and talked to Marco. For some reason, it felt like I could actually talk to him here, and he would hear me. I felt like he answered me and put his thoughts in my head. He told me that he couldn't have peace until I was better. This morning, I needed his forgiveness."

"Did you get the forgiveness? Did you get any more answers?"

"Yes, I felt like Marco told me that Shamus was right, that I wasn't honouring my love for Marco, and he made me feel like you needed my love as much as he did. I couldn't believe Marco would say that because, why would he? I betrayed our vow. So I sat here for hours, trying to figure out whether I really was going crazy and making all this shit up in my head. But now, after hearing your story, I don't think I made it up at all. I think he was giving me his blessing to love you and to be loved by you."

"That was an incredible thing to say, Gabriella. Thank you." He took her hand and kissed it, holding it to his lips longer than he should have, processing all she had said. He was stumped about one thing. He lifted just his eyes. "Now can I ask you a silly question?"

"Sure."

"Who the fuck is Shamus?"

Gabriella laughed. "The groundskeeper at the inn. He found me walking this morning and drove me here himself. He told me about losing his wife and about honouring the lessons our loved ones gave us while they were alive. He is a very wise man"

Satisfied with her answer, Liam pulled her into his arms and hugged her. Then he brought her mouth to his and kissed her like his life depended on it.

He needed to get them back to the inn. She had been sitting at Kilt Rock for almost seven hours now, and neither of them had eaten. He also had to check on Edward.

He made her stand up as he did. Then he took out his phone and texted Edward, *All is well. R u okay? We will pick up food.*

Edward responded that everything was fine, that he had already gotten food for the three of them, and that he was happy everything was okay.

As they walked hand in hand to the motorcycle, Liam knew in his heart this wouldn't be their last trip up to Kilt Rock. He, too, felt an energy he couldn't explain there.

As he got on the motorcycle then helped her on, he realized he truly was going to get a second chance at love. This time, he was going to enjoy every moment and not take anything for granted.

He started the bike, and Gabriella turned back to look at Kilt Rock. In her head, she heard Marco say, *"Make me proud, mi amor."* She wrapped her arms around Liam, laid her head against his back, and thought back, *"Thank you, my love."*

Chapter 16

Meanwhile, Back at the Inn

Edward checked his emails and phoned his two brothers, wanting to check in on his niece and nephew. He hadn't seen them in a while and missed them. He loved those little ankle-biters so much he couldn't imagine what he would feel like if he had his own children.

He still wasn't sure how Gabriella had managed to survive after losing her whole family. Hopefully, Liam would convince her to take a chance on love again. They were perfectly suited for each other, sort of like he used to feel about Gillian.

Though he had been preoccupied with helping Gabriella, not a day had passed that he hadn't thought of Gillian. He had truly believed she was his soul mate. She had been raised in a fish bowl like him and had been forced to dodge the piranhas in the media, so she had related on a level most people couldn't.

Edward pulled out his wallet and found the pictures he and

Gillian had taken in Brighton on the pier. He remembered when she had seen one of those photo booths and had insisted they take a photo together. She had taken five pounds out of her purse and pushed him in. He had sat down with her on his lap, and she had made goofy faces while he just laughed. He loved how those photos exemplified the true essence of Gillian…or what he had thought was the essence of the carefree girl with her fuck-the-world attitude.

She was stunning at five-foot-seven; with blue eyes; cropped, blonde hair cut at the neck; and always dressed like a gypsy yet had a killer body under all those layers.

He had found out too late that her beauty was only skin deep, and she could be bought for the right price. It had crushed him. She had possessed the power to destroy him, and destroyed him she had. He wasn't sure whether he would ever trust another woman like he had trusted her. He would always hold something back. Although, if Gabriella had chosen him, he might have been able to trust her.

Edward had ordered from the restaurant a full English Sunday dinner, and he heard Liam's motorcycle pull up just as the waiter left. Edward had set the table, wanting a real Sunday dinner where you took what you wanted and had seconds. He opened the wine to let it breathe then went about making three Caesars in what he hoped would be a celebration of his friends' union.

Liam came through the door with his hand locked in Gabriella's. She saw Edward and launched herself into his arms. He had seen her intentions and braced himself as she made contact then hugged her tightly.

"You were right, Edward. Thank you so much!" She pulled her head back to look him in the eyes.

"Hey, get your bloody paws off my girl!" Liam jokingly growled.

"Sod off, old man. You may have her love, but that is only happening since I graciously bowed out of vying for her attention. Had I stayed in the race, you wouldn't have had a chance, old boy," Edward joked, making Gabriella giggle as he placed her back on the floor. She loved when he imitated English nobility.

Liam possessively grabbed Gabriella's hand and pulled her gently back into the fold of his body. He liked her tucked right into his side, his arm draped possessively over her shoulders.

Edward handed out the drinks and raised his glass. "May this be the beginning of your forever."

They all clinked their glasses and took a sip.

Liam swallowed hard and scoffed. "This is disgusting! How do you two drink this concoction?"

"Edward, you might still be in the running, after all," Gabriella said as she pretended to try to pull out of Liam's arms.

He tightened his grip. "You might like Caesars, while I like draft, and I like tea over your lattes, but trust me, baby; you're mine." Liam bent down and sealed his statement with a long, passionate kiss.

"Ahem, gross. I am still here. Hello…"

"Uh, sorry, Edward. What is that delicious smell?" Gabriella said quickly to hide her embarrassment.

"That, my friends, is a celebratory Sunday dinner. Roast beef, Yorkshire pudding, and all the fixings. And *you* thought I couldn't cook! Well, I showed you, little miss she-devil."

"Funny, you have the same serving dishes as the restaurant. It was kind of them to lend them to you after all your hard work," she replied.

"Okay, enough you two. I feel like I am with children when you two start bickering. Let's eat. I am starved." Liam pulled a chair closer to his for Gabriella to sit in.

"Wow, I have never had such a big Yorkshire pudding before," she said as she tore off a chunk, dipped it in the gravy, and then popped it into her mouth. "Mm…"

The friends enjoyed their meal at the table then their dessert and hot beverages out on the patio.

"Don't you think it is funny that we are the only ones staying at the inn? I mean, it is gorgeous, and the weather has improved, yet they still have no visitors," Gabriella commented.

Edward and Liam looked at each other briefly before Liam answered. "Why do you have to question a good thing? Just accept that we are lucky enough to have the privacy and be thankful."

"Oh, don't get me wrong. I am thrilled we are the only ones here, but I feel so sorry for the owner. It is so quaint. I just think they need to advertise better. If more people knew about the inn, then this place would be jammed. I would hate to think they couldn't afford to continue to run this place."

Edward decided they needed to change the topic. "I was hoping we could go golfing tomorrow. Are you interested in learning?"

"What makes you think I don't already know how to play?"

"Sorry, I didn't mean to infer you couldn't play. How long have you been playing?"

"I can't play, but I might have been able to." She winked. "You shouldn't assume. Do you know what assume stands for?" She didn't wait for his reply. "It makes an *ass* out of y*ou* and *me*."

"An ass, all right." Edward shook his head. "Well, do you know what golf stands for? Gentlemen Only. Ladies Forbidden. And, in my opinion, it should have remained that way." Edward laughed as Gabriella stuck her tongue out at him.

She really had become like a sister to him, and he adored everything about her. He didn't have a sister, so it was nice to have a female in his life whom he trusted. Could he have fallen head over heels in love with her if Liam hadn't claimed her? Yup, you bet your fucking life.

A horrible thought entered his head, but he pushed it out as soon as it came. Still, he had it, though. He wondered if he could trust her implicitly if she knew who he really was.

Edward was ashamed of himself for that thought. Nevertheless, life had taught him that everyone would eventually turn on him. His pops used to say that it was "lonely on top," and he used to think his father was arrogant, but it truly had nothing to do with arrogance. And after Edward had been burned the first dozen times by people who had claimed to care for him, he had learned his lesson.

It wasn't his choice to have been born into the royal family. If he'd had a choice, he would have definitely chosen a middle-class English family. He could have fostered real relationships instead of his best friend being paid to guard him. How pathetic was that? He could have a girlfriend who truly wanted just him, and not all the glitz, glam, and pomp that people associated with his life. Being royalty had its perks, but for every one, there were fifty disadvantages.

"Edward, hello…? Where were you just now? We were having a disagreement, and you just zoned out on me. I hope you were thinking about how I was right and you were wrong."

"Yeah, that's exactly what I was thinking," he said without his usual flair or charm.

Gabriella's demeanor wilted. "I didn't mean to hurt your feelings. I was kidding."

"No, no, I know that. You're right. I zoned out, and where I went wasn't particularly a nice place to be." He forced a smile. "I am back and returning to my original question; would you like to learn to play golf?

"I would love to try, although I suck at most sports. But golf looks really easy. I mean, how hard could it be to hit a ball into a hole, right?"

Liam choked on his tea, and Edward jumped right in.

"You did not just say that! Are you shittin' me! Golf is probably one of the most difficult games to learn. It takes skill, concentration, and years of practice to become good. You, little miss, are getting a lesson in humility tomorrow, and you will apologize for that statement."

Liam just sat back and watched his best friend and the woman he loved banter, but he needed more contact with Gabriella. So, while Edward lectured her on the game of golf, Liam yanked her chair even closer, picked her up, and placed her on his lap. Then he wrapped his arms around her and cuddled her like a small child.

She was so engrossed in her conversation that she didn't even acknowledge she was now wrapped up in Liam's arms. She was fighting to sit up properly so she could get her point across to Edward. You could see that little Latin temper sparked and ready to spar.

She truly was passionate and full of life now that she was dealing with her grief in a healthy manner. Liam was proud that she had come a long way. He just couldn't get enough of her, and the passion she exhibited made him look forward to getting her back into their bed. He couldn't wait to feel her lips wrapped around his dick...

As he had those thoughts, he was getting the hard-on of the century. She was driving him crazy as she continued to wiggle around while she talked, moving her hands as fast as her mouth.

167

Finally, he could take no more.

Liam stood up with Gabriella in his arms. "Say good night, angel."

"That's rude." Her eyes flashed. "Edward and I are having a conversation."

Liam rubbed her against his hard-on, and Gabriella got the hint and giggled.

"Good night, Edward, and by the way, we should make a bet about the golf game tomorrow."

"You're on. Name your pleasure. This is going to be like taking candy from a baby." He rubbed his hands together in a villainous way. "Easiest bet I'll ever win."

Edward barely heard her response since Liam had already gotten her into their suite, but he did hear her yell, "Game on, you stubborn, English goat!"

Edward laughed; he loved to get her riled up. He argued with her even when he knew she was right just to see her reaction. He loved her and would cherish her friendship forever.

Liam captured Gabriella's mouth and silenced her. He wrapped one hand into her long, curly hair and fisted it against her scalp so he could move her head where he wanted it. With his other hand, he moved to her knit shirt and undid the buttons, mentally betting against himself that the baby blue shirt would match her bra and knickers. He broke the kiss to confirm he was right.

He looked down and saw that encasing her breasts was a baby

blue and white lace push-up bra. It hugged and lifted her breasts, giving her incredible cleavage. He took pleasure in dipping his head and running his tongue along the cleavage.

He lifted his head. "I love to unwrap you and discover that your bra and knickers match your outfits. Over the last few months, I would look many times at what you were wearing and envision the matching ensemble underneath. You have never disappointed."

"Marco was obsessed with matching my lingerie to my outfits," she quietly whispered, hoping she hadn't just ruined their night.

He noticed her hesitation. "Well, God bless Marco. He is my hero." Liam looked up at the ceiling. "Thank you, Marco. You're the best."

Gabriella giggled before it was cut off by Liam removing her bra then latching on to her breast and sucking deeply, causing her to moan.

While he sucked, he undid his belt and the buttons on his cargo pants. When his pants were off, he unlatched from her breast then gently pushed down on her shoulders until she was kneeling.

As she looked at his impressive erection, he removed his black, long-sleeved T-shirt and threw it on the floor. He gasped as her little hands wrapped around his dick before she then licked up it like she was enjoying an ice cream cone. His hips jutted forwards, and he grabbed her head on both sides. Then he pulled her hair back so he could watch what he had only previously dreamed of.

She circled the head of his dick with her tongue, and he hissed.

Encouraged by his reaction, she took him into her mouth and began to suck, rubbing her tongue along the sensitive part underneath his shaft and dipping down as far as she could go without choking. She rubbed up and down the rest of his length with both hands wrapped around his solid girth.

Liam threw his head back as his eyes rolled. He only held the position for a second, though, wanting to watch her.

When he could take no more, he pulled out of her mouth. He wanted to climax inside of her pussy and not her mouth.

"I wasn't done," she protested.

"Anymore and we would both be done."

He took her hands and guided her into a standing position. Then he reached for her jeans and removed them as quickly as was humanly possible before turning her around so fast her hair whipped around and hit him in the face. He bent her forwards so her hands were on the bed and her ass was pointing at him. Then he grabbed her hips and positioned himself.

"Fucking perfect," he groaned as he slid home.

She was so tight, and he was rather well-endowed. It felt like a little piece of heaven for both of them.

"Oh, God, yes! More, more! Faster! Oh, yeah…That feels so…good," she whispered, feeling every inch of him moving in and out.

Liam removed his hands from her hips and leaned over her body, locking his fingers between hers that were spanned wide on the bed. He held her hands as he pumped hard into her little body.

She lifted her head and threw it back onto his shoulder when her climax hit, her body convulsing. She barely made a sound, yet by the shaking of her body, he knew it was a powerful climax, which only ignited him. He could feel his spine tingle. He lifted up on his toes and gave the final thrusts until he came inside her with a loud groan.

He untangled his hands from hers so he could grab her waist and lift her up, every muscle in his body relaxing after his climax. He fell sideways on the bed with her landing just in front of his chest, both on their sides. He then wrapped his arms around her and pulled her to him, kissing the back of her shoulder and then her head.

"Thank you, baby, for rocking my world. That was amazing," Liam breathed out.

"I never expected to ever experience that feeling again. I can't believe how incredible that felt. It was so freeing. I love you," Gabriella responded quietly, and then she brought her head down to kiss his arms that were wrapped around her.

He hugged her more tightly. "I love you, too…so much, baby." He cleared his throat, nervous about how she would respond to his question. "This might sound like a stupid question, but how are you so quiet when you get off? I can feel your body exploding into a million pieces, but you're almost silent."

She didn't respond for a few minutes, unsure how much she should say without ruining the afterglow of making love.

"Gabriella, I can hear the wheels turning in your head, and baby,

I get it. I am asking, knowing it must involve Marco. It's okay to talk about him. He was your life before me, the same as Raven was my life before I met you. They made us who we are today, and we have to celebrate and share that with each other. I want to know about Marco, and I want to share about Raven. I believe you would have really liked her."

Liam felt her tears hitting his arm as she responded, "Could you get any more perfect? I swear, Marco must have sent you to me, knowing exactly what I needed. I really think he is finally at peace now that we have found each other." She didn't answer his original question, completely overwhelmed.

She turned around and made him roll over onto his back. Then she looked into his eyes and kissed him gently on the lips. Seconds later, she laid her head on his chest and let his heartbeat lull her to sleep.

He rubbed her back, feeling her body relax. He knew he would get his answers another day. This had been an emotional one for her, and she needed to rest her mind and body. They had overcome many hurdles, and they had the rest of their lives to sort out everything else.

He closed his eyes and fell into the most peaceful sleep ever.

Chapter 17

Layers Peel Away

Liam woke up at five a.m. like he had every morning for over ten years, but he had no intention of getting up and leaving Gabriella in bed alone. He needed to hear her thoughts after all she had learned yesterday. He needed to see if she could get past the fact that he had been such a bastard and what he had admitted about his feelings for Raven that he had never breathed to another living soul. The anger and resentment he knew would send him to Hell upon his death had haunted many of his sleepless nights. Unburdening his soul had been freeing, but it also had made him fearful of how Gabriella would feel about him, knowing he had been selfish, ruthless, and cruel to someone he had claimed to love.

He rubbed his hand up and down her back, taking solace in her warm body wrapped so tightly around his. One of her arms was wrapped around his waist and one leg was thrown over both of his thighs, effectively pinning him in place. Her head lay draped over his shoulder, which had fallen asleep three hours ago, pins and needles shooting through his shoulder. He wouldn't move a muscle even to give himself some relief, though. She was sleeping peacefully, something that had just begun to happen over the last couple of weeks.

She had suffered so much. He understood the pain of being left behind, yet Raven had left him with two little miracles he could focus his love on. While Gabriella had spent three years trying to find her place in the world, after her identity and reason to live had been taken away. She had been left to carry on with no one to do it with or for, and no direction on how to survive alone. He hoped she would give him a chance to show her that you could love twice in a lifetime, as he himself had just discovered.

"Good morning, mi cielo. I know you are awake. What are you thinking so hard about?" Gabriella lifted her head to look at him, her hair a beautiful mess, more asleep than awake, but she had an impish smile that took his breath away.

He sighed with relief and smiled back at her with full dimples. "What does *mi cielo* mean?"

"It means my heaven or my sky. You're a piece of Heaven on earth, my saviour."

Liam cupped her jaw and kissed her deeply, loving that she so easily accepted all his faults and was willing to look past them. He felt like that green creature, the Grinch, the girls watched at Christmas time, whose heart had broken its metal cage and grown

174

three times bigger.

She was totally and completely *his* saviour. How could he convince her of that? He couldn't get close enough to her.

After kissing her thoroughly, he dropped his lips to her collarbone, thoughtfully staying away from her neck. He sucked the skin, liking his mark on her body. It gave him satisfaction to leave a mark, indicating to any other male that Gabriella was taken.

Liam rolled her over to her back and worshipped her body. He licked his way down from her collarbone to her shapely breasts before taking one nipple into his mouth, sucking, licking, nipping, and then he turned his attention to the other one. She squirmed as he moved farther down.

He grabbed her legs and placed them over each of his shoulders. He could smell her arousal and saw she was dripping with need. He took the first swipe from just in front of her anus to the top of her slit then enveloped her clit, sucking it into his mouth as he flicked the nub with his tongue, driving her to distraction.

"Oh, my freakin' God, Liam. Please...I can't take anymore...I need you *now*!"

If she wanted to come, so be it. That would only add to his delight. However, he wasn't stopping until he was good and finished. She could come again when he entered her. For now, he was feasting.

She came hard, and he was flooded by her juices, which he happily lapped up.

"I love your taste. I could eat you all day long and never get enough."

Although it embarrassed her, it also floored her.

"Please, Liam, I need you so badly. Please…"

He crawled behind her and shifted her gently to her side. Lifting her leg, he plunged into her in one fluid movement. He then snaked his arm underneath her body to wrap around her, grabbing her breast and pinching the hardened nipple. With his other hand, he held her leg up high while he pumped continuously into her body.

He nuzzled his face into her hair, inhaling her intoxicating scent. In and out, he rubbed along her sensitive walls, the tightness, the feeling of being exactly where you needed to be in the world. This was the best feeling in the world, and he wished it could go on forever.

He could feel her walls tightening and knew he was going to rock her world for a second time.

Quietly, exactly like every other time they made love, she climaxed. He felt the convulsions rock her body, which forced him to lose complete control and follow her into bliss. He moaned as he took those final deep thrusts into her body before he exploded inside of her.

"Fuck…" he moaned.

After he had spent himself, he lowered her leg, but he didn't pull himself out. He was very comfortable in her and saw no reason to leave.

He wrapped both arms around her, feeling at peace.

After what seemed like an hour, but in reality was more like ten minutes, he squeezed Gabriella and whispered, "When you come, I can feel you exploding, yet you barely make a sound."

She smiled, having never realized she did that. She knew *why* she did it; she just wasn't conscious of it.

"I used to be very vocal, but one time, when Gianluca started sleeping through the night, I screamed and woke him up. I had to get up and soothe Gianluca back to sleep, which took over two hours. Let's just say the moment was lost, and Marco and I learned to be very quiet after that."

"I never experienced that. By the time the girls were six weeks old, Raven had started chemotherapy and was very sick from the treatments. We never experienced that passion again."

That saddened Gabriella for both Raven and Liam.

"I am so sorry," she said.

"I now realize I was so lucky to have Raven's love for the amount of time that I did. I have to cherish that and share those times with the twins. Sometimes, the twins say or do something that reminds me so much of Raven, and I tell them about her. That is the greatest gift I can give to them. It took me a long time to realize she taught me that."

He knew he had to change the subject before the sadness overwhelmed them both.

"Moving on. I have a few things I have been meaning to ask

you, and I either forget, or we switch topics. Why are your lady bits shaved? I mean, I love it, but why do you do it?"

She giggled as she thought about her response. "One night, about five months after Mateo was born and I was overwhelmed and exhausted, my mother and papi decided they were going to take the boys overnight so Marco and I could go on a date. Marco bought the most amazing bra and thong set in a hot pink to match a top I had recently bought. It was gorgeous, and I was excited about wearing it. While I was getting ready, I considered the fact that Marco always bought me beautiful lingerie that made me feel pretty, but he got nothing in return.

"I remembered when we were first married and he saw me shave my bikini line. He told me I should shave it all off. Of course, the Catholic in me would never allow me to do something so brazen. However, in order to give Marco something special, I shaved myself completely bare, and when he saw what I had done, he expressed his shock and gratitude the entire night. Marco loved me clean shaven so much he made me promise that, no matter what, I would always keep myself groomed like that. To this day, I can't bathe without shaving and thinking of how important it was to him."

Liam thought about the story, respecting Marco even more for how he had treated and encouraged his wife. He was learning a lot from a dead man.

Next, Liam asked about her always matching her lingerie to her clothing, and Gabriella told him all about In Your Dreams Day.

"The more you tell me about Marco, the more my admiration for the man increases. I think we would have been great friends, and I will be grateful every day for the rest of my life that he cared and nurtured you. I will honour him by carrying on his legacy."

Gabriella felt a lump the size of a grapefruit in her throat and couldn't speak for a few moments. She was thrilled Liam encouraged her to speak and share things about Marco. She didn't want to forget him or the love they had shared. In turn, she wanted to encourage Liam to share about Raven.

She looked into his eyes. "May I ask a question now?"

"Sure, anything you want to know," Liam immediately answered.

"Why do you call my private parts *lady bits*? What is that all about?"

Liam laughed. "When I met Raven, I used to say pussy. She hated it and thought it was derogatory. She put up with it, but when the girls were born and she knew she was dying, she asked me to refer to the girls' private parts as lady bits. It wasn't much to ask, and I didn't want her to think I wouldn't teach the girls to be proper young women."

"She thought a lot about the girls' future, huh?"

She was lost in thought and was aimlessly tracing the tattoo of the black bird that looked like it was escaping his chest. The bird had its head and one wing out of a tear in his skin, or so it appeared to her.

"I sort of figured out that your tattoo represents Raven, but tell me about it."

"Gabriella, I am no Marco."

That confused Gabriella. She was about to respond when he cut her off.

"I am embarrassed to tell you, but you have been so honest. You might feel differently about me when you hear what it represents and why I did it." He stopped for a few moments and gathered his thoughts. Revealing this secret was another thing he had never shared with another living soul, but it was time to let it go. It was time to let his anger go.

"After Raven started to get her treatments, she got really sick and tried to hide it. But there were mornings when I would come upstairs to ask her something about the twins, and she would be hanging over the toilet. I would try to comfort her, but she would act like nothing was wrong. She felt that she had to hide her suffering since she had waited until after the twins were born to start. That made me even angrier and sadder that she didn't trust me enough to share her pain and allow me to help her.

"So, one day when she was trying to convince me that she was fine, and I could clearly see she wasn't, I left in a rage. I phoned my mum and asked her to go and help Raven while I went into town and walked into the first tattoo parlor I found. I told the artist what I wanted and offered him double his normal fee if he could draw it and ink it all in one day.

"I loved her so much, and I was so afraid of losing her. Time was ticking away. I realized I couldn't save my daughters' mum no matter what I did, so I took my anger out on the one person who didn't deserve it. Raven.

"The tattoo is of Raven escaping my chest after taking and crushing my heart with her talons. She left me empty and incapable of loving. I was nobody without her. She was the best part of me, and that died the day I buried her."

Gabriella silently cried. It was horrible to lose the love of your life unexpectedly, but it must have been heart-wrenching to helplessly watch that person be in unbearable pain, slipping away, and not be able to do anything to help them.

"Liam, I am so sorry I made you reveal those things. Please forgive me. I had no right."

"No, angel, you need to know that is who I am. I'm not proud of that person, and I'm not worthy of your love. I'm a broken man," he said in such a sad, defeated voice.

Gabriella turned to face his broken expression and grabbed his head in both hands. "Stop torturing yourself. I get it. I don't think any less of you. I spent the first year after Marco and the boys died blaming Marco for taking the boys and leaving me all alone. God help me, but I blamed him for giving me the world then snatching it away. I hated myself for feeling that way. But you, Liam, you gave him back to me by allowing me to remember the love I shared with him. Please allow me to do the same for you. Let me give you back

Raven and let the guilt go."

Just as they started to kiss, Liam's phone beeped with a text. He bent over to snatch it off the nightstand and read the text, bellowing with laughter as he turned the phone towards Gabriella to read.

Guess since u missed our run and it is quiet, u are having sex. Tell her, if she wants a real man, not only do I give lessons in golf, but I can teach her to scream the roof off. Just trying to help, old man! ;)

"I am going to kill him! Liam, that's not funny!" She smacked him playfully as he laughed. "He is so dead. What an ass. Don't encourage him! I swear he is so paying for that!"

"That's just Edward. He has a way of making each situation funny. He got me through some of the worst times of my life. I owe him a lot and love him like a brother."

"That doesn't mean he won't pay for that comment. I am going to whip his ass in golf. Truthfully, I have been playing for years, but because of his arrogance, I am going to bet against him, win, and watch him fall off his high horse." She rubbed her hands together, thinking about her victory.

Chapter 18

Welcome to His Life

Over breakfast, Edward and Gabriella discussed the terms of their bet, agreeing that, because of Edward's size and skill, she would have twenty extra strokes.

"She-devil, I really believe twenty is taking unfair advantage of you. I mean, I have been playing for over ten years, and I am *damn* good. How about I give you fifty? It only seems fair."

"You know, sometimes you just piss me off with your arrogance. I'll take twenty strokes, thank you very much. Now, what are we betting?"

"When I win, I will take fresh churros daily for the next month."

"Well, in that case, I think that, for one month, you can't have any tea. You have to drink lattes or espresso, and you can't complain."

"You both know I will be the one who suffers the most in the bet, right?" Liam asked. "If Gabriella loses, she won't be in my bed when we return from our run. If Edward loses, I am the one whose ears will bleed from listening to him moan and groan while watching his face every time he takes a sip of a latte."

"Not my problem, old man. Stop keeping her so busy into the night, and she won't be so tired. And you will *so* benefit from my winnings of warm churros every morning."

Liam shot Edward a scathing look at the old man comment. "I'm putting one hundred pounds on Gabriella winning."

Edward laughed. "While I have often heard the phase 'a fool and his money are soon parted,' I now realize what it means. And they do say the mind is the first to go as you age. I'll take that bet and double it!"

Gabriella started to panic. It had been at least four years since she had played.

"Hold on, guys. Liam, I can't let you bet your hard-earned money on me. Please, I am uncomfortable with that. I won't play unless you two drop your bet."

"You have no idea how hard I have to work for my money," Liam responded.

Edward choked on his tea and coughed, hitting his chest to regain his breathing. When he got enough breath back, he looked at Liam and simply said, "Fuck you."

Gabriella didn't understand Liam's comment, but continued on, anyway.

"While you two boneheads act like children, I am off to the

bathroom. I will be ready in five minutes. And I repeat, no money on this game, or I don't play."

After Gabriella left, Edward turned to Liam. "You are not backing out of that bet, no matter what she just said, old chum. You're paying up for foolishly putting your cock ahead of your brain."

"Game on, young fuck."

***

Gabriella listened to Edward lecture her on why most golf courses in the UK didn't use golf carts as they walked to the first hole. The two men were carrying their clubs, and they had gotten a push-pull cart for Gabriella. Liam wouldn't allow her to pull it, though. He had his clubs over his shoulders as he pulled the cart for her. She had tried to wrestle it from him, but he would have no part of it. He wouldn't allow her to do anything that he was capable of doing for her.

"Golf is a sport, and in sports, you get exercise. What would be the purpose of playing if you didn't get exercise?"

Lightly laughing, she looked at Edward. "You're right." His mood seemed off today, so she asked, "What's wrong? I am not being derogatory when I say you seem a little sensitive."

"I have this unsettling feeling. I can't explain it, but I feel edgy and snippy."

She smirked and raised one of her little eyebrows. "It's just the prequel to me beating your ass at your own game."

Edward laughed as he grabbed her French braid and gave it a tug.

Liam watched yet another interaction between the woman he loved and his best friend. Gabriella had on a pair of yoga pants and a T-shirt underneath a black jacket that stored a couple of extra golf balls. Her smile lit up her face, and every thought played out on her expressive features. In a thirty second conversation with Edward, she appeared happy, annoyed, sly, and content.

They decided that Edward and Liam would flip a coin to see who went first, and Gabriella would go after them since the starting point for women was twenty to thirty yards ahead. Liam won the toss and hit his first ball.

When Edward took his shot, he turned to Gabriella and haughtily said, "Beat that, love."

She didn't even acknowledge he had spoken as she turned and walked away.

She asked Edward to show her how to hold the club properly, and he smiled smugly from ear to ear as he instructed her. Then she practiced what he had said before she lined herself up. She hit her ball straight down the middle. With the advantage of the extra yards from her starting point, she was only thirty yards away from Edward's ball.

Jumping up and down, she shouted, "Look, Liam! I'm close to you guys. Look!" She clapped her hands in joy.

Liam couldn't help smirking at her deception and the

enthusiasm. "Good for you, baby. That was a great shot."

Edward was stunned. It wasn't a great shot. It was fucking fantastic!

Before walking away, he mumbled, "Beginners luck." However, Edward soon realized luck had nothing to do with it. The little she-devil could play golf and was fucking good. He had been duped.

As they completed the eighteenth hole, Gabriella couldn't help rubbing it in.

"Well, I don't know about you guys, but I could sure use a celebratory drink. How about lattes for everyone?" She laughed as she dodged Edward's attempt at another pull on her braid.

Liam hid Gabriella behind his back, laughing out, "I'll pay for a real drink seeing as Edward now owes me two hundred pounds. Congratulations, sweetheart."

"No fair! You knew she could play, didn't you?" Edward accused at the same time that Gabriella slapped Liam's back, saying, "I told you two no betting! What the hell? I would have felt bad if you lost."

He should have known better; Liam would never bet unless it was a sure thing.

"Are you fucking kidding me! You would feel bad if it was *him* who lost, but not me. Gabriella, who saved your life? Me, that's who! You little she-devil."

"Wow, add sore loser to his list. Next time, don't judge a book by its cover," she retorted.

The two bickered all the way back to the SUV. Then they climbed inside and drove to the closet pub. The guys had a couple Guinness and Gabriella had a Pimm's Cup, a British drink they had introduced her to. The pub was almost full of people having stopped for a lunch break. They shared wings and chips as the trio laughed and talked about golf. Liam was only half-listening, his eyes darting back and forth around the pub.

He stood up, dug into his pockets, and threw money down on the table when there was a disturbance at the front of the pub. Liam swung his head around, and he tensed when he saw two men approaching, one with a camera and the other with a recording device. He immediately went into security mode.

"Fuck, it's *The Mirror*. Move *now!*" Liam said as he stood and moved in front of Edward.

Edward grabbed Gabriella's hand and started to walk in the opposite direction while Liam quickly texted something as he faced the men.

"Edward, what the hell is going on?" Gabriella asked, confused and a little frightened of the men's body language. She felt her heart speed up and was instantly sweating, her mouth dry and her hands shaking. The panic was tangible and scary. She'd had these feelings before at Marco's trial.

One of the men Liam was standing in front of suddenly yelled, getting everyone's attention. "Edward, who's the new babe? Come on, mate; you know we will find out. Just give it to us now and save us all the aggravation."

Liam took two large steps in front of the two guys and, in a low voice only they could hear, said, "Get the fuck out of here. You know the law about how close you can get to him."

The reporter ignored Liam and yelled over his shoulder, "Edward, can we expect another sex tape? What's your name, sweetheart? What's it like to shag the pony prince?"

Liam grabbed the man by the front of his shirt, growling quietly, "Shut your fuckin' mouth. There are kids in here." Then he turned to the other man and whispered, "You move one fucking inch and I swear I will put a bullet through your brain. If I believe he is in any danger, I have the right to shoot you both dead, so turn around and get the fuck out of here. You both know you cannot be within fifty feet of him."

Just then, the local police showed up and rushed into the pub. They approached Liam and quietly discussed the disturbance. Then they took over so Liam could return to Edward and Gabriella and shuffle them out of the pub.

As they stepped out the door, they found a large crowd had formed. Bystanders had their phones out and were taking pictures of them. Some of them were yelling, "Edward! Edward! Look over here! Edward, we love you! Edward, take a selfie with me! Edward, can I have an autograph? What's her name? Who is she?"

A full-on panic attack had taken over Gabriella. The memories were overwhelming. She felt like she couldn't get enough air into

189

her lungs. If it weren't for Edward's arm around her, protecting and guiding her, she was sure she would have passed out.

Gabriella looked shell-shocked and frightened as Liam herded them into the SUV. He shut their door then hurried to the driver's side, putting the car in gear before flying out of the pub's parking lot. Looking in the rear-view mirror, he saw Gabriella was alarmed, pale, and breathing heavily. He knew she was in a bad place, but he had to make sure they were all safe before he could comfort her.

"Angel, everything is okay. Breathe deeply. I will explain everything as soon as we get back to the inn," he assured her.

Edward snapped out of his thoughts. He moved closer to Gabriella and enveloped her tiny, shaking hands in his. "I apologize. I had hoped my life would never touch yours."

Gabriella was totally freaked out. She had already experienced being attacked by the press once before. The horrible things they had said had brought her to her knees. After Marco's death, when it was proved beyond a reasonable doubt that he had been innocent all along, not one reporter apologized for their cruelty. No, instead, they had simply moved on to their next victim.

Frantically, she turned to Edward. "What do you mean? Why were those men talking to you like that? Why did they have a camera? And who were those people outside the pub? None of this makes sense!"

"We have a lot to tell you, but I am asking you just to be patient until we get back to the inn. Just a few more minutes," Liam responded.

Gabriella didn't answer or speak again, which frightened Liam. He wanted her in his arms. He hoped and prayed she would listen when they explained and would understand why they had kept her in the dark. It was one thing for Edward not to say anything, but Liam had fallen in love with her and shared her bed.

"The press helped kill my family," Gabriella whispered. "The press reported the accident like they had witnessed the whole event. They accused Marco of texting and driving when he didn't even have his cell phone with him."

She took a deep breath and continued with the same haunted, faraway look. "The reason the boys were with us that day at the courthouse was because Mateo was testifying about having his dad's phone. After hearing us discuss the call from the lawyer about how they had traced activity on the cell phone during the time of the accident, Mateo confessed to taking Marco's phone to school because he was playing some candy smashing game.

"With the evidence of the inactivity from the phone records, Mateo testifying, and Marco's cell phone that was in the court evidence locker, Marco was fully expected to be cleared of all charges. We were so relieved. It had been months of hell, and the lawyers had cost us a fortune. If the media hadn't become judge and jury, my family wouldn't have been executed."

Edward lifted his broken eyes and looked into Gabriella's. "I'm sorry you had to experience that, but if anyone in this world understands how you feel, it would be me."

That statement brought Gabriella back to the present. He looked like a hurt, lost, little boy. It frightened her after he had been her rock for the last few months.

"What can I do?"

When he didn't answer, she wrapped her arms around him and tried to absorb some of his pain. In that moment, she decided what he needed was a mom hug. She also realized Edward needed her to be strong for him. She needed to pull up her big girl panties, stop being so self-absorbed, and support him.

Here was yet another man being destroyed by the press. Everyone always denied reading those trashy magazines, but they sold in the millions. She often wondered why people continued to buy the gossip magazines after learning that ninety percent of it was bullshit.

"All I can ask is that you keep an open mind. When we get back to the inn and you hear my story, I pray you understand the reasons for my not telling you sooner."

"Edward, there is nothing you could tell me that would change how I feel about you."

Edward smiled at her, but it didn't reach his eyes. "Remember when you asked us to pick a song that best described each of us? Well, I know my song. 'Welcome to My Life' by Simple Plan."

Liam listened intently to their conversation, concerned about her reaction when she learned how truly they had kept her in the dark.

But his biggest fear was that Gabriella would run to get away from the media circus that would surely follow them.

He had to give Edward credit, though. He was good at keeping her mind occupied until Liam could get them to the inn. Decisions had to be made about whether or not they could stay on the Isle of Skye now that they had been discovered. They would have to make those decisions as a trio—God willing—with everyone's eyes wide open.

"I know that song," Gabriella said, "but I can't remember the lyrics. Do you mind if I google it?"

"Here; use my phone." Edward handed her his cell phone.

She busily looked up the lyrics and instantly remembered the tune that accompanied them. Wow, this was definitely not a song she would have associated with Edward. As upbeat as the tune sounded, the lyrics were desolate.

This wasn't the man who had become one of her closest friends. What could have happened to him to make him believe this about his life? She needed to help him find himself again like he had helped her.

Chapter 19

Get the Freak Out

The owner of the inn met the trio as they exited the SUV. He went directly to Liam and handed him the newspaper, speaking quietly, while Edward proceeded to get Gabriella into their suite.

"I hate fearing the unknown," Gabriella told Edward. "Before I lost my family, my sistas used to tease the shit out of me about refusing to watch movies or read books that made me cry. They accused me of living in a bubble, but in all fairness, I was dealing with kids at the center who had insurmountable obstacles to overcome, so why would I want to add more to my life by listening to the daily news and hearing all the sorrow in the world? Right now, I wish I could stay in the bubble that you, Liam, and I have created and not find out what has you guys so upset."

The door to the suite open, and Gabriella knew her life was going to change again as Liam stalked towards her.

He didn't say a word as he held her in his arms A few moments later, he bent so his nose was just beside her head and breathed deeply to absorb her scent. He couldn't lose this woman now that she held his heart in her hands.

He grabbed a fistful of hair in each hand and gently pulled her head back, looking deeply into her eyes. "Do you trust me?"

She gazed at him, not answering. Not because she didn't trust him, but because she still wasn't sure she wanted to know what was going on.

Liam misunderstood her silence and stepped back from her as pain sliced through his newly exposed heart.

Fuck! He couldn't lose her. He just couldn't.

She saw the fear and misunderstanding in his eyes and stepped forwards, grabbing his large hands. "No, Liam, I absolutely trust you with all of my heart. I'm just scared about what you are going to say." She moved in closer and dropped her head to his chest, hugging him.

It took a minute before she felt his body relax.

The situation was entirely out of control. She needed to hear what they had to say then learn how to deal with it. She could do this, not just for Edward, but also for Liam.

"Let's grab some drinks. I have a feeling we are going to need one to get this over with," Gabriella said as she walked to the kitchenette to snag a couple Guinness for the guys and a glass of wine for herself. She then proceeded to head outside to the patio

195

where most of their conversations had taken place. It felt like a safe place for her.

Liam stopped her before she could go outside. "It's no longer safe for us to discuss things outside. We need to do this in here. Please sit." He captured her hand in his and led her to where he wanted her to sit, never releasing her hand as he also sat down.

Edward sat in the chair across from them, and Liam was just about to begin when Edward stopped him.

"No, this is my story to tell." Edward turned to Gabriella. "You know how much you mean to me, and I want you to know first that we never intended to deceive you. I just loved being simply Edward to you, and not the fourth in line to inherit the English throne." He saw the confusion on her face, so he continued, "I am Prince Edward of Arlington, third son of Princess Emma and Prince Albert, grandson of the King of England."

Gabriella felt panic. Then she relaxed, thinking he was trying to distract her and make her laugh before he revealed what the real secret was. How dumb did he think she was? One of the freaking princes of England! The arrogant, British pig thought that, because she wasn't British, she wouldn't know he wasn't the fucking prince.

"I thought you were going to be honest with me," she said angrily, no longer finding him amusing. "Stop with the fuckin' bullshit and tell me the truth, you ass. Prince Edward," she scoffed. "And I'm really Pippa, sister to the Duchess of Hampshire."

Neither man expected that response and were both speechless,

196

their mouths open and minds racing.

Liam returned to his senses first and took control of the conversation.

"Edward is telling you the truth. He *is* the prince, and I'm his bodyguard. It's my job to protect him with my life, and I consider my job an honour and take it very seriously." Liam sighed. "I might have neglected to share his title, but I have never lied to you. Believe me when I tell you that Edward is, in fact, the king's third grandson."

It was true that Liam had never lied to her. Plus, both of them had done so much for her; they had cared for her and nurtured her out of her depression. They had saved her life. Why would they start lying to her now? Then it hit her like a ton of bricks.

"Get the freak out! Oh, my God! I need a minute to process this."

She replayed all the hints to the truth the men were telling her. Edward always wore a hat and sunglasses to disguise his appearance. Liam did all the talking and organizing. He wore those damn black cargo pants and long-sleeved shirts everywhere and said they were his "work" clothes. He was always on his phone or computer, "doing work." They both were Air Force pilots. The princess was killed in a helicopter accident, and the media had said it was suicide. *Oh, my freakin' God!* Prince Edward's fiancée had sold a sex tape to the press for a reported two million American dollars!

She jumped up out of her seat when it all sunk in, blood

draining from her face. They were telling her the truth.

The men stood up and reached out to grab her, but she threw her arms out and hands up.

"Stop! Don't touch me. Just don't touch me." She bent at the waist again, trying to catch her breath, trying desperately to control her heart rate.

Liam didn't give a shit whether she wanted to be touched or not; he scooped her up and dropped her down on his lap, holding her. He wasn't giving up. She was his life now, and he was keeping her. He would give her a chance to absorb it all, but he wasn't letting her run. He would tie her up until she forgave him. He. Was. Not. Giving. Up.

Edward was spooked, afraid he had now lost one of his only true friends. He was devastated that he was the cause of her current pain, all of it because of *his* deception. Would she walk away from Liam, too, and Liam's last chance at love? Fuck! He had screwed up big time. Would she ever forgive him? He was still recovering from the loss of Gillian. Losing Gabriella would break him. Goddammit! This was turning out like everything else in his life—fucked up. He hated who he was.

She made choking sounds, her body racked with sobs. She leaned back to get more air into her lungs, still choking. When they looked at her, she didn't have tears streaming down her face. She was...No, that was impossible. She was...unbelievable! She was *laughing*. What the hell? Had she finally snapped under all the pressure? Were they the ones who had finally broken her?

Alarmed, Liam said, "Gabriella, talk to me. You're freaking me out! Seriously! Talk to me, please."

She rolled out of Liam's arms and onto the floor, holding her stomach, which felt like she had done a hundred sit-ups, and trying to regain her breathing. With everything else rolling around in her head, she thought this must be what it meant to bust a gut.

Ever so slowly, she regained her breath. Then she turned to the two men who were now looking at her on her hands and knees like she had grown horns and said, "I beat freakin' Prince Edward of Arlington, the king's third grandson…in golf! How is that possible?" Once again, she was holding her stomach, laughing so hard she couldn't breathe.

Both men were stunned into silence. They stood there, watching the little imp laugh her guts out.

Waiting…

Waiting…

Waiting…

Just when she was almost under control, she turned her head. Through her long, curly hair, she looked up at them and burst out laughing again.

A smile formed on Liam's face before he started to laugh at her infectious howling. He wasn't sure if it was that funny, but witnessing her, he was caught up in her loss of control.

Edward thought they were both insane until he realized he had

199

never witnessed Liam lose complete and utter control like this and laugh so hard. Edward started to chuckle. In seconds, all three were laughing uncontrollably. This wasn't how Edward had pictured the scenario, but it might be his last laugh for a while, so he was going to enjoy it.

Liam smiled, realizing for the first time in his life his cheeks hurt from laughing. If he hadn't met Gabriella, he might have gone his whole life never experiencing this feeling. He didn't even have to look to know she was smiling, too.

It took a good fifteen minutes for all three of them to calm down enough to have a conversation.

"I want it written down and signed that I beat Prince Edward in golf, in Scotland to boot, and I want it signed by Edward and witnessed by Liam, and I am not kidding. I will frame it and give it to Papi to hang in the restaurant back home."

This little brat was pushing her luck, and that was what Edward loved about her. She could give a rat's ass who he was; she just wanted credit for beating him at his game. If his being the prince added to that glory, then that was all she wanted.

"If that's all it takes to keep you in my life, I will declare it to the world. I will even let Oprah Winfrey interview me on the subject. But first, I need your forgiveness. I never meant to deceive you. I just wanted to have a real friend with no preconceptions. I wanted to be judged for me and not my family or title."

"I haven't even begun to wrap my head around the fact that one of my heroes is the freakin' prince of England." Gabriella shook her head. "To be honest, I don't know if I will ever consider you *him*. You will always just be my Edward, my friend. I have to treasure what I have in this moment, because I don't know how many other moments I am going to have." She walked into Edward's arms, and he wrapped his warmth around her, breathing a sigh of relief. "I don't care if you are a prince; you will still *not* be enjoying tea for the next month, and you owe Liam two hundred pounds."

He threw his head back and exploded with laughter, but not before he pinched the little witch. He then passed her over to an anxiously waiting Liam, who didn't give her a chance to spout more crap. He kissed her deeply and with passion.

"*Ahem*, still in the room, people," Edward remarked as the couple broke apart. "There are still some things we need to go over before you two can retire to the bedroom. Like, I assume the newspaper has an article about me and my whereabouts, or is it worse than I fear?" Edward asked Liam.

Liam removed himself from Gabriella's hold and walked over to the table, picking up the newspaper and showing them the picture and headline.

"*The Pony Prince and His New Filly.*"

There, under the headline, was a picture of Gabriella and Edward sitting at Kilt Rock with his arm around her and him kissing the side of her head.

"Holy shit! How did they get that picture? And they think we're a couple?" Gabriella gasped in absolute shock.

Edward walked to the table, picked up her wine and his ale, and then handed her the wine, held up his bottle, clinked with her glass, and said, "Welcome to my life." Then he downed the contents of the bottle in one sip. "Seconds, anyone?"

"But you don't get what I am saying," she said. "We aren't a couple. Liam and I are, so why are they suggesting you and I are involved, and why do they call you the 'Pony Prince'?"

That wasn't a question Liam felt comfortable answering, so he let Edward take the lead.

"You have obviously been out of circulation for a while. Six months ago, my ex-fiancée, Gillian, sold a tape of her and I having wild sex while on vacation. The media dubbed me the 'Pony Prince' because of the size of my..." He cleared his throat. "I am relieved to know you are probably the only person in the world who hasn't watched that sex tape."

"I wish I could say something profound and explain why Gillian did such a cruel thing, but there is no excuse," she replied with a blush. "All you can hope for is that she desperately needed the money. Otherwise, she wouldn't have hurt you like that. And, um"— she gestured towards his crotch—"women like that. Trust me."

Edward and Liam choked and coughed, both shocked by her remark.

"Okay, you two, enough already. We have a lot to talk about," Liam tried to rein them in. "The innkeeper just informed me that the media has been calling all day to figure out if this is where we are staying and if he or anyone he knew could tell them who Gabriella is. Therefore, I think it's time we moved on. I have someone dropping off a new SUV with different plates so they won't follow us, but we are going to have to be diligent until this calms down. I am moving on to plan B. We are leaving as soon as we can pack to a safe house in Banffshire."

"Liam, does that include me?" Gabriella quietly questioned. "I mean, I don't want to cause any more problems for you and Edward. I mean, I am a nobody."

"Where I go, you go; no questions asked." Liam was furious at her comment yet tried to rein it in. "And you are not a nobody! You are everything to me, and I love you."

Edward also weighed in on her comment. "I can't believe you just said that. Understand that you are one the most important females in *my* life. If I ever, and I mean *ever*, hear you talk like that again, I will personally kick your ass from here to Canada."

She took comfort from their responses.

Smiling, she said, "I'll go and pack the churros for the ride. By the way, where is Banffshire?"

"Moray Firth coastline. The safe house is on a secluded beach, facing the North Sea. You're going to love it. By the way, fair warning, I will be calling your papi and filling him on the move and what happened with the media. Hopefully, it hasn't made its way to Canada yet, but I need to prepare your family for the fallout, anyway."

Gabriella was starting to see another side to Liam: the take-charge solider. He had said it the way it was going to be, brooking no response.

Her life was taking another dramatic twist, but she was excited. She had finally found a place she felt like she belonged, and it wasn't associated with an address. As long as she was with Liam and Edward, it felt like home.

Chapter 20

The Circle of Protection

The unlikely group of friends headed north towards Banffshire fifteen minutes after their new vehicle arrived, each lost in their own thoughts.

Edward was still trying to figure out if Gabriella's reaction would last since he had lost many friends in adulthood when he had realized they associated with him for his notoriety. As a result, he wondered if she would become star-struck like most of the populous.

Over the last few months, Edward had shared his feelings with her and a few stories about his family, but nothing that the media didn't already know. He was ashamed when he realized he hadn't revealed very much about himself or his family to Gabriella, subconsciously knowing, when she eventually learned the truth about his heritage, their friendship would end.

Then it struck him like a bolt of lightning that he had shared some unknown information that really could cost him some heartache. He groaned.

His mother's letters were a family secret the brothers had been sworn not to reveal for fear of public inquisition. For the writers and the readers of gossip surrounding the royal family, getting their hands on information about his mother's private letters would be like winning the lottery. Her personal thoughts to her children would be priceless. The search for the letters would become endless, almost like the Holy Grail.

He had fucked up again and would be forced to phone his brothers to tell them. He would also have to tell the secretary of media relations so they could deal with the fallout.

He glanced into the back seat and studied Gabriella who was also lost in thought. She was beautiful inside and out, but he had given her a bucketful of information that now made her an extremely powerful woman.

Liam caught Edward's glance at Gabriella and knew Edward was struggling with where the prince's new friendship was heading. He wished he could reassure him. Liam wasn't sure how he knew this, but he would bet his very soul that Gabriella would stay true to Edward and their friendship.

He pondered the fact that Gabriella knew heart-wrenching pain. She understood how easy it was to lose those you loved. She would be like a mother bear with her cub, protecting Edward from everyone. What he wasn't sure about was how she felt about his own betrayal surrounding Edward's ancestry. On top of that, he feared she would run from the media circus that would surely catch up to them.

He knew she was well aware of how overwhelming and cruel journalists could be. Could she survive another round in the media attention? He had to make some decisions.

He was in love with her, and he wasn't walking away. If she decided she couldn't take the pressure associated with Edward's life, Liam knew he would have to find another line of work. He had lost his heart once, and he wouldn't survive losing Gabriella. He would sacrifice anything to have her be a part of his and his daughters' futures.

Gabriella was still trying to wrap her head around Edward being a prince. Normal, everyday people didn't befriend someone in the royal family. Gabriella had never really had crushes on famous people like a lot of her friends. She wasn't sure why. It just seemed those people were characters in a book, almost fictional and unreal.

When you had immigrant parents with a family business, you worked hard each and every day, creating a dream more attainable than meeting and befriending someone famous. At her family restaurant, her papi never treated the local celebrities differently than any other customer. He would say, "Their money is the same colour."

She was embarrassed that she knew so little about the royal family. However, she still had no desire to google his family. *Her* Edward would never be the world's Edward.

207

A smile formed on her face when she went through each hint to the big secret the men had kept. She hoped it was her sorrow that had made her stupid and not her self-absorption. All the clues had been right in front of her all along, but she had chosen not to see them. There she was, living in her little bubble again.

They all emerged from the SUV after the four and a half hour drive. At eleven p.m., Gabriella was shocked by how light it was out.

"Wow, I have never seen the sky so light this late. That is so cool. Oh, my gosh! Look, Edward! If that's where we are staying, it isn't a house. That's a beautiful, big cottage, exactly what I would have chosen to stay in. Oh, I can't wait to see it!"

Liam turned to her. "As soon as Edward and I unload the truck, we will go for a walk on the beach and watch the sunset. That will probably happen around midnight."

She was mesmerized as she moved closer to the cottage. It was, indeed, beautiful, covered in grey stone, accented in dark wood. The two upper dormers and all the windows had window boxes full of colourful flowers. A gate opened to an inner courtyard surrounded by a large, stone wall and a lovely garden. The inside of the cottage was as charming as the outside. This adorable treasure truly belonged in a fairy tale.

When she saw the grounds out back, she was truly blown away. It had a patio made out of flagstone and a beautiful table and chairs handcrafted from old whiskey barrels. Best of all, it overlooked the North Sea and miles and miles of unobstructed beach. She was so glad she was able to share this with Liam and Edward.

For a moment, she was sad that her sons had never gotten the chance to experience this view and the sun setting at midnight. Then she remembered Liam telling her that the boys lived on through her and that, as long as she was seeing something or experiencing something, so were they. She was going to absorb all she could so the boys wouldn't miss a thing.

It turned out that Liam and Edward had to take a private conference call before they went for the walk along the beach, so Gabriella spent her time outside, absorbing all she was seeing. Thank goodness Liam had made her get a warm sweater; the wind was cold.

After finishing his call, Liam got a light jacket and headed outside to be with Gabriella and wait for Edward. He watched his girl at the edge of the cliff, gazing at the sea. He knew she was probably thinking about her family.

He walked up and hugged her from behind. "How are you doing, sweetheart?"

She swiped a tear away and turned to hug him. "You know, before I met you, the song that I compared my life to was "Tears in Heaven" by Eric Clapton, but you made me realize that the boys and Marco are still a part of me. I still have them with me, and I was just sharing this amazing view with them. Thank you, Liam, for showing me how to keep them alive inside my heart."

"They were always with you; I just opened your eyes." Liam

sealed his statement with a sensual, warm kiss.

"Oh, for the love of the devil! You two do realize that mononucleosis is passed through kissing, right? Move along. Let's go and explore the beach. I hope the walkway down the cliff isn't too steep." Edward continued rambling as he led the way.

"See?" Liam said. "Edward proves you can't buy class with a title."

Gabriella laughed. "Did either one of you bring your phone? I want some pictures."

"Of course," Liam responded. "But, with the media hot on our tails and now that you know Edward is the prince, I think, for safety's sake, I need you to have a phone with you at all times."

Gabriella could only nod in understanding as they continued their trek down the path.

At the beach, Gabriella quickly removed her shoes.

"What are you doing? The water is freezing! Put your shoes back on."

"No, I want you and Edward to take off your shoes, too, so I can take a picture of us dipping our toes into the North Sea. Come on, please...for me?"

Liam bent down to unlace his heavy combat boots that she had always thought were motorcycle boots as Edward walked up to him and whispered, "Pussy-whipped." That got poor Edward a boot in the ass, literally.

"Don't make me ask again." Gabriella glared at Edward. "Take off your shoes."

Since Edward was a sucker for this woman, he did as she said.

Liam walked up and whispered in Edward's ear, "At least I get the pussy I'm whipped by."

Edward's response was his famous six words: "Sod the fuck off, old man." But Liam never heard him, laughing too loudly as he walked away.

Gabriella made them stand in a circle on the sand with the water lapping over their toes so she could take a picture. It turned out really cool—two sets of ginormous feet and one pair of little, pink painted toes, standing in the water. She then made Edward take some selfies of the three of them while Liam lifted her up so their heads were all at the same level and you could see the sunset in the background.

She loved these men.

***

The next morning, four of Liam's teammates from Special Reconnaissance Regiment and one from Scotland Yard showed up to revise Edward's protection plan. The team informed them the entire industrialized world had seen the pictures of Prince Edward and his new "love interest," and everyone was trying to figure out who the mystery woman was. Therefore, they would have to be even more conscientious of every move they made.

Edward had feared this would happen, knowing in his gut this was the beginning of the end. He wanted to have a heart-to-heart with Gabriella over all the deception. He didn't want to bring any new heartache into her life and needed to give her the option of distancing herself from him.

Liam decided that they could walk along the beach as long as two members of the security team were watching and following at a safe distance.

As Gabriella and Edward reached the beach, Gabriella went to lock arms with Edward, and he flinched.

"Did I do something wrong? Why are you pulling away from me?"

"I apologize. It's just...now that you know who I am, I realize things have obviously changed for us."

Her expression destroyed him. He had unintentionally hurt her.

In a soft voice, she responded, "If they have changed, that's on you, not me. I'm embarrassed to admit I know very little about you or your family. But, at the end of the day, we are all human. We all bleed the same colour, and I know for a fact that your shit smells as bad as mine."

He smiled at her response but didn't really believe it. Gillian had destroyed his faith in people. Maybe Gabriella needed to know why he couldn't believe her.

In a voice Gabriella had never heard him use, he turned to her and unloaded his frustration and anger. "I am twenty-six years old, and my whole life, I have been sold to the highest bidder. I was going to marry Gillian, make her the mother of my children, share

212

our future together, but even *she* sold me out. It was the last straw.

"I have spent my life dodging maids who go through my dirty underwear, revealing it to the public. I have had classmates include me in adventures so they could tell the story. I have had girlfriends rate and judge and measure me in the bedroom so they could get their faces on the front of entertainment magazines. Even teachers sold copies of my report cards to parade my intelligence, or lack thereof, to the public. God help me, but it has been so bad that chaps I called friends have sold memories of my mum, all for the almighty pound. Gabriella, sooner or later, someone will name your price. You are a sweet girl, but everyone eventually sells me out, and I expect no less from you."

Gabriella recoiled like he had slapped her. He had been her protector for months, built her confidence, but he really hadn't believed in her at all. If he had stabbed a knife into her heart, it would have hurt less.

One of the security officers radioed to Liam that something was wrong when she screamed her response.

"I can't claim to understand what your life has been like, but I do understand the hounding of the media! Unlike you, I didn't have the training or the knowledge on how to deal with their cruelty that nearly destroyed me!

"If you're wondering if I would sell you out for the almighty dollar, you can rest easy knowing I was awarded a *huge* settlement from Marco and the boys' wrongful death, and I have never touched

213

it. Why? Because it's blood money! I didn't want the city's money; I wanted them not to hire crooked cops!

"You want to walk away from me? Go ahead! I have lost so much already that I don't care anymore! I can be out of the cottage in twenty minutes!" With that said, she turned and ran up the beach, sand flying behind her.

She ran like the devil himself was chasing her, tears streaming down her face. She knew she was overreacting, but what he had said had hurt, and hurt badly. When would she learn happiness was short-lived? She would always lose everything she cared for, like she would lose Liam when he chose Edward over her. He had to; he was his best friend and bodyguard.

Why was love always associated with pain?

Edward was stunned, frozen in place as he watched the closest female in his life run as fast as she could away from him.

The two SRR officers radioed that Gabriella was out of control and on the run, and Liam ran to the cliff edge, his heart pounding. He saw Gabriella running for all she was worth up the path. Then he saw Edward safely standing on the beach with Liam's two teammates. He started down the path as she started up.

She was so absorbed in her meltdown she didn't hear or see Liam until she ran full-force into him, nearly knocking him off his feet. She yelped in shock, breathing heavily and crying as he grabbed her.

She couldn't hear Liam or process his words until he shook her

214

hard and yelled, "What the fuck happened, Gabriella?"

She collapsed in his arms, feeling safe. With the way things were going, she would lose that safety net, too.

Edward, waking up from his shock, sprinted up the path where Gabriella had just landed in Liam's arms.

What had he done? He realized he had betrayed her. He had purposely punished her and hurt her before she'd had a chance to hurt him.

He had to try to rectify this colossal mistake. He loved her and couldn't survive if he truly had pushed her away.

For months, he had been protecting and nurturing this sweet, little soul, and in two minutes flat, he had destroyed everything he had accomplished. What a fucking prick he was. As he got closer, he called out to Gabriella, but when she saw him, she yanked herself out of Liam's arms and again ran up the path to the cottage.

Liam was still at a loss as to what the hell was going on. He turned and followed behind both Gabriella and Edward as he listened to Edward beg for Gabriella to stop and listen.

Edward reached Gabriella just as she got to the top of the path. He knew she wasn't listening to him, so he did the only thing he could think of. He tackled her to the ground.

Liam came behind them and grabbed Edward by the scruff of the neck, ripping him off Gabriella with his fist raised and ready to punch Edward in the face.

Gabriella screamed, "No! Stop!" just as the captain of the SRR and the operative from Scotland Yard grabbed Liam's arms, forcing them behind his back before pushing him to the ground face first with a knee in his back.

Liam was beyond furious; in a blind rage. He needed to get to Gabriella who was crying and screaming.

In less than thirty seconds, the two men who had contained him were flat on their backs, and the other two who had finally made it up the path were also on the ground, nursing sore jaws.

Liam again flung Edward away and scooped up Gabriella, not taking a breath until she was safely in his arms.

The security team were reaching for their guns when Edward leapt in front of Liam and screamed, "I'm ordering you to back the fuck off!"

Once he had their attention, he had words with Tom, the captain in charge, explaining that the situation was his fault.

"I don't care whose fault it is," Tom responded. "Liam should never have raised his fist to you. I am relieving him of his duty, and he will be relieved of his service. Now, Prince Edward, move from in front of him."

With venom in his voice, Edward leaned in towards the men. "If any one of you opens your mouth about this, I will make it my life's mission to bring each and every last one of you down. I won't rest until you are all destroyed. Do you understand me?" Edward spit the final comment out of his mouth.

"Go to hell, Edward. I don't need your protection! No one

touches any of my girls and walks away unscathed! I will face the consequences."

"Shut up, Liam, and look after Gabriella. We will sort out our family shit after they leave. And make no mistake, you two are my family."

Edward then turned and escorted the group to their vehicles with their assurance of silence while Liam took Gabriella inside to clean her scraped hands and knees.

Liam grabbed her face and gently kissed her still hiccupping mouth.

She was scared shitless. Not just from being tackled by Edward, but from Liam's reaction to Edward and Edward's reaction to the SRR guards. Those men were intense. She still didn't know how it had gone wrong so quickly. She did know Liam had protected her, she had protected Edward, and Edward had protected Liam. The circle of protection was a continuous loop between the three friends.

Chapter 21

Healing Stones

Edward stood, leaning against the doorframe, quietly watching Liam clean the scrapes on Gabriella's hands. After cleaning each one, he would lift the palm of her hand to his mouth and gently kiss the marks, trying to make it better. Edward was ashamed he was responsible for injuring Gabriella in such a brutal way.

He had never seen Liam in a full-blown rage, and he had to admit it was a little frightening. How stupid could you be to enrage your best friend enough that he was willing to beat you down?

Edward, in a rough whisper with eyes down, said, "I have no excuses. I have hit rock bottom, and I am so sorry."

Gabriella had already forgiven Edward. She knew he had made a mistake and that she had overreacted.

She could feel the tension in Liam's body. He wasn't going to be so quick to forgive.

"Your rock bottom will make for a solid foundation for us to strengthen and repair our friendship," Gabriella said to the astonishment of the two men, her voice soft yet strong and confident. "No one is destroying the circle we have created; not the reporters, not the public, and definitely not any of us. Today is the day every man fears. We are talking about your feelings. You owe me this."

With a loud groan, Liam looked at Edward. "You're going to wish I killed you." He turned to Gabriella. "Do I have to partake? I didn't do anything wrong."

With her mothering voice, she reprimanded Liam, "Funny you should say that. I seem to remember you almost punching your best friend in the face not an hour ago. You need to learn to use your words and not your fists. This lesson is for all of us. Trust me; it will come in handy when you're two daughters begin to date."

"You do know what I do for a living, right?"

"We are going to do anything Gabriella wants," Edward said in hopes of getting on her good side.

***

At the beach, Gabriella searched for a fist-sized stone. There weren't a lot of rocks on this beautiful stretch of beach, but she managed to find the one she needed.

She turned to the guys and showed it to them. "I need fourteen more like this."

"What are we doing with them?" Liam asked.

"We are gathering healing stones. We're going to use the power

219

of words to heal the wounds we have caused. I use this strategy with the families I work with to create positive dialogue."

Liam had bared his soul to her over the last few weeks, and he was still raw from it, now feeling overwhelmed with anger after the earlier incident. He loved Edward like a brother, but right now, he wasn't so sure he could have an open dialogue with him. He couldn't help feeling like talking wasn't going to help. Punching the living fucking shit out of Edward would. Regardless, he would try since it was important to Gabriella.

Once they had collected the rocks, Gabriella sat and wrote on each one then placed them in a basket while the men gathered driftwood. Once they had enough, they started a fire then sat in some beach chairs, facing each other.

"In the basket, I have placed all fifteen healing rocks. When it is your turn, I want you to remove one rock, read the word, and then decide how the word affects you, or you can pass the rock to someone else and find out how the word affects them. Each of us will end up with five rocks, so be careful what you give away; the next word might be more revealing. Your answers have to be from the heart and honest. After you are finished, we move on. No comments are needed; just quiet reflection. Who wants to go first?"

She was blown away that these big, strong, beautiful men were allowing her to try to get inside their hearts and minds. She respected that she didn't have to force them, and it spoke volumes about their character.

"Okay, baby, pass me the basket and let's do this," Liam volunteered, taking the heavy basket and digging into the middle of the stones. He pulled out a rock, turned it over, and read the word out loud. "*Heal.* Wow, okay, give me a minute to get my thoughts together." Liam sat quietly for almost five minutes, thinking. "This is way harder than I even imagined. One word can mean so many things.

"Okay, let me start by saying that all three of us have suffered loss, and if I am going to be totally honest, none of us are healed. Healing takes time. Lots of time. I believe Gabriella has started to heal my heart by understanding my past and not judging me. Edward, I can only hope, when the time is right, some smart-mouth, little lass will waltz into your life and turn it upside down. And, when she comes, you, too, are going to have to allow her a chance to help you heal."

"Well, that's interesting," Edward said, shocked to hear how Liam felt. "If I believed someone as incredible as Gabriella would come into my life and heal me, I would welcome her with open arms." Edward cleared his throat, realizing the importance of Liam's statement. "I'll go next. Pass the basket."

Edward took the basket and chose the rock on top. He turned it over and read out loud, "*Fear.*" He pondered the word for a few moments then passed the rock to Gabriella, seeing the scrapes he had caused. He kissed the top of both her hands then said, "Sorry, sweetheart. I don't know how I am going to make it up to you, but I was terrified I was going lose you, and I had to stop you."

"You don't have to make it up to me. I'm not going anywhere." As she shuffled the rock from hand to hand, she remarked, "Somehow, I knew I would get this one." She took a moment to gather her thoughts. "I overreacted today because of fear."

She took a deep breath. "When I had my second child, I had complications and nearly died. I was told I would never have another child. I remember going to church and talking to God, thanking Him for my life and all my blessings. Instead of asking Him 'why me?' in a negative way, I chose to ask why He chose to grant me with the perfect life. I didn't get an answer until the day He decided to take it all away. I should never have gone to church and said what I did to God, because it made Him realize I did, in fact, have too much, and He took it all away.

"I live in fear each and every day that you both will be taken away from me, too. I try not to let the fear get the best of me, but today, it did. I am sorry, Edward."

She didn't let the guys get a word in before she reached in and took another rock. *Mistake*. Without a second thought, she reached over and passed it to Edward.

"*Mistake*...Where do I start? Both of you know the mistake I made today, but you might not understand why." He took a deep breath. "My whole life, I have never really trusted anyone, and then I met Gillian and trusted her with my whole heart and soul. It was a mistake. I was so hurt I thought I couldn't trust anyone...but I was

222

wrong.

"Liam, I have always been able to trust you. I trusted Raven, and she trusted me. And, Gabriella, I do trust you with every fiber of my being. So, I guess the good thing is I learned from my mistake."

He then reached for the basket and drew another stone. "*Weakness.*" He thought for a moment and realized he really wanted to know how Liam interpreted this word, so he tossed the rock to Liam.

Liam caught the rock and huffed. "Females, plain and simple, are my total weakness. Enya, Ainsley, Raven, and now Gabriella are the only ones who make me weak. I go crazy when I can't help or protect them. I lose all sense of reason, like when I struck out at you today." He nodded at Edward. "I want to wrap them all up in bubble wrap and protect them from the world and anything that could hurt any of my girls. But, no matter how strong or diligent I am, they still get hurt, and I can't do anything. So, they are totally my weakness."

Liam placed the rock on the ground then reached out to grab the basket. He pulled out another rock and read "*Courage.*" Smiling, he handed it to Gabriella, thinking, as much as he had complained about the game, it was eye-opening.

"Courage is something I wish I had," Gabriella began. "I worked with students who struggled to live through each and every day. They are happy just to be alive and have someone smile at them or stop and talk to them. They are strong and courageous to be who they are in a world that isn't always kind or understanding. It takes courage to live a life most people don't think is worth living. Courage is living. That's what they taught me. And because of those kids, I didn't take my life when I lost my family."

She looked at both the men and saw pain in their eyes. She raised her hand. "Don't, please. Carry on."

Liam handed her the basket, and she dug in and pulled out the rock that read *Honesty*. She leaned over and gave it to Edward.

He turned it over in his hands a few times then looked straight at Gabriella. "You ask for honesty, but you never ask for a thing you're not willing to give. I have learned more about honesty from you than anyone else in my life. That is the God's honest truth."

Nothing else needed to be said, so he grabbed the basket and another rock. *Dream.*

"Oh, I am keeping this one. *Dream.* I dream that one day I can find the kind of love that both of you have had with other people. You were lucky to have that love, but then you lost it, and now you found it again in each other. I dream that I am not asking too much. I dream for a family, little Edwards and Edwinas running all over the place, tormenting Liam. That is my dream."

They all laughed then silently all dreamed the same thing for Edward.

Edward pulled another rock. "*Scarred*," he told them, tossing it to Liam.

"How appropriate that you would give me this word. If I had drawn it myself, I would most certainly have treated it like a grenade and tossed it anywhere but in my own lap." He turned to Gabriella. "You were going for the jugular with this one, baby."

He drew three deep breaths then lowered his head and spoke to the sand. "For years, when I looked into the mirror, I saw a man who had been shredded and scarred. He was ugly on the inside. He let down the one person in the world he had vowed to care for. His selfishness and bitterness destroyed someone so pure and kind. But, when he looks in the mirror today, he sees the scars vanishing and healing with the help of an angel." Liam didn't raise his head. Instead, he chose another rock and read the word, *"Believe."* He passed it to Gabriella.

She placed it in the sand then got down on her knees in front of Liam, holding his huge hands in hers. "I believe you saved me. I believe you're harder on yourself than Raven ever was. I believe Raven knew how much you loved her. I believe you're an incredible papi and friend. I believe you love me. I believe we have a beautiful future ahead of us. Most importantly, I believe in you." She kissed the top of his head, then walked over to Edward.

She kneeled down again and grabbed his hands. "I believe you also saved me so I could help you. I believe you are the best friend anyone could have. I believe your mother is so fucking proud of her incredible son. Most importantly, I believe in you."

She got up, took the basket from Liam's side, and drew out another stone while both men held their heads down, tears in their eyes and terrified they would lose it.

225

Gabriella read, "*Love.*" Then she told them, "I love you with all my soul, Edward. And, Liam, you are my heart and my life. I love you and thank you for loving me."

"I don't think this is an exercise in dialogue so much as an exercise in how to make grown men cry. Love you, too, angel, with all that I am."

"Love you, little she-devil. But, next time, I'll take a beating from Liam before a heart to heart with you," Edward scoffed.

She laughed, grabbing another rock. "*Vulnerable,*" she read then tossed it to Edward, laughing more as he rolled his eyes.

"Are you sure there are only fifteen rocks in there? I swear, I feel like we have had at least a hundred." Edward took a deep breath, getting serious. "Okay, vulnerable. I have never, ever been as vulnerable as I have been today. I feel like I have ripped my chest open and made my heart vulnerable. I wish I had played this game with Gillian. Maybe I would have seen a sign that could have made me less vulnerable to her."

He grabbed another rock. "*Strength,*" he read. "I have never met anyone as strong as you. Now I want to know what strength means to you." He tossed the rock to Liam.

Again, Liam reflected on his answer before he spoke. "When I think of strength, it isn't about muscles. I think of my daughters who lost their mum and how their father walks in and out of their lives, yet they never complain. That is strength." He sighed. "They deserve better."

226

He looked into the basket. "There are only three stones left. Let's all put our hands in and grab one rock each. After that, we are going up to the cottage to crank Gabriella's tunes, play cards, cook dinner, and get fucking loaded."

Liam stuck his hand in and waited for the other two. When they all had their hands in, each pulled out a rock.

"*Trust*," Edward started. "I learned today to trust what I know in my heart completely."

Gabriella went next. "*Faith*. I learned today that I have faith. Maybe not in God yet, but in the people I choose to surround myself with."

"*Forgiveness*. I can never have peace until I have Raven's forgiveness, but I can have happiness." Liam ended the game.

Hours later, while Liam and Gabriella slept, Edward snuck down to the beach with a flashlight in hand. He collected each of the rocks, read them, thought about their meanings to him and to his friends, and then placed them in his gym bag. They were more precious than any gift he had ever received.

Chapter 22

Oh, God, Not Again

Edward decided Gabriella had to see the sights of northern Scotland to really appreciate, not only the beauty of the North Sea, but all that the north had to offer. He would love to take her to the exclusive Duff House Royal Golf Course, but he knew everyone would recognize him, and then they would want to know the name of the beauty who could whip his ass at his own game.

He hoped he wasn't interrupting an intimate moment as he wrote his text. On second thought, yes, he bloody well did! Why should he be the only one not getting laid? Screw that.

Hey, old man, you up? Let's take G to scotch distillery and sightsee, or we will be exploring more of our feelings. :(I am starving. Send her out. Coffee is on.

Liam knew immediately who it was when the text came in, but Edward could bloody well wait a few more minutes.

He got Gabriella aroused enough to gently enter her before she knew what was happening.

She moaned as he entered her, never opening her eyes. Her senses, though, were hyper aware of every movement Liam made. God, could it get any better? She didn't think so.

Before she was prepared, Liam brought her to an earth shattering climax. Then, while coming down from her high, she felt the change in his pace and the urgency.

He locked his mouth to hers and, on the final thrust, moaned into her mouth. When he released her mouth, he whispered in her ear, "I swear, the more time I spend inside of you, the longer I want to be there. I love you, sweetheart."

"Aw, Liam. I didn't believe I could ever be this happy and content again. I love you, my saviour."

Liam kissed her again for a few more moments then reached over to the nightstand and grabbed his phone. Reading the text, he chuckled then quickly responded with, *Ah, life is good, is it not, my friend? Scotch, yes. Feelings, no. Be out in 5. Did I say life is good? And put water on for tea. Not all of us are banned. LOL :)*

Before he could place the phone back, it beeped again.

Have I told you I hate you, fucker? I hope your dick rots and falls off.

Liam chuckled harder this time as he got out of bed to head for the shower. Then he turned around and caught Gabriella gawking at him.

229

"Keep looking at me like that, and I will have you again." He quirked his eyebrow at her, and she rolled her eyes. "Edward is starving. He started the coffee. Maybe you should feed the animal before your shower, or I fear he will come to get you himself."

She giggled. There was more to that conversation than she was comfortable knowing. However, she was going to take a moment and enjoy the view of Liam walking to the shower first.

He had the most muscular ass of anyone she had ever seen. It was like looking at Michelangelo's David except for a few claw marks from last night's escapades that she looked at in pride. *Yum, last night was really fun.*

When Liam's ass disappeared from sight, Gabriella jumped out of bed, pulled on some leggings and Liam's T-shirt, grabbed her robe, and then headed out to the kitchen to get Edward his breakfast. She knew he would most definitely come in to get her if she made him wait too long.

As she headed to the kitchen, she realized she didn't mind one little bit that Edward was waiting for her to make him breakfast. She loved looking after him and Liam.

"Did the old goat finally let you out of that bed?" Edward asked, raising his head from his phone.

"There are certain lines I won't cross with you, and anything past the bedroom door is one of them, so let's move on. Do you want a veggie omelet or chocolate chip pancakes again?"

He raised an eyebrow at that. "Do you really need to ask?

230

Pancakes, por favor. I already took out the chocolate chips for you and a fresh bottle of Canadian maple syrup that came in with the last shipment of clamato juice."

"You are so kind, but I'm going to cut some veggies first for my omelet. God knows, Liam will be having pancakes, too."

"Damn right, I will, my beautiful wee chef. Nobody makes pancakes like you," Liam stated as he brushed a kiss on the side of her neck, knowing it would give her the shivers. He then sat across from Edward at the table with his laptop.

Everyone was quiet while working on their individual tasks until Edward lifted his head.

"I'm not sure if Liam told you, but we would like to take you sightseeing and to a famous Scotch distillery."

"I would love to go. I'm willing to try anything. Oh, please tell me the tour guides wear kilts. That would make it all the sweeter."

"Since when have you had an interest in kilts, she-devil? If you want to see kilts, Liam and I will show you ours."

On a fit of giggles, she asked, "You and Liam wear skirts? Oh, my God! This, I have to see. Will you please wear them for me?"

Liam reprimanded her while she poured some of the batter onto the pan. "It is *not* a skirt; it's a kilt. Don't force me to put you over my knee and slap your wee ass until it is bright red."

Barely able to keep from giggling and insulting Liam further, she tried to apologize, but the thought of Liam in a skirt had her coughing in a fit, trying to contain herself.

"I'm sorry, but honestly, I think it would be cute—no, hot, sizzling hot. I have always been curious what men wear under their kilts."

She knows how to work the man, Edward thought. She had turned the conversation into a sexual innuendo, and now Liam would think with his little head and not his big one. She essentially had him eating out of her hand.

Edward needed to watch her more closely and learn. This woman was a master at getting what she wanted. Even knowing that, he would still do anything and everything she asked. *Yup, definitely a master.*

Liam's eyes were glazed over and he was smirking when he answered her with his thick, Scottish accent. "Aye, me wee angel, I have every intention of showin' ye exactly what's under me kilt. It's our pride and joy, the Scottish flower, and ye can watch it grow."

A blush moved up her chest to her face. She couldn't believe he had made the comment right in front of Edward.

***

As they entered the distillery, she was happy to realize that, yes, her guide was wearing a kilt. She blushed again, thinking about Liam's answer and what was underneath that kilt.

Edward saw her looking at the kilt and the blush that crawled up her face. He winked at her, which only added to her embarrassment.

Liam just tucked her more closely into his side, his body vibrating from laughter.

The tour was interesting. She learned a lot about how they made scotch and the pride the Scots had in their most famous drink. She smelled the mash during fermentation in the large vats, the pungency of which just about knocked her off her feet. Next, they headed to a very fancy tasting room where the guide explained they would try the mild, younger scotch first then work up to a twenty-year-old scotch.

Gabriella took a little bit more than she should have, desperately wanting to pick out the vanilla flavour the guide had discussed.

The liquid was strong and hot sitting in her mouth. She couldn't taste anything except pure alcohol, strong and deadly. There was nothing pleasant about this stuff. She swallowed to get the shit out of her mouth and soon realized that was a huge mistake when she went into a coughing fit as she felt the fires of Hell travelling and burning every part of her esophagus. Her body heated as she felt exactly where the hot liquid was in her body, warming her up.

Choke. Cough. Choke. Cough.

"Oh, my fucking Christ! It burns so badly!" She jumped up and down, coughing and flailing her hands. "Quick! I need water! Something to put out the fire! Milk! I need milk!" Gabriella choked out between coughs.

The men were in hysterics.

"Baby, you'll be okay. Just give it a minute," Liam suggested as he gently patted her back while she regained her regular breathing pattern.

"I'm not okay. That stuff is terrible! It's no wonder you made me eat. I needed my strength so I wouldn't yak up that devil's brew. Honestly, how can they charge money—and a lot of money—for *that*?"

Edward couldn't regain his composure as he continued to hold his stomach and laugh. When he was finally under control, he said, "Revenge is best served cold, though in your case, hot. Next time you want us to get in touch with our feelings, remember we have ways to make you pay. I honestly thought your palette would appreciate such exquisitely fine liquor, Gabriella."

"Remember who is royalty here. Not me. I am only a poor girl with immigrant parents and no refinement," Gabriella threw back.

While Edward and Gabriella were bantering back and forth, Liam's phone rang, and he stepped away to answer it.

"Lilith, slow down. I can't understand you. What happened?"

Gabriella and Edward turned at the tone of Liam's voice, seeing he had paled considerably.

"What hospital?...Okay, okay. How are they? Please tell me they are okay...I will be there as soon as I can...I am in Banffshire. It will take me two hours...I need you to be strong. If you see them, tell them I love them and that I will be there soon." With that, he hung up.

"Liam, what's wrong? Please, what's happening?" Gabriella, terrified, knew without a doubt that their world had changed again.

"My girls and my mum were sideswiped on their way to school.

One of the twins is in surgery, which one I am not sure, and I don't know the condition of the other. My mum is being looked after. I need to get to them as soon as possible. I can take you two back to the cottage, and I will call the detachment and get a new protection detail."

"Like hell you will! Give me the keys," Edward said. "I am driving while you call the hospital and get more information." Edward grabbed the keys and started walking quickly to the vehicle with his phone to his ear.

Liam glanced back to see if Gabriella was keeping up. She was running as fast as possible, but she was also sobbing and shaking. He could see she was trying to be strong, though, and he loved her for that.

"Gabriella," he whispered as he slowed down to grab her hand.

She yanked at his hand when he slowed too much, needing him to move faster. She in no way minded being dragged if that was what it took to get them to the girls more quickly.

As he ran, he realized it might be too soon for her to deal with the severity of the situation.

"Angel?"

She jumped into the SUV, mumbling to herself, but she quickly set herself straight and met him head-on. "No, Liam, I can do this. I am not losing my mind. I am doing what I swore to myself I would never do again. I am praying for the girls."

"Gabriella?"

"No, Liam, God is going to answer my prayers this time. He has *my* babies; he isn't getting *yours*. I am just making sure He knows that!"

"I called Tom and informed him we are on the move to Sterling," Edward told Liam. "He is sending a crew to collect our personal belongings and bring them to your house. He asked me if I needed a new detail, and I told him I wasn't leaving you. We are family; we do this together."

Liam was humbled. This time around, he wouldn't shut the closest people out. He would welcome all the support they had to offer him and his girls—his beautiful twins, his innocent, little, dark-haired princesses. They had a smile for everyone and expressed their love freely. They had been through so much in their wee lives. They had lost their mum; their father walked in and out of their lives on a regular basis; and the wee imps never complained or asked for more. Now they were fighting for their lives, and he didn't know how he would handle losing either one of them or both.

Please, please, please, God! Please save my wee lasses.

After saying a little prayer, he looked over to Gabriella. She had her eyes closed, and her mouth was silently moving in prayer. He knew that asking God for help was costing her, but he was thankful for anything that would help.

He grabbed his phone and connected with the hospital. Edward and Gabriella listened to the one-sided conversation Liam was having with heavy hearts.

"Yes, please, I need your help. My daughters and mother were brought in by ambulance this morning. I am on my way, but I'm two hours out and need some information regarding their status...Yes, their names are Enya and Ainsley Connor, and my mother is Margaret Connor. They were in a car accident, and I believe one of the twins is in surgery...Yes, I am their father. Can you give me any updates at all?...Nothing?...Yes, I understand. Can you at least tell me where I should head to when I get to the hospital?...Okay...And if I am in the surgery waiting room, will you relay that I am there so someone can keep me informed on my other daughter's status?" Liam hung up and hissed, "Fuck! I can't get any goddamn information!"

Gabriella grabbed Liam's hand and squeezed tightly, silently letting him know he wasn't alone.

Edward, on the other hand, plugged in his Bluetooth and put on his headset. Then he pushed a button and said, "Secretary." There was a slight pause before Edward said, "Myles, Edward here. I want you to use every connection we have to get a hold of St. Mary of Scotland Hospital. I want the best care money can provide for Enya, Ainsley, and Margaret Connor. You fly in the best doctors and equipment...Anything...I want to be informed of every aspect of their care and needs...Okay, ASAP...And, Myles, don't make me wait." He disconnected the call then stared ahead, lost in thought.

Liam was shocked. In all the time he had known Edward, he had never seen him use his power or connections to get something, and

Liam had never been so thankful.

The three friends sat quietly for over five minutes, waiting for Myles to call back. When the phone rang, Gabriella jumped.

Edward answered, "Myles, you had better have some information for me...Okay, connect him. I will put you on speaker."

"Sir, I am connecting you now to the director of St. Mary of Scotland Hospital, Mr. Robert Booth. Go ahead, Prince Edward," Myles spoke in a very proper English accent.

"Mr. Booth, I assume you know who I am," Edward said in a very aristocratic way.

"Yes, Prince Edward, I am well aware to whom I am speaking. Now, you wanted some information about three of my patients? Is a family member with you, sir?"

"I am the girls' father, Liam Connor, and Margaret is my mum. Can you please tell me how they are?" Liam replied before Edward had a chance.

"Mr. Connor, your daughter, Enya, is in emergency. She is going to require approximately twenty-five stitches across her torso where the seatbelt lacerated her skin. Plus, she experienced blunt-force trauma to her head. We have arranged for a brain scan to confirm if there is any swelling. We are awaiting the results before we can call a plastic surgeon to stitch her torso.

"Mrs. Connor has a broken arm, a dislocated shoulder, and three cracked ribs. We are sending her for a CAT scan on her hip. The air bag stopped her skull from being injured.

238

"Now, Mr. Connor, your daughter Ainsley is in surgery. She also has wounds from the seatbelt across her torso from her shoulder to her waist. Her spleen ruptured, and we are trying to repair a tear in the tissue to control internal bleeding. One of her ribs punctured her lung and has caused hemothorax, which is blood collecting in the space between the lung and chest cavity. We are also trying to repair that. After surgery, we have to send her for a brain scan to see if she has incurred any head trauma.

"I have complete faith in my surgical team, Mr. Connor. They are all in excellent hands and will be cared for like they are our own."

"Thank you, Mr. Booth. I will see you soon," Liam responded quietly.

Gabriella tried desperately not to let Liam see she was crying again, but she couldn't wipe the tears away fast enough.

"Mr. Booth, I want the best surgeons," Edward continued. "Whichever plastic surgeon you get better make those stitches so tiny they are undetectable. You treat this family like you would mine. They are now your number one priority. I have supported this hospital for years and believe in it. Please, don't let me down. If there are any changes, you call this number immediately. I will have the children's father there in under two hours. I hope you meet us with good news. Thank you for your assistance, sir."

"I respect your confidence and await your arrival."

Chapter 23

Touched by an Angel

T he SUV was silent, each passenger lost in their own thoughts or prayers, when the call came in, shocking them all back to the here and now.

"Edward here. To whom am I speaking?"

"*Prince Edward, this is Mr. Booth? May I speak to Mr. Connor?*"

"You're on speaker phone; do you need privacy?" Edward asked with fear in his voice.

"*Mr. Connor, I have an update on your children. Shall I speak freely?*"

"Of course, go ahead. How are my wee girls? Is Ainsley out of surgery?"

"*No, Mr. Connor, but the surgeons have managed to repair the punctured lung and stop the bleeding. They have placed a tube down her throat to drain the blood. They are now moving on to the spleen.*"

240

This is favourable news, sir. We had the top plastic surgeon in the UK flown in, and she has started to repair the laceration on Miss Enya. Her brain scan is being evaluated as we speak, and they tell me it looks good.

"*I am going to ask that you come to the back of the hospital to entrance 'D' for privacy's sake, where one of your associates has coordinated with my staff and is waiting to take your vehicle. I will personally meet you with my team and take you to a private part of the hospital until you are able to see the children.*"

"Thank you, Mr. Booth. By my calculations, we should arrive in fifteen minutes."

"*I await your arrival, sir. Thank you,*" Mr. Booth replied before hanging up.

"Liam, they will be okay. Trust me," Edward said with every ounce of belief he had inside his heart.

Liam took a huge breath and lowered his head into his hands. He rubbed his eyes and tried to regain his composure. His heart had plummeted when the phone had rung, dreading it was bad news.

Gabriella realized he was struggling and gently rubbed his back. Then she moved her hand up to massage his neck, which was a ball of knots, telling him, "This is great news, mi cielo. Everything is going to be fine. The girls are going to be okay; I promise. Hang in there and know we are here for you. I love you, my saviour."

He looked into her eyes and right down into her soul, seeing compassion, unconditional love, and strength.

241

The girls were going to make it. They deserved to know a strong and beautiful woman like this.

He had never stopped to consider if Gabriella wanted to raise another woman's children, but he knew he wanted her to. The girls would flourish with such a nurturing soul, someone who was born to be a great mother and role model. The girls needed a mother's love, and Gabriella needed children to love and protect.

He lowered his lips to Gabriella's and gently kissed her, absorbing all her strength and love.

Edward went flying into the back of the hospital. It was a service area where Edward could pull the SUV right into the docking area and away from prying eyes. The director of the hospital was personally waiting for them in his pristine three-piece suit. The team of three doctors were all in scrubs with stethoscopes around their necks.

The friends jumped out of the truck quickly, made introductions, and shook hands. Mr. Booth and his team then escorted them to a private waiting room to discuss updates on the condition of his family.

"Mr. Connor, not much has changed since our last conversation. Miss Enya is still having her lacerations stitched. We expect she will be in there for at least another hour or two. Miss Ainsley is still in surgery, but we hope she will be out in the next hour. Then we will give her a brain scan, and the plastic surgeon will begin to repair her laceration. Your mum is resting in her room around the corner. I will

242

take you to her immediately."

Liam walked through the door. Then he stopped and turned. "Gabriella."

"I can wait here with Edward. You should see her alone first," Gabriella said.

"Baby, I need you. Edward, let's go."

Edward got up without question. This wasn't the first time he had accompanied Liam into a hospital room. He knew his friend didn't need his words, just his presence.

He turned to see fear written all over Gabriella's face and grabbed her hand.

"He needs you, love. I know you're strong enough to do this." He squeezed her hand tightly in reassurance.

She nodded and walked over to Liam, taking his hand and following him into his mum's room.

When they walked into the private room, they saw Margaret lying down with her eyes closed. Her arm was in a cast, and her face was bruised, hooked up to an IV drip and a blood pressure machine.

Liam released Gabriella's hand, and Edward once again grabbed it tightly to reassure her, as Liam walked up to the side of the bed and moved down to kiss his mother's cheek.

"Liam," she rasped as she opened her eyes and saw her son, a tear slipping out.

"Mum, I'm here. How are you?"

She started to sob, the pain on her face tangible. Her ribs were

243

on fire with every breath she took.

"The twins…Oh, Lord, the twins. I am so sorry, Liam. I didn't see the truck comin'. He went right through the red light. Oh, laddie, I am so sorry."

"Mum, I don't blame you. Stop. The girls are in surgery. We just have to be strong. They are going to need us, so put your mind to rest and heal. I love you, Mum, and I'm glad you're okay."

Margaret Connor was a proud woman. She tried to raise her son's hand to her mouth to kiss him, but every move she made hurt, and she cried out in pain.

Gabriella jumped forwards and tried to soothe the woman. "It's okay. Breathe through the pain, Mrs. Connor. Three deep breaths. Follow me. One…in and out. That's it. Two…in and out. Three…in and out. Good, you're doing much better. Please try to remain calm."

When she had regained her breath, she asked, "May I have a drink, please? I am so thirsty."

"Sure, let me get you one. Hold on two seconds." Gabriella walked over to the bedside table, grabbed the Styrofoam cup that had ice water in it, and took it back to her side. Then she gently tipped the cup so Margaret could take a sip from the straw.

"Thank you, ma dear. That's betta." She winced again in pain.

"Can I make you any more comfortable? Maybe move the pillows to adjust your body into a more comfortable position?" Gabriella inquired.

"No, thank ye. Just havin' my laddie here is comfort enough.

Please, don't let me hold ye up from yer duties."

"Mum, she isn't a nurse; she is my girlfriend. Gabriella Dante, I would like you to meet Margaret Connor."

Nothing could have surprised Margaret more than what her son had just said. She was mulling it over in her head, wondering if the drugs were causing her delusions.

Margaret heard a chuckle from the corner and laid her eyes on a smiling Prince Edward who was trying to hide his mirth by coughing into his hand.

"Edward, cut the nonsense and get over here." Margaret was beside herself in pain, but she needed to get reassurance she wasn't losing her mind.

Edward approached the bed and leaned down to press a quick kiss to Margaret's cheek.

"Hey, Mumsy, you look great. You had us worried. What can I do for you, love?" Edward asked as he moved a stray hair from in front of her eye.

"I need to know my mind is still in its right frame. It took quite a knock. Did I just hear my laddie say that this young nurse is his girlfriend?"

Edward chuckled again. "Yes, Mumsy, you heard correct. That hard head of yours is in perfect working order. Gabriella is his girlfriend. Although, I think there is something wrong with her, because I was also vying for her attention, and she chose Liam over me, so you have to know she might be a little weak in the mind."

Gabriella jabbed a finger into Edward's side that made him jump, and then she made a comment that shocked all in the room.

"If you, Mr. Prince of shit, say another stupid comment in front of Liam's mother, I will knock you on your butt so fast you won't know what hit you, smart ass." Gabriella, shocked at herself, threw both hands over her mouth to stop any more rudeness from falling out. "Oh, my God. I am so sorry." She looked at Liam with regret and embarrassment written all over her face.

Liam had a smile from ear to ear, and she heard a grunt from the bed. She turned and saw Mrs. Connor also had a smile before she winced in pain again.

"Well, I see ye've met your match in this little lass, my boy. And, Edward, ye got what ye deserved. You're lucky I can't raise my arm, or I would cuff yer ear," Margaret rushed out on a painful breath.

"You all do know that I am a prince of England and deserve a little respect, right?" Edward chuckled.

"Courtesy is given. Respect is earned," Gabriella was quick to respond. "You, my dear friend, deserve neither one at the moment. You made me look like a crazy nut job in front of Liam's mother. I will get you back for that. No more pancakes, no more churros—you are officially on my shit list." She covered her mouth with her hand. "Oops, sorry, Mrs. Connor. I mean no disrespect; he just ruffles my feathers, and I can't keep a civil tongue."

"Oh, I can see I am goin' to love ye, my wee lass," Margaret said as she closed her eyes from the pain.

"Mum, I think we should leave and let you rest. We will be back in a little while," Liam whispered as he bent down again and gave her another kiss, squeezing her hand gently.

She was such a strong woman, and it killed him to see her helpless and in pain. If it hadn't been for his mum, he would never have been able to keep his job and raise his daughters. No mother should have to help raise their grandchildren. She should be travelling with friends and joining clubs.

They left her room and went back to the waiting room. Liam excused himself.

Edward turned to Gabriella. "I'm sorry, Gabriella. I wasn't trying to throw you under the bus. I was trying to defuse the guilt Margaret was feeling. I learned to use humour when Raven was in the hospital and tensions were high amongst everyone. I became Raven's confidant. She understood Liam's struggle, so she encouraged the bantering. Please know that it isn't personal. You know I worship and love you."

"*I* am so sorry. I should have known. You have a heart of gold, and I love you with all my heart. You are perfect. My mother would say, the only perfect thing in this world is an asshole, so…thanks, asshole." She giggled as Edward put her in a headlock and gave her a noogie then kissed the top of her head.

Liam came around the corner and witnessed the play of affection. He knew what Edward had done back in his mum's room, having witnessed it many times when Raven had been in the hospital. That was the reason he wanted Edward with him—he knew how to help Liam deal with bad situations. This was a side the world didn't know about Edward. If they ever did, they would respect him more.

"Get your dirty paws off my woman, you barmy asshole," Liam said as he grabbed Gabriella like she was a little doll and placed her next to him on a waiting room chair. He wrapped his arm around her shoulders and pulled her tightly to his side.

"I just called him an asshole, too. Great minds think alike." Gabriella giggled.

"And fools never differ," Edward retorted.

Gabriella didn't respond; she just looked at Edward and stuck her tongue out.

Just then, a man walked in with bags of food for the trio. "Sir, Myles thought you all should have something substantial in your stomachs as you will probably be here a while, and he prefer you not leave this restricted area. Word has gotten around the hospital that someone special is here, and we would prefer they not know it is you. I also want you to know that he has requested off-duty nurses from another hospital be brought in to attend each of the family members in their rooms so that they are never alone. That way, it will keep the gossip at a minimum amongst the staff, sir."

"Good thinking on Myles's part. Thank you. I will call him later."

Gabriella opened the feast and laid it all out so the men could help themselves. While she was working at this task, she, reflected on the fun-loving joker Edward was to her. Until now, she couldn't imagine the noble prince he had been raised to be. Yet, after witnessing how he handled unexpected situations and people with confidence, intelligence, and authority, she had a new level of respect for Edward.

Just as they finished eating, Mr. Booth walked into the room. The trio stood, knowing he had news.

"Mr. Connor, Miss Ainsley has come out of surgery. The team removed her spleen and all the blood from her abdomen. She has had her brain scan, and they are evaluating the results. As soon as the plastic surgeon is finished with Miss Enya, she will move on to Miss Ainsley. If you would like to see Miss Ainsley before she goes in for her next surgery, we can allow you a few moments."

"Absolutely. Can we go now?" Liam asked, knowing he couldn't endure this alone. He needed strength he didn't have. "Gabriella, can you do this?"

"Of course, my saviour. Lead the way, Mr. Booth."

Outside the room, they were asked to gown and mask themselves to prevent infection. Gabriella tied Liam's mask since he was shaking. She didn't say a word when she was done. She simply grabbed Liam's hand, squeezed it in reassurance, and moved through the door.

"Oh, fuck. Oh, wee princess...I am so sorry. Why couldn't it

249

have been me?" Liam said on a sob as he touched Ainsley's head.

The scene was heartbreaking. A tiny girl with long, dark hair and alabaster skin lay in a big bed with a breathing tube inserted in her throat. A gash from her left shoulder to her hip lay open with iodine rubbed onto the skin, and the incision from the lung surgery was bandaged with a large square of gauze. You could see the bruising around the area of her ribs. There was also a square bandage where her spleen had been taken out.

Gabriella wondered how much one little body could take. She prayed silently that God would spare this little wisp of a girl whose body had endured so much already. Tears ran down her face in sympathy for the little girl and for Liam.

Liam lowered his head beside his daughter's and silently wept in fear for his beautiful, wee princess. His control was slipping. After slowly and painfully losing Raven, he had vowed never to lose control again, yet here he was, again in a hospital with absolutely no control.

"Fuck…fuck," he quietly sobbed.

Gabriella moved behind him and rubbed his arm and back as she talked him through it. "Sweetheart, she is going to be fine. Don't you dare give up hope. Trust me, please, mi salvador. She needs your words of love and encouragement. She can hear you. Reassure her you are here and will be here when she wakes up. Let her know you love her."

"Wee princess, Daddy is here, baby. I love you. I need you to get strong. You need to fight, okay, baby? Please…for Daddy. I have someone very special I want you to meet. Baby, she is the answer to all my prayers, and you're going to fall as much in love with her as I have. Okay, baby? Please fight with everything you have. I know you are a fighter. You were the smallest babe, and you fought like a soldier. I believe in you."

Still holding Ainsley's hand, Liam turned to Gabriella and shared a little history about his daughters. "She had to fight for every breath when she was born weighing only two kilos. That's why I call her wee princess. Enya is just princess.

"Raven's body was pushed beyond its limit between the cancer and carrying the twins, so the doctors decided to take the girls a month early. Ainsley here was so tiny, but she fought for her place in the world, and she deserves to keep it." He choked on his last sentence, and tears again filled his eyes.

Gabriella was humbled to be loved by such an incredible man and father.

Just then, a nurse walked in and informed them that Enya was out of surgery. They could go and visit her while they prepped Ainsley for the next surgery.

"Baby, Daddy will be right here, waiting for you when you are done. Be strong and fight wee princess. I love you." Liam kissed her brow through the mask and let a tear fall from his eye.

Before Gabriella turned to leave, she leaned down to Ainsley, touched her hand, and whispered into her ear, "He needs you, little girl, and he loves you. Fight hard, little one." Gabriella kissed her hand then brought it to her heart.

Liam watched Gabriella interact with his youngest daughter. Ainsley didn't know it, but his daughter had just been touched by an angel.

They left Ainsley in ICU with tears in their eyes, and then the nurse led them to Enya's room.

They walked in to find her in a hospital gown, tucked into bed with a nurse sitting beside her, holding her hand and calmly talking to her. Her eyes lifted when she realized someone had walked into the room.

"Daddy!" she cried out, breaking down into a fit of tears.

The nurse would later explain that the little girl was so brave until she saw her dad. Then she didn't need to be strong anymore, because Daddy would make it all okay.

"Hey, princess, how is my beautiful lass?" Liam asked as he approached and kissed her, gently lifting her upper body into a semi-hug to avoid hurting the skin that had just been repaired.

The nurse had told them she wouldn't feel the pain today due to the pain killers, but tomorrow would be very difficult for his princess.

Enya calmed down after a few moments of reassurance. He wiped the tears from her face with his large hands then tucked her hair behind her ears.

"Oh, Daddy! It was terrible! Nana was taking us to school, and

252

someone smashed our car. Why did they do that? Is Nana okay? Where is Ainsley?"

Only the father of a daughter would know to wait for all the questions to be asked before answering. He spent the next half-hour answering all of her questions. When he was done, she looked around and spotted Gabriella.

"Who's the pretty lady, Daddy?"

"Enya Connor, I want you to meet Gabriella Dante. Gabriella is a very special lady. I hope you will get to know and love her as much as I do." By the tone and language her daddy used, Enya knew she was someone special.

Shyly, she turned to Gabriella. "Hi, Gabriella."

"Hello, Enya. It is a pleasure to meet you. Your daddy has told me a lot about you. I hope you feel better soon, sweetheart."

Just as they made their introductions, Edward blew into the room. "How is ankle-biter number one doing? I know you did this to get lots and lots of ice cream, right? Or maybe you just wanted a present from me. Well, my little bug-in-a-rug, I am here, so you can rest easy."

"Yay! Uncle Edward, did you bring me a present?" Enya asked, lying in her bed, looking small and fragile.

Edward bent down, kissed her forehead, and gave a silent thanks to God above that she was talking and responding.

At any other time, Liam would be pissed his daughter had asked Edward for a present, but he was just so thankful she was talking and happy. Right now, he didn't give a shit about manners.

"Would Uncle Edward come without a present? Hold on." Edward stepped out of the room then back in with a teddy bear that had a doctor's mask across its mouth and a Red Cross symbol over its heart. It was at least three feet tall with a big, yellow bow.

"With him in your bed, there will be *bearly* enough room for you. Get it? Bear-ly. See? Your uncle Edward's still got it. How are you doing, little one?"

"I was scared, and I want to go home." Enya got teary-eyed again.

"It's okay, my princess," Liam gently told Enya. "I will stay with you girls until you can come home." She seemed to settle right down.

It ripped his heart when she said, "I missed you so much, Daddy. Please don't leave me."

"I'm right here, baby, and I am not going anywhere; I promise." Liam settled into the chair for the long haul.

Chapter 24

Out of the Mouths of Babes

Liam was lucky to have had Gabriella and Edward for the last two weeks. They stayed with the girls when he left each morning at four a.m. to go home, shower, and get clean clothes. He would then spend thirty minutes each day going through emails and keeping in touch with Tom and the rest of his team.

The trio rotated shifts between Ainsley in ICU and Enya and Margaret. Liam could never have kept his promise to Enya if it weren't for Gabriella and Edward.

Edward's team had taken everyone's luggage to Liam's home and opened up the house after a year of being closed up. The friends took turns going to Liam's house to shower and change. Edward would drive Gabriella to get groceries then to Liam's place. After showering, she would cook some food and bake some sweets to take to the hospital. Meanwhile, Edward would take care of his business.

Liam was beyond impressed with the dedication Edward and Gabriella had to his family.

Gabriella learned that the girls stayed at Margaret's, which was only two houses over from Liam's. There were ten houses attached to the row. They were beautiful brownstones, so different than Gabriella had ever seen: big, grey stones with white shutters, three-levels high. Each window had boxes filled with beautiful red flowers. It looked so welcoming.

Liam's house had four bedrooms and someone—she assumed Raven—had done a beautiful job making it feel cozy. There were pictures everywhere. Photos of Raven and the girls, a few family shots that were taken after the twins were born, and a wedding picture of a much younger Liam and his beautiful, dark-haired, tall bride.

The last one she looked at made her sad. She could tell Raven had been very sick at the children's christening, but the family was full of smiles, making the most of the time they had left.

Gabriella made the sign of the cross, kissed her lips, and touched Raven's picture as a show of respect.

***

Liam walked into the room and saw Edward sleeping on a fold-out chair, and Gabriella on another. The director had arranged for the three adults to have them in the huge room with the children so the girls would know they were never alone. It was another advantage of Edward's pull.

Ainsley had been moved into the room just yesterday, now out of ICU. She was still in a drug-induced coma due to swelling around her brain. However, the breathing tube had finally been removed yesterday after it was confirmed the repair to the lung had been successful.

Liam went over and checked on both of his daughters, kissed them gently, and then went to Gabriella, who was sleeping on her side. He tucked himself under her, and she stirred and smiled when she realized she was lying on top of Liam. She looked into his eyes and saw right down deep into his heart.

"Hey, my saviour, everything okay? Mm...you smell good," Gabriella whispered.

Not wanting to lose their moment of privacy, Liam whispered back as he gently moved her hair away from her face. "Do you remember when you said to me that you didn't know how you could repay me for helping you back to the living? Well, at the time, I was taken aback, offended even. I didn't understand those feelings, but now I do. You and Edward have gone way beyond the call of duty, and I am forever in your debt. Thank you, Gabriella. I love you."

He sealed his statement with a deep kiss, tasting every inch of her mouth. He kissed her as he rotated his hips, and she moaned into his mouth in response.

He had to stop. Otherwise, he was going to blow his load in his clean pants, in the hospital room that held his injured twin daughters and one of the princes of England. *Fuck*! he screamed in his head.

257

"It sucks, doesn't it, old boy?" Edward smirked from his chair beside Ainsley's bed.

"Keep talking, young buck, and you will need a hospital bed," Liam snarled back.

"Daddy, you here?" Enya asked, rubbing her large, blue eyes.

Liam moved Gabriella so he could get up and go to Enya's bed. "Yeah, princess, right here. How are you feeling this morning?"

"Daddy, my tummy is itchy. Help me scratch it, please..."

Gabriella jumped up and went to Enya. "Hey there, hermosa chica." (*Beautiful girl*) "Listen, you can't scratch your stitches; otherwise, you will open them. I have some cream the nurse gave me. Can I clean the stitches then rub the cream on your tummy? It will help with the itchy feeling."

"Please, Gabriella, anything that will stop the itching!" Enya begged.

"Do I hear the ankle-biter complaining? How about if I tickle you until you pee that bed?"

"Edward, not appropriate and a bit brutish, don't you think?" Gabriella defended Enya.

Just as cheekily, Enya pointed her finger at Edward and said, "Ha-ha! You got in trouble, Uncle Edward."

"Just wait until Gabriella turns her back, ankle-biter. Then I will get you." He curled his fingers and made a monster face.

Enya just giggled, knowing her uncle was being silly while Gabriella started to clean and rub the cream on Enya's stitches.

Enya then proceeded to ask the same question she had every hour for the last five days. "Gabriella, how come Ainsley won't wake up?"

Gabriella, a firm believer in telling children the truth within reason, said, "Her body needs to heal a little bit longer than yours. And she needs all of her power to do that, so the doctors are letting Ainsley sleep."

"How do you know so much? Do you have kids?" Enya inquired.

Everything stopped. It seemed like every bit of oxygen had been sucked out of the room. The men held their breaths, frightened the innocent question would push Gabriella over the edge.

Liam had started to walk towards them when Gabriella answered his princess.

"I do, hermosa chica. I had two beautiful, little boys, but they no longer live on earth. They went to Heaven with their daddy to be with God," she answered without tears and with heartfelt honesty.

It broke the men's hearts, but Liam was so proud of how far she had come. He waited to see what would happen next.

"I bet they know my mum. She died when we were babies, and she lives in Heaven, too," Enya answered as straight forwardly as Gabriella had been with her.

Gabriella finished with the cream and gently kissed her forehead as she pulled the hospital gown down. "I think you might be right about that, because someone brought your daddy and Uncle Edward to save me. I bet your mom and my family met and decided to put us all together so we wouldn't be so lonely anymore." Patting Enya's cheek, she continued, "Okay, hermosa, are you good now, because I am going to go and rub some cream on Ainsley's stitches?"

Just as she went to move away, Enya grabbed her hand. "I'm glad you're not lonely anymore, and thanks for helping me with my itchy tummy."

Now Gabriella's eyes really did fill up with tears, but she smiled as she walked towards Ainsley's bed.

Liam had never been prouder of his first born child. *Truly*, he thought, *out of the mouths of babes.*

Not three minutes later, Mr. Booth and a doctor walked in and asked Liam to step outside to discuss the children's progress.

Edward noticed Liam tense up, uncomfortable that he was being asked to go out of the room, so he got up and followed Liam out for moral support.

"Mr. Connor, nothing is wrong, but we have to make some decisions, and I prefer not to do it in front of Miss Enya. Your mother is doing better and can be released today, providing there is someone with a health care background to help her at home and assist her with physical therapy. Next, Miss Enya is also ready to be released. Miss Ainsley, if all goes as planned, should be ready to go home in a couple of weeks. Now, I know you wanted to keep the girls together, but for Miss Enya's sake, I really think she should be at home. Her recovery will speed up with the change of environment, and when Miss Ainsley comes out of the coma, she is going to be in a lot of pain. I don't think you want Miss Enya to witness her sister in that condition."

Liam breathed deeply as he rubbed his head, trying to figure out logistically how he could make all this happen.

"I will stay here with Ainsley," Edward jumped in. "Get your mum and Enya home with Gabriella's help. The nurse with your mum now can assist her at home, and then I will make sure a rotation of nurses is available to help her until she is able to care for herself. Gabriella can look after Enya while you get them all settled. Then get some rest and come back to the hospital later tonight or tomorrow morning and relieve me for a while. The three of us can all jockey back and forth until Ainsley comes home. That way, both girls get equal amounts of attention."

Liam was again confounded by Edward's generosity. "How much more can I take from you, my friend?"

That comment pissed Edward right off. Liam had already given Edward something he had been missing his whole life: a middle class family who couldn't care less whether he was a prince or a beggar.

"Would you do it for me? Would you? Of course you would. It's no different than when you followed me to Skye instead of going home to your family. We have always been there for one another. But, if you really want to pay me back, hand over Gabriella and we are even." Edward chuckled before Liam cuffed him upside the head.

"Nice try, asshole, nice try." Liam smirked.

***

"Okay, princess, it has been a long day, and it is time for you to go to sleep. I am going to go and check on Nana. Gabriella will be here until I get back," Liam told Enya as he tucked her in her little twin bed.

"Daddy, please read me another story so I can fall asleep. I'm not used to being alone. Ainsley and me always talk when we go to bed. Please, Daddy? I am scared to be alone," Enya begged.

"I would love to read you a story while your daddy goes to check on your nana," Gabriella offered, having walked in during the conversation. "Would that be okay with you, hermosa?"

"Sure. What do you want to read? Our bookshelf is over there." Enya pointed to the white bookshelf between the two twin beds. "I like to look at the pictures when you read."

"Thank you, angel. I will only be a few minutes," Liam said to Gabriella before he bent down and kissed Enya.

"No rush. Enya and I will be fine," Gabriella told him as she walked over to the bookcase.

She had pulled one book out to read the title when another one fell onto the floor. She bent down to pick it up, and her heart skipped a beat when she looked at the title. *I'll Love You Forever* by Robert Munsch. Her eyes filled with tears as she was transported back in time.

"Are you okay, Gabriella?" Enya asked, wondering why Gabriella wasn't moving. "Why are you crying?" the innocent child asked.

Gabriella stroked the book as another tear fell, whispering, "My boys used to love this book. My youngest loved it so much he made me buy another copy so that he had one all to himself. I always told them that I would read this book at their weddings to let their wives know that I was the first girl who loved them."

Enya gingerly crawled out of bed in her long, white nightgown and came up behind Gabriella. She wrapped her tiny arms around Gabriella's neck and leaned into her back, looking at the book over Gabriella's shoulder. "My daddy always tells me that, if I talk to Mummy in Heaven, she will hear me, so I think you should read me the book and your sons will be able to hear, too."

Gabriella wiped her tears away. "Oh, my sweet girl, that is the best idea I have heard in a long time. May I lie on the bed with you so we can read it together, seeing as you know all the words, and my boys will hear us both?"

"Yes, they are going to be happy with my reading. My teacher says I am the best reader in her class," Enya happily answered as she crawled back into bed with Gabriella by her side.

They read the book three times before Enya and Gabriella fell asleep, and that is how Liam found them—curled up together with a book on Gabriella's chest.

He had just gotten off the phone with Edward, learning nothing had changed with Ainsley. Edward had convinced him to sleep in his own bed tonight.

He watched the girls for a minute then looked up at the ceiling. In his head, he spoke to Raven for the first time. *I know it was you who sent us Gabriella, and for that, I am so thankful.* He then turned and gently moved Enya from Gabriella's arms.

He carefully shook Gabriella until she opened her eyes. "Come to bed, sweetheart." He took her hand and guided her to his room.

Gabriella was sleepy until she entered Liam's bedroom. She skidded to a halt as it hit her like a ton of bricks. She was in another woman's bedroom and was about to get into that woman's bed.

"Liam, I'm sorry. I can't do it," Gabriella whispered, staring at the bed.

"What's going on in that pretty, little head of yours?"

"I can't get into Raven's bed. It's just not right."

Liam was visibly relieved. This was something he could deal with quickly.

He grabbed her head in both his hands, his thumbs smoothing up and down her face as he spoke. "Baby, it's not Raven's bed, nor is it Raven's house. We lived in a flat on the other side of town. The girls and I moved here after Raven passed away to be closer to my mum and so the girls could have all their stuff when I was away, working. My mum looks after the house when I'm not here.

"As far as the bed, no woman has ever slept in that bed. When Raven passed, I was still so angry, and every time I went to bed, all I could smell was her, so I gave the bed to charity and bought a new one."

Gabriella's eyes nearly popped out of her head at Liam's response. Having Marco's scent on her bed had helped get her through that first year, and she still hadn't gotten rid of his or the boys' clothes or possessions.

She was learning that everyone truly did grieve differently. No one way was the right way. The only right way was the one that got you through the day. Now she felt like an idiot for forcing Liam to relive his pain again.

"Oh, God, Liam, I am so sorry. I shouldn't have said that. Please forgive me."

Liam wrapped his arms around her. "Baby, you never have to apologize for being considerate of Raven. That is why I love you so much. You always think of everyone before yourself. Now, enough talking. I need you now. But first, I need a taste of you. I want your lips…both sets." He winked just before he bent down and consumed her mouth.

When the kiss finished, he stepped an arm's length away and looked at her chest.

"Well, that's just plain weird. What on God's green earth are you doing?" Gabriella asked.

"It's ivory, or it could be white or maybe a combination of both, but definitely lace. Yeah, baby, you never disappoint. It is definitely lace," Liam purred.

Gabriella caught on to what he was saying and decided to make it interesting. "Okay, let's make this worthwhile. If you are right on the first colour, I am on my knees. If you are right with the second, you are on your knees. Lastly, if you guessed right the third time, no one is on their knees, no foreplay at all, just right down to business. Choose wisely."

"Oh, baby, the first two are a win, win situation. The third, I'll be dammed if I am getting no foreplay. Let's see...This could be tricky, and not because I am not one hundred percent sure, but because I want it all. I want to change the bet to double or nothing. If I guess correctly, you are on your knees first, and then me. And if I guess incorrectly, we both get nothin', and my balls turn a whole new shade of blue."

Gabriella giggled at the face of pain Liam made. "Okay, you're on, buddy. But I swear, if you are wrong, I am heading right back to Enya's bed."

"Hm...Let's see. It could go either way. Your shirt has both colours in it, but usually, the more dominant colour wins, so I am going to wager...hm..." Liam had one eyebrow quirked and one finger tapping his gorgeous chin with its shadow of dark whiskers. He started to rub his chin, making a rasping sound.

"Oh, forever lovin' Jesus, hurry the fuck up! I'm dying here!" Gabriella huffed out.

"Wow, sounds like the pussy wants to come out and play, and she's getting a little impatient." Liam chuckled.

"Careful, her claws are going to come out in a minute. Pick already. I am counting to three, and then I am going to sleep with Enya. One...Two..."

"Bra: ivory with white lace on the side of each cup with a tiny black bow in the middle of your beautiful breasts. Thong: white cotton panel with ivory lace that wraps around those softly rounded hips and a beautiful, little black bow in the middle under your belly button. Now, not a word. On your knees, baby, and keep your eyes on me. I want you to see what you do to me."

Gabriella did as she was told and then unwrapped her present.

He thought he had won, but really, she felt like the winner.

She undid his belt, pulled his zipper down, and pulled his jeans down to just mid-thigh, in a hurry to get her prize. She yanked at his boxer briefs just enough to get his penis out. When she did, she stroked it up then down, relishing the soft texture Then she ran her tongue up from the root to the tip, swirling her tongue around the head before popping the whole head into her mouth.

Liam groaned then reminded her to keep her eyes up.

He was right. It was totally erotic and powerful to watch his reactions to what she did to him.

She went up and down, using her hands to wrap around his girth. After a few minutes, she felt him twitch before he pulled back. She moaned in frustration, having been enjoying herself.

Without a word, he lifted her up. Then, in one fluid motion, he grabbed the bottom of her shirt and pulled it over her head, throwing it on the floor. He quickly unzipped her jeans then yanked them off. Her thong soon followed.

He turned her quickly, almost toppling her, and snapped off her bra before throwing the last of her clothing to the floor. Then he pushed her face-first onto the bed, and she landed on her arms as he quickly lifted her knees so she was on all fours. He split her legs farther apart and dove his face into her centre from behind.

Gabriella groaned and threw her head back, all of her hair following, and her spine curved down. The man didn't speak many words, but Jesus Christ, he could use that damn mouth.

He licked up her juices and nipped at her clit, sending her upper body up. In less than a minute, he sent her to Heaven and back, continuing to lick and worship every inch of her.

"Please, Liam, please...I need you now," she begged after another ten minutes of unrelenting worship, rotating her hips.

She felt the vibrations of his chuckling, but she decided she would murder him after she got off again.

Liam pulled back, wiped her juices from his face, and then grabbed his dick, placing it at her entrance. He grabbed her hips and pushed right into the hot core of his woman.

In one thrust, he was balls deep, breathing deeply. This was where he was meant to be.

He pulled back painfully slow so he could feel every inch of her inner walls, and she could feel every inch of him.

"Faster, baby, please. I need it faster," Gabriella pleaded.

He accommodated her and began to thrust back and forth. It felt so good.

Gabriella leaned down, absorbing his thrusts, placing her mouth to the comforter so she could muffle her moans. He tightened his grip on her hips to the point that it hurt and she was sure she was going to be bruised tomorrow. Regardless, she knew they were doing a lot more than making love. They were making it as physical as possible to prove they were alive and the girls were alive. Liam had so much tension to release, and if her body was a conduit for that, she would welcome every bruise to prove everything was going to be okay.

"Yes, yes, right there. Yes!" she moaned into the comforter.

Liam felt the tremors of her climax, which triggered his. "Yeah, baby!" he moaned.

Gabriella collapsed on the bed, her hips still held up by Liam.

He bent down and kissed her back. "I am so sorry. I totally lost control. Baby, are you okay?"

"Mm…That was amazing. No, *you* were amazing. Thanks, mi cielo."

Chuckling, Liam pulled himself out of Gabriella and lifted her off the bed. "I have never been thanked for getting my rocks off, but really, you are totally welcome. Let's get you cleaned up then off to bed. I have to relieve Edward at five."

Chapter 25

Reaching Out

I t had been over three and half weeks since she had found out about Edward. Gabriella looked at her phone to see there were ten urgent messages. When had the sistas learned how to send urgent messages? Gabriella had owned her phone for five years, and she didn't know how to send urgent messages. Five messages were from Jocelyn and five were from Dakota. The last three messages said, *"Group Skype chat for Caesar Friday at four p.m. Canadian time, nine UK time."*

She realized the sistas had seen the pictures of Edward and her, and they were jumping to conclusions. And if she knew her friends at all, they hadn't asked her parents for fear of getting Gabriella in trouble. Liam had called her papi, though, and had prepared them, but evidently, he hadn't shared with the sistas. Well, she had one day and six hours to prepare for the inquisition, and she had a lot to do before that could take place.

Enya would wake up from her nap soon, and then Edward was going to drive them to the hospital so they could all have dinner together. That way, Enya could spend some time with her twin before the doctors attempted to take Ainsley off the meds that were keeping her in a coma. First, she had a call she had to make.

Her heart was pounding so loudly in her chest she wasn't sure if she would be able to hear his voice.

His phone rang three times before he picked up.

"Buenos días," Manny answered.

"Bueno días, Papi," Gabriella replied.

She heard him gasp and take a deep breath. She realized she should have called sooner.

"Dulce niña, is it really you? Oh, Dios, I've missed your voice. How are you? Is everything okay? I haven't heard from your man for over three weeks, and I have been out of my mind with worry. If he didn't call by tomorrow, I was going to call him. Is everything all right?"

At first, she couldn't reply. Just hearing her papi's voice made her throat close up. She suddenly wanted to crawl into his lap, have him envelope her in his arms, and make everything okay. Although, she had to admit to herself she did like that her papi had called Liam her man. She hadn't known until that moment that his approval was so important to her, but it was, and she had it.

"Papi, Liam has been…well…his—"

"Gabriella, just tell me what has happened. Do you need me to

271

come there, dulce niña?"

"No, Papi, just talk me through it. Liam's daughters and mom were in a car accident and the youngest one, Ainsley, is still in the hospital. Tonight, they are going to try to bring her out of a drug-induced coma, and Papi, I am scared," she whispered. "What if she doesn't wake up? What if Liam loses her like I lost the boys? What do I say? How do I handle it? Liam saved me, and now I need to be there for him, but I am scared, Papi, so scared. Help me."

"Oh, my sweet, sweet chica, just you being there is enough. You know there isn't anything you could say or do to change the outcome. To stand back and watch you suffer after the boys was the hardest thing I've ever had to do in my life, but there was nothing I could say that would comfort you. We all have to face our own demons. All you can do is pray and ask God for help."

Gabriella cringed.

"Just be you, sweet child. Liam and I have had many conversations, and I think you underestimate what you give him on a daily basis. All he wants or needs is you to be who you are; that is comfort enough for your man. Nobody has the right words, but when you lack words, sometimes a hug can speak volumes."

She thought on his words for a moment. "Papi, how is Mom?" Gabriella was almost afraid to ask. Deep down in her heart, she felt like she had let her mother down when she hadn't been able to take comfort from her. As a mother herself, it would have killed her if she couldn't have comforted her boys in the same situation.

Oh, my God, she thought, that is exactly what her papi had just tried to tell her. She couldn't take Liam's pain for him; she could only be there for him. Now she knew why she had needed to talk to her papi. He was the smartest man she knew.

"She misses you, Gabriella. And I'm not trying to make you feel guilty; I'm just saying it like it is. I am outside the restaurant. Do you want to say a quick hello?"

She hesitated for only a second. "Yes, please."

She heard her papi cover the phone and explain something to her mother. Then her mother came to the phone.

"Gabriella, sweetheart, how are you? I have missed you, my girl." Gabriella could hear the tears in her mother's voice.

"Hi, Mom, I'm fine." She took a deep breath, trying to stop her tears. "I'm sorry. I just needed time to find myself."

"I know, sweetheart. You don't need to apologize. I will be here when you are ready. Get strong, my bonnie, wee lass, and come home to your family."

"Thanks, Mom. I love you. May I say good-bye to Papi?"

"Of course. I love you, too, sweetheart. Oh, and by the way, your old friend Jill from the university came by yesterday. She said she lost your number. She looked so familiar, so I gave it to her. I hope that's okay?"

"No problem." *Jill? I don't remember anyone by that name*, she thought. "Bye, Mom. Love you." She heard her mother pass the phone back to her father. "Papi? I have to go now. We are leaving

273

for the hospital soon. I love you, and thanks for the advice."

"Adios, dulce niña. Te quiero. I am going to the church after I hang up to say a prayer for Liam's daughter and for him. I will, as always, pray for you, too, mi amor."

After she hung up, she felt a sense of peace come over her. She had been blessed with the best parents in the world, and she really did miss them and needed to see them soon.

Just then, Edward walked into the kitchen. "Mm...Something smells delicious. Can I have a taste just to hold me off until we get to the hospital?"

Gabriella didn't answer. She just walked up to him and encased herself in his arms and placed her head on his chest. He reciprocated, wrapping his arms around her.

"What happened? Are you okay?"

"Yes. I just spoke to my parents, and I need the hug my papi would have given me if he were here."

"That, I can do, love. And, if you need it, I can give you the love Liam would give if he were here."

Gabriella smacked his chest and giggled. "Are you ever serious? Actually, on that note, I meant to tell you, when you were handling all the logistics at the hospital, I saw a totally different side to you. I saw Prince Edward for the first time since I met you, and you know what? He's not such a bad guy. He doesn't sound or act like my Edward, but I wouldn't throw him to the curb."

"Well, I am sure my grandfather would be proud to hear you

wouldn't throw me to the curb," he said on a chuckle. "Now, can I have a taste of that lasagna? I'm starving."

"Sorry, but that's a big fat no. If I cut it before it cools, all the liquid will drain out. But, because I love you and knew you would come scrounging for scraps, I saved the leftover noodles and sauce for you. They are on the stove."

"Christ, Gabriella, have I told you today that I love you and you are the perfect woman?"

"Be careful with that word perfect. Although, flattery will usually get you everything with me. Now, when you are done, wake up Enya so we can head to the hospital. I want Liam to have a warm supper, and I want Enya to spend time with her sister."

"No problem. Oh, Liam's sister Megan flew in today. She was at Margaret's when I went to visit. She is going to meet us at the hospital. She wants to see Liam and Ainsley, and then she is going to take Enya to Margaret's so I can be there for Liam after they stop the meds."

"Is there anything I need to know? I get the feeling something is up with Liam and his sister."

"There has been tension between them ever since Raven passed. Megan and Raven were good friends, and Megan thought she should raise the girls instead of Margaret."

That made Gabriella's spine tighten and straighten. "Wow, that was a little presumptuous of her, don't you think? I mean, Liam is their father."

"She didn't suggest it out of malice. She was really just trying to do what she thought was best for all concerned, but she underestimated Liam's devotion to the girls and her mother's abilities to help them stay with their dad."

"Well, I won't judge her if that is what you believe, but I warn you now, I won't stand for anyone disrespecting Liam."

"She-devil, I have seen your fangs, and I don't want to see them again, but I don't believe it will be an issue. When we get there, if you don't mind, could you take Enya to the gift shop and buy something for Ainsley? That will give me an opportunity to talk to Liam about Megan before Enya comes in the room."

"Wow, you really are a sweetheart. I am so finding you a chica I approve of." Gabriella lifted up on her tip-toes to kiss Edward's cheek. She finished with, "I love you, my friend."

**

"Enya, do you see something you would like to buy Ainsley?"

"I don't want to get her a stuffed animal, because Uncle Edward gave her a bear like mine. How about this? It is Anna and Elsa. They are sisters, too. We can play with them together. What do you think?"

Enya was excited over her upcoming purchase, so Gabriella assumed it was perfect. This was the first time Gabriella had ever had to think about purchasing a gift for a girl. She knew she would come out with the perfect gift if she were shopping for a boy, whether it was a truck, building blocks, or water guns—her favourite. She guessed most boy toys could also be purchased for a girl, though. She thought it would be fun to have a water gun fight with Liam and the girls. She would have to remember to buy them when Ainsley came home and the girls were healed.

Gabriella was so lost in thought she jumped when her phone beeped, and a text message came through from an unknown caller.

Hi, this is Jill. I really need to talk to you. Please reply.

Gabriella racked her brain, trying again to remember who Jill was. How could she have forgotten someone she had gone to school with? She would ask the sistas tomorrow. Mom had said she recognized her, so it had to be someone who had come to the restaurant with her back in the day.

"Gabriella, do you like the dollies?" Enya very patiently waited for an answer.

"I do. I think they are perfect, hermosa." Gabriella smiled down at the beautiful, blue-eyed girl.

She had enjoyed helping Enya get ready this morning. She had put the tiny little girl's hair in two pigtails with white flowers attached to the elastic then found the most adorable blue sundress with white daisies to match. Honestly, it was like having a real live doll to dress.

They made their purchase then headed up to Ainsley's room. As soon as Enya saw her daddy, she went running and flew into his arms.

"Daddy! How is Ainsley? Is she awake? Look at what me and

277

Gabriella bought her! We brought lasagna for dinner. I helped make the salad. I hope you like the salad."

"Whoa! Slow down, princess. I can't answer all your questions if you fire too many at once," Liam said as he carried his oldest while he walked towards Gabriella.

He hugged Gabriella to his side then kissed her lips. Then he steered them all towards Ainsley's bed.

"Daddy, answer me," Enya whined.

Gabriella was shocked that it didn't even faze Enya that her dad had just kissed her.

Enya wiggled out of Liam's arms so she could see if her sister was awake to give her the present she had bought. Long forgotten were all the questions she had asked.

Liam turned to Gabriella. "I missed you, angel. Dinner smells amazing. How was your day?"

Gabriella glanced over at Edward. "I guess Edward has already told you that I called my papi today. I even talked to my mom."

"Yeah, he did. Are you okay? I could have called your papi if you needed."

Gabriella felt treasured when Liam offered to do things she was uncomfortable doing, but it was time she took some burdens away from him.

"I called Papi so he could guide me on how to help you. He told me he was going to church after we hung up so he could say a prayer for Ainsley and you. I need to get stronger so I can take some of the pressures off you."

Liam was shocked. Did she not see how much she gave him?

"Angel, look at my daughter. She didn't get dressed like that by herself, and I know for a fact Edward isn't capable of matching that outfit. Smell the room. What other patient or patient's family gets home-cooked meals? I don't know any other man who has his girlfriend taking shifts at the hospital to sit with his sick daughter and, when she isn't here, taking care of his other daughter and mother. Angel, I couldn't do this if it weren't for you and Edward. Thank you, sweetheart." Liam kissed her more deeply this time, trying to reassure her that she had taken a good percentage of his burdens.

"Ahem, keep it G-rated. There are ankle-biters in the room," Edward reminded them.

Gabriella laughed, and then Enya called her father over to show him what she and Gabriella had purchased for Ainsley.

Just then, Gabriella's phone beeped again. Pulling it out of her purse, she read the message.

Please, Gabriella, it is very important. I need to talk to you. Jill.

Wow, she hadn't spoken to this person in years, and now, all of a sudden, it was do or die. Gabriella was annoyed, so she fired back, *At hospital. I will return your text tomorrow.*

Not thirty seconds later, a response came through.

Sorry, I didn't know. Hope everything is okay. I will await your response tomorrow. Jill.

279

Gabriella put the phone away after explaining to Liam that an old friend was trying to contact her. Then the unconventional family sat together like they had done every day since Enya had gone home.

About fifteen minutes after they'd had dinner, Liam's sister came in. Gabriella tensed, not knowing what to expect. However, all of the tension melted away when Liam walked up to his sister without a word and wrapped her in his arms. Megan cried as he gently consoled her, and Gabriella realized forgiveness was an incredibly powerful thing.

"Megan, I would like you to meet a very special woman, my girlfriend, Gabriella Dante. Angel, this is my sister Megan Duncan."

Gabriella shook Megan's hand.

"So you are the miracle worker I have heard so much about," Megan said.

Gabriella blushed. "I'm not sure whom you have been talking to, but I am not a miracle worker. It's nice to meet you, Megan."

"Likewise. It was my mum and Edward here who have been singin' yer praises." Megan's Scottish accent was as thick as Margaret's, and Gabriella had to listen carefully.

"Well, I am honoured that your mother spoke highly of me, but anything Edward says shouldn't be believed."

The room erupted in laughter.

"Aye, so you ken Edward well, I see." Megan laughed back.

"In the room, people, in the room," Edward remarked.

"Megan, are you sure you don't mind taking Enya to Margaret's

280

until one of us can get her?" Gabriella asked.

"Of course I don't. But I have a better suggestion," Megan said. "Why don't I take her to Mum's for a visit, and then I can take her to Liam's place, bathe her, and get her in bed while you all stay here with Ainsley? Although, I would like to spend a few minutes with Ainsley first."

"I would appreciate that, Megs," Liam responded. "I am not sure how long this is going to take. We might not be back tonight, though."

"No problem. Take as long as you need. And, Gabriella, don't worry about cookin'. I'll take care of dinner tomorrow. By the way, thank you for all the food you have been cookin' for Mum. I shared some of the lasagna ye sent her today, and it was amazin'."

"No, no, no," Edward jumped in before Gabriella could respond. "I will make sure Gabriella gets home in plenty of time to cook dinner. I have had your cooking, Megan. No offence."

"That was rude!" Gabriella remarked. "You owe Megan an apology, or this lasagna will be the last meal I cook for you."

"Ha-ha. You got in trouble again, Uncle Edward! You better say sorry to Auntie Megs." Enya giggled, pointing her finger at Edward.

"Megan, you know I love you, and I would never want to hurt your feelings, but I am just going to say…You've tasted her food," Edward responded, not quick enough to learn his lesson.

"Aye, Edward, I have, but I will be cookin' tomorrow, and ye will be eaten' it, you bloody fool. Ye better pray I don't poison ye

281

after that smart-ass comment."

A knock came on the door before a doctor walked in. "Good evening, everyone. I just wanted to let you know that the neurologist just verified that the EKG readings are normal, and we will be removing the IV in the next few minutes."

The smile on Liam's face fell and was replaced by a worried glance at his youngest daughter.

Edward stood. "Okay, ankle-biter, be a good girl and say good-bye to your sister. Then Auntie Megs is going to take you to Nana's house for a visit. But first, come and give your uncle Edward a big, wet kiss."

Enya flew into Edward's outstretched arms and smothered him with hundreds of little kisses while he tickled her, conscious of her stitches. Then she went to say good-bye to Ainsley, her daddy, and Gabriella. She then took her aunt's hand after Megan had a few moments with Ainsley.

Just before she walked out the door, she turned to her father. "Daddy, I dreamed of Mummy last night, and she looked like the picture in my room. She promised me Ainsley is going to be fine."

The room was so quiet you could have heard a pin drop. The only sound was the blood pressure machine.

Liam walked over to his daughter and bent down on one knee so he was eye-level with her. He took her little hands in his and said, "That's good to know, princess, because if Mummy told you, then it must be true. Thank you for sharing. I love you, baby."

He hugged her so tightly she said, "Daddy, I can't breathe."

Liam released his hold, kissed her cheek, and then patted her head. Then he watched her walk away with her aunt.

Gabriella walked to Liam. "You see, my saviour? There are so many forces at play here. She has to be fine." She hugged him, knowing she wasn't going to get a response. He was too consumed by emotion.

The doctors and Mr. Booth entered the room and went to Ainsley's bedside.

Liam held Ainsley's hand and kissed her forehead. "I love you, wee princess. Come back to Daddy."

The IV was removed, and the group stood vigil for over an hour and a half before any sign was detected, which the doctors reassured was normal. If it hadn't been for Edward, the doctor and the director wouldn't have been standing with them, waiting to see if the little girl woke up.

Finally, Ainsley moaned and started to move.

"Wee princess, Daddy is here. Come on, baby. Fight it…Come back to me."

Ainsley started to cry, and in the weakest, little voice said, "Daddy."

"I'm here, baby girl…Daddy's here," Liam told her, tears running down his face as he kissed her little face.

Gabriella turned to Edward and hugged him as tears ran down both their faces. They had gotten the miracle Raven had promised

Enya.

Chapter 26

My Ship Has Sailed

When Edward arrived at six that morning, it killed him to see the pain the little ankle-biter was in, and it was apparent the couple hadn't slept a wink since he had left them the night before.

The doctors weren't kidding when they had said Ainsley would be pain, which kind of surprised them because her stitches from all of her surgeries were healing nicely. But, due to the inactivity of her body, her muscles were sore and cramped up. Ainsley would wake up screaming, and Liam and Gabriella would take turns massaging her muscles. Ainsley's ribs also caused her a lot of pain. That they could do nothing about, except to shuffle her little body into different positions to take some of the pressure off. Edward immediately hired a physiotherapist to help work Ainsley's muscles.

"I will stay with the little beauty; you two go home and get some sleep. I don't want to see either of you until dinner tonight."

Gabriella and Liam went home and were fast asleep soon after. They slept until after one when Liam woke Gabriella as he kissed his way down her body. It might have started out gentle, but much like the last time when he needed reassurance, it turned rough and hard. The bruises that had just faded were now back. This time around, though, it really was more satisfying.

Liam showered and told Gabriella that he was going to the Royal Air Force station, Leicester East, to touch base with his team and to find out what was going on with the media circus they had left behind.

It was four o'clock when Gabriella walked into the shower. It was the first time she had been alone in a long time, and it felt strange. The house was so quiet until she heard her phone beep with a message.

She hurried to it in case Edward was texting from the hospital or Liam needed something.

I hope everything is okay, and I don't want to bug you, but when can I call? Jill.

Gabriella felt guilty after the rude text she had sent her yesterday, so she figured now was probably the best time to catch up and solve the mystery of whom her forgotten friend was. She texted back to call now.

While Gabriella waited, she dressed and brushed her hair. Just as she buttoned up her pants, her phone rang.

"Hello," Gabriella answered.

No response.

"Hello?" Gabriella pulled the phone away and glanced at it to make sure the connection was still there. It was. That was strange. "Hello?" she tried again.

"Gabriella, hi, this is Jill."

"Hi, Jill. Listen, I have to apologize right off the bat. I have been going through some things, and I was very rude yesterday. I'm sorry, but I don't recognize your name. Will you help refresh my memory?" Gabriella hoped she hadn't offended the woman.

"Actually, you don't know me. We have never met. But please don't hang up until you hear me out."

Gabriella's heart started to pound. She wished one of the guys were with her now. Why did this woman want to talk to her? Was she a reporter or one of those stalkers Edward had warned her about? Fuck, she was supposed to be more diligent.

"Gabriella, please, my name is Gillian Wainwright, Edward's ex-fiancée. Please, I need to talk to you. I know you two are dating; I saw your pictures in the paper. I'm sure you must know about me. If I could just have a minute of your time."

Gabriella's entire disposition changed from fear to anger. Who did this bitch think she was, going to her parents' restaurant and lying to them to acquire her private number? Edward had told her Gillian was calculating and heartless. Gabriella wasn't going to allow this bitch to manipulate her. She had met her match.

"Why should I even give you a second of my time after all the

287

hurt you caused Edward?" Gabriella was furious. If this woman wasn't smart enough to take the hint, Gabriella was going to unleash the hounds of Hell on her.

"You don't understand...No one understands. Please, just hear me out for a minute, and then you never, ever have to hear my voice again," Gillian said in an exasperated tone, knowing her chances were slim that Edward's new girlfriend would hear her out.

Gillian had been devastated when she had seen the pictures of Gabriella and Edward. She had been replaced by this gorgeous, petite, dark-haired beauty—the total opposite of herself.

She had hired a private investigating team to research Gabriella and her past. After learning about her, Gillian knew she was only a brief blip on the radar in Edward's memory. Edward loved to rescue people, and by the sound of it, Gabriella was due some rescuing.

This was her chance to see that Edward got some happiness in his life. If it couldn't be with her, then she really hoped it would be with Gabriella. She had to take the chance to try to save her from the same fate that had befallen Gillian.

"I will give you one minute to explain what you want and not another minute more, starting now," Gabriella stated firmly.

"Okay, okay. Listen carefully, Gabriella. I didn't do the things I am accused of." Gillian stopped for a second when she heard Gabriella snort with disbelief. "I know you lost your family, so you have to believe when I say I swear on my brother's grave I am not lying to you. I didn't do what everyone accused me of, but that isn't

288

why I called. My repeated defense of my innocence has fallen on deaf ears for almost a year, so I don't expect anything different from you. Still, I need to warn you."

"Warn me? Warn me about what and why?" Gabriella asked, fearful of the answer.

"Somebody set me up to get me out of Edward's life. I love Edward with everything that I am, and I would never hurt him. But someone wanted him free of me."

"Why would someone do that to you both? How am I to believe you? Why didn't you go to Edward yourself with these accusations?"

"Oh, Gabriella, don't kid yourself. I did everything within my power and my families' to try to reach Edward and convince him of the truth. If you haven't realized already, the royal family is very powerful, and if they don't want you to have any connection, then quite simply, you don't."

"Are you saying someone in Edward's family did this—embarrassed him and you with a sex tape—just to get rid of you? Really? Listen to yourself, Gillian; that sounds crazy. And I think I am crazy for listening to you."

"I think you understand better than anyone how easy it is to be framed for something you didn't do; am I right? You *do* understand." Gillian knew this was the pivotal moment.

Gabriella felt like she had been punched in the stomach. She did know exactly what it felt like to be accused of something. She had lived it with Marco, day in and day out. She knew how it felt to have acquaintances, coworkers, and so-called friends comment on your guilt or innocence. God help her, but there were people who still chose to believe the worst, even after Marco had been cleared. Yes, she knew those god-awful feelings.

Could Gillian be telling the truth, and if so, why was she telling Gabriella?

"I don't know what to say or believe, and I am still unclear as to why you are telling *me* this," Gabriella said.

"My ship has sailed. Edward will never believe I didn't betray him, but maybe I can save you from my fate and save Edward from more heartbreak. You should know by now what a great person he is. He has a big heart and a lot of love to give. He is the most remarkable man I have ever met.

"Someone is trying their best to control Edward's life and whom they see fit to allow in it. I know your history, and I am sure that isn't what they want for Edward, so protect yourself and Edward. Don't trust a soul. That being said, love him, Gabriella. He deserves to be cherished and loved. I wish you no malice; I just want Edward to be happy, and I hope you make him happy. Please, I beg you not to hurt him. If you care for him and treat him right, he will give you the stars and the moon.

"Thank you for giving me the time to warn you. I wish you a life of happiness together. Good-bye, Gabriella."

Before Gabriella could respond, Gillian hung up.

Wow. Just...wow. Could that be true, or was it just another way for Gillian to hurt Edward? She had been trying to warn Gabriella, though.

The wheels in Gabriella's mind worked overtime. She did know how it felt to be wrongfully accused. Could Gillian have been? How very sad for Edward if that were true. The man had been in love with her. Could they have been wronged? Could Edward have been manipulated to believe Gillian had betrayed him?

Gabriella had heard all the conspiracy theories and controversy surrounding the death of Edward's mother. If Gillian were right, though, then Edward needed to know. If Gillian hadn't betrayed him, he deserved the chance at the happiness he so desperately deserved.

She was going to talk to Liam and ask for his confidence. They needed to find out if Gillian really was telling the truth, and they needed to do it without Edward knowing.

***

Gillian hung up the phone with a heart-wrenching sob. That phone call had been the hardest one she had ever had to make. She curled into a ball on her bed and wept for hours. Her phone rang repeatedly, but she chose to ignore it.

How did you recover when your soul knew that its mate was with someone else? If she died tomorrow, she would at least go with a clear conscience. She had tried to protect the person she loved most in the world.

Scattered all over the bed were the pictures the press had taken

291

of Gabriella and Edward. She had also acquired pictures of Edward shielding Gabriella from the press at pubs and pictures of Gabriella wrapped in Edward's arms in the back of an SUV with Liam driving. She didn't have to look at them anymore; she knew every detail of every picture. They were seared into her brain. She was one of few people who knew that look of love and protection in Edward's eyes.

It was final now. Edward had moved on. But how did she? Did she want to move on? Nope. She needed to let her heart bleed. Why stop now?

For the past year, she had been punishing herself for a crime she hadn't committed. She knew why Edward believed it was her who had made the sex tape. One wrong joke had sealed her fate. It had left a tickle in the back of Edward's mind, and because of it, she had been crucified. Damn! Why had she joked around so much back then?

As a typical Hollywood brat, everyone in the world expected her to fall into the same pattern as her mother. She had been blessed with the fairy tale childhood then had it all snatched away in her young adult life, leaving her with nothing and no one.

Stephanie Wainwright had been the gossip rags' number one headliner. After she had successfully pushed Gillian's father away, after years of accusing him of affairs then the death of their son, she had turned to the bottle, and she continued to make a spectacle of the family every chance she got.

Her dad was still Hollywood's most sought-after actor who had just recently married a girl three years younger than Gillian. Her father wanted another son, and it looked like now he was going to get it—the second coming would arrive in two short months.

Damn, she had run out of vodka. She was going to have to walk to the liquor store and stock up. It was going to take more than one forty-pounder to make the pain of Edward and Gabriella go away. Karma was a bitch.

She had sat down to check her wallet for cash when the photo booth shots of her and Edward fell to the floor. As she bent down to pick them up, she leaned too far forwards and fell onto her hands and knees. She tried desperately to pick them up, but her hand-eye coordination was off.

She leaned her forehead down to the ground, while she screamed and cried.

God, she was totally pathetic. No wonder Edward didn't want anything to do with her. He was much better off with Gabriella.

Thankfully, she passed out on the floor and was able to sleep it off, waking up the next morning with the worst hangover of her life. That was saying a lot since she had turned to the bottle for a while after Edward had broken up with her.

While lying on the floor, staring up at the ceiling, she remembered the day she had looked in the mirror and seen a younger version of her mother. She had quickly dumped all of the booze out and decided to become a woman Edward would have been proud of. After months of trying to find a way to get to Edward, she had finally given up and turned to charity work as an escape.

Getting up off the floor, she tried to push her hair off her face, but it was stuck there.

She stumbled into the bathroom and looked into the mirror. There, once again, was Mommy dearest staring back at her.

"Okay, regroup, girlfriend," she said to the frightful mess of a woman staring back at her. "This is the first day of the rest of your life." How many first days had she given herself in the last year? "It doesn't matter. As long as I keep doing it, that's the important thing, right?"

Still talking to the mirror, she continued, "You survived the conversation with Edward's new girlfriend. You did what was right. Now you have to pull yourself together and become a woman Edward would be proud of. No, you need to become a woman *you* can be proud of."

She brushed her teeth then jumped into the shower. Yup, today was the first day of the rest of her life, so she had better get to it and purchase a dress for the charity function she had later this week. Then she was off to Nepal for two months, building homes with Habitat for Humanity.

If she couldn't save herself, maybe she could save someone else.

Chapter 27

Word in Edgewise

At the hospital that afternoon, Gabriella asked Edward to have a coffee with her in the waiting room. When they had settled in, she had to take a minute to try to remember everything she had rehearsed.

"Edward, I'm going to ask you a question, and I want your honest answer. I don't want you to be uncomfortable with anything you decide. Can you do this for me?"

"You never have to ask. Of course I will have sex with you and teach you how to scream," Edward responded on a laugh.

Gabriella went to punch him and, instead, knocked over his coffee, which landed in her lap.

"Shit! That's hot!" Gabriella jumped up and tried to wipe the hot coffee from her white pants.

Edward jumped up, too, and quickly went to grab a towel.

"Oh, love, I'm sorry. I didn't mean for you to get hurt. Whip off those pants, and I will rinse them out."

Punching him in the shoulder, she said, "Seriously? Do you ever stop?"

His smile dropped. "All joking aside, what can I do for you? You're not burned, are you?"

"No, I'm good," Gabriella said as she grabbed his hand and sat down again. "It's Caesar Friday," she reminded him, "and it's going to be like the Spanish Inquisition. The sistas saw the pictures of us, and they want the scoop. They will be relentless, but if you don't want me to speak to them about you, I totally get that and will respect your decision. I know they will respect my confidence. So, are you okay with that?"

He was completely overcome by emotion and couldn't speak for a moment. Edward's mind was in overdrive. It was the first time in his life someone had respected him enough to ask his permission about discussing his private life. Why, oh, why didn't she have an identical twin?

Gabriella mistook his hesitation for anger and disappointment. "Forget it, okay? I never should have asked. Please don't be upset with me. I didn't mean to offend you. It's just...they're my—"

"Stop. Let me get a word in edgewise, please."

Uh-oh. Gabriella had heard that tone before. She had been taken off-guard when he had yelled at her last time. She braced herself for his rant and tried to mentally prepare herself not to take it personally.

"Sorry. Go ahead."

"Stop looking at me like that. We are not having a repeat performance of the beach. You just took me by surprise, but not for the reasons you think."

"Edward—"

"No, let me finish. You are the first person to ever ask me if they could talk about me and my personal life. Do you know how that makes me feel? Don't look at me like you are going to cry right now. I'm a big boy and have learned to accept my life." He took a deep breath. "I give you permission to discuss anything you want with anyone. I trust you and believe in you."

Shaking his head, he continued, "You believe I helped to save you, and yes, maybe I did, but you also saved me. You restored my faith in the relationships I choose to have. You gave me back the real me, and let me tell you, I haven't seen the real me in a very long time. Now, come here so I can wipe all those tears away and hug the woman I respect most in the world."

Gabriella walked into his arms and totally fell apart.

"What the fuck did you say to her?" Liam bellowed, taking a sobbing Gabriella out of Edward's arms.

Edward laughed while Gabriella blurted out in Edward's defense, "It's not his fault. I'm just over-emotional as usual. He just made me so happy."

Liam knew what Gabriella had wanted to talk to Edward about, and he knew she had been nervous. He had already tried to reassure her that Edward would have no problem with it.

"Edward is going to stay with Ainsley and the cute—Edward's words, not mine—physiotherapist. I'm going to drop you off at the house so you can have your Caesar Friday in peace, and then I am going to meet up with Camden to touch base about the girls. I might be late, so don't wait up, okay, angel?" Liam moved Gabriella's hair behind her ears when she continued to cry. He was forever touching her hair. It seemed to soothe them both.

"Now, before you go, she-devil, remember to tell the sistas I am single and love Canadian cougars."

***

In four minutes, she would be getting the fifth degree from Jocelyn and Dakota, and then spilling her guts about Edward. Was she ready? She had guzzled one Caesar already and was on her second, trying to consume some liquid courage.

She had emailed Jocelyn and Dakota, asking them if they minded cancelling the group chat and making it private between the three of them. She was going to be revealing some very personal information about Edward, herself, and Liam, so she needed to keep it to her closest friends.

The computer beeped that there was a call coming in, and her heartrate sped up.

"Hey, Geisha, Pocahontas, how are my sistas? Everything well? I miss you girls so much. By the way, Happy Caesar Friday!" she started with a smile, knowing she was overcompensating, but she also knew she wasn't going to get another word in for the next fifteen minutes.

"What the fuck! Don't even try that shit with us. Sistas, my ass!" Jocelyn fired back.

"What?" Gabriella panicked and went with playing dumb.

"Really, Mingo? The innocent act might work with knock-your-socks-off, hot Liam, and of course, let's not forget Prince Edward of fucking England! but it won't work with us! Cut the shit and let's get to the meat and potatoes. Why the hell are there pictures of you and Prince Edward splattered all over the papers, saying you two are involved? We thought you were involved with hot Liam?" Jocelyn stated.

"Well, you see—"

"There are freaking pictures of you kissing Prince Edward of fucking England! How the hell does that happen? And again, what happened to hot Liam?" Dakota fired off.

Before she could answer, Jocelyn jumped back in. "What are your parents going to think? How the hell did you hook up with one of the princes of fucking England? Please tell me that isn't *the* Edward you were trying to introduce us to. Really? You could have said, 'I'd like you to meet Prince Edward,' and we would have waited until he came back from wherever it was he went. I mean, really? A prince of fucking England for Christ's sake? What the fuck?"

"I just want to say, you all accuse *me* of swearing a lot. I think I might be the tamest of the group," Gabriella very calmly replied.

"Are you fucking kidding us! Of all the things we just said, all you take from that is we *swear* a lot? Well, isn't *that* the pot calling the kettle black?" Dakota fired back.

"I have been getting thousands of calls from friends and acquaintances who are curious if you are the mystery woman in the papers. I scoff and say, 'Really, do you think Gabriella Dante would be dating a prince of England? It has to be her doppelganger'," Jocelyn informed her.

Gabriella settled back and enjoyed her Caesar as the girls continued for another ten minutes.

"Are you paying attention?" Jocelyn snapped.

"I can't get a word in! When you two are finished with your rants, let me know," Gabriella responded as she lifted her feet onto the desk and crossed her left ankle over her right, taking a big sip of her yummy Caesar.

"Sorry," Dakota started. "You're right; that was incredibly rude. So, are you really dating the prince? And what happened with hot Liam?"

"Yeah, sorry for not letting you answer, but it has been crazy around here," Jocelyn said calmly.

"First off, when I was going to introduce you to Edward, I didn't know he was a prince of fucking England, as you so eloquently like to put it. Edward is a sweetheart, and I love him with all of my heart. He is as close a friend as you two, but I am not dating him. I'm still dating Liam, and I am so telling him you guys called him hot. I didn't think I could ever love another man after Marco, but I do. I really and truly love him."

After finally closing her mouth from the shock of hearing Gabriella say she was in love, Dakota asked, "Does that tall drink of water have a twin?"

Giggling, Gabriella answered, "Yup, he totally does. He has two! They have jet black hair, the bluest of blue eyes, and are the cutest people you have ever seen."

"I so want one," Jocelyn declared.

"Me, too!"

"Well, that could be a problem because they are sort of attached to their father, and I am sure he doesn't want to separate his daughters." She winked at the girls' surprised faces.

"Oh, my God, he has twin daughters? How old are they? And what do they think of you? What's their mother like?" Jocelyn asked.

Gabriella spent the next two hours telling them all about the twins' accident, shared about Raven, and talked about everything they had done in Scotland. Gabriella was exhausted by the time she started to tell them about the pictures of herself and Edward. Then she explained about finding out about the prince. She informed them that she would never, ever think of him as the world's Prince Edward.

Gabriella was giggling away with her girls when Liam walked into his office and saw her with her feet propped up on his desk. He

301

came up behind her chair and wrapped his arms around her. Then he bent down and kissed Gabriella on her cheek.

"Hey, how's my girl? I love to walk into a room and hear you laughing." Liam turned his face to the computer screen. "Hey, ladies, thanks for making my girl laugh. How goes it?"

"Oh, my, I am suddenly very thirsty," Dakota breathed out.

Jocelyn smacked Dakota's shoulder and burst out laughing, as did Gabriella. Liam quirked his eyebrows at their antics and looked from one woman to the next, knowing he was missing something.

After that wonderful belly laugh, Gabriella continued right along by telling the women some more things that had happened with the twins.

To the astonishment of the two women on the computer screen, Liam lifted Gabriella up and sat himself down in the chair, placing her on his lap. He cuddled her close as she continued her conversation with them, never missing a beat.

"Uh, hello? Mingo, you do realize hot Liam just repositioned you, right? And now we don't have an effing clue what you just said." Jocelyn laughed.

"On that note, I guess this conversation is officially over. To be honest, I am totally exhausted." She stifled a yawn. "Girls, I can't thank you enough for listening to me and for all the advice. I love you two. Say hi and give hugs and kisses to the rest of the girls."

"Girlfriend, we are thrilled to see you happy again. And, hot Liam, we have you to thank for that. Take care of our Mingo and remember we want to meet Edward at the next Caesar Friday, 'kay, Gab?" Jocelyn questioned.

"Love you, Gabriella. Talk to you soon. Bye, hot Liam. I hope your twins continue to get stronger. I don't know if Gabriella told you, but I am an identical twin, as well," Dakota said then blew a kiss to both of them.

"So I have been told, and I understand that I have another twenty-five years of hell in front of me by the stories Gabriella shared," Liam responded.

"You bet your life, so keep those bodyguard skills sharpened, because those two beauties are going to test you every opportunity they get. Watch them closely and learn their body language for when they tell a lie. It will become your most valuable tool. They know what the other one is thinking and will outsmart you every time." Dakota laughed.

"Thanks for the advice. I think, if I have to interrogate the twins, I want you to sit in on it," Liam finished with a wink.

They all laughed.

"Bye, sistas." Gabriella blew kisses as she disconnected. Then she turned her head to look at Liam. "God, I love them."

"I can tell they feel the same about you, sweetheart. How did they take the news about Edward?"

"They're pretty sure that, if I wrote my life story, no one would believe it." Gabriella chuckled then asked, "How did it go with Camden?"

"He has a friend whose brother-in-law owns an investigation/security company and will take on the assignment. You are sure about this, right, angel?"

"Liam, I would bet my soul that Gillian is telling the truth. I have never felt so strongly about anything in my life. She didn't make or sell that tape. She was warning me to help save Edward more heartache. I know she still loves him; I could hear it in her voice. It was killing her, because she really believes Edward has moved on with me."

"Why call you, then? Why not let someone break up the relationship? If you weren't a couple, then maybe she would have a chance to get back with him."

"I've thought a lot about this. She went to great lengths to get in touch with me. She travelled to Toronto to get my number from my parents. She told me she went crazy from trying to reach Edward when the accusations were made. Who handled that? Was it the team you work with? I'm not even sure where we start."

"Listen to me right now. You are, as of this minute, not involved with this investigation, understand me? I am doing this for you and Edward. This is extremely delicate, so I don't want you to mention it to anyone. I will keep you informed as much I can, but you are never to discuss this outside of this home. I need you to understand me fully and assure me that you understand what I am telling you."

"Liam, you're scaring me. Should I be afraid? Do you think someone will hurt us for inquiring about Gillian and Edward's breakup? Now I am freaked right out! What if I just opened a can of worms, and someone gets hurt because of me? My savior, I won't survive losing you, too." She choked on her last three words, overwhelming emotion in her voice.

Liam hugged her close and nestled his lips into her shoulder. "I won't allow anything to happen to you or me."

"I would never forgive myself if anyone got hurt because of me. I just want Edward to be as happy as we are. We all have our crosses to bear, but Edward has a good heart and deserves to be happy and in love. The man is going to make an incredible papi to some lucky children one day, provided he can fall in love again."

"While we are on the topic of children, I need to ask you something."

"Go ahead."

"Angel, you have been instrumental in the recovery of the twins. I couldn't have done it without you. I don't know how I am ever going to repay everything you have done. I am head over heels in love with you, and the girls are growing to love you just as much…but I want more. I want you to move in with us. I have never even asked if you wanted to be a part of the girls' lives, but I believe they would be lucky to have you. I don't want to rush you. I get that you might need time to think about it, and I respect if you can't do it."

"Liam, I—"

"I can't live without you," Liam interrupted. "I am so afraid that you won't want to be with the girls, and I get that since you lost your boys. But, baby, they are good girls. They won't cause you any problems. It's just—"

"Liam!" Gabriella turned and straddled him. "This is the second time today someone has asked me questions then rambled on for ten minutes, insinuating they know what I'm thinking. Stop. Let me get a word in, and I will tell you. And stop looking at me like I just stole your puppy!"

Gabriella took his face into her hands and dragged her thumbnails over his jawline against the bristle of his whiskers. She kissed his lips gently then said, "I am already living with you and the girls, but I'm not ready to move all my things from Toronto or sell my house…yet. I need time to see if this works. *You* need time to see if this works. Most importantly, we need to see if the girls are comfortable with this arrangement. They have gone through so much in their young lives and especially this last month. Let's take it one day a time. Let's not label it. Let's not force it. If it is meant to be, then let it happen naturally. I love you, my saviour, and I know you love me; that's enough for this moment."

Chapter 28

Direct Hit

Today was the day they were bringing Ainsley home from the hospital. Gabriella awoke before Liam and Edward went for their run. She was planning a very special meal for their first "official" dinner at home. She struggled with saying a "family" dinner, wanting to give Ainsley the same opportunity to get used to her in her environment as Enya had.

She had spent a lot of time at the hospital with Ainsley and had fallen in love with her. Gabriella just wanted Ainsley to come home and not feel like Gabriella had invaded it.

Liam popped into the kitchen to give Gabriella a quick kiss and to tell her they were leaving for their run. After he left, she returned to the sauce she was making for spaghetti and thought about how much she loved cooking, especially when she had a lot on her mind. It was therapeutic.

Gabriella was just dropping in the last four meatballs when the guys came in from their run. Her hips were grooving to "Angelina & Zooma Zooma" by Louis Prima when Liam came up behind her and scared the crap out of her. She jumped as he moved her ponytail to one side and kissed her neck, giving Gabriella shivers. He was freezing, since it was cold outside. A shudder moved down her spine, and she dropped the last meatball.

Edward bent down to pick up the meatball she had dropped at Liam surprising her as he jokingly said, "Brilliant, old man, that's one less meatball for you tonight. By the way, Gabriella, just so you know, you can smell that sauce five houses down, and it smells absolutely heavenly. I think we are going to have to send Mr. Miller a plate; he stopped Liam to find out what you were cooking tonight and said he was drooling from the smell. Mr. Miller wanted to know if your mum was single."

Gabriella giggled as Liam asked, "How's my beautiful girl today?" He was still nuzzling her neck and speaking into her ear. "That smells out of this world. I think Edward and I should have run an extra half-hour this morning. I am *so* overeating tonight." Liam took a deep breath while copping a feel of Gabriella's breast as he slipped a hand inside her robe and tweaked a nipple. He figured they were safe since their backs were to Edward.

"Get your hand off her chest while I'm in the room! I saw her jump. Gabriella, is that proper kitchen etiquette?"

"Nothing gets me going more than seeing my girl dancing in her underwear while making a fabulous meal at six in the morning."

Liam ended his statement with a hard smack to her ass as he turned to walk away.

"Ouch, you bastard, and I'm not in my underwear."

Although cheeky, his words had brought a smile to her face. She liked to make him happy, and if cooking in his kitchen at six in the morning while wearing her nightie made him happy, then so be it. However, he wasn't getting away with smacking her.

She whipped the tea-towel off her shoulder, wound it up, and unleashed it towards his ass. It snapped as it made direct contact.

Liam jumped then spun around with a shocked face. "Damn! That hurt!" He rubbed his stinging ass cheek.

Gabriella laughed at his shocked expression, but it changed quickly, and she knew by the look on his face that she was in deep shit.

She wound the tea-towel back up as she ran towards Edward. "Help me, Edward!" she cried as she tried to hide behind his back.

"Sorry, love, I'm not getting in the middle of you two. You're on your own," he told her as Liam took three steps to reach them.

"Arsehole!" That was her new favourite word since arriving in Scotland.

Gabriella unleashed the towel at Edward's ass as he was walking away.

"Bloody hell!" He jumped and yelped.

Gabriella laughed as Liam threw her over his shoulder. He gave her another good swat on the butt while Gabriella desperately tried to make sure her short robe was covering her ass.

"Shit, that hurts, Liam. Not so hard!" Gabriella whined.

"Don't worry, Angel; I will kiss it better as soon as we get to our room. Edward, after your shower, can you give the sauce a stir and listen for Enya? Gabriella is due a punishment. We will be out in an hour or so."

"No problem, chum. Give her a good thrashing for me."

"Oh, my God, you did not just say that!"

"She-devil, you started this by hitting us with the towel, so don't cry foul on me now. Ten extra thrashes for the last comment, Liam."

"Done," Liam said as she beat on his ass, trying to get him to put her down.

"Put me down, you overgrown ape." *Smack.* "Ouch! Jesus Christ, that hurt! I think I broke my hand on your ass."

"Well, now I have to kiss your ass and your hand better," he commented as he carried her up to his room.

He threw her on the unmade bed and followed her down, pinning her. Then he leaned up and pulled out the elastic band holding her ponytail before running his fingers through her hair while she struggled with all her might to get away from him.

"I am not a *Fifty Shades* type of girl and never will be. Hit me for your pleasure, and I will damn well beat you back!"

He laughed as he started kissing her and removing her robe.

"Liam, please, we can't do this now. Edward will know, and what if Enya wakes up? Please, let's just wait till tonight." She started struggling again.

"We are so doing this now...and tonight. For the first time in my life, I am going to have everyone I love under one roof, healthy and happy. We are celebrating."

He dropped his mouth to hers and consumed her. She relaxed in his arms, stopped thinking, and just started feeling.

His tongue was all over hers, and he was removing the two measly pieces of clothing she was wearing while she started to remove his T-shirt and shorts.

She stopped and asked him to grab her a tissue from the bathroom before they continued.

"You really need a tissue now?"

"Yeah, baby, I do."

He got up in his boxer briefs and headed for the bathroom. She leaned up on her elbows and just watched. She was wearing a huge-ass smile when he walked back into the bedroom.

"What are you up to now, angel?"

"The only foreplay I ever need is to see you walk across the room in those boxer briefs. You look so hot. Way better than those advertisements with David Beckham wearing his underwear."

"You don't really need a tissue, do you? You just wanted to objectify my body." He grinned. "Well, baby, it's all yours. I think you should get on your knees and pay homage to my little friend." He started to pull his boxers off an inch at a time.

Gabriella was drooling as she slid off the bed and onto her

knees, smiling at his reference to his *little* friend. Yeah, right.

She took his little friend that wasn't so little into her hands and rubbed it up and down, enjoying the silky feel. Then Gabriella looked up at him and licked her lips before she circled the head with her tongue.

He groaned as he braced himself then tilted his hips, trying to get closer to her mouth. He grabbed her hair as he guided her mouth farther down his length. She loved the fact that he never forced her to go farther than she was comfortable with. Even on her knees, taking care of him, she felt worshipped.

Gabriella rubbed her tongue on the sensitive vein on the underside of his little friend. Then she sucked hard as she moved up and down a few times, inciting yet another groan of pleasure. She felt a tremor in his legs, a clear indication he was close.

He snapped her up and tossed her onto the bed before lifting her legs and dropping her knees over his shoulders. She leaned back on her shoulders as he wrapped his arms around her hips, holding them in place as he attacked her lady bits. Sometimes, she thought having sex with Liam was like being a performer in a circus. He got her into the weirdest positions.

He feasted, licking, sucking, and worshipping. He latched on to her nub then concentrated on that little bundle of nerves, and Gabriella went wild, shooting off like a rocket.

He released her legs, but he was having a hard time trying to contain her heaving hips. He then did pin her down finally, with her back on the bed, and he plunged inside her with another groan. They moved together, listening to the smacking of flesh connecting.

He was pumping inside of her, trying to make it last, when Gabriella exploded again, which caused the tremors in his legs to come back, bringing him seconds away from coming. She felt his final thrusts, knowing he was about to release inside of her. And when he did, he collapsed on top of her, his heart pounding a million miles a minute.

He lifted his body and moved all the hair from Gabriella's face before encasing her face in his hands as he gently brushed kisses all over it.

"I love you, angel. You truly have completed me and my world." He sealed his statement with another thorough kiss.

Gabriella felt her eyes fill with tears. "You are my saviour and my life now. Thank you for loving me." She gave him a soft, gentle kiss across the lips then said, "Get off. I can't breathe."

He laughed as he stood up then dragged her to the edge of the bed and helped her stand. "Let's shower. Then I have a meeting with Camden. He said he has some information for me. Then I will pick up Ainsley at four."

"Are you sure you don't need Edward or me to come to the hospital with you? And are you going to tell me what Camden tells you?"

"Thanks, angel, but I think I have it covered. Megs is still there; she can help with Ainsley. Edward is going to bring my mum over.

If you will stay with Enya and keep Mum company, that would be a great help. I will let you know later if I can share the information Camden has."

Gabriella didn't want him to know that she was curious about the information Camden had. She knew that, if she pushed, he would pull back, so she pretended to accept what he said.

"No problem. Enya and I have to pop out to the store a little later, but I will coordinate that with Edward."

When she came out of their room after sharing a shower, Enya was sitting at the table with her uncle Edward, eating sugar-coated cereal.

"Good morning, hermosa. Why is Uncle Edward letting you eat that cereal when he clearly knows I would have made you a healthy breakfast?" Gabriella gave Edward the evil eye.

"Uncle Edward said to hurry before you found out that we were eating the yummy cereal, and he said not to tell you he ate three meatballs." She held up three fingers as she batted her baby blues.

"Enya! That was our secret." Edward was so shocked that Enya had given him up.

"Edward, really, you asked this beautiful, innocent child to lie for you? And, on top of that, you know that cereal is loaded with empty calories and tons of sugar."

"Daddy says never to lie," Enya piped in, looking at Edward smugly. "And besides, Gabriella and me are making a chocolate 'money' cake for Ainsley's welcome home party."

Edward looked between them. "First off, there is nothing innocent about the little ankle-biter. She threw me under the bus for a chocolate money cake! And on that note, you feed us sugar in your baking all the time. Sugar-coated cereal is a rite-of-passage in a kid's life, the same as your s'mores."

"Okay, I give up; you win. For the record, I bake with all-natural ingredients and raw sugars, nothing refined, and it isn't bad for you at all. You know, you are going to make a wonderful papi some day, and I want to be there to feed them refined sugar. Lots and lots of refined sugar. Then I will laugh while they torment you."

"From your lips to God's ears. I really can't see that happening, though. I will live vicariously through Enya, Ainsley, and my other niece and nephew."

"One day, Prince Edward of Arlington, you are going to eat those words, and I will be there to tell you, 'I told you so.' For now, do you think you could take Enya and me out to pick up a few things for the party? We need things to bake the money cake."

***

Liam walked into Camden's flat. This was a very delicate investigation, and they needed to make sure they kept it under the radar. They also had to make sure Liam had no ties into the investigation. If someone had gone to such great lengths to frame Gillian, he knew they had to have power, money, and connections. However, no one would ever question Liam going to his brother-in-law's flat, especially when the girls were still recovering.

"Hey, Garret, how's it going, man? Nice to finally meet you face to face." Liam shook hands with the man Camden had set him up with.

"Good to meet you. Let's get right down to it. I only have a few minutes. This will probably be the only time we meet while this operation is active."

Garret gestured him over to some papers on the coffee table. "You were right; something doesn't add up with how the scandal broke and who is behind it. On the surface, all the facts lead to Gillian Wainwright. The payoff from an unidentified source was going into an offshore account in Wainwright's name, opened six months before the tape surfaced. We even have footage of a woman described as Wainwright going into a bank in the Caymans to make the deposit. We have the written testimony of the maintenance man at the hotel who claimed to have seen Wainwright meeting with a mysterious man and handing over the envelope, which we assume is on the tape."

"You're telling me the same info I gave to you regarding the investigation. Give me something new. Is there a chance Gillian was setup, and if so, do you think you are capable of discovering who initiated this public embarrassment? Let's not forget, Gillian's family has a shitload of money and did their own investigation without vindicating her; why?"

"For one, they don't have the computer genius I managed to acquire. He was able to pull the bank's surveillance tapes, and after removing layers and layers from the tape, he says it isn't Gillian Wainwright. Turns out the kid had a crush on the girl and knows every mark on her face. He says he can prove it isn't her. Next, the guy from the hotel got killed when he was side-swiped on the mountain, and his car was thrown off the cliff. Pretty convenient, I would say. I researched the guy who supposedly side-swiped him, and the guy's mom suddenly came into a small fortune. Then the family moved to another part of Mexico."

"So Gillian really could have been setup?" Liam's mind was going in a million different directions. Who would want to break up Edward and Gillian, and why? Could this be his family? Maybe his father? Liam knew there was bad blood there, but he had always believed it was on Edward's side, not the future king's.

"This is just the beginning," Garret told him. "I believe we are onto something here. It could get messy. Are you sure you want to continue? I have no problem doing it, but it might blow up in your face, depending on who initiated it and who funded it. I can't guarantee Prince Edward won't stand a bigger chance of getting fucked around. What are you willing to trade for the truth?"

"That's not your problem. I have my reasons, and trust me, it isn't to take something away from Edward. He has a right to know if someone fucked with his life and his future. How long do you think it will be before you have some hard evidence I can take to Edward?"

"This could definitely blow up, but I'll cover my tracks. No one

317

will ever know who or where the evidence came from. I can't guarantee the same for you once I hand over the intel, but that's your problem, not mine. Like I said, no one will trace it to me. I'm thinking this should all be wrapped up in a couple of weeks, maybe three."

"How and when do you want payment?" Liam asked.

"Here's the deal. You could pay me money, or we could trade info for info. I checked you out, and you have clearance with every agency in the UK. I'm always in the market for intel. It would never put you in danger or a position where it is illegal. Coming to you could save me loads of time and money. All acquisitions would be done strictly through Camden, and we would never trade coin. You help me; I help you."

"Done." Liam shook his hand then walked to the door without another word.

Chapter 29

Best Gift Ever

L iam looked around the dining room table as his family finished their supper. He couldn't believe how lucky he was. His best friend was entertaining his two little girls, and they were laughing at some antic he had pulled. They thought of him as the bee's knees, or so they always told him. "Who knew bees had knees?" was always Liam's response. One or both of the twins always jumped in with, "Daddy! Bee's knees means you're cool. Duh…Look it up in the urban dictionary." That always got a laugh. The twins could barely pronounce dictionary, let alone *know* what a dictionary was. Yet, if Uncle Edward said it was true, then it was written in stone.

Somewhere in that twisted brain of his, Edward thought the girls understood everything. They loved Edward unconditionally because he treated them like equals. Edward proved that every time he was around the girls, and the twins could sense when an adult respected them. Liam had no doubt that Edward was going to be a great dad, and after his meeting with Garret today, if it all worked out the way Liam hoped, Edward could be a father sooner than he thought.

Liam turned to listen to the woman who had given him his soul back. She was telling his mum and sister all about life back in Toronto. She took his breath away when he looked at her. She was so beautiful. Sometimes, when he looked at her, he still couldn't believe she was his. She belonged on the cover of a magazine or in the arms of someone rich and famous, like Edward. But she couldn't care less about things like that. She was Liam's, body and soul.

She was wearing a turquoise peasant top—she had corrected him earlier, saying it was not just a blouse, whatever the fuck that meant. Liam didn't care about the blouse; it was what was underneath that drove him to distraction. He knew without even having seen her get dressed that she had on a turquoise bra with purple stitching on the straps and a beautiful little purple bow in the centre, nestled between her perfect breasts. And under her blue jeans, she had on the matching lace thong.

Fuck, if he had to get up from this table right now, he would be screwed. His dick was doing everything in its power to push its way through his jeans and pay a visit to Gabriella.

Everything his angel thought played out on that beautiful face. She was explaining Canadian Thanksgiving right now. This year, it fell on October 7th, the day after her birthday. She had no idea Liam knew when her birthday was. When he had done her background check, all of her information had come up, and that was one of the things he had made sure to remember.

She continued telling them how Canadian Thanksgiving took place on the second Monday of October and how everyone really celebrated it on the Sunday because of turkey comas.

Liam did a double-take. Had he heard her correctly?

"Did you just say, 'turkey coma'? What the heck is that?"

This caught Edward's attention.

"Another one of those crazy Canadian things. My guess is they swing turkeys around, and if you get hit in the head with one, and you end up with coma, you are the loser," Edward tried to reason, the look on his face one of pure comedy.

"You're such a doofus! Come on, really? You guys are joking me! You have never heard of a turkey coma?"

As Gabriella was speaking about tryptophan and sleepiness, Ainsley got up and headed around the table. Liam thought she was going to him for some TLC, so he gently started to push his chair out, but then she stopped short of Liam and tried to get up into Gabriella's lap.

Gabriella, continuing her conversation, pushed her chair out a little and lifted Ainsley, saying, "Come here, preciosa." She cradled Ainsley in her arms, gently rocking her while rubbing her back.

Megan smiled from ear to ear while Margaret's eyes flew over to Liam's, and she nodded her head with pride. Margaret hadn't seen them interact before, so for her, this was new, but for the rest of the group, it was normal. Gabriella was born to be a mum and had been nurturing Ainsley and caring for her since before she had even come out of her coma.

Yup, Liam knew Gabriella was a keeper.

He had a surprise planned for next weekend, which worked out perfectly for the birthday celebration he intended to give Gabriella.

"Angel, I would love it if we could celebrate Thanksgiving with you. You can make a turkey with all the fixings, and I will Skype your parents. We can celebrate as one large, extended family."

He saw the panic enter her eyes.

She stopped rubbing Ainsley's back, doubt flashing across her face, unsure she could carry it off. She had told Liam she hadn't celebrated any holiday since her family had passed. However, she knew it was now time for new beginnings, new memories, and old traditions mixed with new ones.

Edward instantly picked up on her panic.

"I agree," he said. "Turkey comas for everyone! I will get the turkey, just give me the size."

Without even changing her expression, she said, "Sixteen kilograms."

"Are you bloody kidding me? What are we feeding, an army?" Edward raised his shocked voice, startling a sleeping Ainsley.

Gabriella cooed her fright away.

"It's not just about Thanksgiving dinner, Edward. The next day, it is about turkey soup, turkey salad sandwiches, turkey paella, and turkey casseroles. Of course, not all of that in one day. One turkey can make about ten different meals, but my absolute favourite is the next day when we have turkey salad sandwiches and turkey soup."

"Done! How about a twenty-two kilos one, then? Anything else you need to make this celebration any more authentic?"

"Yeah, I need parmigiano reggiano cheese for the soup and Miracle Whip mayonnaise for the turkey salad sandwiches, but sadly, you can't get it here." She pouted.

"Well, that's a relief. We Brits make the best mayonnaise in the world."

Liam could see the excitement start to build in her as she let her sadness go. "Very funny, you British toad. Let's really do this right. We have to make mulled cider. We need gourds to decorate the table, pumpkins we can all carve with the girls, and we have to find a corn maze for the girls to go through, and a tractor with a wagon to take us through the corn maze. Oh, wow! This will be so much fun. Oh, and for sure, I have to make my famous pumpkin pie. I will get to share some of my family's traditions with all of you. Oh, I can't wait! Oh, Enya and I have dessert still to serve, right, hermosa?"

God bless Edward's twisted soul. Once again, he had been able to take her from sad to happy in the blink of an eye.

Liam mouthed *"Thank you"* to him after Gabriella passed him Ainsley. Then Enya and Gabriella went off to the kitchen to get dessert.

All of a sudden, Enya ran into the room and shouted, "Welcome

323

home, Ainsley!" She then shot off a party popper full of colourful confetti.

Ainsley, now fully awake, screamed with excitement as Enya ran to her with a popper for her to shoot.

Gabriella laughed, carrying in the most amazing three-layer chocolate cake the guys had ever seen. "Five dollars if you shoot Uncle Edward, Ainsley."

"Don't do it, ankle-biter number two. I will get you back," Edward warned, trying to use his influence over the girls to go against Gabriella's offer of money.

"Do it, do it, do it!" Gabriella started chanting, and the rest joined in.

The girls were giggling and laughing as Ainsley moved the popper from pointing at the ceiling to pointing at Uncle Edward.

"No! I'm warning you, number two," Edward said as he held up his hands.

Gabriella, figuring all hell was about to break loose, stepped back to place the cake on the side hutch and away from the line of fire.

Ainsley fired right at Edward, and *poof,* he was covered in thousands of little coloured confetti bits.

Everyone laughed hysterically as Edward turned around and bent over to reach the side of the china cabinet. He pulled out the mother of all confetti cannons and pointed it slowly at everyone, including Liam's mother. That thing was meant to be shot off at a hall with hundreds of people in it, not in Liam's home.

"Don't even think about it, laddie! Or it will be the last thing you do," Margaret said, pointing her finger at him.

Then Edward pointed it at Gabriella, and Liam shouted, "Do it, do it, do it!"

She turned to him with a surprised look on her face, and Liam almost peed himself.

"Liam!" she screamed.

He laughed even harder as Liam's mum said, "Liam. James. Connor. That isn't nice!"

"Really, Mumsy? I seem to remember you telling ankle-biter number two to do it when it was pointed towards me, and now it's not nice?" Edward said, again pointing the cannon towards Margaret.

"I will tan yer arse if you shoot me," Margaret warned to the merriment of the six-year-old twins who burst out laughing.

"Yeah, Nana is going to tan your arse, Uncle Edward!" the twins repeated.

Edward pointed the cannon to the ceiling and pulled the trigger. Suddenly, nobody could see anyone, or anything. There was a snowstorm of a million coloured confetti pieces as the girls screamed in absolute delight.

Liam looked around to see every single one of them and every surface of the room was covered in confetti.

Gabriella spit some confetti out of her mouth. "No cake for you,

Edward!"

Everyone laughed after the shock wore off. Gabriella had to scrape off the confetti-covered icing before she could serve the cake while the rest of the adults cleaned up all the rest of the mess.

It took fifteen minutes before Gabriella announced, "Now that this place is semi-clean, let's have dessert. This is a money cake, and baked somewhere in the cake is a Canadian looney, which is a one-dollar coin. Some Canadians consider it lucky. Ainsley, you get to make the first cut."

Everyone was enjoying the cake and opening the little waxed paper packets with money until Edward jumped up and pumped his fist.

"Winner! I won the wish! Sorry, ankle-biters. Better luck next time."

As he showed off his lucky looney, Liam couldn't hold his tongue. "A looney for a loon—how very appropriate."

Edward toned down his usual response and said, "Sod off, old man. Jealousy will get you nowhere."

"There isn't anything to be jealous of. I have everything I have ever dreamed of sitting right here at this table." Liam leaned over and gave Gabriella a kiss on her cheek.

"Daddy, you got chocolate on Gabriella," Ainsley said as she took her napkin and wiped the cake from Gabriella's cheek.

"What do you wish for, Uncle Edward? Tell us," Enya asked.

"Oh, no, I am not telling. Otherwise, it won't come true. And besides, I am saving my wish for something really important."

Ainsley gave a loud yawn, and her dad realized how late it was for the girls. "Okay, girls, this party is officially over. Go and give Nana, Megs, Edward, and Gabriella a kiss, and then I will help you two get ready for bed."

"Daddy, we want Gabriella to help us get ready for bed. She reads to me every night, and we have been practicing a book to read to Ainsley."

If he weren't so thrilled the girls were bonding with Gabriella, he might have been hurt by Enya's request.

With a big smile, he replied, "Absolutely, princess, if it is okay with Gabriella."

"I would love to help you get ready for bed, but let's read in Daddy's big bed. That way, we can all see," Gabriella replied.

***

Gabriella and the girls had just finished setting the table for dinner. It was the day before their big Canadian Thanksgiving celebration, and everyone was excited. Gabriella was talking to Edward about all the finishing touches they had to do yet for their first holiday together. He had found her a twenty-two kilogram turkey, and they had spent the day gathering all of the things they needed to make this perfect.

Gabriella heard the door open while she was at the stove, checking the rice. She and Edward were still arguing over mayonnaise when Liam came in and kissed her neck, giving her the shivers.

"I have a solution to this ongoing dilemma. *You* use Miracle Whip on the sandwiches, and Edward can use English mayonnaise."

"And where am I going to get Miracle Whip?" Gabriella tartly remarked.

"We have some, mi niña!"

Gabriella slowly turned at the familiar voice. Her hands started to shake, and she dropped the tea-towel.

"This can't be real. How is this possible? Mom? Papi?" She started to cry as she rushed into her mother's arms, and then she collapsed into her papi's. "How...How are you here? When did you get here? I missed you both so much! I can't believe you guys are standing here! Oh, Papi, please don't cry. Papi, please tell me...how?"

Gabriella's papi was so caught up in his emotions he couldn't talk, so she looked at Liam.

"Happy birthday, angel. Tell me, is there a better way to spend your birthday and our first holiday together than celebrating with family?"

Papi, finally pulling himself together, said, "Your man here phoned us a couple a weeks ago and asked us if we could make arrangements for the restaurant so that he could fly us out here to celebrate your birthday. After not seeing you for six months, we jumped at the opportunity."

"Who is looking after the restaurant?"

"This is for you, darling," Gabriella's mom said as she handed her a very large jar of Miracle Whip. "Your brother and Nina are taking care of the restaurant. We made Carlos the sous chef while we are away. We might start travelling more, so this will be a good trial. Everyone back home sends hugs and kisses."

Gabriella left her papi's arms, walked to Liam with her jar in hand, and enclosed him in her arms. "Best gift ever. Thank you. I love you."

"Hello, little novia. My name is Manny, and this beautiful lady is Elia. What's your name?"

Gabriella turned to see her papi on one knee, shaking hands with Enya.

"I am Enya, and my sister is Ainsley."

Gabriella walked over to them and bent down, too. She wrapped her arm around her papi and said to the girls, "This, hermosa and preciosa, is my papi. Papi is Spanish for daddy. And that lady is my mom."

"Okay, ankle-biters, move over. I want to meet Gabriella's parents, too."

They stood, and Gabriella grabbed both of her parents' hands before turning towards Edward. "Edward, this is my mom, Elia, and my papi, Manny. Mom, Papi, let me introduce you to a very important man. This is Edward, the first man I have beaten in golf after not playing for about four years. And I didn't just beat him; I served him his butt on a silver platter. Papi, you would have been

329

proud."

Her parents started to laugh at Edward's expression.

"It is a pleasure to meet you both." Edward shook their hands. "I'm not sure how that rude creature came from such lovely people. I am sure you taught her manners, but I am afraid she may need a refresher course."

"It is a pleasure to meet you, Edward, but you can't possibly be talking about my preciosa niña," Papi said. "She is flawless. Look at her, so sweet and innocent."

Edward choked. "I can see you haven't been around your not-so-sweet, not-so-innocent daughter in a while. Time will tell. It is, indeed, a pleasure to meet you both."

"Isn't he perfect, Mom?" Gabriella asked.

Her mother burst out laughing again and, in a warning tone, said, "Ga-bri-ella!"

"See? Not two seconds later, she proves my point. I know what that means, Gabriella. Manny, pay attention to your not-so-sweet daughter. At least Momma Elia sees through that innocent act."

"I think you misunderstood my beautiful, little niña. I heard her give you a compliment. I'm thinking someone else needs some manners training, and it isn't my daughter." Her papi pulled her in more securely to his side with his arm wrapped around her. He was forever her champion, defending her honour. No matter what, she could always count on her papi.

"Okay," Gabriella said. "Now that I have been vindicated, let me get everyone drinks. Girls, will you and Uncle Edward please set the table for two more?"

***

Edward, bless his soul, had found a farmer with a corn field and had paid him to make a maze and take everyone on a wagon ride. Gabriella had a blast, walking arm in arm with her mom and papi, watching Liam and Edward carefully run with the screaming girls through the field.

After the farm, they went home and carved pumpkins. Between the mulled cider and the smell of turkey cooking throughout the house, Gabriella was in a state of eternal bliss. This had been a great day and a wonderful birthday.

While her mom was in the kitchen, she was making handprint painted turkeys with the girls. She didn't think this day could get any better.

"Okay, I concede, Gabriella. I owe you an apology. I now understand a turkey coma," Edward commented after dinner, rubbing his belly.

Gabriella laughed.

Everyone had devoured the turkey, and it was time for dessert, so she stood up, but her mom patted her hand and said she would get it, and Liam got up to help her.

"Edward," Liam called out a few minutes later, and Edward got up and turned out the lights.

Everyone sang "Happy Birthday" loudly, and Gabriella started to cry as her mom placed her famous green cake in front of her.

Liam brought his chair closer to her after placing the pumpkin pie on the table.

"Grandma, why are Gabriella and Grandpa crying?" Ainsley asked.

Elia had asked the girls yesterday if they would prefer to call them grandma and grandpa, since Liam wouldn't allow the girls to call Gabriella's parents by their first names. This had taken Gabriella by surprise, but both of the girls had jumped at the opportunity, especially after her parents had showered them with gifts.

"Sometimes, when grownups are happy, they cry, and that is exactly why both of them are crying," Elia answered the girls.

Gabriella blew out the candles, and then Edward got up and left with the girls. A few minutes later, they came back in, carrying all kinds of presents.

"Open mine first!" Enya yelled.

"Me second!" Ainsley rushed in.

"Wow, presents? Having everyone in one room *is* my present."

"No, *real* presents, Gabriella. They're more fun," Ainsley assured her.

She opened Enya's gift first. Enya was beyond herself with excitement, and helped open it. It was a child's book titled, *Love Is You & Me* by Monica Sheehan.

"Oh, hermosa, I *love* it. Let's read it together tonight. Best gift ever!"

"Yup, and when Daddy asked me what to get, I said we would like a book. We read all the books until I found the perfect one, and I picked this one because love is *you* and *me*," Enya proudly proclaimed.

Gabriella hugged her and whispered into her ear, "Thank you. It's amazing. I love you, hermosa."

"I love you, too," Enya replied,

"Me next!" Ainsley vied for attention.

Gabriella picked her up and placed her on her lap.

"I picked this," Ainsley told Gabriella as she gave her a small, wrapped box. She let Ainsley open it then lifted out a necklace with a cute, little angel on a silver chain. "Daddy always calls you angel, and you always wear shiny, grey-coloured necklaces."

"Oh, baby, it is beautiful. Will you put it on me? I will cherish it always! Best gift ever. Thank you so much. I love you, preciosa."

It took her a few tries, and Liam tried to intervene, but Ainsley would have no part of him helping.

"No, Daddy, it's *my* present."

He backed off, and she couldn't have been prouder when she got it on.

Gabriella turned around, and Ainsley tapped on her throat where the necklace laid as she declared she liked it.

Next, Gabriella opened her parents' gift—actually, the two girls did. They took the present to the floor, wrapping paper flying everywhere. Then they pulled out a big blanket and handed it to her.

333

"Oh, Mom, it's beautiful! You made it, right?"

"Yes, sweetheart. I started it when you left six months ago. You were always so cold, but now I see it is meant to share the warmth in your new home. Maybe you can wrap yourselves up in it when you read together. Happy birthday, sweetheart."

"Wow, Mom, that's beautiful. Best gift ever. I adore it. Thank you, Mom, Papi."

"No, mi niña, that is your mom's gift. This is mine." Her father handed each of the girls a wrapped box, and they carefully opened the boxes after Papi told them to be gentle.

Inside each box was a beautiful flamenco doll, one in pink and one in purple. The girls were so excited with their presents.

He explained to everyone, "I have always believed that the flamenco dolls were handcrafted after my beautiful Gabriella, and I want you two little girls to have the same dolls Gabriella played with when she was a little girl now that we are a family!"

In one sentence, Gabriella's papi had just gifted her with his acceptance of Liam and the girls, embracing them into the Capello family fold.

She was speechless for a second then burst out in a loud sob. "Best gift ever!"

Her papi walked over to her, and as he went, he reassured the girls that Gabriella was happy. They hugged and sobbed for a few minutes until both of them could pull themselves together.

Margaret and Megan then gave her a beautiful lamb's wool

sweater she had been admiring while shopping the other day.

"That is the best gift ever. Thank you so much. I love it." She got up and kissed Liam's mom and sister.

"Mine next," Edward declared as he handed her two presents.

She opened them herself now that the girls were busy with their dolls. The first one was a framed picture of Edward and Gabriella at the golf course. Beside the picture was a handwritten declaration with his signature, stating that she had beaten him in golf and that she was a better player. She turned it over and saw that he had also written on the back of the picture that she was a she-devil who had tricked him, so it really didn't count.

His second present to her was a T-shirt. She lifted it and saw it was from the *Twilight* book series, and it read "Team Edward." She burst out laughing as she showed everyone what it said.

"I love everything, Edward. Best gift ever!"

"You won't be wearing that, angel," Liam was quick to say. "You can use it to clean the loo."

Without even thinking, Edward spouted, "Sod off, old man. You're just jealous! And I bought it extra small so that it will cling to her chest." It hit him like a ton of bricks that he had just said that in front of the children, Liam's family, and her parents. He cleared his throat. "I apologize. That was inappropriate. But you should know that your daughter could have been mine…if I didn't feel so sorry for old Liam here."

They all laughed at his embarrassment and comeback.

335

She could see in her parents' eyes that they were pleased with how much Edward and Liam loved her.

Liam's mom pointed her finger at Edward. "You're pushing it, laddie."

"Oh, you love me, and you know it, Mumsy."

"One more, beautiful." Liam lifted a large, heavy box and placed it on the table.

"But your gift to me was bringing my parents here," Gabriella argued, "and I don't think you can outdo that. It means the absolute world to me, my saviour, and—"

"I know. Best gift ever. Regardless, I want you to have this." His dimples were on full display.

"I don't say that a lot!"

Edward started to cough.

"Very funny, Edward! But I mean it each time. You have all chosen the best gifts." She turned back to the gift. "Now, what could possibly be in this big box?"

Gabriella opened it to find a rock with the word "take" written on it, and another smaller, wrapped box. She opened the next box to find a rock with "this" and another wrapped box. The next one said, "rock." Then, after that, "and." Lastly, she opened the next small box and there was a little rock nestled in a velvet case.

She turned to Liam who was down on one knee with a diamond ring in his hand. Her eyes instantly filled to the rim with tears, and she couldn't see him or the ring.

"Angel, the moment I saw you, I fell in love with you. You changed my life. I lost my soul, and you found it and gave it back to me. You taught me how to love again and to accept the person I am. You have nurtured and cared for me, my mother, and my girls. We have both loved and lost, and I believe those people we lost somehow brought us together and showed us how to be a family again. You have so much love to give, and I am so thankful I am on the receiving end of that love.

"The real reason I brought your parents here was so they could meet me and the girls face to face. I wanted them to witness for themselves the love we share. And I brought your papi here so I could ask his permission for your hand in marriage. Then I asked the twins for their permission. Next were Jocelyn and Dakota. I even went so far as to ask for Edward's permission. I wanted to make sure everyone who loved you was on board. So, please, angel, take this rock and marry me."

With tears streaming down her face, it didn't take her but a second to reply, "Yes!" And then she screamed, "Best gift ever!"

Chapter 30

A Visit from a Friend

G abriella was sitting in Liam's office with her iPad, writing an email to her parents to tell them how much their love and support had meant to her over her lifetime, especially the last three and a half years. She was constantly thinking about them and what they meant to her.

Yesterday had been a sad day for Gabriella. She had stood at the airport with her new family, saying good-bye to her parents. She was proud of herself since she had kept it together, though a few tears had slipped out.

The girls had broken her heart when they had cried. Ainsley had grabbed her papi's leg and wouldn't let go. Everyone had tried to reassure the twins they would all be together in three months for the wedding.

Papi had been a hot mess between leaving his beloved daughter and his two new granddaughters who had stolen his heart. Her mom had texted Gabriella and said she had been terrified Manny was going to break down the barrier to get back to everyone after they had cleared the first security checkpoint.

Manny was a strong man in every sense of the word…until it came to the girls in his life. Then he became a big marshmallow. Elia was his reason for living. Next, Gabriella, and now the twins were his sweetness, the icing on his cake.

Gabriella and her papi had had many heart-to-heart talks over the last week, but what stuck in her head the most were the words he had spoken about Liam.

"Mi niña, I loved Marco like he was my own son, and knowing him the way I did, I know that he helped you find your way to Liam. I know this because, if I'd had to choose another man for you, I couldn't have done a better job. Treat him well, mi niña. If you do, he will love and treasure you for the rest of your life. Don't compare your past to your future; just accept and treasure every minute you are given."

As she remembered his words, she knew Papi was the smartest man she had ever known.

Her mom was simply the roots that held them together. She knew how to manage everyone with wisdom and grace. Gabriella hoped she could one day offer the girls as much wisdom as her mom continuously gave her. She always let Gabriella make her own mistakes, and if she needed guidance, she would stand back and wait for her to ask before offering. It took an incredibly brave and strong

339

woman to stand back and let her children fall, to teach them to get up for themselves instead of always picking them up. She gave her children legs to stand on and to run with. She was the woman Gabriella aspired to be.

A knock on the door startled her out of her thoughts.

"Come in."

Edward walked in, carrying a blue box with a silver bow. "Hey, do you have a minute?"

"Sure, I was just writing my parents an email. Is there something you need?"

"Now that Liam and the girls are out, I thought we could have a private conversation."

"I don't mean to be rude, but your demeanour is so somber it's scaring me. What is so important that you can't talk to me while Liam and the girls are here?"

"It's nothing bad. I mean, I don't think it is." He shook his head. "I'm going about this all wrong. Forgive me. It is a secret I was asked to keep five years ago, and now it is time that I share it."

"Oh, Edward, you can tell me anything. You know that."

"Okay. First, this is a gift for you, and don't look at me like that. It isn't a gift from me."

"Then who is—"

"I don't mean to cut you off, but this has been weighing on me for a long time now, and I have to get it over with." He took a deep breath. "So, this story starts about five years ago. You know Raven and I were friends, and we became very close as her illness progressed. Well, Raven and Liam lost their way for a short time, and I was their buffer. They did find their way back to one another, but through the hard times, I was a confidant to both Liam and Raven. Both knew the other vented to me and encouraged it, so I am not betraying anyone here.

"Raven knew in her heart that Liam loved her completely, but she blamed herself for the walls he erected. We talked many times about this, and she was convinced that, one day, someone special would walk into his life and remove the walls of bitterness that she believed she had created. It wasn't her fault; believe me." He choked on his last sentence and stopped speaking for a moment, overcome with grief.

Gabriella didn't say a word. She just moved her chair closer so their knees were touching and picked up his hand that wasn't holding the blue box. She squeezed it to reassure him and to let him know he could take all the time he needed.

"Raven gave me this box and its contents to give to you, the woman Liam chose to marry after she passed on. She knew in her heart Liam would find love again, but she told me it would have to be an incredible woman. She said she owed you some explanations, and those words should come from her own mouth, so she gave me a video." He handed her the box.

Gabriella gently untied the bow and opened it. Inside held a memory stick. She cautiously removed it and looked at it with fear and curiosity, her hands shaking.

Edward grabbed her hands. "Love, do you want me to stay with you? Raven made me watch it before she entrusted me with it, so I know what it says."

"Yes, please. I am so scared. What if I don't measure up to the woman Raven wanted for her husband?"

"Raven wasn't the judgmental type. She was kind and loving, and she had wisdom far beyond her years. All she wanted was the best for her family, and I believe she got her wish, but don't take my word for it…Take hers."

He took the memory stick out of her hands and placed it into the computer. A woman Gabriella knew to be Raven came up on the screen. She was wearing a head scarf to cover her bald head and a funky hat. She had the most captivating blue eyes Gabriella had ever seen. The twins looked identical to her.

When Raven spoke, Gabriella was shocked at her accent. She knew she would have to pay special attention so as not to miss anything she said.

Raven tapped the lens of the recorder and started to speak. *"I hope this is working. Hello, friend, I am sure you know who I am, and I wish to God I knew who you were. And, although I have never met you, I know you are someone incredibly special. The reason I know that is because, out of all the people on this earth, Liam would choose to love only two women. One is me, and the other is you. If you are listening to this, it's because you and Liam are engaged or married. Congratulations! I wish you all the happiness in the world. Edward has been a Godsend to me, and he has promised me that he will help you through listening to this if need be.*

"I know I am dying and don't have much time, but this conversation is important to me. I am leaving this world with only one regret, and that is how much my decision hurt Liam. In fact, if I am going to be honest with you, I hurt Liam beyond comprehension, but not beyond repair. I believe in my heart that you are capable of making him whole again.

"If you are a mother or intend to be, then you know the decision I made was the right one. I could never have killed or hurt my children in order to save myself—I have no regrets in that department. What I struggle with is hurting the most loving man I have ever met.

"I know you love him, and to love him is to know how much guilt he carries in his heart over a situation he had no control over. I took away all of his rights when I made decisions that affected a couple, not just one person. Right now, I can hear the words of a song he plays constantly. Stop and listen to the lyrics of the song, "Castle of Glass" by Linkin Park, and then return to me."

Edward stopped the pre-recorded message and pulled up YouTube so Gabriella could listen to the song and read the lyrics. The song was hauntingly good, and she could see why Liam loved it and related to it. She, too, had felt the same feelings invoked by that song.

343

After a few minutes of reflection, Gabriella turned to Edward. "I am ready to hear the rest. I got the message of his state of mind that she wanted me to understand."

Raven continued, *"Now that you have heard the lyrics, you realize how broken and helpless he felt. Had I been wiser, I would have given him a chance to absorb the fact that I had cancer. I would have given him a chance to be active in the decision to reject treatment until the girls were born. After all the facts and seeing the sonogram, feeling the movement of the girls, I know he would have come to the same conclusion I did. However, I took all of his choices away. I panicked.*

"You see, I lost my mum to the same cancer. I know the terrible decisions that have to be made, so I did what I thought was right at that moment. And, in the end, I broke the one person I was trying to protect, so I need you to convince Liam that I forgive him totally and completely for everything we did to each other. I can only wait in Heaven to get his forgiveness. I ask for this gift from you. I swear on my daughters' lives, if I am capable of returning the favour from Heaven, I will.

"Now, my daughters, Enya and Ainsley. They are the light of my life. They are the best thing Liam and I ever did together. They are the absolute best of the both of us. I look at them and can't believe how lucky I am to be their mum. Please love them, and I guarantee they will love you back. It is a miracle that they were even born. They didn't ask to be brought into this world, but they deserve to be.

God has plans for my wee lasses, and I expect they will be great. Please teach them all the things a girl needs from a mother.

"I have left DVDs to help guide them along the way, but if you work with me, the girls will always have the information they need. I am sure it will be hard to raise another woman's children, but mine are worth it. If you have children, look at them and know I would do the same for you. If you and Liam have more children—for Liam's sake and the girls, I hope that you will—the twins will be excellent role models and friends to any other siblings. Just ask Edward.

"Most importantly, I need you to make sure that my girls get tested every year for breast cancer. My hope is that a cure has been found by the time the girls reach that age, but if it hasn't, please, I beg you, monitor their health. If it comes down to it, encourage them to do anything medically and surgically to spare them the same fate that has befallen both my mum and myself.

"Make sure Liam encourages a healthy lifestyle. I have already gotten Margaret's assurance. She will assist until you come along.

"This is a new chapter in your life and our families' lives. It breaks my heart to leave my family, but I now know I am leaving them in good hands. Once you hear this DVD, and I know Liam forgives me, I can finally rest in peace. Thank you for making my family whole again and for giving them a future. God bless you."

When the screen went black, Gabriella heard her own sobs. She also heard Edward softly crying beside her.

"Edward, take me somewhere for a while. I can't see Liam or

345

the girls right now. *Please.* Take me somewhere to think, like Kilt Rock. I need the highest place in Stirling. *Please.*"

"Oh, fuck, Gabriella, I'm so sorry. I thought you were ready for this. Liam is going to fucking kill me."

"I'm not freaking out. I just need to talk to Raven, and I need the highest point in Stirling to do that."

***

When Gabriella had said she needed the highest place to talk to Raven, Edward had instantly thought of Stirling Castle. There was a lookout area on the farthest point on the wall that surrounded the castle. It was also the highest spot over a cliff of shear rocks that looked directly down to the valley below. It had a panoramic view of the area and was exactly what she needed to feel closer to Heaven.

For a girl who claimed to have lost her belief in religion, she spent more time talking about God and the people in Heaven than anyone Edward knew.

Edward had called Myles and asked for him to arrange for him and Gabriella to enter Stirling Castle through the back way and for guards to section the public off from this area for privacy's sake. The last thing Edward needed right now was for more pictures to give away their location.

Myles had just sent him a text saying everything was in place and they could arrive at any time. Edward's contact was Lieutenant Hubert, who would see to any of their needs and would keep that part of the castle open for them until they indicated they were done.

"Thank you again for indulging me during one of my meltdowns. I'm sure you are exhausted after being around me for six months. One day soon, I am going to repay you for all your help and understanding," Gabriella said, although she never turned her head to look at Edward; she just kept staring out the windshield of the truck. She could see they were followed by the same team who took over anytime Liam wasn't available.

"Your friendship is my gift. My life has been enriched from knowing and loving you. I would do anything in my power to see you healthy and happy."

"Thank you. I am already working on a gift for you, though. I hope it will repay some of the kindness you have shown me. By the way, where are you taking me?"

"We are heading to Stirling Castle, Scotland's most famous. It has been restored to its natural beauty and is definitely the pride of Stirling. You will instantly feel the connection you are looking for when we enter the castle. The walls are alive with history and legends. It might seem odd that one of the Princes of England is taking you to a place which was the cornerstone for Scottish independence, but I love the place. It is one of the few places I go to talk to my mum. She fought so hard for what she believed in, and she could relate to the pride of the Scottish people. I'm not sure if you knew, but my mum was half-Scottish."

"No, sorry. I have to admit I don't know much about your family except your mother's unfortunate passing. You wouldn't

347

know I was an educated woman, would you?"

"I like that you don't know a lot about my family. Then I can share how I see my family, not how the media has portrayed us." Edward paused for a minute. "I'm going to ask you something, and if you don't want to answer, that's fine. But, why are we rushing to the highest point, and what do you hope to get out of it?"

"My answer might not make you happy. You might think I'm crazy. But when I was at Kilt Rock, I felt energy there, like I knew Marco was with me. I'm hoping to feel that energy again—Raven's presence. I need to talk to her, and I need her to listen. Crazy, eh?"

"No, love. I would expect that you, and only you, could talk to angels." He grabbed her hand and gave it a little squeeze.

They pulled into Stirling where Lieutenant Hubert met them, and then left them alone on the platform built on the cliff, closest to Heaven.

"If you need me, I am a call away. Good luck."

"No, Edward, please stay."

Without a word, he stood back and watched. After a few minutes, Edward thought she was talking in her head, but then she started.

"Yes, I feel her." She looked up at the sky. "Raven, it's me, Gabriella. I just listened to your message. Thank you. Welcoming me into your family's fold was an incredibly unselfish act. I know you loved Liam with everything you were, and I get that, because I also love him with my whole heart and soul.

348

"You taught him how to love first, and you did a great job. He learned well. He has been my saviour. I don't believe I would be healthy today without him. And I will do everything in my power to convince him of your forgiveness, but you also have to let go of the pain.

"He forgave you the day the twins were born. He knew you were right; he just didn't know how to tell you. So rest in peace, my friend. I will take care of the family you have entrusted me with. I will treasure every moment I have with them. I will treat your daughters like they are my own. You were right; I love them desperately already, and not because they are Liam's daughters, but because you can't help loving those two little imps.

"I'm not able to have any more children, and that's okay. I have an important job ahead of me. Those two little girls are going to get all my love and attention. I will always make sure they know who their mum was, but I'm warning you now; I am going to ask them to call me mama, because I intend to be just that. They will be incredibly lucky to have a mum and a mama.

"Now, you promised me a favour, and I am here to collect. I have promised to look after your family and make them mine, so now I'm asking you to do the same. Marco and my boys, Gianluca and Mateo, are in Heaven. Find them if they haven't already found you and love them. Give them a love only a mother can. Look after Marco and reassure him I am fine and well looked after…"

Edward didn't hear what else she said, his mind wandering.

Tears were streaming down his face from listening to the wee wisp of a woman. How *did* she find the strength? It was killing him, and he was only listening. He hadn't lived her life.

This was his wake-up call. If she could move on after such insurmountable odds, then he needed to, as well. Had he been hurt? Abso-bloody-lutely! But so had she, and deeper than him. If she could find love again, then so could he. No more feeling sorry for himself. Today would be the first day of the rest of his life. Damn, but that woman had given him so much, and she had no idea.

Edward's thoughts were interrupted when she collapsed to the floor of the wall, sobbing. He rushed to her side and gathered her into his arms, rocking her back and forth and repeating his earlier statement.

"Liam is going to fucking kill me."

"Not even God can protect you, wee bastard," Liam growled.

Chapter 31

Water Tight Frogs and Wings

S eriously, Edward, what the fuck happened?" Liam growled. "Gabriella, come here, baby. What's wrong? Are you freaking out over getting married? We can wait. There is no rush."

He had seen her in despair, frightened, sad, angry, and even tears of joy. But when Gabriella looked up into his eyes, he saw something different, something he couldn't place, something he had never seen before.

Liam took the palm of his hand and wiped her tears away as she started to ramble. He couldn't keep up between her hiccups and crying.

"I did it, Liam! I met her! And I liked her! And I am going to look after you and your daughters, and she's going to look after my boys! Liam, don't you get it? They can both rest in peace now, and there is a woman to look after my boys. You told me before she was wise, but I didn't understand how much until today. Oh, Liam, this changes everything!"

Liam looked to Edward for answers, having no clue what she was talking about.

He knew she was upset. The guard detail that was following her and Edward had told him that, and that Edward was taking her to Stirling Castle. Liam had been confused because, when he had left home, she had been happily writing to her friends. What had changed?

"Edward, help me out here. What is going on? What is she talking about?"

Edward saw the fear on Liam's face and addressed Gabriella. "You need to talk to Liam. After what you just spewed, he is baffled by your statement, thinking the worst, and that isn't fair."

Liam's mind was in a panic. The last time he was this fearful had been when he had learned Raven's treatments weren't working and she was dying. *Oh, please don't let Gabriella be sick.* He had thought they had gotten past their difficult times, but obviously he had been wrong. Why were they always going three steps forwards and five back? He just wanted simplicity in their lives.

Gabriella broke his train of thought when she encouraged Edward to tell him.

"Liam, you know that Raven and I were friends, and that I became…"

Raven? He couldn't help thinking, *What the fuck is he doing?*

Why was Edward talking about Raven and further upsetting Gabriella?

He looked at Edward like he was going to murder him. He had better have a good excuse for this, because he was pissing Liam right the fuck off.

"I became Raven's confidant. She told me about many conversations the two of you had. She knew she was dying and wanted to make sure you moved on, and she hoped you would find love again. She told me she tried to tell you about the different chapters in people's lives."

Liam nodded at that, having shared that wisdom with Gabriella months ago.

"She desperately wanted you to fall in love again," Edward continued, "and to create a family for yourself and the girls. Anyway, she believed this so strongly that, before she died, she left a message...for your new fiancée. She entrusted me with her last wish before she died. She made me swear on her life that I would never tell you about the DVD she made for Gabriella."

Liam hadn't been expecting that. It took him out at the knees. He fell down on his ass, taking Gabriella with him. He felt like he was in a fog as he leaned back against the wall of the walkway. What had he meant, *Raven made a DVD for Gabriella?*

Edward bent down to make sure they were both all right. "Sorry, man. There was no gentle way to tell you all this. I couldn't go against the wishes of a dying woman, so I kept my promise. Please forgive me, but she asked so little from me, and keeping her confidence was a small price to pay for her peace of mind."

"Raven thought a lot about how you and the girls would manage after she was gone. She was so frightened that you would become bitter and shun any new relationship. She told me she was putting her trust in fate and made a DVD to give to Gabriella. When she was finished, she sat me down and made me watch it, and then we discussed it. She made me promise, the day after your engagement or marriage, I was to gift it to your bride with Raven's blessing. I was honoured to give her peace of mind when she was struggling with the pain her death would cause all of you.

"So, when you asked me for my permission to marry Gabriella, I had the package delivered to me. This afternoon, after you and the girls left, I gave Gabriella Raven's gift. I sat with her and explained what the package contained. Then we sat together and watched it. Gabriella didn't quite respond the way I expected."

Liam was having such a hard time wrapping his head around the fact that Raven had left a message for Gabriella. What could she have possibly said? Why was Gabriella here at Stirling Castle?

Gabriella was getting out of Liam's lap with that same strange look on her face. "Liam, Raven gave me a gift today. Today, two families truly became one. I will show you the DVD when we get home, but first, there are some things I need to say, and I need you to listen." Gabriella was now kneeling in front of him, holding his forearms, with that same strange look on her face.

354

She was tearstained, but Liam knew in his heart of hearts that there was no sense in trying to clean her face when she would be crying again before they were through.

"This is going to sound crazy, but I need you to just go with the flow and don't pass judgement until you hear me out completely. I told you when we were at Kilt Rock that I went there to talk to Marco because, for some reason, I felt his presence there."

Liam realized at this point that it was just as difficult for Gabriella as it was for him to hear about Raven, so before she continued, he interrupted her.

"Honestly, I was so frightened you were leaving me or that you were sick that I freaked myself out. But, really and truly, I would much prefer to have this conversation in our home rather than on this wall. Not only that, but I could really use a pint right about now, so could we go home?"

"Sure, let's go. Edward, do you mind taking the girls out so Liam and I can have some time alone for a while? I have some food in the fridge I can make before you go."

"No, love, I don't mind at all. I think we will go out on a date; just their favourite uncle, his security team, and his beautiful little ankle-biters. Don't worry; the girls will be safe with me."

Liam couldn't believe he had said that. "Edward, I never worry whether my girls are safe with you. I worry more for you. They can be a handful; are you sure you can manage the two of them alone?"

"Really? Is a frog's ass water tight? Of course I can manage two

355

little six-year-old girls."

"Okay, but don't say I didn't warn you." Liam got up from his seated position by the wall and took Gabriella's hand. Then the three of them walked away.

Gabriella suddenly stopped, turned around, and quietly whispered, "Thank you."

***

The girls were out of their minds from excitement when they found out Uncle Edward was taking them out on a real date to McDonald's of all places then to the movies. They insisted on dressing up, so Gabriella spent the next thirty minutes finding their favourite dresses. She agreed they could wear them, but only if they wore their leggings since it was cold outside. They matched a pair of Wellies to their dresses, one in pink and the other in purple. Gabriella learned quickly that, in Scotland, children had a variety of different designs of rain boots. Then she put their hair in pigtails with fancy bows.

The girls looked adorable as they ran down to meet Edward. She smiled as she watched Edward produce a small bouquet of sweet peas for each of the girls. They giggled demurely and batted their eyes as they turned to their dad and asked if he would put their flowers in water and place them on their nightstands.

Liam rolled his eyes at their flirting and explicit instructions. Little did he know that this was just the beginning of the girls and the dating nightmares he was going to have to endure.

Liam and Gabriella stood on the stoop, hand in hand, to wave good-bye. After closing the door, they stopped in the kitchen to each grab their favourite drinks then headed off to Liam's office. They both felt anxious about what they were about to share together, neither of them able to anticipate the other's reaction.

"Are you ready to do this, Liam?" she asked as they settled into the love seat in his office with his laptop turned on and ready to go.

"As ready as I will ever be," he answered.

"I was so nervous when Edward told me Raven had left a message for me. I was so afraid I wouldn't measure up to her expectations. But, as I listened to her words, I realized she was also giving me her blessing regarding our wedding, and she gave me so much more. Start the video, and we will talk afterwards."

Gabriella curled herself into his side, wanting him to know she was there for him, and felt Liam tense the minute Raven appeared on the screen. She couldn't even imagine how it must feel for him to see his wife looking and sounding just like she had before the cancer had destroyed her body.

He didn't say anything while he watched Raven speak, but he did squeeze Gabriella closer when Raven made references to her. Now she was getting nervous. Had she made a mistake by sharing it?

When the video went black, they sat there, not saying a word. Gabriella needed Liam to speak first, but she knew she had to give him time to process.

Quietly, she whispered, "I'm going to leave you alone for a little while. You need time to think. When you're ready, I will be in your room." She got up and went up to his bedroom where she got in bed and curled herself around his pillow, taking comfort in the fact that it smelled just like him.

She lay there for quite some time, listening to the song by Linkin Park play over and over. Then…silence.

Gabriella heard the girls' voices and jumped out of bed, realizing it was now dark outside. She must have fallen asleep.

She turned and looked at the clock, seeing it was nine-forty. Wow, she had been asleep for over three hours. *Oh, my God*, she thought. That meant Liam was still sitting by himself in the office.

She ran down to meet Edward and the girls.

Edward caught her panic. He cocked an eyebrow at her in question, but she ignored it, not knowing how to answer him.

"Hey, my little hermosa chicas, how was your date?" Gabriella plastered a fake smile on her face.

She looked up at Edward, knowing he wasn't buying her insincere act of happiness.

"It was so cool! I want to be a real life princess, and I want my own snowman," Ainsley proclaimed.

"Oh, preciosa, you *are* a real live princess, and you have a goofy uncle who is way more fun than any snowman. Now, give Uncle Edward a kiss and thank him for your date. It's time to get to bed. It's an hour and a half-past your bed time."

"Aw, do we have to? Where is Daddy?" Enya asked.

358

"Daddy is working. And, yes, you do. He will give you a kiss in a little while. Now, thank Uncle Edward."

Both girls ran into Edward's outstretched arms. He picked them up as they thanked him and gave him big, sloppy kisses.

"I will put the little rug rats to bed. You put on the kettle for tea. Now, ankle-biters, when I bend down, kiss Gabriella good night, and if you both do exactly as I ask, we can have another date next week."

As she kissed each girl, Gabriella said, "Good night, preciosa. Good night, hermosa. I will see you in the morning. Love you, girls."

Edward must have been tickling them, because she heard them laughing while yelling, "Love you, too," as Edward carted them up the stairs.

She put the kettle on then walked over to the office. Very quietly, she opened the door and saw Liam sitting in the dark, not moving, just staring off into space. She closed the door to give him privacy and went back into the kitchen.

Gabriella put a couple pieces of bread into the toaster. She was sure Liam must be starved, but she would have to wait to feed him.

She made tea for Edward and herself and had just finished her toast when Edward walked in. He came up behind her and started to rub her shoulders. It felt so good. She hadn't realized how tied up in knots she was.

"He will be fine. Just give him time."

"What if I made the wrong decision? Maybe I shouldn't have let

359

him see that message. Obviously that is why Raven gave it to you. She must have known how he would react."

"Don't second-guess what you did. You did the right thing for you and Liam. He just needs time to absorb it all. This is how Liam dealt with Raven's illness and death. It's not the first time I have seen him like this. You have to remember that neither one of us really talked about our feelings before meeting you. We learned a lot about the power of words by helping you. But, when in a crisis, we revert back to what we are familiar with, and that is our own inner thoughts."

She didn't say anything, reflecting on what Edward had just said.

He squeezed her shoulders a little more tightly then said, "I think you are keeping quiet just so I will continue to rub your shoulders. You're just using me for my skilled hands and fabulous looks."

She spurted a little laugh.

Gabriella decided she couldn't live in a world without Edward. He had the remarkable ability to use humour, love, and intelligence to help her through any circumstance. It was a shame people would never know this man. They could learn a lot from Edward if they were more interested in the man instead of the myth. However, that wouldn't happen until people stopped buying those trashy papers.

She veered away from her inner thoughts and answered Edward, "You're right, as always. I needed time at Kilt Rock to be with my thoughts about Marco. Now I have to be patient and give Liam the same."

Edward came to her side and grabbed her hand. Then he stopped dead. "What did you just say? And what are you drinking? Well, I'll be goddamned! Where the hell is my phone when I need it?"

"Edward, are you nuts? What are you talking about?"

"Little miss she-devil, do you realize that you are drinking British tea and you just said I was right, and I have no proof! My timing sucks. I needed to record that. No one in their right mind is going believe me."

Gabriella punched Edward in the stomach, maybe a little harder than she intended.

"Damn, Gabriella, where did you learn to do that?"

"Don't poke the bear!"

"Come on, Muhammad Ali, no more boxing. Let's watch some telly."

She followed Edward to the family room where they started watching and an old episode of *Sons of Anarchy*.

***

Gabriella opened her eyes to find the girls standing in front of her. She blinked twice, trying to figure out where she was and why the girls were there. She looked around, realizing she had fallen asleep on Edward in the family room, watching TV. Edward was still snoring softly away, oblivious to the fact that the two little girls were staring at them.

"Why are you sleeping on the couch, Gabriella? And where is Daddy?" Enya asked, and then Ainsley asked why Edward was also sleeping on the couch.

"Edward, wake up," she said as she shook a confused Edward. "Girls, we must have fallen asleep last night watching TV."

"Where's Daddy?" Ainsley asked this time.

Edward took the lead this time, seeing Gabriella was stunned at the question.

She knew the girls sensed something was wrong. Marco and her had always thought they were pulling the wool over the boys' eyes when they discussed his case, but they had been wrong. Kids always knew when something was up.

"Ladies, you know Daddy has a very important job and sometimes has to work long hours and can't always be here, but he left you in our capable hands."

"Yeah, but he always kisses us good-bye," Enya complained.

"I'm sure he did. You two ankle-biters just slept through it. You know how quiet your daddy can be," Edward reassured them, not looking at Gabriella. He knew she would give him away. "Now let's go and make some toast and get the sugared cereal when Gabriella isn't looking."

She looked crossly at Edward.

"Uncle Edward, you're going to get in trouble. I think she heard you," Ainsley whispered fairly loudly with her hand cupped by Edward's ear.

362

"I'll be right there. I just have to grab something from the office," Gabriella said as she rushed to see if Liam was still in the same spot she had left him.

She opened the door to find the office was empty, and her heart sank. She turned right around and headed for his bedroom, taking the stairs two at a time. She yanked the door open. He wasn't there, and the bed hadn't been touched.

"Oh, no. Oh, no. What have I done?"

She felt Edward before she heard him.

He hugged her from behind. "You didn't do anything wrong. He will be fine. Just give him time. I'm going to take the girls to Margaret's, and Megs is going to spend the day with them…after I load them up with sugar-coated cereal. You go and have a shower while I take care of them."

"Thanks, Edward. I owe you again. I'm going to be so screwed when you one day want repayment. Love you."

***

Five hours later, Gabriella sat on the love seat in Liam's office. She was so scared. She hadn't heard from Liam all day. She just knew she had screwed up.

She had watched the video at least twenty more times, trying to understand it from Liam's perspective. All she could see were good things. She also listened to the words of that song a dozen more times, but she still didn't get him.

She sat another hour before the door opened, and Liam walked in. He leaned on the doorjamb with his hands in his pockets and head down.

Thank God he's safe. Gabriella felt the tears flood her eyes. She didn't move, unsure how to handle him. Then she thought, *Oh, no, he can't even look at me.*

The tears started to roll down her cheeks. Still, he said nothing, just stared at the ground. She wiped the tears away as fast as they came, not wanting to be weak. Gabriella wanted to be strong like Raven had been.

However, all she could think was that he must have realized he didn't love her as much as he had thought after seeing Raven in that video.

A few minutes later, the tears stopped, but Liam still hadn't spoken. She guessed, in actuality, that silence spoke volumes. She got up, walked right past him, and then upstairs to pack. She took her engagement ring off and laid it on his pillow.

She didn't know what hit her, but she landed on the bed, like she had been hit by a freight train.

Liam was on top of her and had both of her hands held in one of his. The other hand was moving her hair off her face. He had the beginning of a beard after not shaving for a couple of days and his eyes were no longer shrouded in uncertainty. No, they were wild.

He leaned in so close to her face that she couldn't even focus on his eyes and said, "Don't you ever take my fucking ring off again; do you hear me? Not when you shower, not when you cook, not when we fight, *never. Do you understand me?*"

His growl scared the living shit out of her. Now she was breathing heavily, not knowing how to handle this Liam. She had never seen this side of him.

"And don't fucking look like you are scared of me. You know I would sell my soul before I ever physically hurt you."

Gabriella started to shake from relief, not fear, because he was talking about protecting her and that made her release some of the pent up fear that he wasn't leaving her.

The hand that had moved her hair now pounded the bed once very hard as he dropped his head into her hair.

"Oh, fuck, angel. I am so sorry. I hurt your feelings, and now I am scaring you. Fuck, baby, forgive me. I love you. Nothing means more to me than you. Angel, please, please, forgive me, baby." He let go of her hands and encased her face in his large hands, dropping his mouth to hers.

It started off soft and forgiving, and then it built up to all-consuming. This went on for a few minutes before he lifted his head then started moving his hands around the bed. Finally, he found what he was looking for and grabbed her hand, placing her beautiful marquis diamond back where it belonged.

"Now and forever, baby. Don't forget it."

Gabriella screamed, "Holy shit, Liam! You're bleeding!" His beautiful blue T-shirt that matched his eyes so perfectly had blood on it.

She grabbed it and yanked up, stopping dead in her tracks. He was bandaged up on his chest. Now she really did shake out of fear. What the hell had happened? Had he had an accident? Had he been attacked? She knew his job was—

"Gabriella, stop. I'm okay. It's not what you think."

He got up on his knees and pulled his shirt back down. Then he moved to the headboard and leaned against it. He yanked her into his arms and cradled her.

"You threw me for a loop yesterday. In a million years, I couldn't have predicted how it would feel to have all that emotion shoved at me at one time. Between hearing Raven speak, the content of the speech, and worrying about you…Well, I was overwhelmed. It was a lot to deal with. I now understand why you needed to talk to Marco at Kilt Rock. The fact that she understood and forgave me for my sins was huge. It shattered me. I didn't think I would ever get her forgiveness, but now I have it, and I can truly move on. That was huge, baby.

"But the fact that you trusted me enough to share that with me…Well, I can never thank you enough. So, this morning, I stood on the wall at Stirling Castle, and that's when I figured out that you went there to talk to Raven. I get it, baby. You asked her to watch over Marco and the boys while you watch over and love me and the girls. I get it all, and I am so thankful for you.

"You call me your saviour when you are the true saviour. You make me whole. You are the protector, and I love you now and forevermore." Liam lifted Gabriella off his lap, placed her beside him on the bed, and then he ripped his T-shirt off. "So, after I left the wall, I went to a tattoo artist and he did as I requested." He looked Gabriella in the eyes as he gently removed the bandage.

"Oh, sweet Jesus, it is beautiful." She was sure her mouth was hanging open.

On Liam's chest was the tattoo of the Raven with angel wings wrapped around it now. Written beneath the tattoo was, *"Under Her Wings, Two Become One."*

"Liam, it's gorgeous. I don't know what to say. It takes my breath away."

"It's a tribute to you. You gave me my heart and soul back. You brought together two families and made them one." He gave her a heated look. "Now, enough talking, I need to fuck you like I never have, so get that sweet ass over here."

Chapter 32

Gypsy Girl

The simple life Liam had wished for was short-lived and now put on hold. He realized this as Gabriella sat with him while they combed over the report Garett had given him about the sex tape scandal.

"I knew she was innocent! I just knew it. Liam, why? Why would they do that to him? I don't understand." She shook her head. "They were so happy. He thought he had found his forever. He wanted to build a life with her and have a family. Oh, that poor girl. We have to tell Edward right now," Gabriella said as she stood to get her cell phone.

Liam grabbed her hand. "You can't go off half-cocked. I need you to understand the severity of this. It is a very delicate situation, and it involves some very influential people. It needs to be handled with care.

"I met with Tom when I got the report, and he called an internal investigation. We have already met with Scotland Yard, the king, and his representatives, as well as the perpetrators. I want you to understand these people are very high up the chain of command. This is a serious security breach. If information that the perpetrators have the power to manipulate the royal family is leaked, it could cause untold damage.

"I will allow you to be in this meeting with Edward because I believe you can help him remain composed and calm and, hopefully, stop him from going off. However, I want you to let me handle the disclosure of this deception.

"Myles, his assistant, was involved, and as far as the media is concerned, he alone will be taking the fall. His co-conspirators set it up so that, if the breach were ever revealed, it would appear Myles was the only guilty party, but let me assure you that we have nailed them all."

As Liam continued to explain to her how complicated and deep the scandal ran, she realized how scary and powerful some people were. Liam told her he was putting them all in jeopardy just by insisting Edward needed to know the truth. He informed her that the media relations department was already working overtime on how to vindicate Gillian and keep the damage to a minimum.

"Knowing what I have told you, do you still want to sit in on this meeting with Edward?"

Gabriella didn't hesitate for one second. "Absolutely. Without question, I want to be there for Edward."

Liam texted Edward, and when Edward walked in, he instantly felt the tension in the room.

"Okay, what the fuck has happened now?"

"Edward, sit down. We need to talk to you, and I need you to promise me you will remain calm and hear me out."

Edward turned to Gabriella, trying to gauge what the hell was going on. She looked scared, which made his stomach suddenly clench. He sensed this wasn't going to be good at all.

He walked over and grabbed her hand as he sat down. "Talk to me, love."

"No, this has to come from me," Liam told him. "But I am giving you fair warning that, if you overreact, I will do everything in my power to contain you."

Edward turned to Liam with eyes as big as saucers. "Okay, I get it. Tell me already."

"I'm not going to sugar-coat this. I have just discovered that Gillian was innocent all along. She told you the truth. She didn't commission that tape, nor did she sell it. In fact, she had no knowledge of it. She was setup in order to break you two apart."

Edward lurched back like he had been punched in the face. Then he whipped his head around to confirm Liam wasn't fucking with him. The instant he saw the tears in Gabriella's eyes and her nodding her head in agreement, he knew it was true. But how was this possible? They had done an investigation. They had shown him all the evidence. How could they have been so wrong?

370

Edward's fear was now turning to anger.

"How the fuck is that possible!" He turned to Liam. "You saw the evidence; who could possibly have that kind of power?" Edward began to pace when all colour drained from his face, and he wavered like he was going to collapse. "Please, Liam, I beg you, man. Tell me…Tell me it wasn't my family."

"It wasn't your family. It was people who are supposed to protect you and your family."

Edward exploded. "Who, Liam! I want fucking names!"

He stomped towards Liam, ready for battle, but then Gabriella yelled his name and jumped between the two men.

"Edward, stop! Look at me! You need to listen and process all of this. Sweetheart, I'm not going to lie to you. It's going to rip you apart. Try not to think about revenge, but think about the person who has been hurt the most in this. Gillian."

Edward lost all of his bluster when Gabriella mentioned Gillian. He needed to get his shit together so he could get all the information, and think about his next step.

He sat back down on the couch and told Liam to lay it all out for him.

It took over an hour for Liam to tell Edward the complicated story, and Edward was beyond furious by the end of it. He was mostly disappointed in Myles. He had trusted him for over ten years, considered him a friend. He wasn't even sure why this surprised him, though—everyone eventually betrayed him.

371

Gabriella looked at him, reading his thoughts. "Don't you dare! I have seen that look before. Not everyone has betrayed you. I haven't; Liam hasn't; your brothers and the rest of your family haven't. And Raven didn't. There are two little girls who rely on you to help teach them the value of trust and love. Don't you dare give up on that. We all have had shitty things happen in our lives, but it was you who taught me to stand up, brush it off, and move on. You have the chance to win the love of your life back. Liam and I didn't get that chance, Edward. This is a gift. Don't you dare throw it away!"

All the fury within him instantly evaporated. All he had to do was look at the insurmountable odds his two closest friends had been forced to overcome to survive, let alone find love again, and he knew she was right. He needed to stop feeling sorry for himself and right some wrongs.

"What would I do without you two? I need to get past this. But how did all of this come to surface? It has been over a year."

Gabriella looked to Liam for direction, and he nodded his head.

She turned towards Edward. "Do you remember at the hospital when an old friend of mine was trying to contact me? Her name was Jill. Well, it turned out that Jill is actually Gillian. She saw the photo of us and believed we were together, so she contacted me to warn me to be careful. She told me she was innocent and didn't want her fate to be mine. She said you deserved to be happy. She didn't want to see you hurt again. She still loves you, Edward.

"I know how much that conversation hurt her and the price she paid to put herself on the line. At first, I was so angry I didn't even tell her the truth—that we aren't a couple. I wanted to punish her for hurting you. It looks like I owe her a huge apology." Gabriella walked into Edward's arms and hugged him tightly.

As her warmth surrounded him, he realized he had a chance to make it better, and he would.

***

When Liam and Edward got off the plane in Nepal, the heat and humidity were like walking into a brick wall. The flight had been long, and Edward hadn't slept a wink, too busy trying to think of the right thing to say to Gillian.

How would she receive the news that he knew she was innocent? Would she let him repair the damage he had caused? He had to stop guessing and formulate a plan to get her to understand.

For a year, he had believed she had betrayed him, yet even believing that he had moved on with someone new, she cared enough to try to warn them. He couldn't imagine himself calling her new boyfriend and warning him.

He missed her so much. He hadn't allowed his heart to feel in so long now that the damn thing felt broken, the emotion overwhelming. Gillian had taught him a lot about love, about laughing at yourself, and not taking the world so seriously. He was embarrassed to admit he had forgotten the lessons she had taught him. He laughed and joked all the time, but eighty percent of it was a

373

way to protect himself.

His mind continued to wander as their driver took them to where Gillian was working. He stared out the window at the devastation that still enveloped this city, proud that she was here, working on building new homes for devastated families.

"Edward, stop tormenting yourself. When you explain all the evidence, she will see how you were manipulated to believe she was guilty of betraying you."

"I'm scared, man. Seriously scared. What if she doesn't take me back? I hurt her, and I really don't deserve to get her back. But I love her, and I don't want to live another moment without her. What if she has found someone new? Then what do I do?"

"This wasn't your fault. Don't lose sight of that. So, tell me, how are we going to play this out? Do you want to wait until tonight, or do you want to do this now?"

"I don't know yet. Let me just look at her first. I need to see how my courage holds out. Fuck, I can't believe how nervous I am. My hands are shaking. I wish Gabriella had come; she always knows what to say to calm me down."

Liam was also missing Gabriella. They'd had one hell of a fight over her not coming, but everyone had to keep a clear head and remember they were dealing with very powerful and connected men, and Liam wasn't risking anything happening to her. On top of that, most of the world believed Edward and Gabriella were a couple, and they didn't want to alert the media by flaunting it in their faces then

374

denying it.

They pulled up to the community where Gillian's crew was helping. A foreman walked up to the driver and gave him directions to the house Gillian was currently working on.

Their car moved slowly down the road and pulled into a makeshift driveway two doors away.

"Bloody hell, Liam. There she is," Edward whispered.

He watched her bend down and measure the two-by-four, and then she lifted the circular saw and made her cuts. She looked tanned and way more toned than the last time he had seen her. She was simply beautiful, even covered in dust, dripping in sweat, with her hair held back by a bandana. She made Edward's heart skip a beat.

She was concentrating on a sheet of paper with more figures when Edward slowly got out of the car, mesmerized by her. He stood there, watching her, until Gillian sensed a presence and slowly turned towards the car. Her eyes locked with Edward's, and she wiped her eyes, obviously not believing what she was seeing.

Edward rounded the car and started walking towards her, but she backed up, wildly looking around for an escape route.

"Hey, gypsy girl, I need to talk to you."

"No, it can't be. No, Edward. I'm sorry I called your girlfriend. It won't happen again. Just leave me alone. Turn around and leave."

"Please give me a few minutes in private. I need to speak to you. If you choose not to do it privately, then I'll do it here, but you will hear me out."

"No, you lost the right to tell me what to do over a year ago. You don't get to make those decisions anymore. Leave me alone." Gillian's eyes filled with tears, and her heart pounded. She couldn't do this.

She turned to walk back to the house she was working on, and Edward started to yell.

"Gypsy girl, I know you didn't do it. I know you are innocent. I just found out and came here to apologize. Please hear me out. Don't walk away, Gillian. I'm begging you."

Gillian stopped dead in her tracks and slowly turned. It felt like he had pushed a knife right into her chest. It was too much for her to bear.

He saw she was in so much pain and trying desperately to stop her silent tears.

"How fucking dare you ask me to hear you out!" she screamed at the top of her lungs. "For months, I begged anyone who knew you to listen to me and get word to you! Did you once in the last year call me and ask my side of the story? No! You couldn't give me the benefit of the doubt! You accused me then disappeared. You broke my heart! You never believed in me, in what we had. You said you loved me, but that was a lie! You walked away without even a backwards glance. I had to deal with the fallout by myself. You left me all alone and unprotected!"

She stumbled backwards and fell on her ass. She started to crawl backwards, continuing to yell, "Then you replaced me with a beautiful, lost soul I can't even hate. Go away! We can never go back. What's done is done. Please, just walk away! You have moved on. Please, just let me continue to pick up the pieces of my shattered life."

Liam got out of the car and walked straight for Edward. Everyone in the community had stopped working and were coming to see what had upset Gillian.

Her co-workers and friends adored her. They stepped in between Gillian and Edward, sheltering her from the two men who had distressed her so much.

Edward wanted to push everyone away.

"I didn't know. I swear. Please forgive me. *Please*, gypsy girl," Edward begged, grasping at straws. He couldn't lose her again.

Liam grabbed Edward's arms and forcibly pulled him back as he spoke into his ear, "This isn't the time or the place to do this. It isn't smart, and it isn't safe. You need to continue this conversation in private. You're making a scene. Walk away and regroup. We can meet up with Gillian tonight at her lodging."

As Liam hustled Edward into the car, Gillian's friend Raheem helped her up and loaded her into his pickup truck. As Raheem pulled away, one of the construction workers moved a tractor in front of the driveway, blocking Edward's car and preventing him from following the pickup.

After fifteen very frustrating minutes, the construction crew finally moved the tractor. During that time, Liam had his hands full, trying everything in his power to contain Edward and not let him cause any more of a scene. They didn't need that to be splashed across every newspaper in the free world.

Liam and Edward went back to their hotel, freshened up, and then Edward insisted they head over to the address Gillian had been staying at since she had arrived in Nepal. Once there, they waited…and waited.

After four hours, Raheem walked outside and up to the car.

Edward opened the door. "Where is she? Please, I mean her no harm. I just really need to talk to her."

"I am sorry, but she has left. She left the country this afternoon. She asked me to give you a message once she had a chance to get away. She wants you to find happiness in your new life. She wants you to protect, love, and trust in Gabriella. She said you both deserve some happiness. Those are her words. The next are mine.

"Gillian is a caring, giving, selfless woman. She came to us two and a half months ago, ready to do anything to help. She works harder than anyone here and takes credit for nothing. Every night, after a quick meal and a shower, she would disappear. It took me weeks to find out that she goes to the makeshift tent cities to help the children with their studies. Still, she wants no thanks or recognition. I mean no disrespect, but you were a fool to take other people's truths over hers."

"You don't know anything—"

"No, Prince Edward, I know more than you think. Be enough of a man to walk away. When she needed you, you weren't there. Now she has taught herself how to carry on without you. Let her mend.

"Did you know she nearly lost herself to the bottle? You have the power to completely destroy her, if you push her. If you truly love her, walk away. If she wants you back in her life, she will come to you. As someone who loves and cares for her, I'm telling you to leave her alone. Don't shatter what is left of her heart."

Raheem turned around and walked back inside while Edward stood there for another thirty minutes, just staring at the door Raheem had walked through.

Liam finally walked up to him and squeezed his shoulder. "Time to go."

"I'm afraid, if I leave here, I will never see her again. How could I have been so cruel? I don't deserve her back. I destroyed her. I left her to face the accusations alone, while I went on with my life."

"I know better than most what it feels like to let down the person who counted on you the most, but give her time. If Raven could forgive me, then Gillian will forgive you. Just give her space and time to come to her own conclusions."

Forty-eight hours later, they were back where they had started, standing in Liam's house.

Chapter 33

Wash Your Mouth Out

I don't understand. How could she not even hear him out?" Gabriella asked Liam as she traced the tattoo on his chest.

They were talking in bed while enjoying the afterglow of a hard and rough sexual encounter. It had been the first time they had been separated since they had met, and he knew one hundred percent that he wouldn't leave their bed again.

He had been toying with the idea of resigning from Edward's security detail and relocating from London to Stirling. Maybe he would even leave the RAF altogether and find a job in the private sector. One thing he knew for sure was that he wasn't spending another night away from his angel.

"Look at it from her perspective. She was wrongly accused, and the person who was supposed to protect her and love her before everything else rejected her and didn't listen to her. I can't imagine what I would do if the same thing happened to me and I couldn't reach you. I would go out of my fucking mind.

"Gillian then starts to move on with her life, and one day out of the blue, she suddenly is vindicated by the person who hurt her the most. Well, fuck, I wouldn't trust it, either. And to top it off, she believes you and Edward are a couple. That has to sting like crazy."

Gabriella was quiet while she considered what Liam had said. She knew she was totally biased when it came to Edward, but Liam was right; Gillian was suffering.

Knowing what she had to do, she pulled away from Liam and got out of bed.

"What are you doing, angel?" Liam asked, enjoying watching his girl strut around the room naked. Her long hair sometimes blocked his view, but then it would move, and he would have another perfect view of her beautiful body. She wasn't the same woman who had been self-conscious and uncomfortable being naked around him six months ago. Now she was all his. He was the luckiest bastard in the world.

"I need to contact Gillian. She needs to hear his side." Gabriella fretted until she located her phone, and then she scrolled down her messages until she found Gillian's. She started to text, her fingers flying over the keyboard.

We need to talk ASAP.

She pushed send and stared at the phone, waiting for a response. Not two minutes later, a ping indicated she had a response.

Not happening. Have a nice life!

Gabriella typed, *I am going to throw your words back at you. Hear me out. Then you never have to hear from me ever again!*

As she waited for Gillian's response, she crawled back in bed to join Liam who was leaning against the headboard, watching her. He moved her so she was in front of him, between his powerful legs. Then he wrapped his arms around her and rested his chin on her shoulder so he could read the texts.

Ping.

Not fair. I was helping you. Let sleeping dogs lie! Gillian wrote.

Not a chance in hell. Give me the same courtesy I gave you. I am not giving up!

Gabriella had already formulated her next text and was going to send it if Gillian didn't respond. It took almost twenty minutes before she heard the text alert chime.

Fine. Tomorrow @ 10 a.m. 5 minutes; that's all you get.

Thank you. You won't regret it. I promise. :) Gabriella responded.

Gabriella was so happy, thinking she could do this. She could give Edward what he had given her—his life back. She hoped. She probably wouldn't sleep a wink due to trying to figure out what magical words would change Gillian's mind.

Ping. Gabriella hadn't expected another text.

I already do! :(

***

Ring...Ring...Ring...

382

"Ah, hello?" Gabriella whispered with a groggy voice.

"Who is it, baby? Is everything okay?" Liam asked in a gruff voice as he rolled towards her.

"Oh, you bitch.! I can't believe it. I trusted you. You're fucking sleeping beside Edward right now. You're lying next to him when you take my call. Who the fuck does that?" Gillian screamed into the phone.

Gabriella instantly sat up to look at the clock beside the bed.

"Gillian, it's five forty-five a.m. I'm not sure where you are, but in Stirling, it is early. I was expecting your call at ten. And it's not what you think."

"I don't have to think. I heard Edward! That's it. I'm done. Don't contact me again."

"No, no, please, Gillian. It's Liam's voice, not Edward's. Liam is in my bed," she rushed out, hoping Gillian hadn't hung up on her.

Gabriella waited for a response, fearing Gillian had hung up.

"And they say I'm the twisted one. How dare you? Is one not enough? You have to sleep with Edward and his bodyguard? You sick bitch!"

After clearly hearing the profanity and the tone Gillian was screaming through the phone, an infuriated Liam snatched it away from a shocked Gabriella.

"Gillian, Liam here. Look who's jumping to conclusions now! Stop for one second and hear my fiancée out. Media manipulation, Gillian, plain and simple. You should understand that." Liam's two

383

sentences were short but bloody powerful.

He handed the phone back to Gabriella, feeling confident his point had been received.

Knowing Gabriella would want privacy for her girl talk, he decided to go for a run.

"Your fiancé? Liam is your fiancé? I don't understand."

"I was never involved with Edward. He is my friend. I love him, but my heart and soul belong to Liam. The media created the story that Edward and I were involved."

"But I saw the pictures and the footage from the pub. I saw how Edward looked at you. Trust me; I have only ever seen that look given to one other person, and that was me. He does love you, Gabriella."

"Yes, he does love me, but he isn't *in love* with me. Gillian, he found me at one of the lowest points in my life and nursed me back to health, mentally and physically. He never gave up on me. But I'm like the sister he never had. I owe him so much, and I know for a fact that he truly only loves one person, and that, my friend, is you."

Gillian started sobbing. "It's too late for us. That ship has sailed. He never truly loved me or trusted me enough to weather the storms. We were fooling ourselves that it could work. It was better we found out sooner rather than later."

"Better for whom, Gillian? He has been devastated by the breakup. He hasn't dated a single soul since you. He has even told me that he will never have children, because he could only ever imagine his children with you as their mother. Now does that sound like a man who isn't head over heels in love with you?"

"You don't understand. Too much has happened, and it can't be repaired. Sometimes, love just isn't enough."

"Then you're right; I don't understand. Is he breathing? Are you breathing? If you are both breathing, then that means anything is possible and can be repaired. I know you researched my history. Liam told me what you said to Edward in Nepal. I would give anything to have another shot with my family, but I can't. That isn't fixable; your situation is.

"Stop being stubborn, open your heart, and let your mind wander. Think about what your children would be like and how sad it would be if they never exist because their parents were too stubborn to see past their own hurt. If you aren't willing to do that, then maybe you aren't the woman Edward needs. Are you going to continue to punish yourself just to make Edward pay for something he was manipulated to believe?"

"You're killing me. I need time to think."

"I can give you that, but if you need any questions answered, call me. And, Gillian, I am so sorry I didn't tell you Edward and I weren't a couple. I am so protective of him, and I was afraid you were going to hurt him. Please forgive me. Where are you now?"

"No offence, but I really need time, even for your apology. Our last conversation nearly destroyed me, and I'm not sure I trust you to keep my whereabouts secret. How do I know you aren't

385

manipulating the truth? Give me time. I need to make the right decision for me."

"Absolutely. I get it. You will learn to trust me, though, and we will be friends. I guarantee it. Be safe and don't work too hard. I will talk to you soon," Gabriella said as she hung up the phone.

Gillian looked at the phone in her hand and smiled. Gabriella knew where she was. She had told her to be safe and not to work too hard. She had figured out Gillian was still in Nepal. Smart woman. Maybe they would be friends.

***

"Edward, will you set another place at the table? A friend of mine said she might be stopping by."

"You collect women friends like the Pied Piper collects rats. Do you have some magical flute that entrances them? Because, honestly, I could really use that," Edward said with a smile, the first real one anyone had seen out of him in over three weeks.

The blended family were preparing a meal together in celebration of the girls finally getting a clean bill of health from the doctors today.

Their family dynamics were adorable. Liam refused to sit at the head of the table because he wanted Gabriella beside him, so the twins each got the head of the table. Liam and Gabriella sat on one side and Edward on the other.

Gabriella had just made them say a prayer of thanks for each other and for the food. She hadn't returned to her religious beliefs, but she did believe in spirituality and Heaven. She wanted the girls to be comfortable talking to their mom.

Just after the prayer, the door bell rang, and Edward said he would get it.

"Thanks, Edward, but I'm not sure how my friend would feel about one of the princes of England answering our door," Gabriella said as she walked away.

Edward turned to talk to the twins. "Ankle-biters, since you girls have a clean bill of health, I would like to take us all to Balmoral Castle and ride some ponies; what do you think?" Edward had been promising them that since they left the hospital.

Ainsley and Enya both clapped their hands and said, "Yes. Yes, please." Then the girls instantly started asking Edward what colour the ponies were and what their names were.

Edward had just lifted his fork to his mouth to steal a bite of food before Gabriella walked back in and said, "Everyone, I would like you to meet my friend."

Gabriella stepped out of the way, and Gillian stepped forwards.

Edward's fork fell out of his hand and hit the plate with a clank. "Bloody hell, gypsy girl!" he whispered, not believing his eyes. He stood up so quickly his chair fell backwards, making a loud bang.

Everyone's attention turned to Edward.

"Daddy, Uncle Edward just swore. He said bloody and hell," Enya was quick to respond.

"You're in trouble, Uncle Edward. You're going to get your

mouth washed out with soap," Ainsley added.

"I can do that if you want, girls, but it will have to wait until after dinner. I'm famished, and it smells delicious in here," Gillian responded with a smile.

Edward continued to stand there with his mouth hanging open.

"Close your mouth, Uncle Edward. You're catching flies," Enya told him, and they all laughed.

"Gillian, please sit down beside Edward and let me introduce you to the girls."

"We know who she is, Gabriella. That's Auntie Gillian. Hey, Auntie Gillian, where have you been? We missed you," Ainsley proudly announced.

Gillian walked over to Ainsley and gave her a big hug and a kiss. Then she did the same to Liam and Enya before making her way to Edward, who was still standing in shock. She kissed his cheek and pressed her finger under his chin, pushing his mouth closed. She then bent down and picked up his chair, and he plunked himself down with Gillian's assistance.

Gabriella and Liam were smiling from ear to ear as they started to pass the food, and the twins continued to talk about ponies to Edward.

"Uncle Edward, you aren't answering. Uncle Edward!" Enya whined.

Edward was still in shock.

"I think Uncle Edward needs a few minutes, princess," Liam

388

said. "It has been a long time since he has seen Auntie Gillian. We can talk about ponies another day. Let's find out what Auntie Gillian has been up to."

Gillian took over the conversation, telling everyone about building houses. She told the girls about the earthquake in Nepal and reassured them it would never happen in the UK. Then she talked about the children in her village who had lost everything. The girls asked lots of questions, and Gillian answered honestly. The twins decided they wanted to help build houses, too.

"Munchkins, you are too young to build houses, but there are still things you can do. You can collect books that you don't read anymore and ask your classmates to do the same. And maybe, with your help, we can fill their school with books."

"Gabriella, when we go to school tomorrow, can you talk to our teacher?" Ainsley asked.

"Sure, I think that would be a fabulous idea. On second thought, we should talk to your principal. We can organize a bake sale to raise money for supplies the school needs and organize donations of books for Auntie Gillian's community."

Liam was so proud of how his girls instantly referred to Gabriella for help. She had been mothering them for months now, and it showed. The girls trusted her and respected her opinion.

Liam turned to Edward. He wanted the same feelings he was experiencing for the prince—to have the love of a good woman and children he adored.

Edward still hadn't said a word. He was only eating because Gillian had ordered him to. His mind was too muddled with confusion to do anything else. Why was Gillian here? Had she forgiven him? *God, she is so beautiful.* He kept staring at her out of the corner of his eye.

After dinner, he heard Liam tell the girls they were going to go out for ice cream so Uncle Edward and Auntie Gillian could talk.

"But, Daddy, Uncle Edward loves ice cream. Can't he come?" Ainsley begged.

"Uncle Edward and Auntie Gillian want to catch up," Gabriella told her. "We can have our ice cream, go to the park and play, and on the way back, we will pick up a pint of Uncle Edward and Auntie Gillian's favourite kinds of ice cream. How does that sound, girls?"

"Oh, okay. Uncle Edward, Auntie Gillian, what's your favourite ice cream?" Enya asked.

In unison, they answered, "English toffee."

Edward turned towards Gillian, and she smiled.

Liam watched his youngest daughter pull on her Wellies as she said, "You both like the same ice cream; how silly is that?"

"Daddy, is there something wrong with Uncle Edward?" Enya asked as they were walking out the door.

"No, baby, everything is finally right," Edward heard Liam tell his daughter as the door softly closed.

Edward stood there for a few minutes, trying to figure out what to say. His heart was pounding, his palms were sweaty, and he tried desperately to come up with something intelligent to say. However, his brain was on overload, and he could only think of one thing.

"Why?"

"Why, what?"

"Gillian, don't play with me. Why are you here?"

"Gabriella can be quite persuasive when she wants to be," Gillian replied.

"How did you and Gabriella end up having a conversation? How was she able to reach you when I have been unsuccessful? I have had a team of investigators trying to track you down for over three weeks," Edward asked with confusion.

"I didn't want to be found. By sheer luck, Gabriella contacted me the day I turned on my phone to retrieve my contact list before I threw it away. Edward, I needed time to think after Gabriella explained all that had happened."

"So, what did you come up with?"

"I don't really know yet. I needed to talk to you before I could make any concrete decisions. I am balancing on a very thin rope right now. I could go either way. Tell me what happened. Why did you have such little faith in me? I thought you loved and trusted me."

"I did, but the people who masterminded our breakup made sure I would believe them. They had been bugging our bedroom for months, and when you said we were so hot together and should make a sex tape...Well, those words were used to convince me you

391

had betrayed me. They used our private conversations and set you up with your own words. Then they ensured we had no verbal communication; therefore, you could never defend the accusations against you. I'm so sorry. I don't know what else to say. I know it sounds lame, but that's all I have. I can't change what they did to us. I'm embarrassed that I was so badly manipulated. I have never, not for one second, stopped loving you, though. I missed you, gypsy girl."

Gillian looked at Edward with tears running down her face. She saw him move towards her to comfort her, but she couldn't allow that until she had said her piece.

She moved back, seeing the pain and defeat on Edward's face. She didn't want him to misunderstand her.

"I never stopped loving you, either. I have tried to make myself a better woman so you would be proud of me, and I could be proud of myself. I nearly lost my battle with the bottle, but I didn't want to become what everyone expected me to be—my mother. Therefore, I threw myself into charity work.

"I am so proud of what we have accomplished." She smiled through her tears. "The community in Nepal became like a surrogate family to me. I still have a lot of work to do there.

"When the pictures of you and Gabriella were published, I thought you had replaced me. I was devastated when I learned all that had happened to her. I knew you had rescued her, and I knew whoever set me up would do the same to her because of her background. I knew, if I wasn't royal material, she definitely wasn't. So, I phoned her and warned her. That night, I fell off the wagon again and scared myself straight."

Edward thought about everything Gillian had just said to him. Then he filled her in on how he had discovered the truth.

"Gabriella knew you were innocent and still loved me after your first conversation with her. She knew how much I still loved you, so she asked Liam to investigate privately. He uncovered the truth, and they told me. Two hours after telling me the story, Liam and I were on a plane to Nepal.

"Gillian, I am sorry this happened. I know I broke your heart. I won't lie and say it wasn't my fault, because it totally and completely was. You were right; I didn't trust what we had. Life taught me not to trust anyone, but Gabriella helped me to see that, yes, I do have people in my life I can trust. If you can forgive me, I will never make that mistake again."

Gillian walked into Edward's arms and brought her mouth slowly to his. He got his first taste of her in over a year, yet it wasn't enough.

He tilted her head up and deepened the kiss. She tasted familiar, sweet, and right. He moaned as he tried to consume her mouth, and she purred.

They were so lost in each other they didn't hear the family enter the house.

The girls ran into the room, and Enya yelled, "Auntie Gillian is washing Uncle Edward's mouth out with her tongue, Daddy."

Chapter 34

Full Moon a Rising

Liam had phoned his mum to see if the girls could spend the night so Edward could have his imitate reunion with Gillian. He didn't want to say it out loud, but he knew those two could shatter glass with their antics in the bedroom. It was the most he could do on such short notice.

Liam couldn't leave them completely alone or check them into a hotel until the media had been dealt with. And the twins had just gotten back to school; otherwise, they could all travel to Balmoral Castle for a few weeks.

Liam was on the phone, explaining that to his team, when Gabriella interrupted him and said she could home-school the girls for a few of weeks. She desperately wanted Gillian and Edward to have the time to reconnect in private.

After the twins were safely nestled at Nana's house, the four adults sat in the living room with their favourite beverages, making plans for the next few weeks.

Gillian hated to be the bearer of bad news, but she needed everyone to understand.

"Edward, I love you, and I don't want you to misunderstand my next remark, but I have to be back in Nepal in two weeks. I made commitments, and I don't intend to break them. I am making a difference in Nepal, and it is important work. The last time we were together, I gave up my life to accommodate yours. When we broke up, I had nothing. If this is going to work, I need to retain my independence as well as create a life with you. Do you understand?"

His initial reaction was to feel hurt by her words. After all, he wanted to spend every second with Gillian. Didn't she also want back what they used to have?

It only took him a few moments to realize he needed to put her first, and he needed to understand her fears and concerns. She had changed over the last year, and he was proud of the woman she had become.

"Gillian, I can honestly say I want to spend every minute of the day with you, but you're right. We need to find a healthy balance that is beneficial for both of us. We need to take it slow and rediscover each other. I'm going to lay my heart on the line here and say I will take whatever you are offering. I love you and need you in my life." Edward gently pulled Gillian to his chest and laid a hot, wet one on her. He couldn't stop touching her, afraid that, if he let go, she would disappear again.

Liam interjected quickly. He needed to organize their next move then get the hell upstairs before the room ignited from the lust. There was sexual tension surrounding Edward and Gillian that was palpable, any little spark was going to set the room on fire. He knew he was going to hear the explosion tonight, but he truly did not want to witness it.

"Okay, so here's the plan," Liam started. "The media relations office needs a week or so to work out how the public will be informed about the scandal. We don't want to announce Gillian's presence yet since she still has work to do in Nepal, and I don't want the press to hound her. Public relations are also going to announce Gabriella's and my engagement and explain Gabriella and Edward's friendship.

"Balmoral castle is still open to the public with limited hours during the day. Amongst all the cottages for the workers on the property, there are a few vacant ones in a remote corner of the property kept for guests of the royal family when the main castle is full. We will take one cottage, and you two will have the other. Let's just make this a vacation and have some fun. But, Edward, I warn you now; I will try to give you two as much privacy as I can, but you promised my two little hellions you would teach them to ride ponies, and Edward, payback is a bitch."

They all laughed.

Liam stood and scooped Gabriella into his arms. "Say good night, angel. By the way, I'm cancelling our run in the morning,

Edward. I have a feeling you may want to stay in your warm bed just as much as I do."

"You bet your life, old man. Good night, Gabriella. Good night, Liam," Edward responded.

As Liam was walking out of the room, he heard Gillian say, "You were right, Gabriella. I don't regret it."

Gabriella responded, "Be happy, my friend. You deserve it!"

Edward sat beside Gillian, staring. He still couldn't believe she was there. He ran his hands through her hair. It was so soft and smelled exactly as he remembered, like gardenias. After smelling her hair, he wanted more, so he yanked her closer to him. Then he nestled his nose into the back of her neck and inhaled.

God, he loved the smell of her perfume. That scent had haunted him for the last year. He couldn't pass the perfume section of a store without seeking out her familiar scent. It never smelled quite right, though, because it was the fragrance mixed with her unique scent that was so fucking intoxicating.

He twisted his fingers into her hair and pulled so that she fell onto his lap. Now she was staring up at him with lust-filled eyes, her head in his lap, her body stretched out on the couch. He wasn't ready to take her yet. No, he needed to reassure all his senses that she was back where she belonged.

He looked her over from the tips of her toes to the top of her head. She wore no polish on her toes. He quickly scanned her hands—no polish there, either. He lifted her hands and examined them closely, finding she had calluses all over them. They weren't soft like he remembered. They were dry and cracked, but they were strong and beautifully shaped. Her long fingers were good for playing the piano, she had always said.

He brought her well worked hands to his mouth and kissed all the calluses, proud she carried the marks of her determination and dedication. Next, he looked down at her outfit: a long, flowing, patterned skirt; with an off-the-shoulders, purple, bohemian styled top. Lots of necklaces hung around her tanned throat, and bangles adorned her wrists. She could have stepped out of the cartoon version of the *Hunchback of Notre Dame*. She was his own spectacular gypsy girl.

She swallowed deep then licked her lips as she watched him assess her. Fuck, he couldn't wait to get her mouth on his dick.

He had smelled her, looked at her, touched her, felt her, and tasted her. Now he had to get her naked and start all over.

He slipped her top down, thrilled to discover she had no bra on. Staring back at him were her hard, pebbled nipples, screaming out to be pinched, and that's exactly what he did. *Shit, could this day get any better?*

He pinched the red, little raspberries and gave a little twist. She moaned deeply and ground her hips into the couch. He then bent and licked away the pain while he pinched and twisted the other one. She gasped then held her breath until he licked the pain of that one away.

They needed to take this upstairs where his room was. It had

399

been so long since Edward had had sex that he knew he wasn't going to last long the first time. He was going to blow his load, which would take the edge off, and then he was going to spend his time enjoying the second round.

Gillian went to pull her top up, but Edward refused to let her. He liked the added excitement of maybe getting caught.

She jumped and giggled as Edward walked behind her, groping her. On the second landing, he wrapped both arms around her and grabbed her breasts, holding each one in the palms of his hand, trapping her nipples between his fingers, and then he squeezed. She yelped from the unexpected pain and pleasure.

"This is only the beginning," he whispered in her ear. "I want to hear you begging me for your release."

Gillian couldn't have imagined being this happy one month ago. She had a lot to be thankful for. She was living the dream her head hadn't let her heart have for the last year.

When they walked into Edward's bedroom, he attacked. Her skirt, hipster panties, and bohemian top were gone in under five seconds. There she stood, with only four necklaces, nine bangles, and one funky shelled anklet.

She turned slowly to face him, and he growled, looking at her from bottom to top.

The second time of reintroducing himself to her, he started at her face and worked his way down. He saw her redder than normal nipples, her flat stomach, her belly button ring, and then his eyebrows hit the top of his forehead and his smile grew huge across his face. She had trimmed what little bit of pubic hair she had into a heart.

"Well, fuck me three ways to Sunday. Bloody hell! Tell me you did that for me, gypsy girl."

"I did," she whispered, pleased with his reaction.

He walked up to her and consumed her mouth then dropped to his knees and kissed her heart. He pulled apart her lips and licked up her essence. Her taste was like an aphrodisiac, and he lost his mind.

He grabbed her by the hips and threw her on the bed. She bounced a bit, leaned up on her elbows, and then opened her legs wide as she watched him strip off his clothes.

His lack of patience caused him to get tangled up in his shirt. Suddenly, material was ripped, and the mangled shirt was lying on the floor.

"Touch yourself. Give me something to focus on," he told her as he toed off his shoes and reached for his belt. He tried twice before he was able to slip the button from the hole. The pull of the material over his hard-on made getting the button and zipper down next to impossible.

Gillian saw his struggle and impatience. "Let me."

Edward stilled as she got to her knees in front of him. If he didn't calm down, he was going to come in his pants like a thirteen-year-old lad.

Gillian kissed his tummy while she worked to free him of his pants. He was so absorbed in the feel of her mouth he didn't realize she had managed to get his pants around his ankles.

When she tapped his ankle, he lifted his foot, and soon, the next one followed. She looked up at him. She had forgotten how big the man really was.

She wrapped her fingers around his girth with both hands and stroked him a couple of times then lowered her mouth to his dick, humming from the familiar taste of him. That one hum did him in and had him yanking himself out of her mouth before spraying her body with his seed.

"Fuck, baby, sorry. Just looking at you did me in. You're so beautiful. But when your warm lips wrapped around me, it was more than I could take."

Edward rushed to the loo then back into the bedroom with a warm cloth and cleaned Gillian before laying her across the bed.

He lined himself up to her core and said, "I'm clean, baby. I haven't been with anyone since you."

"Stop!" Gillian yelled as she pulled back. "Condom. I'm not on the pill."

"Seriously, baby? Are you kidding me? I don't have any. I wasn't expecting this. I'll pull out before I come. I promise." Edward was beyond desperate to get into Gillian, and he was close to begging her for it.

"No way. I'm not rekindling this relationship with an unwanted pregnancy." Gillian could just imagine the headlines if that happened. No thank you, no sir, no way in hell! "Ask Liam!"

"I will never live this down. That bastard will remind me every day until my dying day."

"Then go to the store."

"Fuck, fuck, and double fuck. I will be back in a second." Edward swore as he grabbed the towel he had just thrown on the floor.

He ran down the flight of stairs to Liam's room and knocked loudly.

"Not now!" Liam yelled with a strained voice.

Edward pounded on the door then laid his forehead against it, begging, "Listen, old man, unlike you, I haven't dipped my wick into my girl in over a year, and if I don't find a condom, I won't be tonight, either. Please help a brother out. I'm begging, Liam. Seriously, don't fuck me up. Gabriella, I need help here. Please, love, help."

God bless Gabriella. Edward could hear her reprimanding his best friend.

"Liam, don't be like that. We can continue after we give him the condoms. He is desperate."

"Ah, Gabriella, have I told you I love you today? You are the best. Thanks, love."

Gabriella opened the door. "Oh, my God, Edward! You don't have any clothes on!"

Liam yelled from the bed, "What the fuck, man? You show up

403

at my door naked?"

"I told you I was desperate, and if you had come to the door, then it wouldn't have been a problem."

Gabriella grabbed his chin and tugged it towards her. "Edward, focus. These are out of my gift bag the sistas sent me from the *Fifty Shades of Grey* party I joined through Skype. I hope they are okay."

Edward grabbed the handful of condoms, never so thankful. He bent to give Gabriella a kiss on the cheek and saw Liam headed their way.

"You are a lifesaver, and I will forever be in your debt."

To piss his friend off, Edward grabbed Gabriella, dipped her, and kissed her lips. As he did, his towel fell.

Liam grabbed Gabriella out of his arms, and Edward turned, wiggling his ass as he took off upstairs.

Laughing as he went, he yelled, "You're welcome for warming her up, old man."

"Oh, my. Look, Liam, a full moon is rising." Gabriella giggled, watching Edward run up the stairs.

"Not funny, angel. You will pay for that," Edward heard Liam warn as they closed the door.

Edward was taking the stairs two a time. He got to the top and ran into the room, still laughing.

"What did you do? And where is your towel?" Gillian had almost been afraid to ask after hearing all the commotion.

"Pay back for making me beg for the condoms. Here, baby, we

are good for five more times after this one."

Gillian took the other condoms and placed them on the nightstand as Edward opened the package in his hand. With the light of the moon shining in, he was able to see the condom was hot pink with bumps covering it. He turned the package over and read it out loud. " 'Glow in the dark, studded condom. XXL.' Oh, baby, you're in for a treat with this one," Edward said as he rolled the condom on. Yup, they were both going to love this.

He was still hard as a rock, but Gillian wasn't in the same shape as he had left her. He leaned down and fastened his lips to hers, running his tongue along the seam of her mouth, and when she opened, he explored every inch of her mouth. He then moved down to her breasts and licked then sucked as much into his mouth as he could.

His fingers moved to her lower heart, and with his fingers, he rubbed back and forth then dipped lower to find she was soaking wet. He moved the fluid around, coating his fingers, and then plunged two fingers into her. She groaned as he continued to work her into a frenzy. Then she started to beg.

"Please, Edward. Now, honey. I need you now. Don't make me wait…please."

Edward didn't have to be asked twice. He jumped up on the bed, lifted her legs up, and pushed his pink-covered dick slowly in, loving every inch he was gaining.

He was moving too slowly for her, and she was begging for him to speed up, but he had another agenda: to feel and experience all he had been missing for the last year.

He kissed her left calf before turning to her other leg and running his tongue slowly up then down to the shell anklet.

He leaned down as he pushed himself to the root, and she wrapped her legs tightly around him. Then he placed both of his forearms beside her neck, pinning her.

He smoothed her hair away from her face then thoroughly kissed her. He started to thrust harder, feeling heaven, as she wrapped her legs more tightly around him.

He could see her, smell her, hear her groans, taste her mouth, and best of all, he could feel her squeezing him with her internal muscles. He felt her orgasm, heard her loudly scream out his name, and that triggered his own climax.

He didn't let go of her face as she opened her eyes to look at him.

"Gypsy girl, I am so in love with you, and I am so sorry I hurt you. There was never anyone else for me but you. I love you, baby, and I am going to spend my life making it up to you. I will prove to you that I am worthy of regaining your trust. I know it will take time, but I am going to love you every second of every day and definitely into the nights. You are my past, my present, and you are most definitely my future."

Edward sealed his declaration with a kiss, and when he opened his eyes to look at her again, she was crying.

"Please don't cry. I am so bloody sorry, baby. I love you."
Again, he was smothering her in kisses.

Now her body was full-out convulsing with sobs. Edward held her and let her cry. He had a lump the size of a grapefruit in his throat, realizing how many times she must have sobbed like this over the last year, and there had been no one there to hold her or comfort her. Jesus, he felt so guilty.

She was sobbing so hard her internal muscles forced his dick out.

"Well, there is a bright side. My dick is still coloured pink and is covered in goose bumps, waiting to get back in."

She started to laugh, forgetting her tears as she rolled to turn on the light. "This, I have got to see."

Gillian squinted as the light came on. When she turned to Edward, she burst out laughing.

"I love it. That's hilarious. I will have to remember to thank Liam for that in the morning."

Edward moved off the bed and headed for the washroom, Gillian following close behind.

"It wasn't Liam. It was Gabriella you have to thank. It was from her *Fifty Shades* party gift bag."

"I will for sure, first thing in the morning. Do you mind sharing your space?" She asked as squeezed next to him at the vanity. She still felt awkward since she had surprised him by showing up out of the blue.

"Gypsy girl, I want you in my space now and forever." He grabbed her and kissed her again. Then he slapped her ass and said, "Go and pick the next colour and texture you want my dick to be covered in."

As she walked away, he looked in the mirror, surprised at himself. He looked younger somehow, or maybe it was contentment or simply just being in love that agreed with him. For the first time in forever, he was looking forward to the future.

***

Gabriella was making coffee the next morning when Edward quietly came up behind her, grabbed her arm, whipped her around, and hugged her as tightly as he could.

Gabriella screamed, laughed, and then gasped for a breath.

He eased his tight hold, kissed her forehead, and said, "I can never thank you enough…You have taught me more about love and friendship in one year than I learned in my entire life before you. You are full of wisdom, and I believe you are probably the smartest woman I know…and I know a lot of women."

He heard Gabriella make a rude noise in the back of her throat.

"Don't huff like that. It's true. You always know what to say, how to say it, and how to make people hear you. You think not only with your head, but also with your heart. That is a skill not many people possess. You only knew Gillian from the stories I told you and one phone conversation, yet you knew she was telling the truth, and you fought to uncover that truth. I owe you so much for that.

"I love her and want to spend my life making it up to her. She is here because of you. You restored my faith in people, and you restored my faith in myself. I made a mistake with Gillian. I learned from you that I deserve a second chance to make it right. I learned how to respect, love, and trust from you.

"I have always wanted the world for my best friend, but he also got the moon and the stars when he got you. You are going to love getting to know my gypsy girl, as she is going to love becoming one of your friends. I want her to have that because you bring out the best in every woman you befriend. You embrace and elicit their strength, and that is powerful to watch, let alone be a part of."

Edward chuckled. "Who knew the day I plucked you off those boulders that you would change so many lives? I love you, little she-devil, and I thank you from the bottom of my heart for giving me my life back. Now, you better stop crying before Liam gets here, or he is going to kill me."

"Too late, wee bastard. Get your bloody paws off my woman. You've got a couple of thrashings coming your way already," Liam growled as Gillian laughed through her tears.

Edward and Gabriella turned.

On one side of the doorjamb stood Liam, leaning with his arms crossed, and Gillian was mimicking his stance on the other side, tears running down her face.

Edward went to comfort Gillian, and Gabriella sobbed as she walked into Liam's arms.

Gabriella realized at that moment she was exactly where she needed to be: with the people who meant the most to her. Could life get any better? She didn't think so.

Chapter 35

We Do

F rancesca grabbed Gabriella's hand, dragging her back to the dance floor. "Come on, girlfriend; I love this song."

The girls all had their arms up in the air as their hips moved to the beat of the song. Gabriella had been smiling all night, so much her jaw hurt.

Her sistas had all flown to Scotland for two weeks to help celebrate her wedding, and this was her bachelorette party they had arranged for her. Liam had insisted that it be a week before the wedding. He'd had a gut feeling that, when the girls got together, it could be dangerous, and Liam was seldom wrong.

Edward had been instrumental in helping to plan the bachelorette party. He envied Gabriella's group of friends and the closeness they shared. It had been almost a week since they had all arrived like a tornado, and he had gotten sucked up into the vortex. He had fallen in love with each and every woman in the group and understood what attracted Gabriella to each of her girls. They were all so different, yet when they came together, they melded as one.

He had officially earned a place in the sistas when he had arranged a Caesar party for them upon their arrival. They had branded him an honorary sista or "chick with a dick."

Gillian had also been absorbed into the group. She had arrived two nights ago from Nepal. Unfortunately, she only had nine days to enjoy all the girls and loving her man before she had to go back. She had stuck to her guns and the year commitment she had made to the charity.

Edward had arranged aid for the country and their efforts to rebuild the earthquake-damaged area. Having someone famous help raise money and awareness had awarded him a few perks, one of which was visiting his girlfriend privately twice a month. Gillian missed him terribly, but it was important work, and they were both so proud of her accomplishments.

Edward had just completed a course so he could teach at the Air Force Academy in Scotland to keep him out of the public eye. After the scandal had broken regarding Myles and his co-conspirators, Liam had been reassigned as Edward's liaison, replacing Myles. Edward had wanted someone he could trust to be his right hand man, and there was only one man for that job.

Liam put a whole new spin on the position. He refused to move to London and wasn't intimidated by anyone, especially Edward. He also insisted on monitoring Gillian and keeping her safe.

Edward couldn't have been happier. He still lived in the upper room at Liam's place. He knew his future was with Gillian, and he was content to give her time to her spread her wings and find herself. When they were ready to take the next step and create a family of their own, Edward would move out of one happy home and create his own filled with children.

Edward and Dakota had taken on the responsibility of planning the bachelorette party, and it rocked. They had booked a pub by the name of The Knot—Dakota loved the pun. It was rustic, dark, and had a fabulous dance floor. She had arranged for a stripper to jump out of a cake, and then they had a few games planned before the dancing and drinking took them into the wee hours of the morning.

Dakota had the DJ stop the music before she grabbed the microphone. "Sistas, old and new, we are here to celebrate Gabriella's last week as a single woman. Yahoo! We are so proud of you, Mingo. You have come a long way, baby!"

The girls started screaming.

"Because we are who we are, we are having dessert served first. And then, because I promised Liam there would be lots of food to accompany a lot of booze, we will eat and play a few games before we dance the night away."

Two waiters rolled out the biggest cake anyone had ever seen. Most of the girls figured out exactly what was coming out of the cake, so Jocelyn moved a chair to the centre of the dance floor and made Gabriella sit on it.

"I don't think Liam's going to like this, Dakota!" Gabriella said then screamed as the top flew off the cake, and up popped the hot body of a guy in a fireman's suit with a dark-tinted oxygen mask covering his face. He climbed out and started to dance around. Who needed to see his face when he had a body like that?

Laughing her heart out at Gabriella's face as the dancer swivelled his hips around her, Francesca yelled, "This is about you, honey, not Liam!"

Just as the song "Feeling Hot, Hot, Hot," by The Merrymen came on, the dancer started to remove his coat. The fireman had his well-defined chest airbrushed with flames.

"Take it all off, handsome!" the women cat-called.

He bent over so his ass was in front of Gabriella's face and put his hand on his ass between his legs and yanked off his Velcro pants.

Gabriella threw her hands over her eyes, yelling, "No, no! Liam is going to lose his shit."

Gabriella could hear the girls going crazy, but she was afraid to look. God, she hoped the guy wasn't naked.

She barely opened one eye to peek at the stripper and instantly regretted it. He had G-string underwear on, and when he turned, she saw the fire hose design on the front.

"Oh, my fucking God, you have got to be kidding me!" Gabriella screamed, holding her stomach as she laughed.

Her girls were going wild as the stripper danced around each of them. They were putting money in his G-string as he thrust a hip towards them. If they tried to cop a feel, he quickly manoeuvred away from their touch.

Gabriella was cheering all the girls on until the music changed, and Marvin Gaye's "Let's Get It On" blared out of the speakers. The stripper slowly turned, and his focus turned solely on Gabriella. He prowled his way back over to her, placing a hand on either side of her chair, supporting his weight as he proceeded to give her a lap dance without actually touching her.

Dakota turned to Gillian. "Imagine what that guy could do in bed with the way he moves his hips."

Gillian laughed. "No fucking kidding. If I didn't already have the pony prince, I would so do him."

Dakota, who had just taken a sip of her drink, spit the contents all over the floor. "I cannot believe you just said that. You are hilarious! You rock, sista!" Dakota high-fived Gillian.

Gabriella screamed and jumped up, knocking the stripper to the ground as he removed his mask. "Oh, my fucking God, Edward!"

Edward jumped up, threw his arms out, and yelled, "Surprise, girlfriends!"

All the girls erupted in laughter, screaming as Edward ran to the back room to put some clothes on.

Gillian turned to Dakota and hit her shoulder. "You knew?"

"I didn't. I swear," Dakota defended herself. "I hired a real stripper. But someone's getting her wish tonight, you lucky bitch."

Jocelyn was beyond herself, laughing. "That is by far the best prank I have ever seen in my life, and we can't even share it with anyone."

"Liam would kill him if he ever found out, so no one breathes a word, agreed?" Gabriella, still laughing, swore all the girls to secrecy.

Even though everyone standing there knew the bond Liam and Edward shared, Liam would be pissed, but only because Gabriella had seen Edward's ass for the second time in less than six months.

"Gillian, you lucky bitch. He's a prince; he's gorgeous; he's hung like a horse—or so I hear—and when he releases his hose and thrusts those hips, you must end up with a colossal orgasm!" Francesca yelled.

"Oh, shit! TMI, TMI. Stop talking sexually about my best friend and Gillian's boyfriend." Gabriella laughed, knowing that shy, little Francesca was drunk as a skunk, and shit was just falling out of her mouth.

Gillian took no offence. She just smiled and said, "It's good to be me, ladies." She raised her glass and downed the rest of her martini.

They all laughed and moved along for Gillian's benefit, as well as Gabriella's.

Edward chose that minute to join the party, dressed in his jeans and a T-shirt. He walked over to Gillian and pulled her into a hug then kissed her deeply and thoroughly.

"Later, I'll show you that I saved the best hip thrusting for you,

416

gypsy girl."

All the girls laughed, and then they moved on to the party games.

The first game was 'pin the dick on Liam.' Francesca had drawn a life-sized caricature of a cartoon man dressed in an old-fashioned tux with his fly open and a photo of Liam's face on the caricature. She had drawn all different penises and tied them with different coloured ribbons. Each woman was blindfolded, turned, and directed to pin the dick on him. Gillian was thrilled to learn she won that game and opened her gift bag, finding an extra large bottle of lube. Edward smiled and winked at her.

Next was the shot glass trivia game. Dakota and Edward came up with questions about Liam. If Gabriella answered the question wrong, she had to take shot. If she got it right, everyone else took a shot. If they weren't drunk before, they were once that was over, so they stopped the games and decided to dance and wear off some of the alcohol.

At one thirty a.m., Edward swayed as he stood in the girls' loo, trying to hold Gabriella's hair back as she puked her guts out.

"When will I ever learn? If Liam shows up now, I'm fucking dead," he slurred out loud to himself.

"Too late, wee bastard. I thought you had more sense than this. You don't value your life very much, eh? Not only is my poor angel puking her guts up, but someone sent me a disturbing video of a stripper grinding against her. I thought you were here to look out for the girls? What do you have to say for yourself?"

"Help!" Edward yelled.

Gillian came rushing in to defend her man. "I fink she has da flu," she slurred.

"Fuck, I've got a room full of drunken women and one useless, drunk prince. Thank God I brought reinforcements. Tom!" he called out. "Come in the ladies' loo. I need some help."

Tom and his crew took all of Gabriella's friends to the hotel they were staying at and made sure they all got to their rooms safely while Liam took Gabriella, Gillian, and Edward home and got them all settled in bed.

Gabriella puked two more times during the night and felt like death. The next day, she vowed not to drink at her own wedding.

***

Liam and Edward have outdone themselves, Gabriella thought as she peeked down from the upstairs level of Balmoral Castle. *Really, Balmoral Castle? Who gets married in the vacation home of the royals?*

In her mind, Edward would never be associated with the royals. She had never even witnessed him with his blood family. He was part of the family of her heart.

Edward's gift to the couple was throwing them this wedding with all the bells and whistles, including her dress. Gabriella and Liam had given him his life back when they had discovered the truth about Gillian. This was only a small token of his gratitude.

418

The dining room had been setup for the exchanging of vows with chairs for fifty of their closest friends and relatives. It looked like a beautiful, winter wonderland: white flowers with ice blue crystals, chairs covered in white with ice blue organza bows tied to the back. Everywhere, the room sparkled like it was alive.

The main ballroom had been decorated in the same theme. It had a dance floor, and in the four corners stood fourteen-foot trees with white lights, giving the illusion of being outside. There was also a stage for a band and tables where dinner would be served. Never had Gabriella seen a more beautiful setting.

Megan had helped the twins get dressed, and they looked amazing with their ice blue dresses that enhanced the blue in their eyes, resembling something a ballerina would wear in *Swan Lake*. Their baskets were filled with snowflake shaped confetti. She silently hoped there would be no confetti cannons.

The song "Thank You for Loving Me" by Bon Jovi started to play. Manny, recognizing his cue, took his daughter's arm and guided her down the stairs towards the dining room. The twins led the way, throwing confetti as they went.

Liam stood at the front of the room beside Edward and the magistrate. He was dressed in a black suit with an ice blue shirt unbuttoned at the collar and no tie.

Edward was dressed the same as he stood to the left of Liam while Dakota stood to the right, wearing an off-the-shoulder, black, form-fitting, three-quarter length dress with an ice blue, faux-fur wrap draped around her shoulders.

Liam gasped when he saw Gabriella. She was beyond gorgeous. How had he gotten so lucky?

The most beautiful thing Gabriella wore was the smile she directed at Liam. His future relied on that smile. Then he admired what she was wearing.

Her gown had a custom-made, white, form-fitting bodice covered in crystals. It hugged her all the way past her hips then fell elegantly to the floor. It had an underlay of ice blue and beaded crystals for straps. Three crystal strands were draped across her plunging back, holding the dress together. The material started again just above her bum, encasing all of her stunning assets. She truly looked like a snow princess.

Her hair was in an up-do style with crystals weaved throughout, and strands of hair were left hanging down around her face, giving a soft, romantic look. She didn't carry any flowers, not wanting to take away from the dress.

Liam brushed his own tears away as he watched tears travel down Gabriella's face.

He couldn't wait any longer, so he started down the aisle to meet her. He asked Manny if he minded, and when Manny said no, Liam wrapped his arms around Gabriella and kissed her deeply.

As he drew back, he looked deeply into her eyes. "Hey there, angel. Are you ready to complete me? Because, honestly, I can't wait another second before I can call you my wife."

"Nothing would make me happier, mi cielo. As I will tell you every day for the rest of our lives, thank you for loving me, and thank you for saving me."

"Daddy, stop making Gabriella cry. You're wrecking her face paint. And get married already; we have things to do!" Enya scolded.

Everyone giggled at the large man being reprimanded by his six-year-old daughter.

"Yes, princess. Sorry, everyone," Liam replied as he guided Gabriella to the magistrate.

The magistrate took over and married the couple, using their own vows they had written. By the time they were done, there wasn't a dry eye in the room.

After the magistrate told them to kiss, he announced them as husband and wife then turned to the audience and announced he had one more job to do.

"Enya and Ainsley, please step forwards. Each of you take one of Gabriella's hands and one of your daddy's."

The girls smiled with excitement as they did so.

"Perfect. Now, the girls have asked me and their daddy to be adopted by Gabriella today. So we have a few more questions to be asked." The magistrate turned to a shocked and sobbing Gabriella and asked her, "Do you want to adopt Enya and Ainsley Connor today, Gabriella Maria Dante Connor?"

Gabriella replied instantly, "Yes, with all my heart."

"Perfect. Then let's begin." He looked at each of the little girls.

"Do you, Enya, and you, Ainsley, take Gabriella to be your mama? And do you promise to love her and cherish her?"

"We do."

"Do you promise to listen and care for her feelings?"

"We do."

"Do you promise to go to her for help and guidance?"

"We do."

"Do you promise to remember and pray to your birth mum?"

"We do."

"Then, by the power invested in me, I now pronounce you mama and daughters. Today, a family has been joined together, not just as husband and wife, but also as mama, daddy, and their girls. I wish the four of you a lifetime filled with happiness and love. Congratulations, Connor family! Now please move to the side table to put your names and signatures on the marriage certificate and adoption papers. Then go in peace and love, and cherish the family you have created."

"We love you, Mama!" the girls screamed.

Epilogue

Thank You for Loving Me

19 years later...

S o raise your glass with me and congratulate the bride and groom! Ainsley and Joshua, I wish you both a lifetime of happiness. Cheers! And, Joshua, can you get your bride a tissue so she can dry her eyes before your speech? Trust me, man; get used to this job, because the Connor women cry at the drop of a pin."

Joshua did as instructed by Edward then assisted his wife to stand. They walked to the podium, hand in hand.

Once he got Ainsley settled at the podium, he turned around to the curtain behind them and grabbed a big, brown box.

Joshua carried the box to Liam and Gabriella's table where he opened it and handed Gabriella her own box of tissues to the amusement of all the guests. Then he handed a box to both of Ainsley's grandmothers, her aunt Gillian, and Aunt Megan. He then went to the head table and handed one to the maid of honour, Enya, then his mother-in-law's friends. By the time he was done, every woman had a box of tissues.

Next, he went behind the curtain and came back with three of the biggest boxes of tissues anyone had ever seen and carried them to Gabriella's table where he set one in front of Manny, Ainsley's grandfather; one in front of Edward; and the last one in front of Liam.

"Let's not kid ourselves!" he called out to the crowd, who erupted in a fit of laughter and all stood to clap.

He turned back to the podium and saw his wife again crying through her laughter.

Joshua took the microphone and started his speech.

"First, I would like to thank my new family and to tell them I love them. To my new parents, Gabriella and Liam, I can officially call you Mama and Dad now. Although, since the day Liam dragged my sorry ass into your home, you both have been my parents.

"When I first met your family, I was all alone. I had worked my way through the foster care system, only to join the Air Force, trying to find somewhere to belong. Without knowing me, Liam, you brought me into your fold and gave me something I had never had in my life—a family to call my own. I was untrusting and angry, yet none of you ever gave up on me. Who gets to have their mentor and friend become their dad?"

Joshua stopped. He couldn't continue yet, too overwhelmed by emotion. He wiped his tears then looked at his beautiful wife. Gaining his strength from her, he squeezed her hand then continued.

"Gabriella, Mama...I say that with so much pride. You are an incredible woman. You give more love within five minutes of meeting you than most people give in a lifetime. Since meeting you, I have gained fifteen pounds, and I swear thirteen of that are churros."

The crowd laughed.

"Be proud, Mama, that you have raised incredible daughters. I feel so lucky to get one. You say this to everyone, and now I say it to you...Thank you for loving me ... unconditionally.

"To Edward and Gillian, I thought I was blessed with one set of new parents, but to get two is beyond my wildest dreams. Thank you. Edward, thank you for being our master of ceremony and for your kind words tonight." Joshua laughed at the look Edward gave him. "Don't look at me like that. I know you have told me a million times, if I hurt your number two ankle-biter, I will answer to you, and it won't be pretty. Thanks for protecting Ainsley all these years, but that's my job now. I will protect her with my life."

Joshua looked at Manny. "For the first time in my life, I have grandparents. I don't know if anyone knew this, but my whole life, I watched my friends do things with their grandparents, and I always thought that, if I had a grandpa, I would want to learn to fish. Dreams do come true, and I have a stuffed seven-pound largemouth bass to prove it. Manny, I love you. Thank you, Grandpa."

425

Now his attention turned to his sister-in-law. "To Enya and her husband, Thomas, my sister and brother-in-law, thank you for your patience and your friendship. It took me a while to learn that, when you get one twin, you actually get two, whether you want it or not. And, Enya, I want it. You helped us overcome many hurdles. You are truly the sister I always wanted, and I love you.

"To all of Liam and Gabriella's friends, I counted last night, and I realized I have thirty-six aunts and uncles! Thank you all for teaching me about friendship. I learned family comes in many forms, and all of you taught me you don't need to be blood to be family.

"To my buddies, I wouldn't be alive today without you. I love you guys. Thank you.

"To my wife's gaggle of girls, I have nothing to say to you girls, because I can never get a word in edgewise when we are together. All joking aside, you always have Ainsley's back. Right or wrong, you defend her and fight for her. What a gift. Thank you.

"To the family I have never met—Raven, Marco, Gianluca, and Mateo—lessons and love aren't always taught in the here and now. It's the feeling of a breeze passing over you and knowing you aren't alone. It's an idea you swear you didn't think of. It's protecting the future from afar. Thank you."

Joshua turned to look into Ainsley's eyes. He grabbed both of her cheeks and encased them in his large hands. "You, sweet cheeks, are my everything. You are my sunshine on a cloudy day, my smile through a river of tears, and you are the light to my dark. You taught me how to love, and you taught me to trust the love I receive. You taught me to use words instead of lashing out.

"I was so lost and so alone until you gave me a life full of love, strength, and promise. You gave me a friend, a lover, a wife, parents, a sister, a brother, grandparents, friends, aunts, and uncles. You gave me respect and trust, and in six short weeks, you will give me children." He let go of her cheeks and rubbed her big belly full of his daughter and son. Now he wanted to give something to her.

"So, my gift to you is to tie our past family to the future family and name our babies Raven and Marco. Please raise your glasses and toast the luckiest man in the world and his beautiful bride."

Joshua grabbed her cheeks again and said, "Thank you for loving me." He kissed her deeply and long until one of the twins kicked her stomach, and he felt it against his own.

His last thought before being bombarded by family and friends was,   *Life   is   a   gift.*

Acknowledgements

To my biggest supporter, my husband Tony, how can I thank you for always encouraging me to believe in myself? Your love and patience has been unconditional from the day I met you. Every romantic thing I ever write has been inspired by you. You always tell me that I am the smartest woman you know, when the smartest thing I ever did was make you mine. Our love story will never end. You have always made me feel like I am the most important person in your world. Thank you for loving me. I will love you always and forever.

To my four sons, John, Paul, Mark, and Joey, I am so proud of each and every one of you. I love you all with my whole heart and soul. It was a challenge raising four boys, but it was worth it. I love being friends with the men we have raised.

To Eve, you are the daughter of my heart. Love you!

To Isabelle, you are a dream come true. Love you, baby Izzy!

To Nawal I only see great things for us. Love You.

To my Sabo children, I adore and love you guys.

To my parents, Pat and Tony, being raised by the best parents in the world was a gift. Every good thing I write about parents came from you two. Manny and Elia's goodness came directly from you both. Thank you for giving me all of your wisdom and for always loving your little girl.

Now to all my girls, my personal gaggle, I have learned so much from the powerful women I surround myself with. I am in awe when I think of all the different paths we take, yet we still manage to save time for each other. Liz S., it began with you. You're the best. You taught me how to be a good friend. Every young girl should have a best friend like you to walk through their life with. I love you. To Liz D., my Caesar buddy, you rock my world. You make me laugh my guts out, and you are the best Caesar buddy a woman could have.

To my keg party girls and my Caesar buddies—you know who you are—I love and respect all of you.

To the ladies at C&D Editing, Alizon and Kris, you girls are amazing, patient, and so professional. Thank you for walking me through the process. There aren't enough words to say how much I respect you two.

To Mark Da Silva, thank you for turning my words into a beautiful piece of art that became the picture for my cover. You are by far the most talented artist I know. Love you.

To my girls at work, you are amazing. I aspire to be as smart and strong as each of you.

To my old college friends, love you, girls.

To my beta readers, thank you for your feedback and encouragement. I totally respect you girls—well, maybe not Tina. LOL. Just kidding.

Kendra E., Sarah M., Corrine S., Liz D., Eve D., and especially to Charity P.(Webster) and Tina T. (Comma Queen), thanks for making a dyslexic look presentable. Love you, guys.

Last and not least, to my writing partner, Diane Z. Words cannot explain how I feel about you. This book would never have come to light if you hadn't pushed me. We spent a year writing together; you writing your book and me mine. We shared ideas, thoughts, concepts, feelings, and most of all, our love of words. You are by far the most interesting woman I know, and I am thrilled to have shared this experience with you. I love you from the bottom of my heart.

Contact me at: annemariecitro@gmail.com

Made in the USA
Charleston, SC
21 November 2016